NObody's
FOOL

Books by Sarah Hegger

Nobody's Angel

Nobody's Fool

Nobody's Princess

Published by Kensington Publishing Corporation

Nobody's Fool

SARAH HEGGER

ZEBRA BOOKS
KENSINGTON PUBLISHING CORP.
http://www.kensingtonbooks.com

ZEBRA BOOKS are published by

Kensington Publishing Corp.
119 West 40th Street
New York, NY 10018

All Kensington titles, imprints and distributed lines are available at special quantity discounts for bulk purchases for sales promotion, premiums, fund-raising, educational or institutional use.

Special book excerpts or customized printings can also be created to fit specific needs. For details, write or phone the office of the Kensington Sales Manager. Attn.: Sales Department. Kensington Publishing Corp., 119 West 40th Street, New York, NY 10018. Phone: 1-800-221-2647.

Zebra and the Z logo Reg. U.S. Pat. & TM Off.

First Printing: September 2015
ISBN-13: 978-1-4201-3741-5
ISBN-10: 1-4201-3741-7

eISBN-13: 978-1-4201-3742-2
eISBN-10: 1-4201-3742-5

10 9 8 7 6 5 4 3 2 1

Printed in the United States of America

Chapter One

The sign above the glass door to the trendy singles bar scrolled out SCANTS in hot pink neon, blinked twice, and repeated.

"Bugger." Holly yanked her clinging sweatshirt away from her body. You should never ask how much worse a thing could get because Murphy's Law went right ahead and showed you.

The door flew open, and the clamor from the bar roared out onto the sidewalk where she stood. A couple of girls brushed past her, giggling as they hurled themselves into the preening frenzy. On the other side of the window, a mass of beautiful bodies circled each other.

Holly was way, way out of her element. There was no choice, though. According to his doorman, she'd find Josh Hunter in there.

She squared her shoulders and braced for hell. Good thing she had her bloody passport with her.

Holly stepped over the threshold, and the manic melody of singles bars everywhere crashed over her; the clink, the chatter, the bass rumble of male voices juxtaposed against the higher pitches of women. The throb of amplifier and subwoofer underscored the babble and ground out an elemental jungle beat that quickened the blood.

Welcome to the mating ground of genus Homo sapiens. What a bunch of posers. Exactly where you would expect to find someone like Josh Hunter. Proof she and Joshua were an entirely different species. She'd suspected as much in high school. The evidence was now incontrovertible.

Her phone buzzed in her hand and Holly checked the screen.

Emma again. This made it the fifth call in the last hour. What a pity Emma hadn't panicked four days ago, when Portia first went missing.

She stuck one finger in her ear to hear her sister. "Yes?"

"Did you find her?"

"I just arrived in Chicago." Did Emma expect her to fly? Six hours and twenty-four minutes, according to Google Maps, and she'd shaved it to a shade under six.

"What have you been doing?" Emma wailed loud enough to rise above the storm of noise around her.

"Driving." Holly clenched her hand into a fist by her side. *Cool it, Holly.* They were both worried about Portia's disappearance.

Only this morning, she'd discovered Portia missing.

Emma, Portia's twin, had broken down and confessed Portia had left four whole days ago for Chicago. Not only was their younger sister gone, she'd left London, Ontario, without her medication.

The sheer stupidity of it made Holly want to growl.

"Did you find Joshua Hunter?" Emma let fly with her persistent streak. "Portia spoke about him when she called."

"Yes, you told me already." Holly cursed her height as

she levered to her toes to see over the heads in front of her. "I'm looking for him now."

She might not recognize Josh Hunter anymore. A lot could've changed in the years since they'd gone to high school together. Maybe he'd grown another head, to admire the one he already had.

"She didn't sound good." Emma's voice quivered. "You have to find her, Holly."

"I know I do," Holly almost snarled. Four days and Emma hadn't said a word. Holly could barely get her head around it.

A phone call from Portia, flying perilously high and prattling about seeing Josh Hunter, had sent Emma scurrying for Holly and help.

"I have to go." She hung up on Emma, still talking.

The name of her high-school nemesis had knocked Holly off balance for a moment. It was not a name she'd wanted to hear again. She shook it off. It couldn't be helped. The most important thing was finding Portia, and she'd make a deal with the devil if she must.

In his school days, Josh had lived in Willow Park, and that seemed the most logical place for Holly to start. The Hunter house had been down the street from Holly's, and she'd guessed it was where Portia had run into him.

She'd been hanging on to the secret hope of Portia standing on the sidewalk, gazing wistfully at the old family home. If you could call a house you'd only lived in for two years an old family home.

Holly dodged a weaving waitress and stopped.

The two women in front of her spotted each other and squealed like a pair of happy piglets.

Holly waited for the cheek kissing ritual to end.

Cheek kissing gave way to feverish chatter, and Holly finally pushed past. She was on a mission.

Why had Portia gone searching for Josh Hunter? Holly wobbled on her tiptoes and craned her neck past the mass of bobbing heads. It was one of the questions she'd ask her sister when she caught up with her. And catch up with Portia she would.

The house in Willow Park had changed. Dramatically. Holly had been standing outside earlier, wondering where to go next, when the door to the house opened and luck stepped out—trailing spangles and a cloud of perfume. God knows why, but the woman had been thrilled to see her. Holly didn't recall her at all. Fortunately, she had remembered Holly and her sisters clearly.

The woman went on to say yes, she had seen Holly's sister. Portia had been by a couple of days ago, looking for Josh. She confirmed Emma's report that Josh and Portia had found each other and were briefly spotted together. And better yet, had been able to tell her the name of the upscale condo on the Gold Coast where Josh now lived.

Here the bedazzled woman had treated Holly to an abbreviated version of Josh's infamy. Most of it went over her head, but the gist was women and more women, and when was he going to settle down?

Holly ran for cover between the woman's pause and an invocation to God for Josh to stop breaking his mother's heart and get married already.

So, same old Josh Hunter.

Holly had located the condo building easily enough, and a bit of creative truth-bending with the doorman had her standing on the sidewalk outside Scants, exactly the sort of place she would rather chew her arm off than enter.

The crowd in front of her parted and, oh, sweet Mother of God, there he was.

She would have known him anywhere. Like she would know if someone had shoved their fist in her gut.

He'd barely changed since high school except to get even hotter and more chiseled and more—whatever.

Holly huffed in irritation. Low blood sugar made her cranky. She'd been driving all day, having a shit fit about Portia the entire way and steeling herself for coming into contact with Joshua Hunter. So she'd forgotten to eat, and the peanuts on the bar were calling her name. That's all it was.

She sidled past a blonde cackling over the top of her designer blue martini.

Holly dragged her eyes away from the peanuts and eased closer to Joshua. There was no need to tell him the whole story. She'd tell him only what was strictly necessary and nothing more. Right now, she was leaning toward *"I see you're still a prick. Where's my sister?"* This might be the blood sugar talking, and probably not the most constructive of beginnings.

Holly managed to wedge herself between two thirty-something suits who paid no attention to the short woman in the tatty sweatshirt with the whack-job hair but carried on posturing at each other, simultaneously scanning smartphones that jittered and hummed away at them.

From here she had an even better view of him.

He stood with one hand propped against the bar, speaking to another man who had his back to her. The dim lighting in the bar played peekaboo with the finely chiseled lines of Josh's face. His eyes were shadowed, but they were blue. Blue as the inside of an iris, blue as a pansy, blue enough to break a girl's heart and make her want to come back for more.

"Excuse me." One of the suits deigned to look down from his lofty height and notice her jammed between him and his companion. He smoothly sidestepped her, and Holly shifted closer to Josh and the mouth you wanted to suck on.

He wrapped his lips around the neck of his beer bottle. If his face was any less hewn, his mouth would make him look girly. As it was, its full, sensuous sweep made an irresistible counterpoint to the aquiline strength of the rest of his features.

This was so screwed up. Why couldn't Portia have chosen someone else to cling wrap herself around?

Josh laughed at something his companion said. His smile was a broad slash of white teeth across his tanned face; a heart-stopping affair of crinkling eyes and deep, sexy brackets on either side of his mouth. God, she didn't want to have to make nice with him.

He looked up and Holly was trapped. His glance narrowed in on her like a Scud missile.

There was music and the earth moved.

Maybe it wasn't her blood sugar after all.

"I think that's you." One of the suits glanced pointedly at her phone.

Holly's face heated as she jerked her eyes away. She fumbled before hitting the Talk button.

Chapter Two

Josh winced around a mouthful of lukewarm beer. Time to go. He'd been nursing this beer for the last hour and his new book on Sir Isaac Newton was calling him. Age or boredom—who the hell knew?

He'd only come here for a quiet beer to unwind from his day. Granted, this particular bar was a shitty choice, but it was close to his condo, the beer was cold, and the bartender friendly.

A woman pushed through two slick broker types and fumbled a cell phone out of a pair of baggy GAP jeans. Her burgundy University of Western Ontario sweatshirt sneered like a rescue pound mongrel at the expensive Armanis flanking it.

Her brow puckered into a vicious frown.

She could be lost, or in disguise, but she did have the whole I-have-no-idea-exactly-how-hot-I-am thing going for her. A light lurking under a bushel, a diamond in the rough, a girl with an air of *do me, bad boy* she seemed oblivious to.

Not so clueless was every red-blooded male in her vicinity. More than one covert eye went her way.

Dark eyes, gleaming with intelligence and ringed by thick lashes, met his gaze.

A promising start—if he was looking for a pickup, which he wasn't—but still . . . There was something familiar about this girl.

Diminutive and with her face devoid of makeup, she could have passed for fourteen. The air of determination marked her as older, however. Closer to his age, which meant old enough to drink, old enough to drive, and old enough for all sorts of interesting games.

Ten years ago, five even, he'd have cruised right over and worked his smolder. He knew better now.

The woman ducked her head and took a call. A mane of long, wavy hair obscured her face.

The sort of hair a man liked to curl his fingers in.

Her gaze flickered up and over him. Angry eyes under a pair of lowered brows, giving him the eye so evil he almost looked over his shoulder for the true beneficiary.

Whoa!

Women, as a rule, didn't look at him that way. Women dressed like bag ladies with . . . pencils? No kidding. It was definitely a couple of standard number two pencils holding her hair tightly against her head. Women like her almost never gave him the hairy eyeball.

His feelings might be a bit bruised.

Nope. Feelings intact but ego definitely grazed. She kept her hostile glare going. Those eyes could smoke a hole right through him.

Maybe she was gay. Josh winced behind his beer, glad he wasn't voicing any of this out loud. He would sound like an egotistical prick. Okay, women didn't often turn him down, but it happened. Sometimes.

Her glance shifted away. She was aware of him and doing her best not to show it.

He knew her. It hit him out of the blue and he stopped to think. She had the sort of face it was hard to forget. Not pretty, exactly, more compelling, and a blank canvas for every thought running through her head.

And right now she was not aiming happy thoughts in his direction.

She hunched over her phone to hear better.

The love 'em and leave 'em style of his early twenties hadn't left many warm and fuzzy feelings behind him. Still, he came up blank. He was reasonably sure she wasn't one of the bodies littering his youth, but this lady did *not* like him.

"Hey, Jo-osh?" His name was singsonged at him.

And speaking of his youth, right on cue. The timing nearly made him bust out laughing.

His mystery lady stuck her cute nose in the air. The amber glow from the lighted bar counter turned her skin to buttercream and picked out the tiniest golden freckles across her upturned nose.

The disdain rolled across the distance between them in waves.

"Hey, Josh, like, hello." A pair of breasts intruded into his line of sight, right beneath his nose. He faced the owner of the pair.

There were three of them and all looking at him expectantly.

Ah, shit, here we go.

Over the newcomers' shoulders the mystery lady shook her head in disgust. Her eyes raked over him and the posse in front of him and rolled.

Now, that was not entirely fair. He might even be getting a little pissed at her and her attitude. Girls like the trio facing him were knee deep in trendy Chicago bars, which this one happened to be. They were voracious hunters and he'd only been standing here minding his own business. She needn't act like he'd encouraged them.

In the meanwhile, Bambi, Barbie, and Bubbles—or whatever—posed and primped in front of him. Their cheeks pink with a combination of alcohol and excitement.

His heart sank. He could almost script what was coming. It was his own damn fault, ultimately, but there had to come a point when the ghosts of the past went toward the fucking light or something.

"So, like, we were wondering . . ." Bambi/Barbie/Bubbles pursed her frosted mouth at him and stuck out her breasts.

As if he could have missed them the first time around.

Two and three were providing the flanking action, mirroring her movements and throwing in some freestyle hair tossing.

"Hi, girls." His skin prickled. Was he really going to have to do this now? Mystery lady with the judgmental eyes was going to get her money's worth tonight.

"What you sow, you'll reap, mon fils. " His mother's voice clattered around his brain.

He snuck another look at mystery lady and was rewarded with a glare as she spoke into her phone.

Shit. She had a nice mouth, though, full and soft and making his head go interesting places.

Seriously, Hunter? He pissed *himself* off at times. He dragged his player thought train to a halt.

"So, like, we were wondering if you could help us out with something." The trio dissolved into the sort of giggles that told Josh they wouldn't be asking for directions to the library. "We, like, heard you were, like, the most amazing kisser." More pouting, preening, and hair tossing.

Oh, sweet Jesus, not this.

"And then we started talking, and we were, like, all 'I am the best kisser.' No, I am. Whatever! As if! And no, I am. And then we, like, thought it would be cool if you could tell us which one of us you thought was, like, the best kisser."

"Gee, girls." He writhed inside but kept it cool on the outside. They hunted in packs, the interchangeable blondes; they could sense fear and were quick to pounce. "You make me feel so cheap."

"Oh, no." They caroled in three-part harmony. "All you would need to do is, like, kiss us."

"At the same time?"

"As if." The girls rolled their collective eyes. "And OMG, that would be, like, so cool, but, no." Bambi/Barbie/Bubbles's mouths drooped. "It would have to be one at a time."

Mystery lady pretended to concentrate on her phone call, but her pissed-off gaze was locked on him, good and solid. She was hearing the entire vapid conversation, and her lips curled back like she'd licked a lemon. She bared her teeth at him in undisguised contempt.

"Good evening, am I speaking with Miss Holly Partridge?" The voice in her ear was polite, distant, with none of the ooze of a telemarketing call.

She couldn't drag her eyes away from Josh Hunter. "This is Holly."

Typical. It made her want to vomit. She needed to cool it here or she would blow her chances of getting

any information out of the man. One minute he gave
her the most terrific, nerve-tingling eye and now this.
Stay calm. He's a pig, but you need him.

"Good evening, Miss Partridge, this is Sanjay from
Visa Card Protection."

Holly almost dropped the phone as an impossibly
stacked blonde in a minuscule orange dress draped her
arms over Josh's shoulders and sidled closer.

Josh shook his head and laughed.

It was nothing more than token resistance. Women
still plastered themselves over him. Calm flew right out
the window. "Unbelievable."

"I beg your pardon?"

"Um . . . sorry." Holly dragged her eyes away from the
pair. "Who is this?"

There was a momentary polite pause, as if the person
on the other side of the phone took a deep breath. "My
name is Sanjay and I am calling you from Card Protection at Visa."

"Oh?" Relief flooded through her. "Did you find my
Visa card?"

"I beg your pardon?"

"My Visa, did it turn up somewhere?"

Josh caught her looking. *Un-sodding-believable.* A smug
smile followed.

She sniffed and arched an eyebrow at him. He was
pathetically predictable. Oh, God, let Portia not have—

Holly dragged her thoughts away from the dark
hole. Portia couldn't have been that stupid. Only—and
Holly threw him another glare on behalf of women
everywhere—there was no telling what Portia would do.
Look at him, like a pasha surrounded by his harem.
Gross.

"Miss Partridge? Miss Partridge?" Sanjay sounded a

mite less professional. "Are you still there? Are you saying you are unable to locate your Visa card?"

"You have got to be kidding me." Holly nearly exploded as orange micromini made way for turquoise hot pants with a silver bustier.

"I am not joking with you, Miss Partridge." Sanjay soldiered on.

"Huh?"

Hot pants wriggled her breasts into Josh's chest, pushed her unmuffin-topped hips up against him, and writhed like a professional lap dancer.

Men like Josh Hunter deserved to be castrated. Preying on young, defenseless women. He was catnip for impressionable girls and he loved it. She was thinking about Portia and not hot pants, because by no stretch of the imagination did hot pants look naïve.

"I can assure you, Miss Partridge, this is a matter we at Visa take very seriously," Sanjay said. "You must report a lost or stolen card immediately. We at Visa are committed to the growing epidemic of identity theft. Has your Visa been lost or stolen?"

"No." What the hell was Sanjay blathering about?

The bump-and-grind floor show went on.

"Miss Partridge?"

"Yes."

"Has your card been lost or stolen?"

"Neither." Holly took a careful breath. She needed to forget the show and concentrate on her telephone conversation. "Give me a minute."

Her Visa card; the phone call was about her Visa card. Her mind limped into gear. The Visa card she hardly ever used. The one she kept tucked away for emergencies only, the one that was, suddenly and mysteriously, missing. Holly had turned the house upside down trying to find it before she left London. It had been in none of the usual places. A call to Emma had confirmed that Portia had taken it with her. As far as Holly could ascertain, it was Portia's only source of funds for this trip to Chicago.

"I'm not sure," she said, taking more of an interest in the man on the other line. "Why are you calling me again?"

The pause Sanjay took was so deliberately calm Holly winced. There was no reason to look over and see what was happening. No reason at all. She was here for Portia. *Don't even think about him. There.* She was calm and composed and in control of the situation. The card could be a link to Portia.

"I am calling to tell you," Sanjay manfully battled on, "there has been some irregular activity on your account. This is a standard security call, but now you are telling me the card hasn't been lost or stolen. If the card has been lost or stolen the matter is entirely different."

"How?" Holly didn't like where this was heading.

"If the card is missing or stolen, we would immediately put a hold on it."

"Hmm." Not good. She couldn't rely on Portia thinking clearly before she bolted. Portia could be alone in Chicago with only the card for money. Not good at all. "What sort of activity?"

"Miss Partridge, I must insist on knowing if the card is in your possession."

"And I need to know what type of activity we are talking about." Holly went with the best sort of defense. "This call is recorded, correct?"

"Yes, Miss Partridge." Sanjay audibly gritted his teeth. "This call is being recorded for quality control and training purposes. Where are you currently, Miss Partridge?"

"What? Oh, in a bar." Safe enough and totally the truth.

"Are you currently still in Canada?" Sanjay's tone said he was not going to be fobbed off with half answers and evasions.

"No." She couldn't lie outright because they had computers to track that sort of thing. You saw it on TV all the time.

"May I ask where the bar is situated?" Sanjay's voice vibrated with the determination of a man in pursuit of the truth.

"Chicago." It should be safe enough. Portia was definitely in Chicago. Somewhere. God knows where. Josh Hunter might well know where.

Holly turned to face him again. "Son of a bitch."

Josh had a pair of painted-on skinny jeans wrapped around him. One of her legs was firmly wrapped around his hip as her perfect, probably cellulite-free hips thrust at his crotch.

Sanjay was deadly silent on the other side.

"Not you," she said into the phone. "Someone else."

They didn't cover these sorts of contingencies in the training program and Sanjay defaulted to standard operating procedure. "Miss Partridge, this is most irregular. I am going to have to put a hold on your card."

"No." He couldn't do that; it would be a disaster. "You can't put a hold on the card."

"I most assuredly can, Miss Partridge. Under suspicious circumstances, I am duty bound to place a hold on your account. You should consult your nearest branch at your earliest convenience."

"Don't do it." The idea of Portia alone and without funds in Chicago made her want to throw up. Around her, people were giving her the beware-the-crazy-lady eye slide. "Please, don't do that. If you put a hold on the card, she won't have any money."

"She?" Sanjay pounced, his voice swelling with imminent triumph. "Am I to infer the Visa card is not, in fact, in your possession?"

Holly groaned. How stupid could she get?

Sanjay was, clearly, a man who could see the winner's tape stretched out before him. He put on a burst of speed and cut off any response Holly would have made. "Your agreement strictly prohibits the use of your Visa card without your express knowledge or consent."

"I didn't say *she*. You heard me wrong." Holly's heart sank. She'd blown it.

Sanjay's voice surged as he gave her the legalese at the bottom of the agreement nobody ever bothered to read. She could almost hear him stepping up to the winner's podium, another victory in the fight against fraud, the sounds of "O Canada" playing gloriously in his ears. "I would suggest you consult your nearest branch in the morning. Thank you for your time, Miss Partridge."

"Don't you hang up on me!" Holly flew way past caring what the people around her thought. "Sanjay? Are you there? Sanjay?"

The thirtysomething suits took a step away as her voice rose.

"*You* are the son of the bitch. I meant *you*. Did you hear me? Sanjay? Sanjay? Is anyone listening to this recording?"

Josh broke the vacuum seal Bambi/Barbie/Bubbles had around his neck.

Holly.

Holly Partridge.

Holy Holly Partridge.

What were the odds of meeting up with her again? Excellent, apparently.

He shouldn't have given in to the impulse to piss her off and encouraged the trio. Her glare had done it. It brought out the worst in him. Just like it always had.

Damn, a thirty-year-old man reduced to a Pavlov's dog–type reaction under the disapproving glare of Holy Holly Partridge. He shook his head at himself.

Her accent had clued him in on her identity. The sexiest tangling of vowels he'd ever heard, and he'd first heard it when he was sixteen. Not quite British, not quite Canadian, a touch Venezuelan, and a whole lot raspy. It still stroked up his spine like a cat's tongue. It did more for him than the combined attempts of the tightly toned trio.

Holly Partridge, the girl who'd almost toppled him from his throne as king of the tenth grade. Live and in the flesh after all these years . . . and not having much luck. Not if the way she was yelling into her phone was any indication.

She jabbed her fingers murderously at her phone as if she could somehow reach the person on the other end and impale them.

Holy Holly Partridge had only ever looked at him as if she wanted to scrape him off her shoe. Man, it had stung.

There he'd been, undisputed teenage stud of not only Willow Park but all the North Side, and he'd even made inroads into downtown Chicago. An arrogant young prick with a matching 'tude.

Holy Holly Partridge hadn't given a shit. She hadn't been impressed and she'd let him know it any way she could. Like she was doing right now.

Flinty deep eyes and a toss of her honey-brown mane.

She'd curl up her wide, wide mouth as if she'd been kissing a nettle. Man, she'd bruised his overinflated ego.

Josh laughed to himself. She was still cutting him down to size. It was the weirdest thing. He hadn't thought about Holly in years and now she popped up all over the place. Only the other day her little sister had managed to track him down. Now, here she was in person. What were the odds?

"Well?"

Fuck.

Bambi/Barbie/Bubbles waited and writhed like enthusiastic puppies.

"I tell you, girls. I'm going to have to pass."

"Ahh."

"I've got somewhere I need to be." Josh indicated Holly, working away at a bowl of peanuts like her life depended on it. A frown puckered the skin between her eyes.

Chapter Three

"Holly Partridge." His breath stirred the wisps of hair around her nape. A warm ripple slithered down her spine and she shivered. Her heart yammered loudly in her ears and drowned out Taio Cruz.

Play it cool.

"That's Holy Holly Partridge to you." Holly plastered on a smile and turned. She wasn't sixteen and hiding the world's largest, most hopeless crush anymore. She could handle him. She snapped her fingers mentally and made eye contact.

"Ah, you remember."

"Kind of hard to forget." The years rolled away and they stared each other down, both of them stuffed to the gills with teenage hormones and adolescent angst.

Around them the activity in the bar thumped.

"You look well." An understatement, but she wasn't going near the truth. She drew in the citrusy waft of expensive cologne. He smelled all kinds of wonderful.

Over his shoulder, his former playmates clustered together and watched with matching expressions of disbelief.

It was a jarring reminder of who she was dealing with,

and Holly grabbed onto it. The jelly in the pit of her stomach hardened and she got right back on track. "I seem to have interrupted something."

"Not at all." A charmingly boyish grin crept over his face. "About what you saw before, I think I should explain."

The smile set up a visceral tug somewhere deep inside her. She stamped it out. "Don't." It came out as a bit of a snarl and Holly regrouped. "So, Josh, how are you doing?" She cringed; way too loud.

His eyes widened with a wicked glint. "I'm well." The corners of his beautiful mouth turned up. His eyes drifted over her. "And how are you doing, Holly?"

Holly squirmed inside, acutely aware of her GAP jeans versus whatever he wore. Holly didn't even have the name to go with his clothes, but she got expensive. Grace, her other sister, would identify the outfit in a second. *Get a grip.* She needed to stay on topic and not get flustered. "I'm good," she said. "You?"

"Good." His eyes danced with unholy glee.

They'd already covered that and she wanted to crawl under the bar.

Holly did a mental ten count.

"So, what brings you to Chicago?" His smooth rescue only made her want to scream louder. He was probably doing it on purpose, loving every moment of her awkwardness.

"You, actually." It came out in a rush.

Up went one of his eyebrows. "Me? Should I be flattered?"

"Probably not." Somehow she forced her smile to stay put.

He leaned closer. "Now, that's a real shame."

Was he flirting with her? He couldn't be flirting with her. His eyes held her captive. Breathing got difficult.

Wow. He looked incredible, like every girl's deepest, dirtiest fantasy. She'd die before she let him know.

The bartender delivered a glass of red wine.

Holly glanced at the glass and up at the bartender.

He grinned and motioned to Josh. "Compliments of the gentleman."

"You bought me a drink?" The full glass of red gleamed and winked at her, but she might choke on it first. Or accidentally slip and toss it over his dark, silky head.

"You looked like you needed it." He motioned toward her phone.

"Oh, that." She shoved her phone into the back pocket of her jeans. "Nothing I can't handle."

He smiled at her. The slow creep of warm eyes, white teeth, and laugh lines was like a baseball bat to the back of the knees. *Smile with me,* it coaxed her. *Let your guard down and let me in.*

"So, what can I do for you, Holly?" He made it sound like a proposition.

As if she would ever be dumb enough to go there.

"You said I was the reason you were in Chicago?"

"Um . . . yes." Holly clenched her teeth. She needed to focus here. "I believe you recently saw my sister?"

"Yes." He stopped and seemed to consider something for a moment. "It is still Holly Partridge, isn't it?"

"What?" It took her a moment to catch on. "Yes, it's still Holly Partridge." Of all the antiquated, chauvinistic, sexist assumptions . . . "And even if it wasn't—"

"Relax, Holly, I'm just messing with you." His chuckle snaked out and stroked the nape of her neck.

Her face heated. "It doesn't matter." *You need this man. Stand down.* "I believe my sister was last seen in your company?"

It blasted out like an accusation.

Up went his eyebrow and he straightened, out of her space. "You make it sound like a bad thing." An iron undertone laced his voice.

Holly dialed back on the antagonism. There was no need for details, especially not with him. "I need to find Portia. I came to Chicago to find her and it's important I do so as soon as possible."

His eyes narrowed thoughtfully, as if he was processing what he heard. "I ran into her a few days ago."

Hope flared. "You saw Portia a few days ago? How many days?"

Her sister could cover an awful lot of ground and get into a whole load of trouble in a few days.

"Two or three."

"Where?"

"I ran into her in Willow Park." He took a sip of his beer. Imported, of course. "To tell you the truth, I didn't recognize her immediately. I remember you, Holly, but your sisters . . ."

He shrugged. "I went to see my mother and I saw Portia standing outside Brooke and Christopher's house. Didn't that used to be your house?"

"Yes." Brooke! That was the woman's name. A vague memory of a plump blonde in English class flickered. She needed to stay on track. "And you saw her again? After the time outside the house, you saw her again, didn't you?"

He crossed his arms over his chest. "What's going on, Holly?"

Holly bit back a groan of impatience. Why couldn't he just answer the bloody question?

His eyes bored into her, as if he could uncover every secret she had.

Holly rubbed her arms to dispel the prickling sensation clambering over her skin. "I don't really . . ." She clamped her teeth together before she said too much. "It's important. So, could you tell me what you know?"

He stared at her.

"Please?"

"Wow." He chuckled and stared down his perfect nose at her. "That nearly broke your jaw coming out."

Holly resisted the urge to fidget. That pretty face hid a formidable brain and she needed to bear that in mind.

"You still don't think much of me. Do you, Holly? And after all this time?"

"I . . ." The right words wouldn't come. It sounded petty and ridiculous when he said it.

"This is crazy," he said. "We haven't seen each other for years and we're both behaving like teenagers." He took a deep breath. "Let's backtrack."

He gave her one of his knee-wobbler smiles. "You came to Chicago looking for Portia?"

"That's right." She nodded, grateful for the reprieve. If he could be a grown-up, it was beneath her dignity to keep behaving like a child. "Portia called home two nights ago and was talking about you."

His eyes grew a shade wary. "What exactly did she say about me?"

"I don't know, exactly," Holly said. "She spoke to my other sister, Emma."

His face got guarded. The charming smile vanished, as did the twinkle in his eyes.

"All I know is she spoke of you, and that you were together."

"We are not together," he said. "Not in that way."

"I never—I need to find her." Holly didn't want to go there. "It's important, and if you could tell me where she is, I would greatly appreciate it."

He absorbed this, his keen gaze calculating, as if sensing there was a lot she wasn't telling him. "I can't."

"Why not?" Frustration welled to the surface, and Holly blinked to keep his face in focus.

"Because I don't know."

"Are you sure?"

"Yes, I'm sure." His voice became grim. "Just what did Portia say?"

"I told you." Holly's control slipped. "I didn't speak to her, but judging by what Emma said, it sounded like there was . . . more."

"Like?"

"Ah, gee, I don't know." Was he kidding her? Holly's temper cracked. "You tell me, Joshua. You were the one draped in women not five minutes ago. So, you tell me what more there is."

"There's my Holly," he said.

"What happened with my sister?" Holly rose on her tiptoes and stuck her chin out in his direction. She meant business.

So did he. His eyebrows shot down like a pair of gathering storm clouds and his eyes went colder than ice. "Nothing happened with your sister. And about what you saw earlier—"

"It doesn't matter." Disappointment rose, bitter and sharp at the back of her tongue. Now what the hell was she supposed to do? She'd been banking on finding Josh Hunter and having him lead her to Portia. Where the hell was Portia now? She wanted to scream and her voice grated out through her teeth. "Is there anything more you can tell me?" It still came out harshly. "About Portia."

"I took her to lunch because it was the right time of day and I remembered her, vaguely. She wanted to make it more. I didn't. End of story."

"Really?" She couldn't keep the skepticism out of her voice.

"Yes, really." His jaw tightened. "What did you expect?"

"From you? Nothing." Her voice shook. She'd wasted all this time on a dead end. "I should have known when I saw you earlier."

"About that—"

"You haven't changed a bit." Her mouth ran on like it was on rails. "You're the same as you were in high school."

"And how was I in high school?"

"A conceited jerk. You used women like they didn't matter. I despised you."

"Despised?" He jerked back. "That's kind of strong, isn't it?"

"Thanks for the drink." She grabbed the glass and tossed it back. "See you around."

Chapter Four

The humidity oozed around her as Holly left the air-conditioning of the bar. The quiet brought instant relief, but the air was so thick she could almost taste it. Sweat popped up over her skin and slithered down her sides and spine. She wanted to take off her sweat-shirt, but all she wore underneath was a threadbare white tank.

Another decision she hadn't taken the time to think through when she left this morning. It wasn't like her to be impulsive. See, you don't prepare for all contingencies and this was what happened.

Her father was a projects man, ex-British Army, and how many times had he trotted out his little mantra: *Proper planning and preparation prevents piss-poor performance.* That was about it for fatherly advice on Francis's part, so it ought to have stuck. If this had been either Emma or Portia, she would have kicked their butts for rushing off like this.

She was going to kick their butts anyway, not the least of which for forcing her to renew her acquaintance with *that* man.

Emma popped up on her phone.

"Yup?" Holly was past pleasantries.

"Did you find her?"

"Nope, but I found Josh Hunter." And didn't that go splendidly?

Holly blew the tendrils of hair off her face. They floated up briefly and nestled back against the clammy skin on her face and neck as she hurried toward her parked car. Inside was a bottle of water and more air-conditioning. She could be in Willow Park in thirty minutes to start the search in earnest.

Thanks to Sanjay, the bastard, Portia was now out of funds as well. The worry fastened around her throat. Her mouth went dry and she swallowed past the rush of what ifs flooding her brain.

"And?" Emma's voice dragged her attention back to the phone.

"And he doesn't know where she is." And he could still get under her skin with the speed and ferocity of a tropical parasite.

"Now what?" Emma wailed down the line.

"Now, I start looking." Finding a hotel sounded tempting, but Portia was out there somewhere and she wouldn't get any sleep anyway. "Do you know if Portia has any money with her, other than the emergency Visa?"

"She has a bit." Emma sounded hesitant. The knot in Holly's stomach tightened. "But she should be okay with the card, right?"

"Um, about the card . . ." Holly trudged through the sticky night toward her car. "We've hit a bit of a snag."

Emma went silent on the other end.

Holly recounted her conversation as quickly as she could. She'd screwed things up there. It was too easy to lay all the blame on Josh Hunter, but she'd lost her temper and she should have known better. She did know better.

"No." Emma sucked in a breath. "What will she do for money? Do you know what happens to people in Chicago? You have to find her, Holly."

Tell me something I don't know.

A black SUV sat wedged in the slot in which she expected to find her Toyota. She must have parked farther from the bar. "Did you call the police?"

"Yes," Emma said. "There isn't much they can do because she's in the US. I contacted the Chicago police."

"You did?" Holly was momentarily distracted. It wasn't like Emma to take the initiative. "What did they say?"

"Not much." Emma's voice flattened again. "I e-mailed them a photo of Portia and explained the problem. They said they have a small unit that takes care of at-risk people and they would keep an eye out for her."

Holly ground her teeth together in frustration. God, this was impossible. "Okay." She tried to sound positive for Emma's sake. "I'm going to drive back to Willow Park and start showing her picture around."

"Do you think it will help?"

"I don't know, Emma. It's all I've got right now. Unless you have a better idea." Holly's temper rose to the surface. Silence greeted her, and she hauled back on it quickly. "Listen, I'll call you later. Keep on the police."

She hung up and retraced her steps.

She couldn't blame this whole screwup on Emma. True, she should've stopped Portia from going. At the very least, she should've said something earlier, instead of running interference for her twin. Holly hadn't even noticed Portia was gone until Emma let the cat out of the bag.

Holly was angry with herself as well. She should have

realized Portia was missing, for God's sake. The twins lived in the same house, and Emma was a crappy liar. She'd been trying to give the twins space. Trying to wean them off their dependence on her. They'd turned twenty-four on their last birthday. It was time for everyone to get on with their lives. Steven had been nagging about it for months.

Hadn't that worked out wonderfully? Holly wanted to kick something, hard. She should have seen something like this coming. She, more than anyone, knew the signs of a bipolar cycle.

She'd just been so relieved to see Portia stable and getting on with her own life, she hadn't wanted to see what was staring her in the face. Stupid. How could she not have recognized the signs of Portia off her medication: the irritability, the insomnia, the chattering incessantly, the inability to concentrate?

Looking back over the past two months, it was all right there. Portia had done everything short of written her a note. Bloody, bloody hell. She'd grown up watching Melissa rocket up and down through most of her childhood.

And Holly was more and more convinced this was all about their mother.

Melissa had died here in Illinois. Portia was much younger then and didn't remember most of the details. Holly had done her best not to fill in the blanks. It would only be natural for Portia to feel some sort of special bond with Melissa. Portia was so like their mother sometimes.

The familiar anxiety tightened around her chest. Bugger it, she didn't want to think about Melissa.

The wind carried more hot air and pushed it against her clammy skin. Being back in Illinois brought up the memories. Memories best left in the past.

Holly stopped walking. She definitely hadn't parked this far away.

Her car was probably on the other side of the road. She walked toward the foyer of the upmarket condos that housed Josh Hunter.

The doorman was still at his post behind a marble desk. He'd been reluctant to tell her where Josh could be found, but he was even more nervous she would take up residence in his hallowed foyer.

There were cars everywhere, but none of them her familiar metallic blue roof. Confined pools of light spilled over the walkway from the bars and restaurants but provided scant illumination.

The buildings on either side of the street were full of activity. The city would be awake for hours yet. Summer in Chicago meant heat and humidity and an exuberant celebration of the absence of winter.

Holly was back to staring at the pink SCANTS sign as it went through its familiar motion. It must be here. She'd parked it right near the condo.

Holly backtracked, slowly and deliberately.

Cars were jammed in, bumper to bumper, on either side of the road, constricting traffic to a crawl. Not one of those cars was hers. The condo building loomed up in front of her. Mentally, she ticked off the cars parked between here and Scants. Not an older-model metallic-blue Prius among them.

It couldn't be possible. Her clothes were in her car, the few she'd thrown in a bag, and her extra cash. And fuck, shit, dammit straight to hell—her passport. This was not good. Not good at all.

Holly ripped off her sweatshirt. Perhaps she'd parked in another street. No, she'd parked it here, on this street, and nearly right outside the condo. Because she'd thought, at the time, what a good omen it was to find such convenient parking.

Do not panic. This was not the time to panic.

A strong gust of wind chased along the street and engulfed her in its hot, oily breath. Her dry mouth mocked the bravado that made her down the glass of wine. The buttons of her phone blinked up at her, daring her to dial and make it real. Holly pressed the numbers: 9-1-1.

The dispatcher was as sympathetic as Nurse Ratched, but she did promise to send a patrol car at some indeterminate point in the future.

Holly disconnected the call. The buildings on either side loomed over her. All around people filled the buildings with laughter and chatter. Alone and friendless, in the middle of Chicago. Shit.

The wind got enthusiastic and tugged at her jeans and jerked the wet tendrils of hair off the back of her neck. She had exactly fourteen dollars in her pocket and her phone. Nothing more. She was stuck in Chicago, murder capital of the United States, trying to track down Portia, who was out there with no money, caught in the vortex of a bipolar high. She dialed Emma to give her the good news. When her brain worked again, she would find a way out of this.

The phone rang to voice mail. Holly gave a short bark of laughter. Now, Emma wasn't answering her phone. Holly left a terse message. Surprised her voice sounded calm and clinical when panic boiled up her esophagus and clogged her throat. What a pity she couldn't add not being around when her car got stolen to the ass-kicking tally.

The first drop landed with a wet squelch on the side of her nose. Its friends and family followed in short order, like somebody had kicked over a bucket in the sky. Holly threw back her head and roared.

"AH FUUUCK!"

She was a split second ahead of nature as it roared back down at her. The heavens wrenched wide open, and a deluge of sultry, sticky rain thundered down and all around, bouncing off the concrete and the cars in a thick, creeping stream. Death, taxes, and the truth that it never, ever rained, it always sodding poured.

Holly stood there, staring at the place her car had been, the downpour pelting against her skin, and panicked.

Josh ducked out of the rain beneath the overhang outside the bar.

Holly made a pathetic sight. She'd lost her pencils in the downpour and her hair clung like rattails to her face and back. She stood with her head bent and her shoulders slumped, water pooling in the bottom of her jeans and splashing over her Converse sneakers. The rain had plastered her clothes to her body.

Time to get very wet. He snagged a complimentary Scants umbrella and prepared to best his dragon. Despise him now, did she?

"Hi again." Josh almost took a self-preserving step backward as the blast from her eyes broadsided him. He held the umbrella over both their heads.

"Ah, perfect." She threw her hands up. "This is all I need right now. Why did I think it couldn't get any worse?"

Josh inched the umbrella over her head. Rain streamed down his neck and under the collar of his shirt. In seconds he was as wet as she was. "Is something wrong?"

"What do you think?"

Her body thrummed with tension, her hands clenched by her sides. He got the feeling this was about more than the rain.

"I wouldn't bother." She snarled at the hot pink canopy above her soaking head. "Keep it for yourself. That pretty shirt of yours must have cost more than my car is worth."

She was probably right, but this wasn't the time to say so. "Where's your car?"

"Not here."

"Okay." She was right about the umbrella. The rain bounced off the canopy and streamed over the edge and down his head. "Should we—?"

"My car is not here because it's missing." Her face grew flushed as the volume rose. Anger emanated off her in waves.

"Is it—?"

"Because some miserable, fuckwit, son of a bitch, asswipe, bastard, pissant, dickhead, wanker, prat, git stole it. They stole my car."

And thar she blows!

Not good. Her car had been stolen. It explained the standing in the rain.

She went quite red in the face. "They stole my car." The level of rage reminded him of his mother trying to get her three six-foot-plus sons to do her bidding.

Josh was impressed and a bit scared for his life. Holly got mad good and proper, and her swearing was near legendary. He wasn't sure what a wanker, a prat, or a git were, but they couldn't be good.

Ah, dammit! Her nipples pressed against the nearly

transparent fabric of her shirt. Her voluminous diatribe floated over his head.

He needed to focus on the problem.

"Are you looking at my breasts?"

"Um . . ." There wasn't much he could say as he had—totally against his will, of course—been ogling the cinnamon-tinted peaks of her nipples. "Are you sure?"

"You are such a dog." Her eyes disappeared into narrow lines of death.

"Are you sure your car was stolen?"

"I'm standing here without clothes, money, a passport, and a bloody car and you're getting your ya-ya's out. Weren't those girls in there enough for you?"

The Bambi/Barbie/Bubbles thing swung back to haunt him. "About that—"

"I don't care." She stormed to beat the crap out of the weather. "They stole my car and everything in it."

"I'm sorry," he said. Words failed him. The situation sucked, no two ways about it. "Did you call the police?"

"Of course I called the bloody police." She waved her hands around as punctuation.

Josh kept a sharp eye on her hand punching through the air. "What—?"

"Did you think I was standing out here waiting for the car to magically reappear? Or perhaps you thought I was waiting for a big strong man to come and tell me what to do?"

Actually, she'd hit perilously close to the truth. He'd been about to offer his manly arm for her rescue. "You're getting wet."

"You don't say?" She glared up at the umbrella.

He kept the umbrella right where it was. There had to be something he could say to make this seem a little less dire. But nothing came to him. His eyes burned to drop down and get another look. *Do not look at her breasts again. Do not look at her breasts again. Do not—*

"Would you like to wait where it's dry?" Inspiration, when it struck, was dizzying.

"Where?" Her eyes narrowed. Her freckles stood out against her skin in a way that was totally adorable, and she'd probably eviscerate him for even thinking it.

He pointed across the street. "My condo is over there."

"I know that."

"You do?"

She ground her teeth and gave a long-suffering sigh. "Yes. I went there first and your doorman told me where to find you."

"Philip told you where to find me?" Philip needed to be a little less free with the information. Not really the issue right now.

"Yes." Her chin stuck out in open challenge.

He'd ask Philip later and have a much better chance of surviving the encounter. Also lessen the risk of imminent drowning.

"You can see the street from my window." Josh motioned to a wide picture window on the top floor. "You'll be able to see when the police get here."

"Of course you have the penthouse." She scoffed and threw her hands up again. "Tell me, Joshua Hunter, in your charmed existence, has anyone ever had the temerity to steal your car?"

"Er . . . no." She made it sound like a bad thing.

"Typical. Sodding typical."

"Someone once stole my iPhone," he offered by way of consolation.

She snorted and crossed her arms over her lovely breasts.

The rain subsided to a steady torrent. The cuffs of his

pants were wet. He must be as prissy as his younger brother said because the pants were D&G this season, and he liked them. "The condo." Getting out of this rain would be a good move. "Would you like to wait there for the police?"

"I have to find Portia." Her lips tightened into a straight line. "I don't have time for this. I have to find her."

Her eyes gleamed fever bright, and Josh had the horrible feeling she held back the tears by sheer force of will. "She could be anywhere and she isn't—I have to find her."

"But first you need to speak to the police and they're on their way." His gut screamed at him. There was a story here. "Did you say your money and your passport were in the car?"

Her shoulders drooped and she heaved a huge sigh. "And my clothes."

Not good. "Okay, first things first, let's get out of this rain."

"I'm not going to your lair."

His damsel refused to be rescued. Not really surprising.

"What about the foyer?" He mentally congratulated himself for his quick two-step shuffle. "You can wait in the lobby until the police arrive."

"Okay."

"And then we can talk about what else we can do to get you out of this mess."

"Don't patronize me." She sloshed after him to his building.

"I'm not patronizing you. Now, be a good girl and come along."

He was sure if she'd been close enough she would

have done him bodily injury. Josh allowed himself a small smile as he led the way into the building.

"Good evening, Mr. Hunter," Philip greeted him. His eyes widened at the drowned rat person standing dripping water over the marble floor. "Ah, I see your masseuse found you."

"My masseuse?"

"I improvised," she said between clenched teeth. "I didn't think he would believe I was your girlfriend."

"Oh, I don't know." Josh's gaze swept her from top to toe. "I'm not *that* picky."

"Go away." She stuck her chin out and her lip quivered.

His gut tightened. Shit, he hadn't meant to upset her that much. Time to stop being a dick.

"I don't want your help and I will die right here, right on this shiny floor, before I take it."

She probably would, too. He certainly wasn't making her night any better.

Philip paled. There was probably something in the bylaws of the building prohibiting death in the lobby.

"I will wait here for the police and then I will decide how to get *myself* out of this mess."

Josh wished her luck with that attitude. He'd offered his help. She'd turned him down.

"I am terribly sorry, Mr. Hunter; she said she was your masseuse and I saw no reason to doubt her. You have a hairdresser who comes to the condo, and your grooming technician."

A rude noise emanated from the human puddle. "*Grooming* technician?" Up went one of her dark brows and Josh flushed. He wished Philip hadn't felt the need to explain. "Is that, like, a beautician?"

A suspicious noise burst out of Philip.

Josh stared him down.

Philip coughed.

"I believe grooming is as important for a man as it is for a woman." It didn't sound quite as impressive when voiced aloud. *Jesus wept.* Thomas was right. He was in danger of becoming a girl.

Josh stalked over and punched the button for the elevator. The doors swished open and he stepped in.

Tomorrow morning he planned to engage in a blood sport, and after that, it was a trip to the Home Depot. He needed to buy something turbocharged with the destructive capability of a small nuclear device.

"Oh, by the way, Philip." He stopped the doors of the elevator before they could close completely. "Miss Partridge is a talented masseuse. You should get her to give you a foot rub while she waits. Go ahead. It's on me."

Chapter Five

Josh brewed himself an espresso—the coffee choice of real men everywhere—and stood at his window watching the fun.

Damn, her car stolen and everything in it. He ignored the twinge of conscience trying to make itself heard.

Holly Partridge despised him. She didn't want his help and she'd been quite clear about it.

The rain had stopped, transforming the street outside his building into a Turkish bath. In among the billowing clouds of steam stood Holly Partridge, gamely making herself understood by two cops. They were going to love this. A Brit, a Canadian and a South American all rolled into one feisty package.

The female cop leaned against the squad car, her face a mask of public servility, while her male partner attempted to understand Holly.

The man had Josh's sympathy.

Holly waved her arms around like she was directing traffic.

He couldn't hear what she was saying from up here. She hadn't been shot yet, so he guessed she hadn't let fly with her toilet mouth. Probably that cute accent of hers saving the day. Or the local constabulary had no idea what a git or a prat was either. He had an inkling about a wanker.

The police had arrived quickly enough, before he'd given in to his chivalric impulse to take her a dry shirt and a cup of coffee. Knowing the attempt would probably get him vivisected, he'd stayed put.

She'd pulled her sweatshirt on and was pinwheeling her arms around at the cop. She'd barely grown since high school and she'd been tiny then. Her curves had filled out very nicely, into a firm, ripe armful of woman, surrounded by bristling, deadly body armor.

What the hell had he done to piss her off so badly? Josh grinned over his espresso cup. He'd definitely exacerbated the issue by giving in to the impulse to taunt her. He laughed out loud. The look on her face had been priceless.

He didn't much care what people thought of him anymore. Most never bothered to get past his exterior, and Josh rarely wasted his time correcting them. It shouldn't trouble him that she'd left tonight with her poor opinion reinforced, but Josh was surprised to find it burrowed like a tiny splinter under his skin.

Fifteen minutes later, he checked, and Holly was alone.

The police cruiser eased into the traffic and down the street, away from her.

Her head dropped and her shoulders slumped. How a woman with a mouth on her like that managed to look quite so dejected beat him, but there it was. She was Dickensian in her tatty, oversized clothes, with her tangled hair hiding her face.

Don't fall for it, Josh. Don't be a total sap.

Holly Partridge was as tough as old shoe leather.

She crossed her arms over her chest and stood on the sidewalk, as if she had no idea what to do next.

It was a far cry from the battle drone who'd shoved her way into Scants an hour earlier. Something about that sister of hers was off. Earlier, Holly had seemed close to desperate to find Portia, and that didn't sit right either. Portia was old enough to take care of herself; but then, Portia had given him a seriously twisted vibe.

Holly's chances of finding her sister now were nearly zero.

Josh ground his teeth together. Unless someone stepped in and helped her.

Don't do it. He moved away from the window.

Holly didn't want his help. She'd been quite clear on that point. Besides, she'd got here on her own. If her car was stolen, she could always whistle up a broomstick. He chuckled at his little joke.

He would just quickly take another look and see if she was still there.

She dug in her pocket and hauled something out.

He pressed closer to the glass for a better view.

She counted out money in her palm.

"Damn. Damn. Damn. Damn. Fuck it. Damn." Josh reeled away from the window and stomped toward the intercom beside his front door.

"Yes, Mr. Hunter?" Philip responded.

She was a prickly, foulmouthed, bad-tempered viper who hated his guts, but one of Donna's boys would never walk away and leave a woman in trouble. It was ingrained in them, despite rigorous attempts to break the conditioning.

"Miss? Excuse me, miss?"

Holly jerked her head up quickly. "Yes?"

Against the glare of the security lamps, Josh's toady doorman waved to get her attention. "Please, miss?" The doorman squinted at her. "Won't you please come inside where it's dry?"

"I'm fine here, thank you." Her voice wobbled slightly and she clenched her jaw. She refused to cry. This was only a bump in the road. A huge, sodding mountainous bump in the road.

"It's stopped raining now." She gave him a jaunty nod. There was no way she would lose it in front of an audience again.

The doorman hovered around the double glass entrance doors. His tone became cajoling. "I could make you a cup of coffee, or I have water. Or pop. Perhaps you'd like a nice, cool Coke?"

As satisfying as a dignified refusal would be right then, Holly stopped herself. A nice, cool soda sounded perfect. And she may as well face facts; she barely had enough to buy one for herself.

The doorman looked relieved as she turned and trotted toward him.

She needed a good emergency plan. Emma would be as much use as tits on a tortoise.

Grace.

Grace was the answer.

She followed the doorman back into the wide, spacious lobby and comforted herself with the knowledge that the soda would probably be billed to Josh Hunter and the rest of the beautiful people who shared his building.

Philip was a man of his word and produced the promised soda, with a glass and some ice.

Holly perched on the edge of a large indoor water feature and stretched her toes in the sodden canvas of her Converses.

The lobby was mostly covered in honey-toned marble, polished to such a sheen she could make out her wavy reflection between the darker veins of amber running through it. A stately orb of crystal took pride of place and hovered over the mere humans who scuttled beneath its beneficent rays.

The lobby was air-conditioned, and between the cool air and the cooler soda, her brain had kicked into gear. She would call Grace and get her to book a hotel with her credit card. Perhaps she could even track down an all-night car rental. Holly pulled a face. Did you get all-night car rentals in Chicago? She shook her head. She couldn't afford to think negatively.

In the morning, Holly could tackle the bank and call the embassy and see about getting a new passport. This was the United States, for God's sake, and anything was possible. Her glass formed a ring of condensation on the marble and she used her thigh to wipe it clean.

The elevator door swished open with the well-maintained mechanism of expensive condo rates.

Josh stepped out, a gym bag slung over one shoulder. He'd changed into a T-shirt and a pair of jeans. It didn't make him look one iota less gorgeous. Wherever he was going, he probably wouldn't get kicked out of bed tonight.

She tried to push the sodden tangle of her hair into something approaching civilized.

"Thank you, Philip." He turned to the doorman and indicated her with a jerk of his head.

"No problem, Mr. Hunter. I gave her a pop."

"Good work."

Holly glared down at the offending empty glass. It was no use, though. She still didn't feel sorry she'd drunk it.

A set of keys dangled from Josh's index finger as he

strode toward her. It wasn't right a man could walk like that. An easy, feline lope that made her want to slap a pair of six-shooters around his lean hips. He stopped in front of where she sat and glanced down his perfect nose at her.

Holly braced for whatever wisecrack he had brewing in his pretty head.

"We don't like each other much, but I'm going to help you."

"Say again?"

"You need help and I've decided to help you." He nodded. "Chalk it up to some latent feeling of child-hood sentimentality."

Oh, man, wasn't he a laugh a minute. "Good one, pretty boy."

"I mean it." He shifted the gym bag. "I'm going to help you find your sister."

She half-believed he might be serious. She wanted to stand so he wouldn't be looming over her, but she also didn't want him to know she was feeling intimi-dated. In the end, she settled for leaning back on her arms, dropping her head to the side, and staring up at an angle. It wasn't the most comfortable position for her neck, but it did have a sort of *Rebel Without a Cause* air to it.

"Is your neck stiff or something?"

"No." Her cheeks burned.

"Anyway, as I see it, you're in need of help and I'm going to give it to you."

"Are you serious?"

"Quite."

"Get real." Like she would believe that?

He raised one eyebrow. "Right back at you, babe. You have no transport, no money, no passport, ergo no way to get home, and nothing but the clothes you're wearing."

"I have my phone."

Up went his eyebrow again. "How comforting."

"Don't call me babe either." God, he was a cocksure son of a bitch.

"Note to self." His jaw tightened. "Don't call me pretty boy."

No way in hell she was agreeing to that. Holly stood up. It didn't help. He still lurked a good head above her. "I didn't ask you for help. I don't even want your help."

They locked eyes.

"That's true," he said. "But you're getting it anyway."

"Back off, pretty boy."

His eyes narrowed at her and his nostrils flared.

It was a bit thrilling, in truth. Holly stood her ground, prickles of sensation coursing up and down her spine.

"Don't you need to find your sister?" His voice grew silky smooth, but she wasn't going to fall for his trap and relax her guard.

"I do."

"Good." He adjusted his grip on the gym bag and nodded, as if the matter was settled. "The first step is to see what we can find out about your sister."

"Hey." The steamroller went right over her head.

"I'm pretty sure she's not hanging around your old house in the middle of the night, but maybe we can stumble across something useful." He turned and strode off across the lobby, headed toward an exit door partially concealed by a bank of glossy green foliage. "Come on. Babe."

"Where?" And dammit all if she didn't trot after him. It was his help that got her moving, not some deeply conditioned master/slave mentality—the finest of the species holding dominion over the lesser beings, or some crap.

"That's what you need to tell me." He said it patiently, as if he were afraid she wouldn't get his meaning if he used too many big words.

"I don't know where she is, genius." Holly almost plowed into his broad back as he stopped suddenly.

He frowned down at her. "You must have some idea."

"I think she's in Willow Park," she said. "But I was there earlier tonight and I couldn't find her."

"So where were you going?"

"When?"

"Earlier, before your car was stolen."

"I was going back to Willow Park."

He made a soft moan of irritation and turned to loom over her. "You're not making any sense. I seem to be missing some pieces of this puzzle."

"You are missing a great many pieces of the puzzle." He absolutely was the most condescending ass on the planet. "But, as this has nothing to do with you, you are going to carry on missing those pieces."

His eyes narrowed.

Holly straightened her shoulders and glared back. Blue clashed with black and held. Neither of them moved a muscle.

Somewhere *El Düguello* wailed.

"Fine." He threw up one hand. "But I'm going to Willow Park right now. You make up your mind if you want to come along."

He slapped open the exit door and disappeared.

Holly narrowly caught it before it swung back and banged into her. She followed him down the stairwell feeling ridiculous.

His jeans weren't tight, but they framed his spectacular ass.

If she was looking, which she wasn't. It just happened to be there.

Oh, get real, Holly. She lost patience with herself. She was so checking him out. It couldn't be helped. He'd always been a rather superior specimen, and she'd have to be dead from the neck down not to notice. It didn't mean she liked him, though, because she didn't.

She stood there for a moment, warring with herself. It was a brief but bloody skirmish, and in the end the need to find Portia won. Right now, she was screwed without him. The idea got stuck in a wad in the back of her throat.

He stopped at a door at the bottom of the short stairwell. "Did you say something?"

"Nope."

He ran one hand through his hair, raking his fingers across the scalp. "Come on, Holly. Stop being so god-damned stubborn. You need help and I'm offering. After you've found your sister, you can go back to hating me. Okay?" His tone got smooth and persuasive, like he was selling youth elixir, which was why she was floored to feel her hackles starting to lower.

"It's no big deal." He continued to dole out the charm. "Let me drive you over to Willow Park to have a look around. Have you called the police?"

"Yes. Why are you being nice to me?" Holly waited for the other boot to drop.

"I am nice." His voice bounced off concrete and back at her. "You're probably the only woman I know who doesn't think so."

"Lucky me." He was probably right about the only woman thing.

"Now, get your ass down here." There was a tense pause, then his jaw went granite. "Please?"

Pathetically easy, but rather satisfying all the same.

Holly hopped down the steps and followed him into the parking garage.

There weren't many cars and all of them were expensive. She skirted a vintage Bentley and paused in midstride to admire the lines on a cherry-red Ferrari.

Josh bent down to open his car and she stopped dead in her tracks.

"That's your car?" She burst out laughing. This was priceless.

"What?" He ruffled up. "It's a nineteen sixty-seven series one and a half XK-E Jaguar."

Holly laughed harder, and he raised his voice over the sound of her cackles rebounding around the parking garage. "It might interest you to note that Enzo Ferrari said it was the most beautiful car ever built."

"Oh, I'm sure he did." Holly gasped to get her breath back. "Because that, my friend, is a penis on wheels."

"Get in."

Chapter Six

Holly had to admit the XK-E was a thing of beauty as they growled their way out of the parking garage and onto the streets. The recent downpour had done nothing to dampen the atmosphere. There were people everywhere as Chicagoans enthusiastically joined the tourists in painting their town red. Summer in Chicago: one festival after another and a constant party in between.

She tried Emma and got her voice mail. Now she had two sisters MIA. Maybe she should try the police unit Emma had called. And say what? She didn't know where to start. Until this moment, she'd never regretted not forking out the extra money for a smartphone.

The man next to her had one of those, pimped out and bristling with information. Siri probably flirted with Josh Hunter, too. Holly fought back the helplessness and stared out the window.

The car roared through the street, Lake Michigan a mysterious glitter on one side. People everywhere getting on with a good night out and so far removed from the despair pressing her.

On the opposite side of the road from the lake,

towering monoliths of glass loomed over their older stone brothers. Somewhere among these buildings wandered Portia, alone, sick, and penniless. The black hole pressed closer.

She wasn't going to cry. She didn't cry.

Holly blinked her eyes furiously and fixed her gaze on the buildings. New condo developments sprang up, as always, but for the most part it was the same.

Josh maneuvered like a typical native. You didn't so much drive in Chicago as aim. The rule of the road was more along the lines of he who dares, and accomplished with a single-minded determination to add to the prevailing chaos. The result was a gridlock onto the highway that kept them there for long precious minutes.

She needed a distraction or she would climb out of the car and start swinging.

Holly stole a look at her companion. Part of her mind refused to wrap itself around the fact that she was here, now, and with him. And he was being useful. Holly tensed as a taxi swung across two lanes to come to a brake-grinding halt two hairs from their left bumper.

Josh didn't flinch, which meant he was either immune or brain dead.

She needed to get a grip here and relax. He was helping her. She didn't have to like it, but if it meant she might find Portia sooner, then it was all that mattered.

"So." Holly winced as a large delivery van pulled so close she could see up the driver's nose. "You seem to have done rather well for yourself."

"You sound surprised." He glanced in her direction while playing chicken with another driver for a small gap in the traffic ahead of them.

"No." She unclenched her fingers from the side of her seat. In school, lots of other kids—and by that she meant girls—would look at Josh and see only the pretty package. She'd always known a lot more lurked beneath. "What do you do?"

"Nothing, at the moment." He thrust down hard on the horn and she nearly leaped out of her skin. "I recently sold my business and now I'm looking for something new."

"What did your business do? Shit! Watch out for the . . . never mind."

He grinned like a pirate. "We wrote software. Financial stuff, for the most part, stock market analysis, that sort of thing." He shrugged. "We came up with a winner, started making good money, and someone offered to take it off our hands."

"For a sizable fee?"

"You got it."

"Hmph."

"And you, Holly Partridge? I already know you're not torturing some poor husband. Perhaps you're raising a charming set of five illegitimate children or setting the corporate world of Canada on fire?"

"And why would you assume I'm not doing all of the above?"

"If anyone could, it would be you." Josh smiled.

Holly got a warm little glow inside.

He didn't look like he was mocking her.

There was a compliment in there, and rather a big one. It made her feel churlish because she was only sniping at him to avoid telling him what she did. Which was a good job, a stable job, but it wasn't selling software for big bucks, living in a slick condo, and driving a vintage sports car.

She cringed. Her job supported herself and two sisters. She was doing fine. Holly shifted in her seat. Her wet jeans slurped against the leather as she moved. "Those girls at the bar?"

"Uh-huh?" He stared fixedly ahead as his shoulders tensed.

Had she hit a little chink in the Josh Hunter armor of awesome? Here was salvation and an evasion all dressed up and waiting for her to take it out. "What was that about?"

"I've been trying to tell you." The corner of his mouth twitched. "I thought it would piss you off. Did it?"

He turned those big blues on her and gave her a look naughty enough to make a nun toss her coif over the windmill. The man could pack a whole lot of sex into one terrific eye meet.

"Maybe." Her tongue suddenly stuck to the roof of her mouth.

"You were looking at me like I was something left on the bottom of your shoe and . . ." He laughed. "I didn't recognize you at first. You were giving me the stink eye and I went with the sixteen-year-old option as a reaction."

"And the girls were happy to play along?"

"They approached me." He was all wounded dignity and maidenly outrage.

Like hell.

"So." Holly had to get this straight. A horn blared in her right ear and she nearly leaped across the central console into his lap. "Those girls came up to you and wanted to play group spit swapping?"

He grimaced. "Yup."

"Without you doing anything to encourage them?"

"My hand on a Bible." He raised one hand in the air and put the other over his heart.

"Hold the wheel." Holly gasped, as he depressed the accelerator and lurched forward a few feet. "Does that sort of thing happen to you a lot?"

"More than I would like." He inched into a spot

she wouldn't try to fit a moped. "And a lot less than it used to."

This was freaking unbelievable. "Roving packs of strange girls randomly demand you suck face with them? What are you? Some kind of X-rated version of the Pied Piper?"

He gave a bark of self-deprecating laughter. It was, kind of, appealing. "Well?"

He blew out a long breath. A faint stain of color crept up over his sculpted jaw. He was blushing. "Okay, it's kind of my fault."

She was totally fascinated now. "Oh, I need to hear this."

"When I was younger and more shallow . . ."

Holly made a rude noise.

He gave her a level stare.

Holly dropped her eyes first.

"When I was younger and shallower." His expression grew grim. "I used to do things like that. They were, sort of, my thing. If you know what I mean?"

"Your thing?" This was good. It simply never occurred to her someone this beautiful and self-assured ever did any of the cringeworthy stuff mere mortals floundered around in.

"You know, um, like my angle."

"Your *angle?*"

"Jesus." He rapped the steering wheel. "You're a real hard-ass, you know that?"

Holly smirked.

"My angle, my thing with girls is what I mean. I used to use lines like that to pick up girls," he said.

"What?" *Freaking unbelievable!* Holly turned fully sideways. No easy feat with wet jeans in a bucket seat.

Josh threw her a quick glance and rapped his forehead on the steering wheel once, and then again, as if he hadn't quite achieved his original objective. "This is humiliating." He stared at the windshield. "I would, for instance, walk up to a group of girls, work myself into the group, and suggest . . . um . . . a sort of game."

"Game?"

"Er . . . um . . . yes. Like the one those girls suggested."

"You didn't?" Holly was torn between disbelief and horror at the sheer audacity.

"I did," he said in a small voice. "I sort of had this article written about me. An online blog thing about Chicago's bachelors, and it was mentioned in there." Color climbed up over his cheeks as he spoke. "And since then, every now and again, one of those games resurfaces and it happens like it did tonight. I only did it tonight to piss you off. Normally, I don't. I mean, I haven't for . . . years."

Holly spun around in her seat. The extended car hood snaked across the road, low and lean.

"And that worked for you?" She couldn't quite believe any woman could be that stupid.

"Like a charm." He gave her a huge unrepentant grin. "You would not believe how well it worked."

"Hmph."

He had a near-perfect profile. Nauseating.

The traffic eased and they were able to crawl onto the highway. He picked up speed.

"Of course," she said, not wanting to give him the last word, "it only works because of the way you are. Anyone else would have their face slapped."

"I'm funny and I'm charming?"

Oh, that was a good one. "It's because you're hot. It has nothing at all to do with your personality."

Through the open window the wind cooled her face. Somewhere in this city, her sister was hiding. Portia was on a high when she left, but what goes up surely must come down, and that was what scared the pants off Holly.

"So you think I'm hot?"

Holly jerked her attention back to her companion. He looked altogether too smug for her liking. "You know you're hot."

"But you think so?"

Was he fishing? "What do you care?"

Why exactly had she started this line of conversation? Holly wriggled in her seat. Her jeans made rude noises against the leather and she stopped. She was being a wuss. Holly Partridge was a fully actualized, independent, master—in the generic—of her destiny. This conversation was not making her uncomfortable.

He glanced in her direction. "But you do?"

"Lots of girls do." He was like a terrier with a rat.

"Yeah," he said and grinned at her. "But lots of girls don't want to rip my arms off and beat me to death with them."

"And your point is?" He'd given her a rather pleasant visual to go with.

"When you say I'm hot, you mean it."

"Okay." She rolled her eyes, not sure why she was allowing herself to be dragged into his game, but going anyway. "I think you're hot. Happy now?" Boy, like his ego needed any more stroking. "I think we should start looking—"

"How hot?"

"For the love of God." What did he care if she thought he was hot or not? "Drive the bloody car."

"I am driving the *bloody* car." He slid her a sidelong look loaded with something that made her stomach quiver and her head go meandering off over the hills and dales again. "I want to know how hot. On a scale of one to ten, one being the average campfire and ten being a runaway forest fire."

Holly cursed the small, insistent throb beneath the surface of her skin. "Inferno."

"Really?" He pulled his mouth into an upside-down smile and then flipped it right over into a broad knee trembler that made her blood thicken and flow like lava. "Good to know."

Her face flushed and she tugged at the sweatshirt sticking to her damp body. She wished she hadn't brought any of this up now.

"Hey?" He tapped her arm. "Messing with you again." His smile took any sting out of the remark. "You looked like you needed a laugh."

And she did. Holly's irritation slid away.

"Truce?" He glanced in her direction. His blue eyes softened momentarily, and then he ruined the moment with a wink. "Until we find your sister or your car. Then we can go back to all-out war."

Holly laughed. She couldn't help herself. "Okay, truce."

The tight knot of worry in her belly eased a little.

"We'll find her, Holly." He squeezed her hand briefly and then let it go. Call her crazy, but she believed him.

"I brought you some clothes." He indicated the bag he'd flung on the backseat. "At least they're dry."

"You did?"

He narrowed his eyes at her. "I'm a nice person."

Grudgingly, Holly admitted it was certainly a nice thing to do. She leaned over and grabbed the bag. Her shoulders rubbed against his, and the heat of him rushed all the way to her toes. She moved away quickly and pretended to examine the contents of the bag. Nothing fancy; some sweatpants and a T-shirt.

"Is this yours?" Holly dragged out the T-shirt.

"Yes, it's mine." He clucked his tongue. "I would never be so gauche as to give one woman's clothing to another."

"You," Holly said, "are too smooth for your own good." On an impulse, she read the label and swore. "This is Hugo Boss."

"So?"

"People don't buy Hugo Boss T-shirts, for the love of God. They buy them from the GAP or Sears or . . . or Walmart. They do not buy them from Hugo Boss."

"Put it on." He shook his head. "And Hugo Boss makes great T-shirts. I like the way they fit."

Holly wriggled out of her sweatshirt. She tossed the damp, stinking mess onto the backseat.

Josh's eyes flickered in her direction.

Holly wanted to groan. Her nipples were clearly outlined against the fabric of her tank top and she whipped the T-shirt up to her chest. It smelled of Josh, crisp aftershave, and warm male.

"Shouldn't you take that off as well?" he suggested in a husky voice that shot straight through her in a bolt of lust, as surprising as it was unwelcome.

"I can't change in the car."

"Of course you can." He indicated the thinly spaced traffic now they were out of the city center. "Nobody will see, including me. I have my eyes on the road and I promise not to look, but you should get out of those wet things."

What a dog; cool as a cucumber, totally in control of this game. He was such a smug son of a bitch. But Holly Partridge never backed down from a challenge.

She whipped off the tank top and tossed it in the back. The car lurched and swerved.

Holly barked her elbow against the door as she managed to dive into the concealment of the T-shirt. *Gotcha!*

"Jesus." He jerked his head back. "You should warn a guy before you do something like that."

Holly luxuriated in the warmth of the T-shirt. It was steaming hot outside the car, but the wet fabric of her sweatshirt had seeped into her bones. He was right, though. Hugo Boss did make a rather fine T-shirt. She reached for the button of her jeans.

His eyes slid in her direction.

"Eyes on the road." She undid the button and slid down the zipper. The sound rippled through the silent car.

It took her longer than anticipated. Wet denim in a bucket seat made for some concerted wriggling. Holly was panting by the time she managed to hurl her sopping jeans after her sweatshirt.

He had excellent powers of concentration.

She didn't bother to check the label on the sweatpants. They were probably worth more than her apartment. Her legs slid easily into them. He had those typically male slim hips, so the sweats did catch on her hips, but she tightened the drawstring anyway. The pants were laughably too long. She hauled off her soggy Converses and rolled up the cuffs.

He was right. She was immediately more comfortable. There was a bottle of water in the bag and she pounced. It was cool and fresh, and Holly kept glugging until there was nothing more to swallow. She lowered the bottle with a sigh of satisfaction.

One side of his mouth turned up as if he was laughing on the inside. "Thirsty?"

"Uh-huh." Did he have any idea how sexy that look was? Of course he did. He probably practiced it in the mirror. Holly rummaged through the bag again discreetly, under the guise of putting her soaked clothes away. She came away disappointed. Between Josh, her car, and the police, she'd managed to ignore the problem for most of the night, but her stomach was now feeling abandoned.

"You're hungry," he said, proving that while he had the morals of an alley cat, there were definite advantages to this temporary truce.

He took the off-ramp to the north.

They were almost in Willow Park. Something should be familiar.

The quiet night left the long arterial street virtually deserted. Years ago, prostitutes and dealers had plied their trade down this road. Now the community living on either side had reclaimed it. Tire and service shops flashed past the windows, a couple of motels now serving mostly truckers, a Korean barbeque and . . . indoor golf? Holly turned her head to ask. There. In the near distance, its yellow arches beckoning—McDonald's!

Josh pulled over and she could have kissed him.

Chapter Seven

Josh watched her. He seemed to be doing more of it as the night wore on, but Holly fascinated him.

She ate like a cat: quick, neat, and with the sort of concentrated attention that assured him he would lose a hand if he reached for a fry. The smell of burger filled the car. He never let anyone eat in his car, but she hadn't wanted to stop and he hadn't even put up a fight. He shouldn't have worried.

Nothing got away from Holly; no crumb, no morsel, no trace of two Big Macs, both with fries, and three chocolate chip cookies. To be fair, she did offer him one of the cookies, but only after she'd worked her way through everything else and washed it down with a large latte and another bottle of water.

"Better?"

"You have no idea." Holly slumped back in her seat. "I was in such a hurry to get here I forgot to eat this morning."

"Are you going to fill me in on what's up with your sister?" He had to ask because he suspected there was a whole helluva lot more to her story.

"Nope." A guarded expression slipped over Holly's

features, like a curtain descending. *Thanks for watching, that's all folks, have a safe ride home.*

He could've seen that one coming. She didn't trust him and she clung stubbornly to the belief she didn't like him. Holly's secrets lay sticky between them, and he wanted to fight his way clear. They'd butted heads constantly in high school, but he sensed a lot more behind *despised*, and he was going to get to the bottom of that, too.

"Okay." *Slow and easy does it.* "Why don't you tell me what I did in high school that has you bent out of shape?"

"What do you mean?"

There she went again, with the duck and weave.

"What did I do?" Josh leaned over until she had nowhere else to look but right at him. "Why are you pissed at me?"

Her eyes narrowed. "You seriously don't know?"

"I seriously don't know." She glared at him; he held her gaze. "Tell me."

"I'd rather not." She tilted her ski-jump nose and turned her head.

What a ball breaker. Josh laughed to himself.

"What's so funny?"

"Oh, nothing." She played it cool, but Josh bet she seethed inside, dying to demand if he was laughing at her and nearly killing herself not to.

"We should be looking for Portia," she said.

"You're a woman; you can look and talk at the same time. Now tell me what I did."

For a moment, she wavered. "I don't think so." She shook her head.

"Why not?"

With her pencils sacrificed to the rainstorm, her hair curled and writhed down her back in a tortoiseshell mass. He wanted to touch it to see if it was as alive as it looked.

"We called a truce," she said in a reasonable tone. "I don't want to get into anything. I want to find Portia and go home."

"Doesn't a truce mean trusting . . ."

She made a slicing motion with her hand, clearly meant to shut him up. It worked well. "Anyway, like you said earlier, it's long in the past and it doesn't matter anymore."

Except Josh got the distinct feeling it still did. He parked the car halfway down the main street of Willow Park. "Where do you want to start?"

Josh had barely finished clipping her seat belt when her head dropped back and her eyes closed. Exhaustion clung to her face in a slack-jawed pallor. They'd combed Willow Park from one side to the other. He'd worked his phone like he was launching the space shuttle, but in the end he drew a blank. It was now well past the witching hour and they'd given up for the night.

Holly hadn't come quietly. There had been one more street and one more person to ask until, finally, the sidewalks rolled up and the good families of the neighborhood went to their beds. Alone on an abandoned street in a dead neighborhood, even Holly was forced to concede defeat.

Joshua slid into the driver's seat.

In sleep, her face relaxed. The delicate bone structure made her fascinating, as opposed to classically beautiful.

It was the sort of face that grew on you. Not a pretty face, but a smooth oval that owed its charm to glorious skin and a sinful mouth. Her mouth was made for kisses and laughter and sliding over skin. The way she compressed those soft, generous lips into a grim line was a crying shame.

A woman like Holly snuck up on you. You started out thinking she was passably attractive. Then you watched the play of intelligence, humor, and life march across her features and she transcended to fascinating. Until, one day, you couldn't remember a time she didn't knock you on your ass. As a teenager, renowned for only dating the prettiest girls, his interest in her had confused him. As a man, he could see she had the sort of looks to keep a man entranced.

She got under his skin. Folded into the seat of his car, she resembled a shapeless bundle of sweats, but Josh had spent most of the night watching the sway of her ass. She moved like a set of steel drums laid down a smooth reggae beat in her head. A fluid glide to a silent rhythm rocked her hips from side to side and drew his eyes like a lodestone. His sweats hung tantalizingly low on her hips. He wanted to run his tongue along the line of the waistband and dip beneath. He wanted to bury his face between her thighs and draw in the unique scent of her.

"Oh, shit." Now he had wood and the timing was so off, it made his head hurt. He banged his head against the headrest to shake some of those dog thoughts out.

She snuffled in her sleep, deepening the creases between her eyebrows. She frowned too much. Holly carried a heavy load.

He wanted to lighten it for her, not make things worse by hitting on an exhausted, worried woman.

What was the deal with the sister? There was a lot here he didn't know, and it made him determined to find out. He'd been tangled up in enough needy women to recognize the yawning pit of Portia. There wasn't enough love, nurturing, or tenderness to fill the endless cavern of need.

Holly, on the other hand, kept everyone at arm's length. If there had been any way to avoid accepting his help, she would have jumped at it. As it was, she'd gone along grudgingly, bitching and taking shots at him all the way.

"I didn't sleep with your sister," he'd said earlier tonight. Josh wasn't sure she believed him.

She'd posed the question and turned away with a speculative gleam in her molasses eyes when he gave her the answer.

He wasn't sure what was happening behind those dark-as-sin eyes. And he really wanted to know. He wanted her trust and he'd spent the night trying to earn it.

Her head slipped and he carefully rearranged it so her neck wouldn't get stiff.

Why was he making this his problem again?

He let his fingers linger on the warm velvet of her skin for a moment.

Idiot. He slipped the car into gear and eased onto the deserted streets. The tires made a silky hiss against the road. Some misguided sense of chivalry had him in this up to his neck. And yet—and this was the real shocker— he didn't mind.

Life had lacked a certain purpose lately anyway, and what better distraction than a feisty, pint-sized burr of attitude, full to choking with repressed emotion and secrets. It should have been enough to have him running screaming into the hills.

He couldn't say he had a type. He did know what he didn't want. He didn't want a ball breaker, a reactionary basket case with so much baggage it clattered along behind her like the chains of Jacob Marley.

Laura. Another face he hadn't seen in years, though it was never far from his thoughts. Another damsel who needed rescuing. Only he'd fucked that one up six ways to Sunday.

Holly made another of those soft snorts.

Except here he was and, apparently, quite happy to stay for a while. He'd do better this time.

He checked his watch. It was almost four a.m. and the highway reverted to raccoons and litter. As he eased over the bridge, the traffic got busier. Even at this time, there were still some hearty party animals on the go, but it had quieted down substantially. The car's engine echoed loudly in the concrete tomb of the parking garage.

His passenger didn't stir.

Josh stuffed her wet things into the gym bag and tossed it over his arm. He walked around the car and eased open the passenger door.

She was curled into a tight ball that made him smile. Man, she was a bite-sized bundle of tangled-up trouble. And still, he reached in and carefully hoisted her into his arms.

She was surprisingly solid for such a small woman. It must be the weight of the massive chip on her shoulder.

He eased into the lobby, where Philip counted down the last few hours of his graveyard shift.

Philip hit the elevator button for him and smiled at Josh's passenger like an elderly uncle.

"Good night," the old doorman whispered as the elevator doors swished shut.

Josh put her down to open the door to his condo.

And Holly woke up.

Being Holly, she went from sleep to full alert in under point two of a second and came up swinging. "What the hell are you doing?"

The pit of his stomach dropped.

Her cheeks flushed and she braced her arms akimbo. Her hair was flattened against her head on one side, making up for it by springing free and wild over the rest of her head. She looked certifiable. She looked like she was going to hand his balls to him.

"I'm not doing anything." Exhaustion slammed him. From the other side of the door, his bed called. "You fell asleep in the car and I carried you up here."

"You should have woken me. You had no right to put your hands on me." She twitched like an angry cat.

"You were fast asleep. I was trying to be nice." He reached for his last scrap of patience.

"I'm not some helpless, frail female who needs a big strong man to sweep her into his arms and make her problems disappear."

Josh leaned back and straightened the crick in his back. Big strong men also got sore backs from carrying ungrateful women up several floors in the middle of the night. Enough with this crap. He was being a god-damned gentleman here, and a little appreciation would be nice.

"You know what, Holly? Fuck it."

Her mouth dropped open and her eyes widened.

He'd shocked her. Good. He opened the door to his apartment and strode in, leaving it open for her. He would grab a couple of hours sleep before he got up to train. After that, she could get back to giving him crap.

"What does that mean?" She trailed him into the condo, still looking bellicose.

Josh shrugged and didn't look at her. If he did, he might give in to temptation and wring her neck. If he could work up the energy, he might actually feel taken advantage of. He had given up his night to take her where she wanted to go, followed her around like an obedient serf, and asked how high when she said jump. He'd been insulted, mocked, and challenged every step of the way. She'd even called his XK-E a penis. He loved his car. It had taken him months and months to find it and even longer to have it restored.

"It means what it says. Fuck it." He hauled two bottles of water out of the fridge, slapped one on the counter for her, and downed his in almost one gulp.

"Close the door," he said over his shoulder as he strode down the corridor. Just fuck it. "Towels are under the basin in the bathroom and the sheets on the bed are clean. Knock yourself out."

Holly winced as the door slammed behind him. *Oops.* Perhaps the last bit had been rather rude? Okay. She hadn't behaved well at the end there. Actually, bitchy might come closer to the truth. And while she indulged a brief masochistic foray toward truth, she would have to concede her behavior for most of the night might, possibly, be judged as less than stellar.

He'd been rather wonderful tonight. Patient, understanding, and compassionate, and the thrust and parry of their verbal sparring had been a welcome distraction. Other than those first few moments in the bar, Josh Hunter had been nothing like the arrogant jerk she'd gone to school with. To be fair, she hadn't made much effort all those years ago to get to know him. The Josh Hunter who had given up his night to help out an old school adversary was the sort of man it was hard to keep at arm's length.

He'd completely taken her by surprise with the carrying thing.

She'd been asleep. For the first time in more years than she could name, Holly had been safe and warm and cherished. It had been such a sublime feeling, like floating on a happy cloud. She'd woken to find herself engulfed in unadulterated Josh. For a moment, she'd wallowed in the flood of sensations.

Hard on the heels of reveling came the sensory overload of the warm, citrus smell of him, the luxurious press of soft fabric over hard muscle beneath her cheek and the sure embrace of a pair of powerful arms. At which point she'd panicked.

She was really mad at herself. She wasn't supposed to want to curl up like a kitten and have Josh make her purr. In her imaginary world, her meeting with him had gone differently. She'd been poised and calm, having concluded a multibillion-dollar deal or received a Nobel Prize for her groundbreaking work in economics. In her scenario she was cool, aloof, and cutting. Also, in her world, Josh was sixty pounds heavier and losing his hair.

What didn't happen in Holly land was the emotional roller coaster she'd been on for almost twenty-four hours now. In her little fantasy, she was not fluctuating rapidly between arousal and distrust, gratitude and suspicion, and like and despise. It was rather exhausting, and she might have overreacted.

"I'm sorry," she called out to the shut door. "I got a fright and took your head off and I'm sorry."

Nothing.

Holly turned away and let out a soft whistle of appreciation. The old loft had been turned into an open-plan condo with exposed brick walls and large industrial ductwork running along the ceiling. One side of the condo boasted floor-to-ceiling vaulted glass windows facing Lake Michigan. A stainless-steel and granite kitchen ran along the opposite wall. The furnishings were minimal. The big leather couches looked comfortable, and the dining room table crouched ready to seat any number from one to twelve.

One or two large modern canvases took pride of place on the bare brick walls. Holly promised herself a closer inspection in the morning. She turned in a circle and took it in. The condo was beautiful, but there was a sense nobody lived in this space. The kitchen counters were clutter free and spotless; there were no socks or coffee cups left for someone to clean up.

Holly grabbed the bottle of water and wandered over to an open doorway. It was an office, dominated by a massive oak desk. Again, ruthlessly tidy and contained. The top of the desk was clear of paper and a laptop sat front and center on the leather blotter.

She crept to the next door and saw a bedroom. Like the rest of the apartment, it was a showpiece. She eased her way into the room.

All white bedding contrasted sharply with the deep mahogany sheen on the furniture.

Holly slipped off her shoes and put them carefully beside a formidable tallboy. She stopped and bent to neaten them up. It didn't help. Her soaked black Converses stuck out like a set of dog's balls in the pristine perfection of the room.

A large vase of lilies made dramatic sweeps against the dressing table.

"Ah, bugger." The mirror was not her friend. Her hair hung like a tattered old mop head down her back. Dark, tired smudges underlined her eyes like a raccoon's, and Josh's clothes hung on her as if she were a child playing dress up.

It wasn't good.

She edged around the jamb of a door set beside the mirror and peered inside. A black marble and glass bathroom, large enough for a decent frat party, glared at the intruder. The cool floor caressed her feet as Holly tiptoed across it. The shower bristled with chrome. Spigots, showerheads and faucets gleamed at her. It was too much to hope for a simple on/off lever.

Holly turned away, defeated, and slunk back into the bedroom. A shower would have to wait until the morning. Portia would have to wait, too, and as much as she hated to admit it, she needed sleep. Outside the bedroom window, people were still out and about. The thick glass deadened sound in the condo.

The bed wasn't exactly welcoming her with its arctic white, but Holly was past the point of caring. The apartment was cool and comfortable after the humidity of the night, and her feet carried her to where they wanted to be. She should get undressed, but she was warm and dry in her borrowed finery and the idea died instantly. Holly flipped back the duvet and slid beneath in one quick movement, trying not to touch too many surfaces on her way in.

She gave a small whimper as expensive orthopedic support met her tired body. The sheets were clean and fresh, and a goose down duvet wrapped around her like a maternal cloud. At least she was sure it was goose down because it cradled her as close to heaven as she could get right now.

Tomorrow she would find Portia and deal with a pissed-off stud muffin. And if she, somehow, managed to achieve half of that, she may as well give world peace a crack.

Chapter Eight

Holly woke up still tired and with a dead weight in the center of her chest. She lay still, listening to the small sounds of someone, probably Josh, moving about on the other side of her bedroom door. The events of the previous day filtered back to her. She had to find Portia, and find her today. With a groan, she rolled over and grabbed her phone.

Fourteen missed calls, thirteen of them from Emma and one from Steven.

Holly suppressed a twitch of guilt. She'd barely waited long enough to leave Steven a message yesterday before heading for Chicago. Steven got rabid about roaming charges, so she texted instead. Holly kept it brief, explaining where she was and that she'd be back in a day or two.

Emma answered on the first ring.

"Hey, Em."

"Where have you been? I've been trying to reach you for hours."

Holly jammed the harsh words back down her throat. Worry made Emma unnecessarily brusque. Holly rubbed her gritty eyes before answering. "We were looking for Portia last night. It got very late, so I was probably sleeping."

"But you didn't find her?" Emma's voice wobbled.

"No, Em, we didn't," Holly said softly, not wanting the threatening tears to start on the other end of the phone. "I'm going to try again today. I promise I'll call as soon as I have something."

"Promise?"

"Promise. Are you okay?"

Emma heaved a laden sigh. "No, I'm awful. I'm nearly sick with anxiety. I think I might even have an attack. I haven't slept since Portia left."

Holly opened her mouth to ask why, if Emma had been so concerned about Portia, it had taken three days for her to tell Holly her sister was gone. It seemed unkind; instead, she asked, "Did you get the message I left last night?"

"Yes." Emma's voice got higher and more over-wrought. "Your car was stolen?"

"Uh-huh, and everything in it." Holly kept it calm.

"Oh my God." Emma paused. "Everything?"

"Yup." Holly tried to stretch the cricks in her back. "Clothes, money, and my passport."

"What are you going to do?" Emma whispered.

"I'm going to need your help."

"Me?" Emma's voice rose on a squeak. "What can I do? I'm here in London and you're all the way over there in Chicago."

"Em." Going into a screaming frenzy wouldn't help this situation any.

"You know I'm not good at this sort of thing, Holly. You know that about me; it distresses me." Emma cranked up the panic.

"Emma." She put some starch in her voice. "Listen to me carefully."

Emma whimpered and went silent.

"Are you listening, Em?"

"Uh-huh."

Holly wasn't convinced, but she forged on. "Emma, I am going to need you to organize a way for some money to get to me. I think you can use PayPal or something similar."

"Holly." Emma went all breathy. "I don't know how to do that."

"Neither do I, but if you go to the bank they'll tell you how to do it."

Holly counted slowly to twenty.

Emma sniffed. "Okay."

"While you're there, I want you to get the credit card sorted out."

"It's your credit card," Emma said. "Why can't you do it from there?"

"Because." She would have to spell it out clearly. Emma wasn't stupid, but if she could possibly get somebody else to do the thinking for her, she would. "I have no identification. My entire wallet was in the car: driver's license, passport, everything."

"But—"

"And you are the other account holder, and as such you have rights on the account."

"Oh? What about the car?"

"I'll call the insurance from here."

"Good idea." Emma sounded relieved.

"Do you think you could look in my files and send me the policy number?"

"Yes," Emma said.

"Good, Em." At least it was a step in the right direction. "Do it as soon as you can and text it to me."

"Okay, Holly." Emma went quiet again. "Will you find Portia today?"

"I'm going to do everything I can." Outside the window, the city moved into a new day. The sounds from inside the apartment grew louder. It was time to go. "You keep calling the police and . . .". The words got stuck, and she forced them past the knot in her throat. "You might want to start calling hospitals."

"Holly." Emma's voice quivered. "You don't think she's—"

"Don't." Holly couldn't stand it if Emma voiced the unthinkable. So far, there'd only been that one incident, right before they'd got her sister on medication, when Portia had veered too close to hurting herself. Those were two hours Holly never wanted to live again.

"What the hell were you thinking?" It slipped out of her mouth before Holly could stop it. "You know how unstable she is and you let her go."

A long, dead silence followed, and then a sniffle. "You're so mean."

Dread fastened its claws around Holly's throat as the sniffle grew to a sob. Emma was crying. It's what Emma did when confronted. It's what Emma did when she was sad. It's what Emma did when she was angry. It's what Emma did all the bloody time, and Holly didn't have the patience for it this morning.

"I'm here in Chicago and I have a place to stay, but I would like to be able to take care of myself." Holly steeled herself. "I need some money, so please organize it as soon as you can."

And she hung up.

The phone weighed in her hand. She almost called back to check if Emma was all right. She shrugged it off. Emma would be fine because she was sitting at home in London in an apartment Holly paid most of the rent on, with all her things around her. Emma wasn't in another country, wearing someone else's clothes, and relying on a man who'd gone to bed angry with her.

What was needed here was caffeine and a shower. Both of which were going to involve Josh. But first there was an apology owed. She hated the idea, but there it was.

She found Josh in the kitchen, standing beside one end of a central island and staring at his open fridge.

He wore a pair of exercise shorts, some running shoes, and nothing else. The chorded muscle on his arms and chest slid beneath smooth tan skin as he leaned into the fridge. His athletic shorts hung low on his lean hips beneath a perfectly ripped set of abs. He must have been exercising. A fine sheen of sweat created a light-and-shadow play across his upper body.

He tipped back his head and drank from a bottle of water. His throat moved as he drank and, right on target, a large trickle of water escaped over his chin, stroked his throat, and disappeared into the carved groove between his pectorals.

Holly followed the drop into a line of coarse, dark hair disappearing beneath his shorts. She peeled her tongue off the roof of her mouth.

He turned and caught her standing there like a starstruck tween.

Holly dragged her eyes away; a guilty blush crept up her neck. She didn't like the whole muscle thing. Much.

"Good morning." His greeting was polite enough, but missing a smile or any trace of warmth.

Holly stopped halfway to the island. "Good morning."

"Did you sleep well?" He tossed his empty water bottle into the recycling bin. The bottle hit the sides of the bin with a clatter and dropped.

"Yes, thank you." Jeez, so polite she almost bobbed a curtsy.

"Would you like juice? Coffee?" His smile stopped way short of reaching his eyes.

Holly trod the few remaining steps to the island warily. She was at a distinct crabby and grimy disadvantage. "Coffee, please?"

Dark stubble shaded his jaw, and against the warm tan of his face, his eyes were piercingly blue and colder than a blast from the air conditioner. "What kind?"

"Hmm?" Holly tried to regain her balance. The combination of his crazy, sexy body and detached civility wound her up tight.

"What kind of coffee would you like?" He indicated a stainless-steel beast squatting against the far wall like it belonged in an Italian café.

"Oh?" Of course he had one of those. "Latte?"

His body was, honest to God, sculpted like one of those men you saw in aftershave commercials. What was the matter with her?

"Sure." He turned to the coffee machine and twisted and pulled at knobs and levers. Rippling, lovely things happened beneath the skin of his back.

Holly pulled up a stool and enjoyed the view. "Um, Josh?"

"Yes?" He half-turned to glance at her over his shoulder.

"About last night?" Holly had to raise her voice above the hissing and gurgling of his machine. "I wanted to say sorry for taking your head off."

"Whatever." He frothed the milk. There was no point in trying to talk over the noise. Holly regrouped as she waited.

"Look." She tried to catch his eye as he put a steaming cup of caffè latte in front of her. "I was tired and worried and I had a knee-jerk reaction. It was nice of you to go to the trouble of carrying me up here and—"

"Don't sweat it, Holly." He reloaded coffee grounds. "I'm going to help you find your sister and then we'll go our separate ways. There's no need to even get into this."

Holly opened her mouth to argue and shut it again. She didn't have to be friends with Josh to find Portia. She didn't have to get any closer to him than politeness demanded. She could keep him at a healthy distance and still benefit from his help. It was the perfect deal.

Except it didn't sit right.

Josh made an espresso for himself.

He didn't look mad. His movements were smooth and controlled, no jerking or slamming things about. An impassive mask settled over his face, as if she had ceased to exist outside of the realm of the strictly necessary.

"I really am sorry."

"Fine. Apology accepted. We were both tired." He shrugged one muscular shoulder and leaned his hips up against the counter.

The lure of coffee won and she took a sip of her latte. Holly moaned. A man who made a cup of coffee like this was worth risking the bear cave. She drank half the cup in the loaded silence.

Josh thumbed through his phone.

She should probably leave him alone to get over himself. But she wouldn't be Holly Partridge if she did that. "No, it's not fine. Because you were great to me last night and I behaved badly. I was tired and cranky, and I have this propensity to shoot off at the mouth before I think."

He sipped his espresso and studied her over the rim of his cup.

The heat spread all the way down to her toes. At least he'd made eye contact. "I'm sorry I was such a bitch."

"You think I slept with your sister," he said.

"I was probably wrong about that." Holly managed to look contrite.

"Probably?" He glowered. "Definitely."

Wow, he was seriously pissed about that. "Look, Josh, what was I supposed to think? Given the past and what I know of you."

"I'm not that kid anymore. I cleaned up my act after—" He clenched his jaw. "I cleaned up my act."

"Okay." Holly held up her hands in surrender. "You didn't sleep with my sister."

"And you called my car a penis."

Holly opened her mouth and shut it again. "I shouldn't have said that." The car *was* a penis, but she kept it to herself. "Are you done being mad now?"

"I'm not mad."

"Yes, you are."

"No, I'm not."

"Yes, you are."

"No. I. Am. Not." There was a glimmer of life through the permafrost.

"Are, too." Holly poked.

"Holly." He stopped on the cusp of yelling at her, but at least he couldn't freeze her out when he was irritated.

"I'm not worth the sulk," she said.

He groaned and dropped his head forward. "You are the most irritating woman I know."

"Gosh." Holly went back to her coffee. "That's quite something, considering all the women you know."

He strode forward and planted his elbows on the island, putting his face level with hers. "Someone should have wrung your neck by now." Up close she could see how long and thick his eyelashes were. A ghost of a smile chased across his face.

"Most people find me easy to get along with," she said.

"Oh, yeah?" He folded his arms over his chest.

Holly's eyes strayed over the bulge of muscle the action initiated.

"Name one."

She had to think. "Steven." Most of the time. "He's always saying I'm easy to get along with." For always, substitute sometimes, but still . . .

"And Steven is?" He kept it light, but Holly sensed a sudden tension creep back into the kitchen.

"My boyfriend."

"Boyfriend?" There was nothing alarming in his tone, but Holly got a shivery sensation over her skin.

The loaded atmosphere in the kitchen made her want to babble. "Technically not a boyfriend. He doesn't like that term, but, yes, we have a long-standing arrangement."

Something hot and primal flickered across his face but was instantaneously gone again. "Is he going prematurely bald from all the hair you make him pull out?"

"Ha, ha." She attempted to lighten the atmosphere. "Steven has a full head of hair, thank you." It struck her how close his face was to hers. She would only have to lean forward a small bit. Until her mouth touched his mouth. Holly sat back and raised her cup.

"What do you mean by arrangement?" The weird tone was back in his voice.

Holly's guard slipped into place. "Why do you want to know?"

"I'm curious and we've exhausted my love life."

Holly snorted into her latte. "I doubt we've even scratched the surface of your love life."

"Tell me."

"Tell you what?" Holly hedged, not sure she wanted to discuss her relationship with Josh.

"How long have you and Steve been an item?"

"His name is Steven; he doesn't like to be called Steve. And we've been together for six years."

He whistled. "Sounds serious. You going to marry him?"

"No," she said. "We don't believe in marriage." And they didn't, or else they might be married by now. Or not. It didn't matter. "Marriage is an outdated institution."

"Really?" He tilted his head. "Since when?"

"Oh, come on, Joshua." What was it Steven said? "The idea of a man and a woman staying in a monogamous relationship for years and years is antiquated."

Josh raised his eyebrows.

Holly squelched the tiny part of her that was just as doubtful. "People change, they grow, and most of the time they grow away from each other. The world moves too fast these days to hold on to some sort of sweet, outdated romanticism."

"Really?"

"Yes, really. Marriage was only a secure position for women who had no means of supporting themselves once they had children. Nowadays, women don't need a safeguard; ergo women don't need to enslave themselves in an institution that fundamentally disadvantages them."

He grunted and narrowed his eyes. "That's quite a theory you have there, Holly. What does Steve say?"

"Steven." He was doing it on purpose. "And we are in perfect agreement on the matter."

"Help me here, Holly?"

She bristled at the soft underlying challenge in his voice.

"How does this theory of yours work in practice?"

"What do you mean?" Where the hell was he going with this?

"How does it work?" He shrugged. "According to you, the idea of a man and a woman in a long-term, monogamous relationship is antiquated?"

"We have an open and mature relationship." Holly huffed and drained her coffee cup. She couldn't quite meet his eye. This bit always stuck in her throat when Steven brought it up. She wasn't going to share that with Josh.

"'Open and mature'?" His eyes didn't waver from her face, and the skin on her neck and cheeks warmed. "How open? Like seeing other people open?"

"Yes. No. I don't know. Steven and I believe in not putting labels on things and restricting them. We enjoy what we have and take each other as we are."

"Interesting," he said, challenge overloading every syllable. "And how open have you been in this relationship, and how open is Steve the Swinger?"

"He isn't a swinger." Holly's hackles came up. "And I have never felt the need to have my needs met outside of our relationship." She never asked and Steven never told her if he did. She didn't want to think about that.

"So Stevie keeps you happy and satisfied, does he?"

"Yes."

"In bed?"

His question rocked her back. Where did he get off asking her stuff like that?

"I don't have to answer that." Holly leaped to her feet, done with this conversation. "That is absolutely none of your business."

There was nothing wrong with her relationship with Steven. It was the way both of them liked it.

"You know what I think, Holly?" Josh calmly ignored her outrage and turned back to his coffee machine.

"No, and I don't care."

He chuckled, but not nicely. "I think you're kidding yourselves."

"I don't care what you think." Her voice rose, and she was sorry now she hadn't left him to sulk.

"I think your Stevie has got this rigged to suit himself."

"What bloody rot. You have no understanding of a . . . a mature and . . . giving relationship that allows both partners to develop and grow."

"You're right." He turned and propped his hips on the counter. "I don't know anything about that. I tell you what, though, Holly. I sure as hell wouldn't let some other man touch my woman, and I would make damn sure anyone who came sniffing around her knew it."

"That's barbaric and sexist."

"Could be, but I don't share, and I sure as shit wouldn't share you."

"It's a good thing we'll never have to put that to the test."

He crossed his arms over his chest. He opened his mouth, shut it again, and shook his head.

"What?" Holly demanded.

"Nothing." He grabbed her coffee cup. "Do you want another one?"

Storming off versus another cup of coffee; no contest. "You have no right to attack my relationship. You're only doing this because you're still mad about last night."

He made a rude noise and turned to make her coffee.

Holly was forced to study his rather delicious back and fulminate in silence. A caveman like Josh Hunter would have no way of understanding the kind of sophisticated bond shared by two self-actualized adults.

He put a fresh latte in front of her and stood on the other side of the counter looking delectable.

"Who are you to judge anyway?" Holly narrowed her eyes at him, but he remained impervious to her displeasure. "You bounce from one woman to another."

"Used to." He held up one large, rough finger. "I've grown up since then. I remain faithful to one woman for as long as I'm seeing her. And I'm sorry to break it to you, Holly, but any man who says he wants an open relationship is trying to get the milk without buying the cow."

She gaped at him. Outrage boiled up inside her. "You're disgusting. And what you're saying is utter bullshit."

He tilted his head to the side and stared.

"That is such crap. Steven is nothing like you." She was inches away from tossing her latte at him. "He's comfortable with his feminine side. He always understands my feelings and needs. He doesn't crowd me or try to turn me into a possession. He is cultured, well read, thoughtful, sensitive, and considerate."

His eyes bored into her.

Holly glared right back. She wanted to fry him with her eyes.

Suddenly, he shook his head. "You know what, Holly? You're right." He walked forward and propped his elbows on the counter in front of her. "Your relationship is nothing to do with me. If it works for you, great."

She sensed more. "But?"

He shrugged. "You're a beautiful woman, you're smart, funny, and strong as hell. A woman like you deserves a man who is in it so deep he doesn't want to see daylight again."

"Oh." She deflated like a balloon. "Some of us don't want that sort of relationship."

"Really?" His face softened and took her breath with it.

"Yes, really." Holly's hand trembled and she almost dropped her cup down on the counter. Coffee sloshed over the rim.

His gaze searched her face, too close and too intent.

"I need to get dressed." She just about leaped off her bar stool and ran away. The sweatpants tangled with her feet and ruined her exit. She stopped and tugged them up again. Josh Hunter didn't get her at all.

In it so deep he doesn't want to see daylight again. The girl in her sighed. How would that feel?

Not like her. She yanked the sweatpants up. She wasn't that sort of girl. Today, she would contact Grace and have Grace book her a hotel.

Josh Hunter messed with her head and she let him. He didn't know her. And he for sure didn't get her or Steven. Tracking him down had been a mistake. She should have left the man in the past, where he belonged.

He had no right to judge her or to make her feel . . . restless.

Truce! Like hell!

She stalked into the bathroom and slammed the door behind her for good measure. It gave off a satisfying reverberation through the apartment. Holly approached the shower and stopped. She'd meant to ask Josh how to use it. But it would be a cold day in hell before she did that.

She strode toward the chrome and granite monster occupying almost the entire length of the back wall. She was an intelligent woman. She could work this out without having to ask for his help. The various dials and levers stared back at her. Okay, this couldn't be rocket science. You had hot and you had cold.

"Do you need any help?"

Holly jumped and leaped around. "What the hell are you doing?" Her eyes bugged out of her head. "I could have been naked in here."

He leaned on the doorjamb, looking like an open invitation to be a bad, bad girl. "Now why didn't I think of that?"

Holly's face heated to the hairline. She opened her mouth to blast him, but her mind had emptied.

"Anyway, I brought you these." He held a package in his hand. "These are some briefs, never been used. Your clothes are on the bed. I put them in the dryer earlier this morning, so they're good to go."

"Thanks." Holly forced it past her teeth. He was being considerate and her anger sounded ungracious.

"Now who's sulking?" He gave her a satisfied grin, which made her want to smack his face.

"You had no right to say what you did." Holly was horrified to hear her voice shake a bit.

"You're right. I should have kept my opinion to myself." He moved toward the shower and started turning things. "Okay, this is for the overhead spray." He launched into a rapid-fire explanation, forcing Holly to pay attention.

She desperately wanted to keep arguing. He didn't understand how things were between her and Steven. If he did, he wouldn't be saying such inane things.

"I take it you want to head out as soon as possible?"

Holly gave him a stiff nod.

"Okay," he said. "I'll get changed and we can get some breakfast." He adjusted the temperature for her and stepped back.

"Start with a shirt." She didn't get why he insisted on walking around like some pinup.

"Why, Holly." He folded his arms over his chest. Biceps

bulged beneath the skin. The son of a bitch was doing this on purpose. "You don't think I'm hot anymore?"

"Out." Holly pointed to the door.

He took a step toward her. "Are you sure?"

Holly backed away, cursing herself for being such a wimp while at the same time responding to a base need for self-preservation.

He took another step, and so did she. His bare skin radiated a heat that enveloped her and her breath got tricky, like breathing through smoke. Her back hit the vanity and she stopped, helpless as he closed the distance.

He leaned forward and put his hands next to her hips, caging her between his arms. "There's a spare toothbrush in the vanity," he said against her ear.

Her skin broke out in goose bumps. "Um, thanks."

He was much too close.

She pushed against his chest with both her hands. The skin of his chest burned an impression onto her palms. Her hands stuck to him as if fixed there. Holly gave a stronger push. "Just back off."

"Careful, Holly, you might hurt my feelings."

"Then I'm aiming too far north." She snatched her tingling hands back.

The door shut on him laughing.

"I'm only using you to find my sister." She glared at the solid panel of wood, willing it to turn into his smug, insufferable face so she could kick it.

"Sure you are," came the cocky response.

Chapter Nine

Holly locked the bathroom door before she shed her clothes. It might have taken an engineering degree to turn it on, but the shower was heavenly. Water streamed over her tired muscles and worked pure bliss on her aches and kinks. She allowed herself the small luxury before reluctantly snapping off the jets, long before they'd worked their magic. She wouldn't put it past Josh to get impatient and bang on the door.

She wrapped herself in a huge, fluffy towel before carefully sticking her head around the bedroom door. On the bed were her clothes, as promised, and the un-opened package of boxer shorts. Holly picked them up and examined them. This was as close as she intended to get to being in Josh Hunter's pants.

He'd thrown her off balance before, but she would recover. She was thirty years old and she didn't need to behave like she had in school. She would be firm, assertive, and polite. The impulse to storm off was childish, and there was no need cutting off her nose to spite her face. He could help her and, right now, she needed help.

Holly put the comb on the dresser to good use,

working through the snarled mess on her head. Her scalp was raw by the time she had untangled the worst of the knots, but she was much calmer. She patted her hair into a semblance of normal. It was going to dry into a crazy mess of curls, but there was nothing she could do about it.

Holly pulled on her clothes. That was better. She was back again. Her phone buzzed as she opened the door and stepped into the hallway. It was a message from Steven, wishing her luck with Portia and asking if she would be back by the weekend. He had a faculty dinner he wanted her to attend with him.

"Ready to go?" Josh appeared in the hallway, showered and dressed in jeans and a casual shirt. He looked a million dollars to her buck thirty.

Holly firmly tucked her insecure teenager back in its place and gave him a cool smile. "Yes, thanks to you."

"We should get you some clothes." His gaze scanned her from top to toe.

The idea of new clothes sent a bolt of delight through her. The teenager clamored to be set free and spend, spend, spend, but Holly wouldn't let her.

"No money, remember." She tossed his offer back as if she didn't care about clothes and certainly didn't care what other people thought of her clothes, which she didn't. Getting dressed up to impress other people was superficial and pointless.

"I can buy you some stuff to tide you over," he said.

"No, you can't." No way in hell she wanted to owe him even more. She brushed past him and got a knee-threatening whiff of warm man and citrus. "I already owe you more than I can possibly repay."

"I'm not keeping score," he said from behind her.

"I am." Holly ignored the frown thundering over his eyes. "Now, what's our next step?"

"Food," he said. "There's a great place down the street."

"I think we should get going straightaway." Holly didn't want to spend precious time over a meal. Portia was still out there. Somewhere.

"We have a bit of time." He gave her a reassuring smile. "I've been busy this morning, and I can tell you about it while we eat."

"Busy doing what?"

"Finding your sister." Josh dug his keys out of his pocket and strolled away.

Holly followed in his wake, grabbing her damp shoes on the way past.

"Aren't we going to get something here?" The gourmet kitchen would have made a foodie weep for joy.

"I don't cook," he said, as if it explained everything.

"Then why . . ." She motioned toward the kitchen and stopped. "Never mind, but you'll have to buy."

"But of course." He grinned at her over his shoulder. "A barbarian like me would never let a lady pay for her own meal."

Holly glared at his back. "You looking for trouble, pretty boy?"

He stopped in the hallway outside the apartment and turned to look at her. "I tell you what," he said with exaggerated patience, "you stop calling me pretty boy and I'll stop pushing your buttons."

"As if you knew which buttons to push," she said.

The look in his eyes said he wasn't buying.

"Deal." She held out her hand because she might as well face it, he so did know how to get a reaction out of her.

He enfolded her hand in a warm clasp.

Happy tingles danced out from the point of contact.

She held on to his hand longer than strictly necessary. She dropped it. "Are you going to feed me or what?"

"I'm going to feed you." He stared at her. He did that a lot, as if he was trying to piece her together. "And then I'm going to tell you about the progress I've made."

Holly backed two steps away from him and out of line of sight. Josh Hunter needed to stay out of her head. "I should call my other sister, Grace."

"Do you need a phone?"

"Nope." Holly stood at the elevator as he locked the door. "It was the one thing not in my car."

"We should call about getting you a passport," he said as the elevator car arrived and they stepped in.

She would put it on her list. Holly dialed her sister.

The elevator stopped on the third floor and a woman got in.

"Hey, Josh." The woman's attractive face split in a warm smile of welcome that could have lit up the sky.

Well dressed, attractive, twentysomething with killer shoes—your basic nightmare. "Haven't seen you in a while." The woman cooed and fluttered at Josh.

Here they went again. Holly barely stopped her eye roll in time.

"Hi, Michelle." He gave the woman a friendly enough smile, but it was cool and nothing like the way he smiled at her.

So not the bloody point.

"What have you been doing with yourself?" Michelle pressed closer to Josh.

Josh stepped closer to Holly. "This and that."

"I bet you have." Michelle followed and put a red lacquered hand on his arm. "All party, party, party in your world."

"Well, you know me," Josh said. A tiny muscle jumped in the side of his jaw.

Holly tried not to look like she was listening.

"We all know you." Michelle simpered and stroked his arm. "And you know if the party should ever swing my way . . ."

The jaw muscle went into overdrive. "I'll keep that in mind."

The elevator pinged to a stop and Michelle stepped out. She turned and waggled her fingers at Josh.

He gave a tight smile and jabbed the Close Door button.

"Is she—?"

"No." His jammed his hands in his pockets.

Holly stared at him. He didn't react to the woman at all the way she would have expected. "You don't have to hold back because of me."

His angry gaze nearly blasted her right out of the elevator. "And you're so sure I would?"

"Well, I—"

"Because you know me so well. Right, Holly? Josh the player, the pretty boy. Never lets a hot ass pass him by. Even if she's married."

Holly had no idea where that little tirade had come from. Seems Josh Hunter had a couple of his own buttons.

"This is Grace." Her sister's brusque greeting rescued her.

"Hey, Gracie, it's Holly."

"Oh, hi." And immediately her sister's voice grew guarded.

Grace had left home for university at eighteen and never looked back.

Holly had elected to stay with Emma and Portia and look after them. There were times when she resented Grace her freedom, but it didn't take a genius to understand Grace's choice. Grace had seen her gap and taken it.

The elevator stopped at the lobby and they stepped out.

"This isn't a good time," Grace said.

"Josh, *darling*, is that you?" A curvy blonde stepped right in front of Josh. "You look great."

The blonde eyed him up and down as if she wanted to take a lick from his toes to his head. She crowded Holly to the side.

Josh gave the blonde his cool smile and greeted her. Then he stepped around the blonde and took Holly's elbow.

"Yes, I know you're probably at work." Holly bit her tongue from pointing out it was never a good time for Grace to hear from her family. "I'm sorry, but it's urgent."

She spoke quickly, before Grace could launch into the million and one reasons why she couldn't have this conversation now. A million and one reasons why she didn't want to be dragged back into the messy Partridge family.

"Is someone ill?" Grace liked to pretend she didn't care, but Holly detected the smallest note of something in her sister's cool question that Grace was still there. Inside the big shot corporate lawyer with the perfect, big shot corporate mover-and-shaker husband lurked the same Grace Partridge who used to sit at the kitchen table with her big sister, Holly, as they weathered the storm raging around them.

Josh steered her through the glass entrance doors and into the morning. The sun bounced off the pavement and speared her in the eyeballs.

"It's Portia." Holly cut to the chase as she blinked furiously against the light. "She's gone missing. She left four days ago and told Emma, but Emma didn't say anything until yesterday morning."

"Say that again." Grace's voice grew clipped and abrupt, like it did when she was keeping a tight rein on her emotions.

Holly repeated her story.

"Emma is so damn stupid sometimes," Grace said. "What reason did she give for keeping this from you?"

"I didn't ask." Holly didn't need Grace holding forth on the subject of Emma. "Anyway, it seems Portia called and scared Emma, and that's when Emma got the bright idea to share. I tracked Portia to Chicago, but I'm drawing a blank here."

Dead silence settled over the phone.

"Is she off the meds?"

"Yup." God, it made Holly's head want to explode. "I searched her room before I left. She's been off them for a while. It's hard to tell how long, but there's at least two months' supply in her dresser."

"Ah, shit." Grace took a deep breath. "She went to Chicago? What the hell for?"

"Emma is convinced it has something to do with Melissa."

Grace gasped. "Do you think she knows?"

"I never told her." Holly threw a cautionary look at Josh, but he was busy air-kissing another woman, this one quite a bit older, but still looking at him as if he hung the moon and stars.

"I don't think she knows." But what if Portia did know? Then they could be heading for a major freak-out. She and Grace, by tacit agreement, had kept from the twins the full and ugly truth. "But I think Emma is right. This has definitely got something to do with Melissa."

Josh took a pair of shades from his top pocket and slipped them over her nose.

The relief from the morning sun was immediate. It was hard to resent a man who kept making the bad things go away.

He kept his grip light as he guided her down the street, his touch warm through the bulk of her sweatshirt. A small trickle of sweat tickled its way down her side. She could take Josh up on his offer of buying her clothes, but already the murky waters of obligation lapped at her chin.

"Did you call *him*?" Grace never said their father's name. And neither of them called Melissa mom. They were so screwed up.

"Do you think I should?"

"Why bother?" The anger rode Grace hard and came crackling down the phone lines. "He's too busy with his new family, and at least they aren't ugly and broken like his old one."

"Ah, Gracie." The unbearable weight of her sister's sadness settled over her shoulders. She'd been unable to protect Grace from this. The twins were seven years younger, and she'd kept the worst of it away from them. But Grace, two years her junior, had been right there with her, front and center and directly in the firing line. "He is the way he is."

Latin temperament, their father had called Melissa's illness. Her behavior had been blamed on her hot Venezuelan blood. It made her a handful to live with. She was fiery and passionate and prone to dark moods, but there was nothing wrong with his wife. He'd left for work each morning and never bothered to ask how the girls got to school, got fed, and managed those things that kept life running smoothly. It had taken Holly until the middle of her teens to put a name to her mother's behavior.

"Don't make excuses for him," Grace said.

They reached a small, bistro-style restaurant, and Holly delivered the rest of the bad news to her sister. The hostess, naturally, wriggled around Josh eagerly. She led them to a table, but stopped to chat with Josh before she left.

"Are you all right?" Grace asked.

"Um . . . yes, I'm all right."

Josh exchanged greetings with a young couple at the table next to them.

"I have some help."

Josh excused himself from his conversation and took a call, listening intently to the person on the other side.

"Who?"

"Er . . . you're not going to believe this."

"Tell me." Grace's voice livened with interest.

"Josh Hunter."

Josh glanced up at the sound of his name, but Holly shook her head.

"You're kidding me!" Grace's voice yelped loud over the phone lines.

"Nope."

"You're serious?"

Holly held the phone away from her ear as Grace cackled loudly.

Josh's brows shot to his hairline.

"Josh Hunter is helping you?" Grace gasped, and Holly brought the phone back to her ear. "How the hell did that happen?"

Another short explanation was needed, with Grace yukking it up all the way. Grace sobered abruptly. "Portia went looking for him? What the hell?"

"My thoughts exactly."

Across the table, Josh finished his call and hung up.

"Is he still hot?"

"Uh-huh." Holly raised her voice. "And he's sitting here. Right now. Right across the table."

Josh sat back, a small smile playing around his mouth. "Can he hear me?"

"Yes, he can," Josh said.

"You have got to be shitting me." Grace gave another short bark of laughter. "You hated that guy. Didn't he do that thing to you at some sort of dance?"

"Yup."

Josh's eyebrow shot up in query. He was getting every word of this.

Heat crawled up Holly's face. "Anyway, it's water under the bridge."

"Really?" Grace snorted. "Because as I remember it, you cried—"

"Yes. Well." *Ground, open, right now!*

Josh leaned forward, making no attempt to disguise his interest in her call.

Holly shot Josh a weak smile. "He's been great."

He raised an eyebrow at her.

Holly squirmed a bit. "I'd have been up to my neck in it without him. He found me after my car was stolen and has been helping me ever since."

"Do you need me to do anything?" Grace was all business again.

"No, that's fine, I spoke to Emma." Grace made a rude noise. "If she doesn't come through in a day or two, I'll call back."

"Call me if you need anything else and keep me posted."

"I will. How's Greg?" Holly asked out of obligation.

Grace paused. "Greg's good."

"Is everything okay with you guys?"

"Of course it is." Grace made an impatient sound. "Greg is fine, I'm fine. We're fine."

"That's great." Holly backed off. "I'll call you in a couple of days and tell you what's happening."

"Okay." Grace sounded unenthusiastic. "Holly?"

"Yes."

"I love you," Grace blurted out. "I wanted you to know."

Holly's throat tightened. Grace loved her; they were sisters, but she didn't say it much. The unexpected expression of love caught her off guard.

"I wanted you to know," Grace said. "And I know it can't be easy taking care of Emma and Portia."

"We get along." Her heart swelled into her throat and she suddenly wanted to cry. Except she never cried. Never.

"Those two get along because of you, Holly," Grace said. "I know you put your own life on hold for them." Grace gave a dry, humorless laugh. "For all of us, actually. You've been there for all of us and I love you for it."

"I love you, too, Gracie." Holly disconnected the call and focused on the table's wood grain. Tears threatened beneath her eyelids and she blinked them away. No crying.

"Everything all right?" Josh's voice, soft with concern.

Nope, everything was definitely not all right. Grace had opened up a tender place. "I'm fine. Let's order."

"What dance?"

"It doesn't matter." She wasn't going to get into that, now or ever. "It's over and done with. Let's concentrate on Portia."

His eyes narrowed.

Drop it, just please, please drop it.

"Let me tell you what I've been doing. This is what I've found out." Leaning his elbows on the table, he moved into her space.

Holly moved back. It was hard to concentrate when

he was within touching distance. She got all hot and flushed and stupid.

"Portia spent last night in a hotel in Bucktown. She tried to use the same credit card this morning, but it was refused. The credit card was in your name?"

"That's right." Okay, so now Portia was officially out of funds, unless she had cash with her. Not okay at all. "My phone call, in the bar yesterday, it was about that."

"Ah." He tilted his head as if he wanted to ask more.

"Is that it?" Holly prompted.

"No. It seems she had enough cash on her to pay for the room when she left the hotel a few hours ago."

At least Portia had been safe up until this morning. "So where is she now?"

"That I don't know." He made a wry face. "Yet. She's disappeared again, but at least we know we're closing in on her."

"How did you get this information?" Holly had to ask as he ordered more coffee for them.

"I know some people." He shrugged. "Money leaves a trail, and I know lots of money geeks."

"You know everyone." Holly rolled her eyes at him. "Most of them women."

"But not all." His jaw tightened.

Holly grunted.

Right on cue, he produced his stay-back smile and waved across the restaurant.

Holly gave him a flat stare and he laughed. "People like me. I told you before, I'm nice." He tapped one finger against the tip of her nose. "Even if I was an ass in high school."

Holly's cheeks heated. "So what do you suggest this morning? To find Portia."

"I can make a few more calls, but I need you to level

with me." He let her get away with the dodge, but the questions built behind his eyes.

"I don't want to talk about high school," Holly said.

"About Portia." He threw her a minatory look. "I need you to level with me about Portia, first. And then we can get to high school."

"What do you mean?" She could hear the prevarication in her voice, and so could he. Up went one eyebrow as he called her on her evasion.

Holly lifted the menu. She swore those eyes of his could ferret right into the back of her brain.

He reached over with his index finger and lowered the menu until he could stare at her eyeball to eyeball. "There's something going on and you're not telling me."

Holly opened her mouth to deny it, but he shook his head slowly from side to side, and she snapped her mouth shut.

"Come on, Holly. There is so much here you're not saying. I don't need to hear your life story, but I'm trying to help you and I need some answers."

Holly wrestled with herself. He made it sound so reasonable.

He sat there and waited.

Holly wanted to tell him—she sensed she could trust him with Portia at least—but the words wouldn't come.

"Let's start with this." He gave a long-suffering sigh. "Why doesn't she have her own money or credit cards? Why is she using yours?"

That was an easy one and Holly answered promptly. "She can't be trusted with money because she's been known to give it away or go on these huge spending sprees." Holly tapped the table for emphasis. "And now she doesn't have any money. We have to find her fast."

"We will." He made it sound like a sure thing. "And you weren't bothered she had your credit card?"

"The limit on the card is fairly low." Holly pulled a face at her own stupidity. It had honestly not occurred to her until he said it. "And it seemed the least of my concerns."

"Okay." He nodded. "Now tell me the rest."

"Like?"

"Holly." He trapped her hand beneath his. "You're such a hard-ass, you know that?"

"It's not that." Holly shifted in her seat, tugging her hand away from the safe warmth of his. "It's a trust thing."

"As in, you don't have any?"

"Maybe." Holly screwed her face up. Talking about this was like a mosquito bite you couldn't reach. "And also, you and I, bad history, you know."

"Uh-huh." He pulled the corners of his mouth down. "Let's put that aside for the moment and concentrate on finding your sister."

"Okay." Holly tapped the top of his hand as it lay on the table. "I'm not sure why you're helping me."

His jerked a tiny bit. "Does it matter? Isn't it more important that we find Portia?"

When he put it like that, she had no argument.

"You can yell at me later, when we've found Portia." He trapped her fingertips between his. Warm shocks of energy sizzled up her fingers and along her palms. "But I can be a whole lot more effective if you trust me with the truth."

"I don't really do the trust thing." Damn, this was harder than she could have imagined.

"I'm getting that." His grin was a pure, bad boy flash of white teeth.

Heat crept over her skin and her heart gave a jump.

"Emma and Portia live with you, right?" He frowned in thought.

"Right."

"Why?"

Holly cursed herself as her bristles snapped to attention. "What do you mean, why?"

"Oh, come on, Holly." He raised an eyebrow again. "Three grown women living together? It's like something out of another era."

"We like it that way." Holly hated the defensiveness in her voice. "And we live together because we can't afford any other way. It's not everyone who comes up with some software brainstorm—"

"Whoa." He grabbed both her waving hands and pinned them to the table. "I'm not judging. Honest to God."

Like hell he wasn't.

"It's unusual and there's got to be a good reason for it. And I suspect it's the same reason for all of this and I'm asking you to tell me. So, Holly, enough with the sidetracks; let's hear it."

Across the table she locked eyes with him. *Don't do it.* The teenage girl was out and on the rampage again. *He can't be trusted. He's mean and he hurt you.*

Josh waited her out.

You can trust him, her intuition whispered. He'd been straight up with her since she'd talked to him at Scants. She was the one keeping secrets that could end up hurting her and her sister.

"Portia isn't well." *Just tell him,* yelled her instinct. A lifetime of secrets rose up in defense. "I live with them because she needs taking care of and she can't work a regular job."

He sat forward, his eyes keen and alert. "Are we talking about some kind of mental illness?"

Holly nodded, not wanting to speak the words. Her heart raced and she took deep breaths to steady it. She was overreacting. It wasn't such a big deal, but she didn't talk about stuff like this. Not even Steven knew the full story. Even after all these years, the habit of keeping it hidden and secret was almost too powerful for her.

Her father had ingrained it in them. The Partridge family didn't talk about what went on in their house. They didn't tell their secrets to anyone. And they didn't stay anywhere long enough for anyone to guess the truth.

"Okay." His face grew thoughtful. "But you're going to have to give me more. Is she dangerous?"

"To herself," Holly admitted. "Portia is bipolar."

"Ah!" He nodded. "That sucks."

It was such an understatement it drew a reluctant smile out of her. "Yes," she said. "It really, really does, and now she's here in Chicago and I'm not sure what she's doing for money and I need to find her before she crashes."

He sat patiently, waiting for her to finish her explanation.

"Portia is having an episode." The words came easier. "Her moods will cycle wildly. When she's up, she's flying higher than anyone, and when she's down . . ." She didn't want to finish her sentence.

"Why Chicago?"

Holly shrugged and tried to keep it light. "You might not remember this, but Melissa, my mother, died in Willow Park. We think Portia is fixating on Melissa and her death."

"I remember," he said and his face softened

"Portia is still in the early stages of the disease, but it's progressive and it's a vicious process of cycling through ever worsening highs and lows." Holly hurried on before he interrupted with more questions she didn't want to answer. "Strange environments stress her, and she needs to avoid those sorts of stresses. We may have lived here as kids, but that was a long time ago."

He absorbed the information in silence. "Why me? Why did she come to find me?"

"I don't know." With relief, she led him away from the rocky waters of Melissa. "Perhaps because she heard Grace and me talking about you all those years ago. You were quite the topic of conversation in our house."

"Because you despised me?"

Holly nodded. "Because of that."

"Okay," he said. "So let's find your sister before she gets into trouble."

"Yes." The weight lifted off her shoulders. He wasn't going to ask about Melissa.

"I've got an idea." He reached for his phone. "Are you hungry?"

The ghost of a smile chased across her mouth. "I could manage something,"

He scrolled through his contact list. "Okay, order yourself a feeding frenzy and I'll make a call."

Chapter Ten

"Who?" Dr. Richard Hunter gaped at his receptionist, nurse, and general thorn in his side.

Carmen gazed back at him with her pale eyes; cold and calculating like something on a fishmonger's block, they glittered behind the lenses of her round glasses.

"Joshua is on the phone." She enunciated, carefully and loudly.

His waiting patients swiveled their glances in his direction and stuck as they sensed blood in the water.

"Your brother," Carmen said. "The one who lives downtown?"

"Josh?" His face heated, but he still couldn't quite believe Josh was on the phone.

As per usual, her expression remained exactly the same. "You have another one who lives in Chicago?"

Richard had grown a thick skin working with Carmen all these years. She was about as pleasant as a barracuda, but she was plugged into the medical network of Chicago and could, and occasionally did, get things done for him.

Richard could count on one hand the number of

times his brother had called him, and it was normally on the cell. Richard reached to pick up the phone.

"This is the reception phone." Carmen put one plump hand over the phone. "Use the one in your office."

Richard opened his mouth to argue with her, but their audience watched each word as if it were their personal soap opera. He stalked down the hall to his office, the tattered remnants of his dignity creeping along behind him.

"Josh?" He put the phone to his ear. "Is everything all right?"

"I need your help."

Richard gave a surprised bark of laughter. Unfortunately, he'd just taken a sip of his lukewarm coffee and he choked. Coffee freckled the manila patient files on his desk and he dabbed at them. Carmen was going to have a cow. His lab coat had escaped mostly unscathed, but he had to take several more hacking breaths before he could respond. "You want my help?"

"Are you laughing?" The guard came up on Josh's voice.

"Nope." Richard worked on the coffee stains. "I was choking. I don't think you've ever asked for my help."

"I'm sure I have," Josh said.

Christ. He could say the sky was blue, Josh would come back and say it wasn't. Probably. Only a year separated them in age and they'd been competing fiercely since the day Josh entered the world. Actually, Richard blamed most of it on Josh.

"I'm as sure you haven't. Not even when you were a kid." Richard chuckled at the memory. "You must have been the only three-year-old in the country trying to tie your own shoelaces."

"I was a fast developer."

"You were trying to do what I did."

"That's bullshit."

"Oh, yeah?" Richard settled in to enjoy the taunt. "So how is your triathlon training going these days?"

"Screw you."

"Ten hours and fifty-six minutes," Richard said with relish.

"No problem," Josh said.

Richard smiled. Josh would beat his time or die trying.

"What can I do for you?"

He wasn't smiling five minutes later when he hung up. Josh was heading for a whole ugly, crapload of mess. Bipolar disorder was not something you took lightly.

Holly Partridge had been behind him at school and he could only form a vague outline of a short, rather determined girl. Not surprising. At the time, he'd only had eyes for one girl.

Richard allowed himself a great, stupid, soppy grin. He still only had eyes for one girl.

He told Josh what he knew about the condition, which wasn't much. He would look into it more closely tonight. There was something more, however, that he could do. It was risky, though. It would require some groveling and some humility. It would put him in debt and it would take him a lifetime to pay off that debt. But a brother was a brother.

He braced for impact and picked up the line to reception. "Carmen, I need to ask a favor."

"I'm going to have my morning coffee in five minutes."

"Actually, it's more for Josh than for me."

"Speak to me." *Gotcha!* Richard allowed a triumphant smile to split his features. Apparently, not even Carmen was immune to the Josh magic.

* * *

"Hey?" Josh said.

She sat beside him, curled and almost fetal as he headed back toward the city.

A day of trawling the streets, asking anyone and everyone if they had seen Portia, had resulted in a big fat zero. Josh had called in all the friends and contacts he had and now there was nothing to do but wait and see.

"We'll find her." He uncurled one of Holly's small hands from her raised knees.

She'd kicked off her shoes and sat with her knees hunched up to her chin. The anxiety had built in her as the hours dragged past, but no tears.

Laura had cried a lot, especially toward the end.

Josh got the sense Holly rarely cried, but her despair squatted toadlike in the car between them.

She put up a token resistance but let him take her hand.

Josh smoothed her fingers. It was a small hand, almost like a child's against his own. Her nails were neat and short, the skin dry with slight calluses across the pads, as if she often carried things or worked with heavy grips. It was a capable hand, a functional limb that served its owner.

Her sigh seemed to come all the way from the sole of her Converses. She dropped her head back against the seat but left her hand quiescent in his.

"Nobody's seen her," she said, as if she couldn't quite credit it. "How can one girl be invisible? I was sure someone would have seen her."

"Someone has." He wanted to put his mouth into the center of her palm and make a visceral connection. The urge to comfort her rode him hard.

Holly would fight him.

He did it anyway, pressing his mouth against the slightly roughened skin. Trying to communicate with his touch that she wasn't alone in this.

She gasped and turned her head to stare at him.

"Someone has seen her." He released her hand and leaned forward to turn on the ignition. "We haven't found that person yet, but I have everyone I can think of looking. Sooner or later, we're going to get some good news."

Holly frowned at the hand he'd kissed. "What's with you and the touching?"

"I'm tactile." He eased into the light traffic. And with her, he wanted to go tactile over every inch of her, but it was more than that. He wanted to wrap her up and shield her from all the shit swirling around her. He needed her to know he had her back. For now.

Holly stopped and waited as a woman stepped into their path.

"How are you, Josh?" Brunette, stacked, gorgeous hair and killer smile—Holly barely even paid attention.

Josh responded to the girl like he did with the others as they made their way across his lobby.

Philip was on duty, and he waved and smiled at Holly.

She dredged up a response as Josh admired the small dog tucked against the capacious bosom of a woman who was eighty if she was a day.

He was your basic chick magnet, that's all there was to it. No woman was immune. It wasn't as if he flirted with them either. Like now, he listened attentively to a description of the dog's various ailments. It sounded as if the creature would be better off put out of its misery. But Josh bent his dark head and paid attention, as if he had nothing better to do and nowhere he needed to be.

"Is this your young lady?" The octogenarian turned and fastened her sharp eyes on Holly.

Josh slipped an arm around her waist and tucked her into his side. "Holly is a good friend, Mrs. Sherman."

Holly's stomach slid south.

"Friend?" Mrs. Sherman leaned forward with a wicked twinkle that coaxed a smile out of Holly. "A woman doesn't keep a man like this as a friend, dear."

Josh stiffened beside her.

The woman winked one eye caked with plum-colored shadow. "A man like this is strictly a playmate." She jerked her head at Josh.

Holly was rendered speechless. She wanted to protest that he made a great friend, but they weren't friends. Allies, perhaps; old acquaintances, definitely.

Josh's face hardened into a blank mask as he said his good-byes to Mrs. Sherman before tugging her toward the elevator.

Again with the touching. Her forearm tingled beneath his palm, and it didn't totally suck, or suck at all in fact. She could have shrugged off his light clasp, but for some reason she left it there.

Holly didn't get it. Sure, he had a smart mouth and could throw down the charm like a matinee idol, but the best parts of Josh were the glimpses she caught in between all that. The caring man, the patient one who'd spent his day doing everything he could to help her find Portia. "Why do you let them think those things about you?"

"What things?" The mask remained in place.

"Assume that you're shallow."

He shrugged, but the muscle ticked in his jaw. "People see what they want to see, Holly. And I reckon I've done enough to earn my reputation anyway."

Sarah Hegger

It sat wrong with her. "I promise not to call you pretty boy anymore."

"Ah, Holly." The flirt slid over his features as smoothly as oil over water. "Does that mean my charms are fading on you?"

Nope. She dragged her eyes away from his megawatt smile. His charms were only getting more appealing, and they had very little to do with his beautiful face and sinful body.

Josh was impressed. "Where do you put it all?"

She'd worked her way through most of an extra-large pizza. It wasn't as if the food was even a sensual experience for Holly, like some women were about chocolate. No, she fed the machine. And the machine needed a lot of feeding.

Her eyes widened and she swallowed her mouthful. "I don't know, but I always seem to have space for a bit more."

She glanced at the piece of pizza in her hand like she dearly wanted to eat it but didn't dare.

Man, she was fucking adorable. Josh laughed and nudged her hand toward her mouth "Don't pretend you don't want it."

She grinned and bit down with her straight white teeth.

He liked making her smile. Holly didn't do enough of it. And he especially liked it when he could make her laugh. He got a smile now as she went back to her eating. It made his chest burn with a curious sort of warmth.

Another thing he liked was having her here, and that surprised the shit out of him. He'd broken another rule of a lifetime by letting her take up residence in his place. One night was understandable, given her circumstances, but he'd brought her home with him tonight as if she belonged there. First, he'd let her eat in his car and now she was in his haven. If he didn't watch out, she'd be making space in his underwear drawer and alphabetizing his music.

He wasn't sure what it meant, but the more time he spent with her, the less it seemed to matter. He couldn't stop touching her. His hands wouldn't stay off her.

Tactile, my ass. He kept the laughter inside as he got up and put on some music. The cool Latin rhythms of Santana filled the condo.

He grabbed the empty pizza box and went to the kitchen.

Holly uncoiled from the floor and walked over to the window.

He could sense her worry gnawing away at her insides. Actually, there seemed to be rather a lot fighting for space in one small container. Being around her was like sharing space with a can of pop. If he shook, he was never entirely sure what was going to come out. So many contradictions wrapped up in that tiny bundle. He wanted to make sense of them all.

Her hips swayed to the music, drawing his gaze like a lodestone. Her hideous jeans hid the full swell of her hips, but every now and then he caught a flash of the smooth line of her small waist or, even better, the taut curve of her belly. He wanted to run his hands over those curves, stroking down until he could move around and cup her ass.

She had a body that made a man want to touch and worship. Her skin made his mouth water. He wanted at what lay beneath her butt-ugly sweatshirt. He hated the fact she hid her dangerous curves. Then again, there was a lot of her she kept hidden, and he wouldn't accept it. He wanted to unwrap her like a Christmas present. She was a foreign country, an uncharted territory he had to explore and conquer.

Man, he was losing his fucking mind. It must be the near permanent lack of blood to the brain. Holly had enough weight on her shoulders right now to sink someone twice her size. He pulled a bottle of red from his wine rack and scanned the label. It was rather pathetic. He was walking around semihard, knowing only a jerk hit on a vulnerable woman. It was like being sixteen again. Only this time, he was going to play it better, even if it killed him or caused permanent brain damage.

The dickhead of a boyfriend didn't deserve a woman like Holly. Just the thought of another man putting his hands on Holly had Josh's gut tightening in a feral ball of *mine, all mine.* If Stevie the Swinger was too fucking dumb to see what he had, he deserved to lose it.

Holly moved gently from side to side, dancing as if she inhabited the slow Latin rhythm.

Josh rolled his tongue back into his mouth.

And in that instant he was back in the school gym, watching Holy Holly Partridge move her body in a way teenage boys only dreamed about. It had lost none of its potency, and his libido responded with a *hell yeah!*

Josh wrestled it back under control while he poured the wine and carried a glass over to her by the window.

She startled slightly out of whatever place she'd been lost in. Her sinful mouth kinked up in the corners. "Red wine? How did you know?"

"I guessed," he said. Holly made him think of red wine: rich, understated, and improving on each taste. Fuck! When the hell had he degenerated to thinking in shitty poetry?

"And you guessed right." She took the glass from him and raised it to her nose. She closed her eyes and took a long appreciative sniff before lowering the glass to her mouth.

He leaned against the architrave surrounding the window and tried not to stare too obviously at her lips.

"It's part of why the girls like you." She moved away, putting physical distance between them.

Josh tamped down on the desire to follow.

She threw herself onto one of his large leather sofas. The cushions huffed air as she slumped into them. She put her head back and stared at the ceiling. "This waiting is driving me crazy."

"Something will break," he said. "We have enough lead in the air now, it's only a matter of time."

She gave a rough bark of laughter. "Yeah, time we don't have." She propped her feet on his coffee table. "If I think about Portia, out there alone, I think—" Abruptly, she sat up and pinned him with a gaze. "Let's talk about something else."

"Okay." Josh let his agreement hang out there and counted on Holly not being able to remain silent for long.

"You confuse me." She didn't even last ten seconds. "The way you are with all the women." She made an expansive gesture with her free hand. "It's like you're such a player and that's the way you are in my head, but . . ."

"But?" He hid a grimace behind his glass. Holly picked up on stuff way too fast for comfort.

She lifted her head to stare at him. It was more of a glare, but he kept his expression polite. "But I've been watching you today." She dropped her head back down as if it was all too much effort. "These women, they're all over you. And you, you've got this great big hands-off sign over your head. It's not what I expected."

"What did you expect?" He sipped his wine and squirmed inside. He hated talking about this shit, but at the same time he sensed she needed to know. If nothing else, she might trust him a bit more.

"You always say the right thing, or do the right thing, and women . . . melt. How do you do that?"

Josh sensed a loaded question and weighed his answer carefully. "I like women," he said. "I'm a mama's boy. Richard was almost a carbon copy of my dad. Thomas was always on his own mission. And I liked being with my mom. I think that's why I'm always easy in female company. Women sense that and are comfortable with me."

She made a rude noise and pulled a face. "Oh puh-lease, you're still a player."

"No, I'm not." Laura had taken care of that.

Her eyes narrowed. "Those girls at the bar?"

"I explained about that. I did some stupid shit when I was younger. I know better now."

Lips pursed, she studied him and sipped her wine.

"I'm not a player, Holly." It was the truth, so help him God. "I like women; I'm not going to lie to you. I like women and I certainly was quite a boy when I was younger, but I don't need the thrill anymore. I'm not looking for the conquest."

He took another sip of his wine and braced for the questions he could see building in her eyes.

"What happened?" She sat up and tucked her legs underneath her like she was settling in for a long chat. "Some woman break your heart and you saw the light?"

"No." Laura's face slammed through his memory and he couldn't meet Holly's mocking stare any longer. "I broke her heart. Broke it in so many tiny pieces, I didn't think she was ever going to be able to put it back together again."

"Oh." Something flickered through her eyes and she stiffened.

He deserved all the judgment she heaped on his head and more. The old familiar pain grabbed his chest and squeezed. "Her name was Laura."

"You going to tell me more?" She cocked her head.

No, he wanted to yell. But his big mouth opened anyway and out it came. "My dad was furious with me. He warned me about Laura, that she was fragile, but I was so jacked up on my own arrogance and flying high, I didn't listen. I broke up with Laura, broke her fucking heart, and my dad found out."

"And?"

"And he died thinking his middle son was a heartless prick." Shit, his dad's eyes were branded into his brain. Disappointment, disillusionment, ashamed of his son.

"What happened to Laura?" Holly's voice, soft and soothing like a balm on the raw place.

He took a fortifying slug of his wine. He never wanted to forget Laura, his harsh reminder of how fragile another being could be. "She left Willow Park about a year after I broke up with her, moved to LA. I looked her up on Facebook. She got married, has a little girl now."

"So she's all right now?" Holly's dark eyes bored right into the soul of him and he dropped his gaze.

"I think so. I never contacted her after—" He needed to change the subject, now. "Too much of a coward."

Holly shook her head, her hair a dark cloud around her face. "It's probably better that way."

He'd like to think so, but he knew different.

"And your dad?"

The regret scalded his throat in a dry burn. "The last conversation I had with him was the fight about Laura. He died thinking I was a selfish asshole."

"No." Holly took a sip of her wine. "I remember your

dad; he loved his boys. He might have been mad at you, but I think he knew you better."

The hold around his throat eased. "It's a nice thought."

"Is that why you keep these women at a distance? Because you don't want to hurt one of them?"

He could lie, and damn, he was tempted, because the truth didn't cast him in a stellar light either. But Holly had this thing about her, this sort of rigorous honesty, and he didn't want to lie to her. "Now I'm more careful to be honest with the women in my life, but as for the others . . ." His face heated. "Women are attracted to the reputation."

"Women like you because you're hot." She snorted into her glass.

"That's part of it." Women had been telling him they liked the way he looked since kindergarten. "The problem is, that's all they see. The way I look and the reputation and that's all they want from me."

Another bark of laughter escaped her. "And you want more than that?"

"Is that so hard to believe?" He pushed away from the wall and walked toward her. He went still inside, some part of him hanging on to hear her answer.

Her eyes widened and she took a hasty sip of her wine. "No."

"Even though you hated me?" The relief lightened his mood instantly.

"Not that again." She groaned. "Anyway, I didn't hate you, I despised you."

"My mistake." His apology earned him a dry chuckle. Damn, he liked her laugh. He liked making her laugh even more.

"And you may as well be the first to know, I've downgraded despise to mild dislike," she said with a prim nod.

her wine. He wanted behind those walls she built up around her.

"You also learn how much it means to have a home," she said, surprising him.

It wasn't much, but it was another one of those tiny chinks in her armor. Through them he caught tantalizing views of the woman she kept hidden behind her ugly jeans and faded sweatshirts.

"Yeah." His home life had been very different. His mother and father had, for the most part, had a good marriage. His father, Des, was the sort of old-fashioned man whose word was his bond, but it also made him a stubborn, intractable ass sometimes. Richard took after their father. At least he had been as stubborn and set in his ways until his recent marriage.

Josh was always closer to his mother. Like most middle kids, he was often cast adrift between his overachieving big brother and Thomas, the baby. Some baby. All six foot four of heaving bulk. Thomas had been home for Christmas, tanned like leather and almost blond from the Zambian sun.

Despite their differences, though, they had been well cared for and loved. Des and Donna had erred on the side of the old-fashioned when raising them, but Josh was grateful for it now. A man's integrity defined him, and his strength was a responsibility. It was why he still wished he could go back and redo that last conversation with his father. To assure Des that he got it now: women were to be nurtured, loved, and cherished. Holly would have his ass for even thinking it.

"Yeah," he said. "I bet it does."

"Still." She pulled the corners of her mouth down. "I've seen some amazing places."

"Like?" Outside the bank of windows, the sun made its way down and the soft pink light bathed her intense features, making her appear vulnerable. She did a good job keeping that part of her hidden, but it was there. "Where did you go after Willow Park?"

"First my father got some work on a project in Dubai and then we moved on to Malaysia."

"Tell me."

He nearly ground his teeth to stubs as the shutters came down and she disappeared from view.

"Dubai was hot and compound living. Malaysia was wetter, but still hot, and we lived in a small apartment."

"I'm sure there was more to it than that." He pushed to see if she would let him in again.

"I suppose." She pulled a face. "My father got married again in Malaysia."

"Really? How was that?"

"Boringly predictable. Young new wife is not happy to share space with grown daughters of former wife. I can't blame her," she said after a short reflection. "I was pretty much set as the family matriarch, Grace takes shit from nobody and the twins were teenagers in every sense of the word. It was a lot."

"And your mother? What about her?"

She didn't move a muscle, didn't breathe.

He'd hit pay dirt.

Her stillness swirled like a vortex between them. "I don't talk about my mother," she said in a cold, still voice.

"No?"

"Back away from the cliff, pretty boy."

"Okay." He held up his hands in a gesture of defeat. "But I would like to register my objection to the term—again. And have it put on the record I prefer the more gender neutral term *stone-cold fox*." He threw down the charm and eased out of the moment as he safely tucked away the snippets of information he'd gleaned.

Holly Partridge responded with a smile and sipped her wine. She didn't know it, but he was a man who loved a puzzle, and he was slowly and painstakingly putting the pieces of her together. She was a sweet, tempting enigma he was unraveling and drawing inexorably closer. Holy Holly Partridge had no idea, but she was in big, big trouble.

Josh had a sneaking suspicion he might be in the same sort of difficulty.

Chapter Eleven

It came to Josh in a dream. Didn't it always? You could spend your waking hours racking your brain for the answer and it wouldn't come. The harder you tried, the more elusive the solution became. It hid, laughing its ass off at you, waiting until you were drifting somewhere between the nether and the now, and then it hit you like a knee to the balls.

Josh rolled over and groaned. He wouldn't sleep anymore tonight, or this morning rather. Holly sleeping down the hallway had played havoc with him for most of the night. Before Laura, he would have cruised on down the hall and tried his luck. What a dickhead he'd been. He'd made a promise to his dad at the funeral that he would do better. Not until Holly barreled back into his life had he been seriously tempted to break that promise.

It didn't stop his libido from prowling in its cage and snarling and clawing at the restraints. Watching her pert ass sashay away from him into the spare bedroom took an act of self-discipline worthy of a medal. The door had closed behind her and he'd stood there like an over-eager, horny puppy, holding his breath and willing her to turn and give him the signal, even the smallest sign, that it was on.

He sat up and swung his legs over the bed.

The conversation tonight must have got his subconscious moving because he'd finally locked onto the last conversation he'd had with Holy Holly all those years ago. Maybe despised wasn't too strong after all.

He had some groveling to do. Josh went to throw water on his face. Coffee first.

Holly battled to fall asleep and stay that way. Her mind wouldn't rest long enough for her to drift off. She was worried about Portia for certain. And Emma, which was pretty much a perpetual state. Also, there had been a tone in Grace's voice that had got her thinking.

However, it wasn't family churning in her mind in the wee hours of the morning. Nope, that dubious honor belonged to Josh. He kept popping into her mind and sticking with the stubbornness of old bubble gum on the bottom of your shoe.

Their conversation tonight had been enlightening and disturbing. It was easier to keep him at arm's length when she could put him into a neat box and label him *trouble*. A more sensitive and caring Josh presented way more danger.

Even with her limited experience, Holly got that she was attracted to Josh. Blisteringly so.

Steven barely shifted the needle out of tepid.

Josh, on the other hand, redlined it all the way, and it made her twitchy and uncomfortable in her skin.

Some people weren't designed for the grand passion. They weren't made that way, and she was one of them. Sure, every once in a while she got the feeling perhaps she was missing something. And there were times when she got restless, dissatisfied even. Relationships, however, weren't built on chemistry and wild, unruly surges of emotion.

She was a pragmatist and a realist. Take Romeo and Juliet, for example. She would have checked for a pulse before offing herself, which she wouldn't have considered doing in the first place. As such, she had no trouble recognizing how colossally insane it was to be attracted to a man who, up until two days ago, she wouldn't have spat on if he were on fire.

The worst part being she liked him. God knows he could make her laugh, but he also had a way of knowing what she needed and when she needed it. It made her feel special and treasured. Her feminist soul writhed like a worm on the hook, but it couldn't be denied and she relished every moment of it. He got her in a way Steven didn't even come close to.

Steven! Holly didn't want to think about Steven. Her disloyalty sickened her. Six years was a long time to invest in someone. She would bet Josh Hunter hadn't had a relationship lasting six years.

A noise outside her room grabbed her attention and she snapped on the light switch. Footsteps padded down the hall toward the kitchen. It was probably Josh.

She turned off the light. Holly lay in the dark like a quivering vestal virgin, frightened he might have noticed and terrified he hadn't. He was messing with her head.

A soft knock on the door and Holly froze, at least the part of her brain responsible for coherent thought. She battled to hear much over the insistent drumming of her heart.

"Holly?" Quiet enough it wouldn't wake her if she were asleep, but loud enough to be heard if she wasn't. She could pretend not to hear.

"Yes?" *Way to go on the keeping-your-distance thing.*

"Are you awake?"

"Why?"

Josh's chuckle made her smile. *Super job of keeping a level head on your shoulders, Holly.*

The door opened a crack. His silhouette shadowed the doorway. "Too late; I already saw your light."

"What do you want?"

"Don't ask leading questions, Holly." He padded toward her on near silent feet.

Holly pulled the covers up to her chin. They were alone and she was in bed. A small thrill of deliciousness snaked through her as he moved closer.

"I had an epiphany." The bed dipped beneath his weight as he made himself at home.

"What the hell are you doing?" She glared through the dark at him.

His hip bumped hers and she scooted over. "I'm sharing my epiphany."

Holly struggled into a sitting position, feeling way too vulnerable lying on her back. "Get off my bed."

"Jeez, you're a grouch." He settled his weight on his hands.

"It's the middle of the night." *And you're in my bedroom, on my bed, and my nerve endings are breaking into a happy dance.*

"Really?" He got comfortable. "Hey, stop kicking me."

"You're on my bed and I want you off."

"Just wait." He fastened his big hands around her legs below the knees. She could hear the laughter in his voice and make out the light flash of his teeth. "I want to talk to you. I was going to wait until morning, but you're awake, so I might as well get this over with."

"Get what over with?" Holly wriggled her legs. "Let go of me."

"Only if you promise not to kick. God knows what you could hit in the dark."

"Are you turning weird on me?" The dark was too intimate, and she leaned over and snapped on the light. Mistake, because she got a good look at Josh and her pulse leaped.

"Shit." He recoiled and let go of her legs to cover his eyes. "And no." He shook the bed as he laughed. "I am not turning weird. Man, Holly, you're a crazy woman. It's probably why I like you so much."

He dropped his hands and grinned at her. He was only half dressed in a pair of track pants and his hair was mussed, as if he'd been running his fingers through it.

Holly's hand twitched to brush it straight.

"Why don't you do us both a favor and put a shirt on?" She looked pointedly away from the warm, hard muscle perched within inches of her hungry fingers.

"You could always give me my T-shirt back." He indicated the one she was wearing.

Holly threw him a withering glance and folded her arms over her chest.

He pulled a regretful face. "No?"

"Why are you here, Joshua?" He needed to go before she did something stupid.

"Actually . . ." He ran his hands over his face. His expression grew serious. "I was lying in bed, thinking about you, and I got it. All of a sudden."

Oh, damn but that did hot and shivery things to her. "You were lying in bed thinking about me?"

"It was the night of the Valentine's dance, wasn't it?"

Her mind shifted, so fast it made her gape at him. She was sixteen going on seventeen, and he was the boy who made her heart go pitter-patter. The same heart skipped a beat and started again sluggishly.

It was, indeed, that night. It was a night she had replayed again and again in her teenage mind.

"The reason you're mad at me is that night." He didn't seem to need any response. "I asked you to dance and you said no."

Holly's throat was dry. The night was burned on the back of her brain. "Actually, I said I made it a point never to dance with anyone who was prettier than me."

"And I said, 'Then you must never dance.'"

"And everyone laughed," Holly said.

It was in the open and Holly was—deflated. It sounded inconsequential, one of those childish interludes that came and went, over as fast as it had begun.

"Fuck. I was an insensitive little shit when I was a kid." He broke the silence. "It was the first time any girl had ever said no to me and I didn't take it well."

"No, you didn't." Holly tried to dredge up the hurt and the self-righteous anger, but it wasn't where she'd last left it.

He sat on the end of her bed without morphing into a monster. What she had was a rumpled, sexy man wearing a ferocious frown and looking as guilty as hell.

"You were a little shit," she said. "It crushed my teen-age ego."

"Yeah." He nodded. "I can see how it would. Is there an expiration date on apologies?"

"But it wasn't entirely your fault." Holly surprised herself with that one. She was even more amazed she meant it. "It was a very bad time for me, and your rejection came on top of some other stuff that had nothing to do with you."

"It was a mean thing to say." He shook his head. "I had forgotten all about it. I never meant it, you know?"

"It *was* mean," Holly said. "And it did hurt, but I think there was probably a lot more going on than just that night." Okay, that was some sort of half-assed evasion. "I know there was a lot more going on."

"I only found out later your mother had died. I tried

to come around and apologize. I got to the door, but the movers were there. You were leaving." His shoulders shifted up and down in one of his habitual shrugs. "And I guess I put it away and forgot about it. It is why you hate me, right?"

"Despise."

"Mildly dislike," he said. "I was young and stupid, Holly." He gave a short laugh. "You want to hear the funny part?"

"What's the funny part?" she asked when he remained silent.

"I was so hot for you," he said.

Holly's mouth dropped open and she shut it. Josh had been hot for her? She would never have guessed that. She made some vague, choking sound of disbelief.

"Man, was I hot for you, Holly."

Searing heat shot through her core. Holly shivered and brought her knees up to her chest.

He took one of her hands and threaded his fingers through hers.

She was hypnotized by the way her palms seemed to throb in time with the steady pulse of her blood through her veins.

His thumb brushed the inside of her wrist. "I used to watch you all the time when you weren't looking. It blew my tiny mind I was crazy for the girl who was making my life difficult. You had this short pleated skirt." He stopped himself and cleared his throat. The smile he gave her was pure predator. "That was one hell of a skirt."

"You're making this up." It shocked Holly how much she wanted to believe him.

"I swear to God, I'm not." He raised one hand like he was taking a vow. "And you." He tightened his fingers around hers. "You were cool and aloof. It made me want to go ape shit. I could get any girl I wanted, any girl." He wasn't being arrogant. That was the way it had been.

"But the one I wanted didn't want me. I didn't like the rejection."

"You were laughing with your friends," she said. "Over by the door to the gym. You were looking at me and laughing. I thought you only came over as a joke."

"You thought wrong," he said. "My friends were laughing at me. They said I didn't stand a chance."

"They were right, you didn't."

"Apparently not." He made a rueful face. "Anyway, I was lying in bed feeling like the world's biggest shit because I saw that look on your face again. As I said it, you got this look on your face, and I knew I'd hurt you far more than I meant to. I only meant to salvage my pride. It occurred to me it might be time for an apology."

It was a bizarre feeling. She'd been hugging this close since she was sixteen. It should have taken an Act of Congress to make it go away. "Okay."

"Okay what?" His gaze drifted to her mouth.

"Let's hear this apology."

"I really am sorry, Holly. I shouldn't have said it, and I should have apologized long before now." His eyes went deep, deep blue, almost purple. A girl could drown in eyes like his. "If my dad had known about that night, he would have been ashamed of me then, too."

Huh. Apparently a sincere apology would do the trick. And she had to get real here. Perhaps Josh had only ever been the proverbial straw. It had been an awful two years.

By the time the family arrived in Willow Park, she and Grace had given up trying to fit into new schools. The sisters stuck together and got through the school day as best they could. There was no point making new friends. The family would only be leaving soon, and with Melissa getting worse by the day, there was no way to invite their new friends home. The Partridge family circled the wagons to keep their secrets.

Her mother's illness spiraled out of control during Holly's last year of high school. Holly had isolated herself from the rest of her class, desperate to hide the truth from friendly, interfering eyes. Her schoolwork was the one thing she could master, and she'd thrown her spare energy into it. So had Grace, but for different reasons. Good grades were going to be Grace's ticket out of the insanity.

"Holly?"

"Yes?"

"Would you like to dance with me?"

"Now?"

"Yes, now. Better late than never."

"Get a grip." For an insane moment, she nearly said yes, but that was a bad idea for more reasons than she could name. She pushed against his solid shoulder. "I'm not going to dance with you. It's four in the morning and you are just too smooth."

He rocked back. "So that's a no?"

"It's a no."

"So if I can't make up the dance, how can I make it up to you?"

"You don't have to." This honesty thing was like a contagious disease. "Because if we're laying it all out there, I have to confess I may have had a small crush on you as well, and it was part of why I reacted so . . . strongly." It tumbled out of her mouth in a rush and her cheeks were hot by the time she'd finished.

His teeth flashed in his darker face. He cupped a hand around his ear and leaned into her. "Say what, Miss Holly Partridge? You're going to have to say that again. I'm not sure I understood."

"You heard me." She squirmed as his grin widened

across his face. "Until I realized what a stupid git you were."

"And a prat?"

"And a wanker." Holly's smile widened across her face.

"All boys are wankers, Holly." His voice grew wicked. "It's because we spend nearly all day thinking about girls."

"Ew!" She pushed him with her feet.

He held her ankles still. "Let's discuss your crush on me instead. Why don't you tell me all about it?"

He walked his hands up the outside of her legs, bracketing her hips.

"It's old news now," she said.

He'd moved closer to her, putting his mouth within range. "Does this mean I'm forgiven?"

All one of them would have to do was lean forward. "Maybe."

The thrum of desire pounded against her eardrums, reverberating through her body and pooling between her thighs.

His answering desire glinted clear in the slumberous heat in his eyes as they caressed her face and moved down over her breasts.

Her chest rose and fell sharply as her breathing got messy.

"I'll take a rain check on that dance." His voice stroked along her senses.

He felt it, too, and the knowledge jacked up her heart rate and she pressed her thighs tightly together. *Oh God.* She still wanted him as much as she had when she was a girl. Except it was more potent now; it was a woman's need her body understood and craved.

He leaned forward and she sat there like a mongoose watching a dancing cobra as he moved closer. His cheek was slightly rough against hers. "I think I should get out of here."

"Uh." It was meant to be a vehement denial, but it sounded horribly ambivalent.

He got up and left. "Good night, sweet Holly."

Holly deflated so fast her head whirled. She wouldn't have made much effort to stop him if he'd wanted to stay. Thank God he hadn't forced them both to that conclusion.

Josh shut the door behind him with a soft click. He could damn well forget sleeping now. He was so hard he ached. God alone knew how he'd got up and walked out. She was as turned on as he was; he had felt the heat coming off her skin. Unlike him, however, she wasn't too thrilled by the idea.

He wanted to make love to Holly Partridge. He wanted to love her long, hard, and sweet like she deserved. To make love to her until those tiny brackets of dissatisfaction disappeared from the corners of her mouth.

Fucking limp dick Steven couldn't do that.

But now he needed to run or he was going to turn right around and finish what he'd started. His man beast yowled and whined as he pulled on his running shoes.

And exactly when had the man beast done anything but lead him into trouble—by the dick? "Shut the fuck up."

Chapter Twelve

Holly didn't know when Josh slept, or even if he slept, because by the time she got out of bed the next morning he was gone. Needless to say, she hadn't gotten a lot of sleep after his wee hours visit.

A text from Steven hadn't helped. He wasn't sure she would be back in time for his faculty dinner and informed her he would be taking Judith from the languages department.

It didn't bother Holly one bit. And, for the first time, she wanted to know why it didn't and if it should.

She padded across the floor and tried to ease the tension creeping into her neck.

Her skin felt stretched too tight to contain all the shit going on inside her. The various parts of her life had assigned places, little boxes to keep them neat and orderly. As long as the order was maintained, she could cope.

Josh refused to stay in his box of *that ass from high school*. And then there was Portia, who had bust out of her little compartment and run for freedom.

Six days since Portia had left Ontario. Two days of scouring Willow Park and still no Portia. The steady tick of time passing in her head grew louder. It fought for attention with the increasing clamor of what ifs.

Holly couldn't go there or she would lose it.

She wandered through the tomblike quiet of the apartment into the kitchen. Looking for something to do, she opened the fridge and checked out the contents.

Josh had agreed to stop for groceries yesterday, amused by the notion that she intended to cook a meal from scratch.

Holly pulled a carton of eggs from the fridge and cracked them into a bowl. They inhabited two entirely different universes, she and Josh. Their worlds may have briefly intersected in high school, but that was some time ago.

His condo was the bomb. Part of her plain envied his charmed existence. Her mundane world revolved around paying the mortgage and making ends meet. It seemed at times as if she had skipped her youth and gone straight to middle age. No teenage rebellion or twentysomething rocking out and setting the night on fire, only responsibilities and more of the same the next day.

Holly added milk and seasoning and whisked the eggs. Now she was thirty and there were days when the noose grew too tight. She only had herself to blame. Emma and Portia were dependent on her, and she kept it that way. She never insisted the twins make their business turn a profit or live on their own.

The twins dithered around, playing shop and living with their big sister, and it was getting pathetic.

Codependent, Grace had accused her of being, and there was enough truth to the accusation to get Holly fighting her way out of the corner.

The eggs hit the pan with a happy sizzle and Holly pushed at them.

"Hey."

She jumped and turned to greet him, her cheeks hot. "Hey."

He'd been running, and she kept her eyes trained on his face and away from his tanned, sweaty chest. His shoulders filled the doorway to the kitchen.

Holly turned away. "I'm cooking breakfast."

"I see that." His voice came closer. "What are you cooking?"

"Eggs." Holly stirred the eggs in the pan. "I'm cooking enough for both of us."

"Great." He came up behind her and her brain stalled. The heat coming off him was worse than the heat of the stove in front of her. He was having that effect on her again. She tried to ignore it, but his hands were firm and hot against her hips. "I think this is the first time someone has ever cooked in this kitchen."

"Um?" She tingled at every point where he touched her. Her sense of order slipped further away and she needed it back. It all pressed down on her, fighting for space she didn't have inside—Portia, her, Steven, Josh and this crazy thing going on between them. Her breath came out in a juddering sigh.

"Holly?"

"Yes?"

"Is everything all right?"

"Everything's fine. Great." Her voice rose and Holly cringed.

He dipped his head over her shoulder. "Is it Portia?"

Holly's pulse quickened as his whisker-roughened cheek skimmed against her ear. "Partly."

"So what's the other part?"

"You." Her voice came out ragged. "You're freaking me out. Everything is spinning out of control and you're making it worse."

His hands tightened on her hips before he let her go and stepped back. "Okay."

"No, it's not okay." Holly dragged in a deep breath. It was that or totally lose her shit. She took the pan off the heat and placed it on an unlit burner. Her heart roared in her ears as she snapped off the gas and turned to face him. "Cards on the table? In the spirit of our truce and all?"

"Let's see what you got." He dropped his hands from her hips and moved back a step.

Holly slid from between him and the stove. She relaxed with some distance between them but moved to the other side of the kitchen island just in case. "I think you're flirting with me, and I can't deal with it when I need to concentrate on finding my sister."

"I know how important finding Portia is to you." He planted his hands low down on his hips and dropped his head. The back of his hair stuck to his neck in an absurdly vulnerable way. "And if you really want the truth, I'm trying my damnedest not to flirt with you. Apparently it's an epic fail."

"Oh."

A ghost of a grin chased over his mouth. "Are you speechless?"

"A little."

He laughed. "I like you, Holly, but I'm also trying not to be the asshole who hits on the girl with bigger things on her mind."

"Oh." It was all she had. Her mind emptied and heat prickled beneath her skin. She wished she hadn't opened this can of worms because now she had a committee meeting happening in her head. Parts of her were ridiculously happy at the idea of him wanting to hit on her and another part knew she absolutely shouldn't be. This was so many kinds of wrong it nearly blew her mind.

His eyes deepened to indigo. "I meant every word, Holly, but I'm not going to leap on you or make a dick of myself."

"Are you saying you're attracted to me?" Holly nearly banged her head into the fridge. That was the question she'd asked?

His teeth flashed white across his face. "Yup."

Shivers chased over her skin. Her knees got iffy and she edged her butt onto a stool. Oh boy, she was way, way out of her league. "I can't."

"I get that." His face grew taut, but his voice was as calm as ever.

"Good." She ignored the quiver of disappointment in her gut. "Because nothing could happen, even if you were . . . attracted, which I'm not sure you are. But if you were, it couldn't, so it's all good."

Shut up, Holly. Close your mouth and stop speaking.

He crossed his arms over his chest and leaned his hips against the counter. "Why are you so sure I'm not attracted to you?"

"Why?" Holly gaped at him. She could write him a book on why not. "There are many reasons why."

"Give me one."

"Okay." Holly ordered her thoughts. "You and I, we might as well live on entirely different planets. You have all this." She gestured to the condo around them. "And you go to places like that bar."

He stayed silent, listening.

Holly warmed to her theme. "Even your sports shorts are fancier than anything I own."

He unfolded his arms and gripped the counter on either side of his hips.

"I don't do casual, and you have girls throwing themselves at you. And look at you and look at me." Holly waved her hands between the two of them.

He raised an eyebrow. "And by this you mean . . . ?"

"You're beautiful," Holly burst out, her face growing hot. "Dammit, you only have to look in the mirror to see it."

Josh stilled.

Holly almost stuttered to a halt, but her mouth didn't get the idea. "I'm not like you. I'm not like those girls in the bar."

"Can you forget those girls?"

"No." And God help her if she ever did forget. "I can't because they're what your life is about. I'm not one of them. You have to see that."

"Anything else?"

"Yes. No." Holly ground to a flustered stop. "It doesn't matter because even if all of that was out of the way, there's still Portia. And Emma. I have responsibilities and I can't just . . ." She waved her hands again, out of words.

The exhaust fan hummed in the silence.

He kept his gaze on her and Holly couldn't look away.

"I don't like games," she said, breaking the deadlock. "I don't like them. I don't know how to play them."

"Okay." He pursed his lips. "I think you sell yourself short, but let's go with it. You don't like games?"

"No."

"And you're sure I'm playing games with you?"

Holly blinked at him in confusion. "Well, what else?"

"Oh, I don't know." The corners of his mouth turned down. "Like, maybe I do think you're incredible and I really like you."

The breath rushed out of her as if she'd been winded. Men like Josh Hunter didn't fall for girls like Holly Partridge. Except he'd told her last night how much he'd liked her in high school, and he was standing here, looking effortlessly gorgeous and telling her the same thing. Holly put her hands up as if to ward him off physically. "Don't."

"Don't what?" A small frown creased his forehead. He straightened from his slouch against the counter.

Holly's mouth went dry. "I don't do this sort of thing. I'm not sure what you want from me." Her voice shook. "I'm not sure what all this is about. You and me, and what you said last night and now." She waved her hand expressively. "Here."

A shadow of a smile ghosted across his face.

"You're laughing at me." It scraped against her raw emotions.

"No." A smile broke free over his face. "You're so honest it takes me by surprise every time."

"I don't play games." Holly stamped on the rush of panic bubbling up inside her.

"Okay." He strolled around the corner of the island. "You keep saying it. I think I might be getting the message."

The air between them compressed as he strode over to where she sat. Grasping her stool, he spun it neatly until she faced him with her back to the counter. He leaned down until his arms rested on either side of her hips, pinning her on the stool. "Let me return the favor."

His eyes flickered over her mouth and lingered before reaching her eyes. He kept his stare direct and keen.

Holly forgot how to breathe. She even forgot how to move, just slumped there with her heart going like a steel drum.

"No games and no bullshit. You are overbearing, difficult, argumentative, and prickly as hell, but it doesn't seem to make a difference because I like you anyway."

"Thanks." She wasn't happy with his description of her, but he'd probably earned the right over the last couple of days. She'd been all of those things and more. Besides which, her brain stuck on the other thing he was saying; the thing about liking her.

"And most of what you say is true," he said. "We do live different lives and we desperately need to find your sister. And you know what I'm going to do about it?" He cupped her face between his big palms.

"What?" The quiver in her belly took over her vocal chords.

"Nothing." His lips burned her forehead in a light kiss. "I'm going to keep my hands to myself and help you find your sister."

A bigger surge of disappointment shot through her. "You are?"

"I am, because that's what you need the most right now." He nodded. "But as for the rest of what you said, about someone like me not liking someone like you, that's total bullshit."

"No, it's really—"

"It's my turn to speak." His hands tightened on her jaw. "You're beautiful, funny, clever, and so incredibly loyal to your sisters it blows me away. You throw your whole heart into loving someone and it leaves me in awe. Any man would be lucky to have someone like you in their corner, Holy Holly Partridge."

Her insides melted into a puddle and slid into her

Converses. She really wanted to believe what he said, but she knew better. "I'm not—"

He shook his head. "I'm not done yet. You're also sexy as hell, and since you want the cards on the table, brace yourself, because I might have a bigger crush on you now than I did in high school."

No amount of bracing could have prepared her for that, and she blinked at him like a rabbit in headlights.

"Now ask me what I'm going to do about that."

"What are you going to do about that?" Had her brain left the building?

"Absolutely nothing." His beautiful eyes filled her vision.

When her lungs worked again, she dragged in a deep breath. "Okay."

A naughty grin split his face. "Unless you throw yourself at me like those girls in the bar, and then all bets are off."

"You're messing with me."

He laughed softly. "Only partly."

"Which part?"

He dropped his hands and straightened. "I think I'll take a shower now."

Holly sat in a state of paralysis as he stalked across the condo to his bedroom. He left the door ajar.

The shower turned on.

He would be stripping off his shorts and climbing under the spray. What would it be like if she followed him? She wanted to march down the hall, rip off her clothes, and climb into the shower with him. She wanted to grab his big hands and put them on her body. She wanted to press her skin against his and have his mouth hot and hungry on hers. Yes, she most definitely wanted all of those things, and it scared the crap out of her.

She dropped her head into her hands. God, when had things gotten so bloody messy?

The shower snapped off and her mind constructed an image of a hard, wet body stepping out of the shower.

A phone rang in Josh's room and he answered it in a deep murmur.

"Holly." The urgency in his tone jerked her out of her head. "It's Portia. We've found her."

Chapter Thirteen

Holly texted Emma and Grace from the car. Silently, she urged Josh to go faster.

He ducked and wove through the labyrinthine streets of downtown, but it wasn't fast enough for Holly.

Despite Josh's assurance that his brother was already there, Holly wouldn't be able to relax until she actually clapped eyes on her sister and could judge for herself how bad it was. The police had picked up Portia, behaving erratically, outside a small preschool mere minutes from where they'd searched yesterday.

The preschool had noticed Portia talking to the children through the fence and were concerned by her behavior. The school had called the police. The police had taken Portia to a hospital with a psychiatric ward where she could be evaluated. Richard, Josh's brother, had found her. Actually, Josh said, someone called Carmen had put the pieces together.

Holly was grateful to whoever it was.

Josh didn't bother her with small talk or try to bolster her with platitudes.

Holly couldn't have managed much of a conversation. A sick feeling of familiarity shaded the entire scene. The tight-lipped driver, the car ducking through the city, the terrible feeling of part relief and part terror, even the traffic rushing past the window, sounded the same.

This was like a nightmare trip down memory lane. Her in the front and Grace in the backseat. Their hands tightly clasped behind the central console as Holly reached back to hold her sister's hand. A wave of dizziness slammed her and Holly wanted to throw up.

She had to get it together or she would be no use to Portia.

So many times she had glanced over at her father driving. His face would be set and grim, and Holly had desperately wanted him to reassure her. Perhaps squeeze her hand and tell her everything was going to be all right. She wouldn't have believed him, but she'd wanted the comfort all the same.

"We're almost there." Josh's eyes were like a fixed point in her crazy, lurching reality, and she clung to his quiet confidence.

Holly went back to staring blindly out the window. Her eyes stung and she blinked them to clear the sudden misting. She was glad he was here and, irrationally, it made her furious with him.

Josh had no business being nice. His kindness weakened her. It made her want to melt and cry.

Holly couldn't afford to cry. Deep inside was the hard knot that was her strength. It ran like a steel rod through her center, iron and impenetrable. She drew the ability to cope from there.

Josh pulled into a large, tarred parking lot and drove straight to the emergency entrance. "You go; I'll come find you after I've parked. Richard is waiting for you."

Holly jumped out of the car, slamming the door behind her.

"Richard is inside and I'll be there as fast as I can," Josh called through the open window.

"But how will I—?" He was already driving away.

Her head spun. Helplessness pressed down on her. She forced her legs toward the entrance.

Glass doors swished open.

"Holly?" A more rugged version of Josh approached her.

Holly almost burst out laughing at the uncanny resemblance.

"I'm Richard Hunter," he said in a deep, gravelly voice. "I'm sure you want to go straight to your sister."

Holly followed Richard's tall form inside. The smell backhanded her. The combined odor of illness, humanity, and antiseptic solution washed over her and her knees locked. She hadn't been in a hospital since the last time with Melissa. Muted white light, nondescript walls scarred from the scrape of gurneys, brisk footsteps tapping on the stippled floor. It crashed into her, paralyzing her.

Richard stopped and walked back. Concern clouded his eyes. Blue. A lot like Josh's eyes.

"Holly?" His voice seemed to come from a distance and she turned vaguely in the direction of the sound. "Are you okay?"

She couldn't find her voice beyond the choking tightness in her throat. She needed to assure Richard she was fine, but the words wouldn't come. Saliva flooded her mouth and she clenched her rolling belly.

Shit. She was going to throw up.

Plastic chairs neatly lined against the wall in rows. There were people in those chairs, discombobulated faces wearing a variety of expressions her rapidly scrolling mind couldn't decipher.

Plastic chairs that clung to the back of your legs and

made sweaty, sucking sounds when you stood up. She and Grace used to sit in plastic chairs, backs to the wall like they were facing a firing squad. They had waited, but nobody noticed them, not Francis or the harried-looking doctors, rushing about with their white coats fluttering around their legs. Occasionally a nurse or someone's relative had taken pity on them and tried to engage them in conversation.

The anger writhed inside her chest, almost strangling her with its intensity. She'd been angry then, too. Angry with her mother for doing this, angry with her father for pretending it wasn't happening, and angry with herself because she wasn't able to stop it. It was sitting in plastic chairs outside emergency rooms Holly had learned not to cry.

Tears were pointless anyway. Tears didn't change anything, and they didn't make anything better. You could cry and cry until there was nothing left, but in the end you drowned in the salty river of self-pity.

Richard spoke to someone over her head. Vague words floated above and around her.

"Holly?" Josh dragged her back to the present. His hand was warm beneath her elbow and she turned toward him. "Do you need to sit down?"

His face wove into focus, beautiful and familiar, with concern tightening the skin on his forehead and chasing haunting shadows through the indigo of his eyes.

"No." It came out louder than she'd intended.

He frowned and tightened his grip on her arm.

"No." She got her voice under control. *Breathe.* She sucked at the air. *Breathe and keep going. There's no other choice. Breathe, dammit, breathe.*

Richard spoke, and the words *panic attack* slapped her in the face. Holly snapped her spine straight. She did not have panic attacks. Carefully, she disengaged her arm from Josh. "I'm fine," she said to nobody in particular.

"Are you sure?"

"Holly?"

They stared at her with twin expressions of concern, but she had it under control now.

"Where is she?" Her voice, perfectly controlled but emotionless and clinical, as if it existed outside of her. "Where is Portia?"

A woman in a white coat strode down the corridor toward them. "Josh? Is that you?"

Of course she was a friend of Josh's. Holly almost laughed hysterically, but she didn't think she'd be able to stop.

"Carmen says you know my patient?" Fatigue lines bracketed the woman's eyes and mouth, but she was still lovely.

Of course she was. Why would Josh hang out with anything less than perfect?

Perfect brushed Josh on the forearm. "She won't tell us her name or anything, and she has no identification on her."

"Portia," Holly said. "Her name is Portia and she's my sister."

The woman transferred her attention to Holly, still keeping her eyes on Josh for part of her explanation.

Portia had been there overnight. They were waiting for a psych evaluation, but the woman shrugged and tightened her mouth; it wasn't always possible to make things move at the pace you wanted. The system . . . the words blurred around Holly. Portia was uncooperative but lucid and physically fine. Josh performed the introductions, but Holly barely listened.

"She's bipolar," Holly said.

The doctor's eyes widened slightly. She was probably used to that and a whole lot more if she worked emergency.

"She's been diagnosed?" Finally, lovely lady doctor turned her full attention on Holly. "And she's not on medication?" A slight frown marred the woman's smooth brow.

"She doesn't always take it." Holly winced at the defensiveness in her voice. It wasn't her fault if Portia refused to take her medication. It wasn't her fault Portia was bipolar. If she kept saying it, perhaps there would actually come a time when she believed it. "She doesn't like the way it takes away her highs."

The woman nodded her blond head, as if she expected as much. "Do you know what she's on?"

The ground firmed up beneath her, and Holly talked lithium and other mood stabilizers they'd experimented with until they got Portia an effective cocktail.

"She's calm now," the doctor said. "She's still refusing any form of sedation, but she's calm enough for us to wait for a psych evaluation. I'll take you to her."

The doctor walked down the corridor and motioned for Holly to join her. Josh and Richard dropped into place behind her, a phalanx of strength at her back.

They were there, with her. It was odd and unfamiliar. She forced her attention back to what the doctor was saying.

"So she's gone down." If she stuck with the facts, she'd get through this. "She was on a high when she left and it was only a matter of time. She left her meds behind." It made her want to scream just saying it. "We knew what was going to happen next."

The doctor nodded. "She's been off her medications

for some time now," she said. "She didn't tell us much, but we ran some basic blood tests when she was first admitted. She told us she wasn't taking anything and her blood work pretty much confirms that."

The doctor turned left down a corridor and through a set of double doors.

It was quieter in this part of the hospital, and the knot in Holly's belly loosened.

"We wanted to run some further tests, but she got quite insistent that we not. She's worried about the effect of the tests on the baby. I would guess her pregnancy had something to do with her coming off the medications as well."

Holly nodded, but the roaring in her ears muted all sound.

The doctor talked on. "I made some calls last night and the results are inconclusive either way. There's no real hard proof for either taking the medications or not. It's a preference thing, and also a matter of understanding that once the baby is born, the postnatal depression could be off the charts."

Time slowed to a crawl as the other woman's mouth moved and sounds came out, garbled noise that didn't make any sense. A dislocated stillness settled over Holly as she waited for the doctor's last statement to catch up with her. Around her, the sterile hallways lurched before righting themselves.

Josh and Richard were just standing there.

Her insides were numb. Her brain stuck. "Pregnant?"

She must have stopped moving because the doctor carried on for a few steps before heading back toward her. "You didn't know?"

She clucked her tongue and tucked her hands into her coat pockets. "I was sure you would know, otherwise

I wouldn't have said anything." Her eyes darted over Holly's shoulder to Richard. "I didn't think it was confidential. I would never have said anything otherwise."

"We'll take it from here," Richard said.

Her vision tunneled in on the other woman.

Pregnant?

There was that bloody word again.

The doctor was upset, and Richard said something to placate her. With one last look of regret, the woman turned and hurried away. The heels of her flat shoes squished on the corridor as she walked.

Josh stood behind her. He was breathing hard, the harsh sort of accelerated sound of someone in shock.

No. It was her breathing.

Josh's warm hand beneath her arm sent ripples through her system, threatening the wall of ice around her.

Holly shook off his touch. She needed to be strong. She needed to be impenetrable.

"Portia is pregnant." It made sense now—this insane pilgrimage to find their mother, the coming off medication and the secrecy.

Emma must have known.

Josh stood close to her, ready for her to lean on him, ready to support her.

Holly took a deliberate step away. She kept her eyes locked on Richard.

"You didn't know?" Richard raised his eyebrows.

"No, I didn't know." She straightened her shoulders. "Let's go see her."

Chapter Fourteen

Holly wanted to grab hold of her sister and rock her like a baby. The relief buckled her knees.

Portia sat on the edge of a stripped bed in a curtained-off cubicle. Beside the precisely folded blanket sagged a white plastic bag labeled "personal belongings."

She was taller than Holly if they stood shoulder to shoulder, but right now, Portia looked about twelve years old.

Holly dug her fingers into her palms as she stayed clear of the emotional vortex hurtling around her feet. Her sister needed her to take charge, the way she always did.

Portia glanced up as the curtain rings clattered against the rails, her eyes glassy like a wounded animal's.

Melissa stared back at her, slumped and dejected, sitting on the edge of her bed, her hair hanging in tangled streamers around her face.

The smile wavered on Holly's face. She fixed it in place with determination.

This was Portia, not Melissa, neatly dressed in jeans and a T-shirt, with her hair braided down her back. Her face was clean of makeup and, physically at least, she seemed fine.

"Hey there." Holly kept her distance, tense as she gauged Portia's condition. Holly beat back the bitter tide of hopelessness. Just as Portia was not Melissa, Holly was also different than she'd been back then. She was older now, more capable and able to manage.

As an adult, Holly understood much more. The disease was difficult to cope with and virtually impossible without medication. It came and went with vicious randomness, disappearing as fast as it came and plunging everyone into eviscerating hope. Because the one constant was that it always came back and it got worse.

The child who'd lived through those dreadful, terrifying lows wanted to run and scream. Holly could almost hear a voice in her head urging her to run and not look. Perhaps if Francis had been there to help, to explain or to comfort, it would have been different.

It made her hover, for a second, on the edge of stupid, pointless regret. Holly shook her head impatiently. Francis was who he was, and she was way past the point of expecting him to change.

"Holly," Portia said in a dead voice.

"Hello, sweetheart." Holly approached the bed. "I've been looking for you."

"I didn't do anything." Portia's dull gaze tracked her motion. "They said I was frightening those children, but I didn't do anything wrong."

"I'm glad I've found you. I've been worried about you." Holly eased onto the bed beside her sister. She kept her tone light and noncommittal. Her fear for Portia battered at the tight confines Holly placed around it.

Like a cornered animal, Portia would sense Holly's fear and use it to fuel her combustible emotions. Holly was the anchor for Portia. If she slipped, got angry or upset, everything would spiral into disaster.

"I came as soon as I figured out where you were." Holly kept talking as if everything was normal. As if they weren't sitting in a hospital room at all. "But I had some trouble."

Portia tensed beside her.

"My car got stolen." Holly forced a small laugh. "You hear these things about Chicago. You never think it's going to happen to you." It was a feeble attempt at conversation and fully deserved the disinterested silence with which it was met. "Your medication was in my car."

"I don't want it."

"Yes, I saw from the bottles." *The medication you haven't been taking.* A surge of anger blindsided her and she swallowed. She wanted to shout at Portia and shake her. This wasn't rocket science. This was a simple equation. The medicine keeps you stable. When you are stable, you are capable of leading a normal, fulfilled life. Therefore, take the medication.

Except it was bigger than not taking her medication. Portia was keeping all kinds of secrets.

It was naïve of her, but Holly hadn't known Portia was seeing anyone. Worse, she hadn't even known the twins were sexually active.

Emma lived like a nun. Why should Portia be any different?

Well, she was, way different. The twins weren't still children, for God's sake. Of course they were having sex. Some bipolars were known to be extremely promiscuous.

Holly had read about it. She wasn't blind or uninformed. She should have been prepared. "Is that because you're pregnant?"

"They told you?" Portia glared at her, braced like a naughty child for her punishment.

"I just found out." The impotence rose up and she pushed it down. There was so much rushing through her brain it was difficult to find a clear space.

Pregnant and alone was one thing. It was difficult enough to be a single mother. And this pregnancy would produce a child because that was the way it went. A small, defenseless child who would need to be kept secure and nurtured.

Not cleaning vomit off her mother's face when she lacked the will to get out of bed, or terrifying rushes to the hospital in the middle of the night when life got to be too much. No child deserved a life like that. "Did you stop taking your meds because you were pregnant?"

Portia nodded. "I read about it online. I did the research and decided it would be better not to take anything while I was pregnant."

"Uh-huh." It was getting harder for Holly to keep the anger out of her voice.

"I was fine for a long time," Portia said. "But I don't think I'm fine now."

"No. I think you're having an episode. What do you think?"

Portia nodded, and then her face crumpled. "I'm sorry, Holly. I'm so, so sorry."

And what else could Holly do but hold her and stroke her back until the sobs gentled?

It was all fucking pointless. There was no comforting this away. It wasn't something a kiss and some love would ease. A good cry and a night out with some girlfriends wouldn't touch this.

Hopelessness slunk into the cubicle and wavered like a tangible presence before Holly.

Portia was pregnant.

Holly tightened her arms around her sister. God help her, she loved Portia, but it wasn't enough to help her swallow the bitter pill of resentment. And who would help Portia bring this baby into the world and raise it? *Congratulations*, a bitter voice mocked in the back of her mind, *you are about to be a mother.*

"What am I going to do?" Portia's shoulders heaved under the strength of her sobs.

"The first thing is to get you out of here." Holly hated these cubicles. They were all the same, weary and soul-less, like the collection of human misery had seeped into the walls and floor.

Portia was just one more to the tally.

Her resentment was selfish and unworthy of her. The battle armor of coping fastened around Holly. "Then we're going to try to get you home as soon as possible. You're always better when you're home and where things are familiar. Right?"

Portia nodded slowly. "I want to go home."

"Good."

"Can we go now?" Portia sounded like a young child.

Holly gritted her teeth against the surge of irritation. "Well, there may be a small problem until I get a new passport."

"I didn't lose my passport," Portia said. "I hid it."

"Okay." One obstacle overcome.

"It's not good for me to be here," Portia said. "I need to go home."

"Yes, don't we all?" Home to their nondescript, three-bedroom apartment just off campus. It didn't fill Holly with peace. It hovered in front of her like a layer of cling wrap over her nose and mouth.

Josh approached the cubicle where Richard said Holly's sister was being kept under observation. This was some heavy fucking shit. He should've been running in the other direction as fast as his legs could carry him, but he wasn't. It hadn't occurred to him not to get involved.

"Josh." Richard caught his forearm, his brother's face grave. "This is big. Are you sure you want to get involved with this? This is some heavy fucking shit."

"Exactly what I was thinking." Josh gave a bark of laughter as his brother's words neatly echoed his thoughts. "I'm still here, though."

"Josh?" Richard's eyebrows lowered heavily over his eyes.

Josh sensed a lecture in the air. *Jesus.* Richard could be such a supercilious prick sometimes.

"I've got this." He cut his brother off.

"But it's—"

"I've got this."

Richard gave him a hard, searching stare but released his forearm and stepped back. "Want to tell me why you're getting yourself into this?"

"Haven't got a fucking clue." Josh shrugged. "But it's got something to do with that small brave woman in there."

Richard's face gentled. "Okay, but you know where I am if you need me."

"I know that."

"Good."

On the other side of the privacy curtain, Portia huddled like a child against Holly.

A wave of fierce protectiveness staggered him. Not for Portia but for Holly.

Portia was much larger than her older sister. Taller and larger framed, but Holly held her nonetheless, arms stretched to physical capacity to contain the weeping maelstrom in her arms. And wasn't that just like Holly? She'd give damn near everything if she loved you.

"Um, there was one thing." He stepped back toward his brother and let the curtain fall shut. "I thought I should take them to Mom's place. Maybe Portia will be better there until we can sort the passport thing out."

Richard moved up to peer silently over his shoulder.

Holly and Portia were locked in their private communion. It was one of a handful of unguarded moments Josh had seen with Holly. Her face was wistful and melancholy, her head hung in defeat.

Richard murmured his agreement about the house.

More than anything, the look on her face got to Josh.

Holly wasn't helpless, and she didn't give up or give in. At times she was only marginally more congenial than a ferret, but she didn't allow herself to be brought down.

Josh wanted to make it go away for her. He wanted to rush in and take the burden off her dainty shoulders and heft it around for her. The only thing stopping him was that she'd probably cut off his balls before she allowed it.

Holly caught sight of them and her face settled back into the fierce lines he was used to. Only in flashes did he catch the softer, hurting woman.

"Hey," he said. "Richard will see to getting her released, and we were thinking maybe we should take you two back to my mother's house."

"Joshua?" Portia stuck her head up and wriggled free of Holly's arms. She scooted off the bed and got to her feet. Her eyes gleamed at him, tears swelling up in their depths. "Joshua."

"Hello, Portia." Something was very off, and the skin on his nape prickled.

"I thought you'd never get here." Her cheeks flushed pale pink and her hands drifted over her stomach as she gazed at him with the sort of abject hero worship that made his guts tighten.

Over her head, Holly frowned, her dark brows a violent slash across the peach of her skin.

"We had some trouble finding you."

"I've been waiting to tell you our news." Portia's lashes lowered over her eyes and she took a step into his space.

"Our news?" He was getting a bad, bad fucking feeling here.

Portia put a hand to his chest. "About the baby."

It was an elegant hand, with long fingers and clean nails at the tip, stark against the fabric of his shirt, and he took it away. He had a sort of surreal, out-of-body thing taking over.

"Portia?" Holly came up behind her sister and touched her on the elbow.

Portia shook Holly's touch off.

Holly's midnight eyes went dark as an abyss.

"Are you happy?" Portia beamed adoration that made him want to gag. She touched her flat belly almost reverently. "You are happy, aren't you? About the baby?"

"Portia, I don't understand." The world seemed to tip and reel under his feet. He was very much afraid he did understand.

As if she were his lodestone, Holly drew his gaze. Her eyes gleamed hard and black as pitch.

"Oh, Joshua." Portia launched toward him, her arms like manacles around his neck.

Instinctively Josh wanted to shove her away, but he stopped the impulse and grasped her arms and pulled them from around his neck.

"It doesn't matter now because you're here. You came,

darling. I knew you would come. As soon as you found out about the baby, I knew you would come. Are you happy, Joshua? Tell me you're happy about the baby."

"Jesus." Josh stepped away from her as if she was radioactive. His mind blanked as he tried to form the denial in coherent sentences. He shook his head and kept his eyes on Holly. "No."

Holly stood frozen in place, her eyes wide with shock and her face pale.

"No." His glib tongue totally deserted him. Now, when he desperately needed the right words, his ability to speak had abandoned him. Helpless rage surged through him.

Portia tried to get closer to him, and his hands shot out and held her at bay. "No."

Why was Holly looking at him like that? "I never touched her."

Questions crowded her expression.

Portia's eyes filled with tears. "But Joshua?"

Holly put her arm around the younger woman's waist. She murmured quietly to her sister.

Portia subsided into a wounded silence.

The slow boil of his temper simmered below the surface of his skin. He clenched his fists until his knuckles ached. He didn't dare lose it here. "Let's get back to the house and then we can talk."

Holly had that stubborn twist around her mouth, like she might refuse.

"You have nowhere else to go and we need to sort this out," he said.

"What's wrong, Joshua?" Portia stared up at him. "Aren't you happy?"

Christ. He wanted to shout a denial. He wanted to physically force the lies back into her mouth.

"Josh?" Richard's hand was strong and sure on his arm. "Not here and not now."

"It's not—"

"I know," Richard said.

A hot, sweet wave of relief flowed over him. The blood drained to his extremities and he wanted to sit down.

"I know you," Richard said.

Josh nearly hugged his brother. He settled for a nod and a slap on his shoulder.

"And I can count," Richard continued in a quiet undertone. "Not even you can work that fast."

Chapter Fifteen

Josh parked in front of a Willow Park red brick Edwardian that showed signs of being lovingly restored.

"This isn't your condo." Holly spoke for the first time since they'd left the hospital.

Portia was jammed in the tiny backseat and she leaned forward, between them, to look out the window.

"No, it isn't." Josh got out of the car and walked around to open the door, but Holly got there before him. Already helping Portia out.

"Where are we?" Holly asked as he hauled Portia's bags from the trunk. She'd followed him around to the back of the car.

Portia stood to one side, listlessly looking around her.

"We're at my mother's house. I mentioned it earlier, before—Christ!" Josh stormed up the neatly paved pathway to his mother's front door.

A week ago he'd been living the life of Riley and now this. The Partridge sisters had tracked him down and systematically dismantled his perfect life, piece by piece. What the hell was he thinking, still standing in the middle of the wreckage and helping them do it? If he had any good sense left, he would pack them off to a motel and walk away.

Holly stood beside his car, the one she'd called a penis, in her badly fitting clothes and looking like she bore the weight of the world on her slim shoulders.

His muscles clenched in protest. He wasn't going to pack them off anywhere.

"And your mother is okay with this?" Holly had a good game face, but her vulnerability shimmered in the air around her.

He must be the only person on the planet, Holly included, who got how fragile she was. And did that make him an idiot or the rest of the world blind? Fucked if he knew either way.

"My mother isn't here." He cranked the key in the lock with more vehemence than necessary. The door jammed, reminding him it needed more finesse to open the old girl. He needed to get it together. He gently twisted slightly to the left and up. The door opened. "And if she were, she would be fine with this."

"Why here?"

The woman was going to kill him. That was for damn sure. She couldn't take a helping hand without checking it over to make sure there wasn't a concealed dagger. The anger bled out of him.

Life had taught Holly that lesson. His chest ached for her. She'd always taken care of her sisters at school, and it looked like she still was.

"It's quieter and there's more space. I thought it would suit . . . your sister better." He couldn't even bring himself to say Portia's name. He knew she was sick, he got it, but naming him her baby daddy scraped him raw. Worse was the suspicion that Holly believed her. God knows, the lady had no high opinion of him in the first place.

The two women trailed him into the entrance hall, looking around them like a pair of stray cats. Josh opened another door and motioned them through. "The kitchen," he said. "Make yourselves at home. There probably isn't much here, but I'm sure you can find a cup of coffee. None of the bedrooms are being used; pick whichever one you like."

"Where are you going?" Holly's voice stopped him.

The truth? He was going to drive around the block as many times as it took to get his frustration under control. He needed to talk to Holly, but not while his fight/flight reflex held the reins. "I'm going back to the condo to fetch some stuff. I'll pick up some basics. Anything specific you need?"

The way his day was going, he braced for one of them to ask for tampons.

"No." Holly shook her head. "We're good."

Of course they didn't need fucking tampons. One of them was pregnant. *Ah, Christ.* It crashed down on him. How the hell was he going to deal with this?

Holly couldn't believe he'd slept with Portia. Even if she had no faith in him, she was a math whiz kid. She could add the months, same as Richard had.

The ground beneath him was unstable and shifting and he didn't like it. He needed answers and certainty and things to fit into place. Even if Holly did believe he hadn't fathered Portia's baby—what then?

Holly tucked Portia into bed. She ached like she was a hundred years old.

"Whose room is this?" Portia looked around her with cursory interest.

"Thomas's," Holly said. "He's the younger brother. Wasn't he in the same year as you?"

"I don't remember." Portia rolled over onto her side and ended the conversation.

"No," Holly said, as if she hadn't been dismissed. "Actually, I believe he's a few years older than you. Didn't he have a skateboard?"

A big blond boy beamed underneath his graduation cap from a photograph on the bedside table. He wasn't as dark as his older brothers, but the clean, handsome lines of his face marked him a Hunter brother. That and the direct, unwavering glance of those clear blue eyes. All the Hunters were good-looking boys, but Joshua still took the blue ribbon.

She pushed down a huge sigh. Josh Hunter was going to be a problem in her life again, but for a whole other reason. She wanted to tuck herself under the strong, clean line of his chin and have him tell her everything was going to be all right.

God, he must be mad enough to chew nails right now. Mad enough to want nothing more to do with the Partridge sisters.

This was insane. Two days ago she'd have put her head on a block she would never see Josh Hunter again. Just a smidge over forty-eight hours later she needed to be near him so much she ached with it.

Portia's eyes drifted shut and Holly made a move to climb off the bed.

Portia's eyes popped open. "Stay." Her sister still didn't look at her but closed her eyes. "Stay, Holly, like you used to when we were little and we couldn't sleep."

But you're not little anymore.

Her sister's face relaxed as she got drowsy.

You're not little anymore, but I'm still stuck on the end of the bed, watching you sleep. It had to be some kind of deep and meaningful metaphor. What the hell? She wasn't going to do metaphoric today. Holding her head up on her shoulders was more than enough.

The room was like being part of *The Dangerous Book for Boys*. Everything was neat and in its place, but the room still spilled testosterone in messy, invisible leaks. Boy stuff littered every surface, rugby posters of big men with cabbage ears and battle-scarred legs and arms rubbed shoulders with Miss September of the surgically enhanced body.

Portia lay still under the bold diagonal stripes of the duvet. The red contrasted harshly with her wan features.

Holly smoothed back a strand of her hair. Questions she couldn't ask bubbled up, and she distracted herself by reading book titles.

Trophies propped the ends of a row of books on the rickety bookshelf. Charles Dickens and Jane Austen kept time with *The Principles of Statistical Thermodynamics* and *Advanced Calculus*. A raft of engineering tomes made Holly tired looking at them and, right beside them, an extensive collection of science fiction and fantasy.

The contrast to Josh's clinical condo struck her. All of Thomas Hunter lay around her, for her to see and understand, a visual clue to the man.

Josh's beautiful, perfect condo gave nothing away. Rather like the man himself, a beautiful disguise hiding the real man beneath it.

Portia's chest rose and fell in a more relaxed rhythm.

Holly got comfortable while she waited. The men in this family liked their beds big. The king mattress swallowed her and Portia.

Holly had helped her bathe and washed her hair

before tucking Portia into bed. Portia was tired and overwrought. A good night's sleep wouldn't cure her, but it would certainly help—stability was the key. It was the most important thing for Portia. She needed things to be secure and familiar. Stress was a trigger, and Holly did what she could to mitigate the effect on her sister's life.

Melissa hadn't stood a chance with their vagrant lifestyle.

Portia's eyes grew heavy.

A fist of sadness clenched in her chest. It was such a large, crushing disease against impossibly frail Portia.

"Are you still there, Holly?"

"I'm here, Portia."

Down the hallway, the low murmur of voices indicated the brothers were in the kitchen.

Josh had returned some time ago with the unmistakable growl of the XK-E. He'd stayed as far away from them as he could this evening, and Holly didn't blame him.

What were they talking about? Probably her and her screwed-up family. The old horror of having their secrets found out tightened in Holly's stomach.

Francis would have been horrified at someone seeing behind the perfect facade the Partridge family presented to the world: Francis, the world traveler and professional engineer, with his beautiful Venezuelan wife and their four lovely girls. It was the picture the family preserved at all costs.

Your girls are not so lovely. They are broken and scarred, and you've left them behind now that you have a new family to play with. One of them has the same disease as her mother, the other is a flake who does what she can to perpetuate the myth that life is a fairy tale. The second oldest has ruthlessly constructed her world in an ordered and antiseptic fashion that has no space for messy and ugly. And your oldest daughter . . .

She must have made a sound because Portia glanced over. "Did you say something?"

"No." Holly closed her eyes. She was tired; that's what was wrong with her. It had been an eventful day, all things considered: the stress of looking for Portia, the relief of finally finding her, and the shock of the pregnancy.

Tomorrow was another day. Holly stretched her mouth in a grim smile. Unfortunately, it threatened to be the same as today.

Chapter Sixteen

Holly couldn't quite summon up the energy to do anything about her hunger.

She wandered into the kitchen, a large, homely room. Unlike Josh's condo, there were signs of life everywhere. The notices pinned to the fridge, the jumble of boots and coats in the corner, and the collection of misshapen pottery lined up on the windowsill. School projects from long ago, proudly on display.

The bench protested as she pulled it out and sat. The surface of the table was scratched and scarred from years of use. It was large enough to seat three boys and their friends comfortably. It was a place waiting for its family to come and fill it up.

Holly put her head down on the table. The faint tang of furniture polish soothed her, and she pressed her forehead to the cool wood. She would rest here for a while and then get something to eat. In the quiet, a rooster clock on the wall ticked, and Holly let herself be lulled by the rhythm.

The bench rocked as someone sat, and she turned

her head, not surprised to see Josh had joined her. "Hey?"

"Hello."

"She's asleep?" He had to cock his head to maintain eye contact.

Holly nodded. Her head was way too heavy for her shoulders and she left it where it was.

"What are you doing?"

"Feeling sorry for myself."

"How's that working for you?"

Warm yellow light stroked lovingly across the fine angles of his face. Lucky, lucky light. "Not so good. How are you?"

His jaw tightened. "Honestly?"

"What the hell, go for it."

"I'm still a bit pissed."

She ached to trace the beautiful lines of his remote profile. His eyelashes were almost absurdly long. "About the pregnancy thing?"

"I am not the father." His voice was raw with suppressed feeling.

"I know that."

His expression changed so quickly, it was almost comical. "You do?" He turned to face her, and a frown creased his forehead. "You gave me this look at the hospital, as if you were convinced I'd done it."

"I can count, Josh." And she was an old hand at the Portia Partridge take on reality. "Portia is over four months pregnant. Even you have your limitations."

He put his head down on the table, facing her. "I would prefer it if you'd said you knew it wasn't mine because you trusted me."

She did trust him, oddly enough. It wasn't that. "I think we've covered my trust thing."

"Holly." His face had an austerity to it, like a Dutch masters' painting, "I never touched your sister."

"I know." It was the only tiny glimmer of okay in this monumental balls-up. "Portia constructs her own reality, and right now, you're it."

"Lucky me," he said, but some of the tension drained out of his features. His gaze slid over her face and the corners of his mouth quirked up a bit.

"It'll pass eventually," Holly said. "She'll find something else to fixate on."

He absorbed her statement with a nod. "Have you been sitting here like this for long?"

"Nope."

"Because it's not comfortable."

"I told you." Holly sniffed in a way that even she found pathetic. She didn't care. "I'm having a pity party."

"Wanna talk about it?"

"Nope."

"Do it anyway," he said and sat up.

Holly let the silence draw out as she put her thoughts in order. "It's the baby." Christ, she was such a selfish bitch to be even thinking this way. "I can't be glad about the baby."

"Because it means you'll be taking care of it?" He shifted closer.

"I don't want to take care of another person." It sounded bad saying it out loud, but Josh's expression didn't change. She'd half-expected him to rear back in shock and disgust. "And what if it's like Portia or—" Holly choked off her surge of panic. "It's not always hereditary, but it sure does increase the chances." And now they had another little genetic time bomb on the way. "You were right, this sucks. I want . . ."

No point in even finishing that thought.

"Holly?" Gently, he moved strands of hair away from

her face. "It's not wrong to want things for yourself. It's only wrong if you take those things at the expense of someone else."

"I know." The lack of conviction in her voice fooled no one. Her head got all that, but the older sister in her still wasn't buying.

"I want to hold you," Josh said.

Oh, yes, please, please, please. A small sob caught in her throat. "You can't."

"Why not?" The soft touch of his fingers on her cheek was heavenly.

"Because I'll lose it if you do." If he held her now, she'd never want to stop leaning on those strong shoulders. A stray tear slid down her nose and landed on the wood in front of her. "I don't cry."

"Why not?" His leg pressed against hers, warm and solid.

She scrubbed the traitor away with her palm. "Tears are pointless."

The bench scraped on the wooden floor as he got to his feet. The loss of him left her bereft. Until he slid his long legs on either side of hers, cradling her body with his.

She had to scoot forward to the edge of the bench to accommodate him, but she did it anyway. And because there was nowhere she'd rather be right then than wrapped in a cocoon of Josh.

He leaned over and kissed her on the cheek. His lips pressed warm and soft on her skin. "I think we can risk it."

He settled his big body behind her.

Holly closed her eyes and let it be.

He surrounded her with his warmth and comfort. His breathing huffed loud in her ear and his heartbeat pulsed strong at her back.

Holly didn't feel alone as she lay quiescent in his arms, and she didn't feel burdened. She was safe and peaceful and she let the feeling seep into her bones. She didn't have to be herself. "Josh?"

"Hmm." His voice vibrated through her chest.

"What if I'd said yes that night and we'd danced?" Holly kept her eyes closed. She didn't want to open them and confront tonight.

"We would have danced," he said and chuckled softly.

Her back vibrated as he hummed a couple of bars of "Truly Madly Deeply."

"You remember?" Holly grinned.

"My mother says I'm a sensitive soul." He tightened his arms around her, tucking her more securely into him. "I notice these things."

"What was I wearing?"

"A short dress."

"Good guess." Holly laughed.

"A green dress with some sort of flower pattern."

"Butterflies," she said, close enough to be impressive.

"I was more focused on the body than the dress." It should have ruined the moment, but somehow—it made her smile wider.

"So, if I'd said yes?" Holly shifted. "We would have danced?"

His thighs were rock solid. It must be the running. "Hell yeah. And I would have collected about twenty bucks from my buddies."

"You bet on me dancing with you?" She tried to work up some outrage.

"Damn straight, but you turned me down and I ended up losing big."

"You deserved it."

"You're right." He nuzzled the curve of her ear.

It sent a lovely shiver over her skin and Holly gave a small, contented hum of appreciation.

"If we'd danced, I would probably have copped a feel," he said.

Holly snorted with laughter.

He joined in, and they sat there and laughed. His hands shifted until they rested on the waistband of her pants. His fingers brushed her skin as their chests rose and fell together.

A different sort of tension coiled in her belly. Beneath her sweatshirt, her nipples beaded, tight and expectant.

His erection pressed against the base of her spine.

"Josh." Her skin was sensitized. It was so good, and it shouldn't be. Her defenses were melting.

"I know, Holly." He edged his hips away a tiny bit. "I only want to hold you, to be close to you."

Holly nearly protested the loss. "Is this you doing nothing?"

"You got it. This is me being your friend when you really, really need one."

Unshed tears pressed hard at the back of her eyelids. A friend, someone to lean on. Shit, she'd never had one of those. "Have you ever been friends with a woman?"

"Nope, but I think I'm doing quite well so far. What do you think?"

The smell of him curled around her. "I think women don't look at you and see friend material."

"I don't care what they think." He snorted. "What do *you* think?"

"I don't want to think."

His arms tightened around her. "That works, too."

God, Holly could lie like this with him forever, even with the constant hum of sexual tension between them.

"What if I wanted more than a friend, for tonight?"

Her own daring left her breathless. She needed this, him, and this was great, but it wasn't enough.

He went still before he spoke, his voice rough around the edges. "I would make myself want to puke by reminding you that you aren't in a good place to be making that sort of decision."

"People say it's the best sort of comfort." Holly's blood pounded in her ears.

He blew out a long, tortured breath. "You're not making it easy to be a nice guy."

"I know." Holly folded her hands over his. "But I don't want to be reliable, sensible Holly tonight." She moved her head until her cheek was pressed to his. "I want to pretend it isn't real."

"You want comfort sex," Josh said. The bench scraped as he surged to his feet. "And I'm going to have to say no."

Chapter Seventeen

Holly's heart gave a vicious twist in her chest.

Josh was turning her down.

"Don't look like that." He ran impatient fingers through his hair.

Holly tried to school her features into a mask, but she was too worn out to give it a decent effort. "Like what?"

"Like I'm rejecting you, because that's not the case, sweetheart."

Holly snorted. She sat at the table and he stood poised for flight. It sure looked like rejection from her angle.

He took a step toward her. "I'm trying to do the right thing."

Holly spent a lot of time theorizing about moments like this. As a grown woman, in charge of her own life, including her body, she could make whatever decisions she wanted. Holly dropped her eyes to the front of him, where his erection pressed full and impressive through the fabric of his pants.

He wanted her, but he was doing "nothing."

Enough. Enough thinking, planning, strategizing, waiting. Enough making sure everyone else got what they needed. Well, damn it to hell, Holly needed a little something, and it was four feet away from her and waiting for her to make her move.

Energy crackled through her. Holly stalked him, her feet slapping on the wooden floor.

He tensed, his eyes narrowed as he watched her approach.

He was much taller than she was and she had to virtually climb him like a maypole. His chest was hard and hot. Raising her body, his cock branded her through their clothing, and it was like a match to dry tinder. She didn't doubt the wisdom of what she was doing. Thinking didn't even come into it. She wanted and she needed.

Holly grabbed a hank of his hair and tugged his mouth down to hers. His hair was soft and silky beneath her fingertips as she held his head still.

His eyes flared. "Be sure, Holly, because I don't have a lot of good intentions left here."

"You're overthinking this." She fastened her lips over his.

He gripped her hips, tugging her flush with him. "Ah, baby, if you stop me now, I'm going to cry like a girl," he said as his mouth took over.

"I'm not going to stop you." Holly panted as heat twisted her up inside.

Josh groaned deep before claiming her mouth with a single-minded ferocity that thrilled her.

Holly reveled in the power she had over him.

His big body pressed closer, leashed strength in the hard muscle demanding a combustible response from her.

She needed this, needed him. Like this she wasn't contained, careful Holly, taking responsibility and keeping her family on track. Here she was desirable, beautiful, all woman and passion.

The kiss grew wild, a fiery mating of teeth and tongues that swept her along.

The taste of him roared through her, and there was no more thinking.

He lifted her onto the solid wooden table with thrilling ease. His erection was hot and heavy through his jeans and she ground herself on him.

Her fingers fumbled with his shirt.

He helped her and sent buttons flying across the kitchen.

She spread her fingers over his flesh, enjoying the contrast of hot, silken skin over hard, unyielding muscle.

"Josh." She pressed her forehead on his chest. His skin was hot against her face, the insistent drum of his heart heavy under her ear.

He tipped her chin up for access to her mouth, the line of her jaw, the sensitive skin of her throat. His tongue skimmed her ear, sucking the lobe, sending electric shocks coursing down her neck and back. "This is for you, Holly," he said. "Just for you."

Yes. Holly arched her neck to give him freer access.

He didn't need any more of an invitation and swooped down, putting hot, wet kisses along the line of her throat. Until he reached the curve of her shoulder and he breathed deeply.

"My favorite part of a woman." It came out as a sigh.

He bit lightly before he brought his mouth back to hers for another drugging kiss.

Holly's bones turned to water as he kissed her. His sure hands brought her flesh to life.

"Velvet." He cupped the weight of her breasts.

Her nipples peaked hard and ready for his touch as he brushed his fingers over them.

God, it felt so good, perfect. She gasped her approval.

He tugged up her shirt and gained access to her breasts. With a growl of appreciation, he bent his mouth toward her. He licked a nipple and blew softly until it reached aching hardness.

More. Holly arched her back, offering her flesh to him. Soft whimpering noises escaped her throat as he brought her nipples to aching points of sensation that shot straight down to her core.

"So beautiful." He sucked lightly on the underside of her breasts, laving the skin with his tongue, moving along her ribs and onto her stomach.

Holly sucked in her stomach and wriggled beneath him.

With deft fingers, he worked the fastening of her jeans. He tugged them down her thighs and sent them sliding across the floor.

This was what she craved. It scared her and thrilled her all at once. Holly opened her mouth to protest, but he kissed her as he nudged her butt farther back onto the table. Excitement drummed like a pulse between her thighs.

She grabbed the waistband of his pants, tugging at the button. Her hands slipped inside to touch the hard, throbbing length of him, and he sucked in his breath. With shaking fingers, she pushed down his briefs until she could stroke him.

His cock pulsed in her hand. He grabbed her wrist. "No."

Holly moaned her protest. She wanted to touch him, brand his skin like he did hers.

"There will be time for that." He spread her hands

above her head before skimming his mouth down her body.

He grasped the elastic of her briefs and pulled them off. "I've wanted to do this for as long as I've known you."

He pushed her thighs apart and stepped between them.

"Josh."

His gaze skimmed hot and demanding on her exposed flesh, but she didn't feel shy or vulnerable. His eyes worshipped her. He dropped to his knees, his mouth searing on the inside of her thigh as he pushed her legs up and apart until she was completely exposed to him.

"Shit, look at you." His mouth tracked higher, and she writhed in anticipation.

Her hands tangled in the silky strands of his hair, tugging him closer, wordlessly demanding he get on with it.

She stuffed her hand in her mouth to stop the scream as his mouth discovered her needy flesh. He hummed his enjoyment as he worked his lips and tongue over her. He took his time, exploring the aching bud of her clitoris and sucking gently, laving her.

It was too much, and Holly went off almost immediately under his mouth.

He spread soft kisses over her stomach as Holly drifted back down. She melted onto the table beneath her and there was a gentle throb between her legs.

"That was—" Holly couldn't find the words.

"Don't say nice."

Holly laughed.

He leaned over her and kissed the skin of her neck. His hair was mussed where her hands had gripped it.

She pressed her face into the spot where his neck and shoulder met and inhaled the scent of clean man and laundry detergent. She had been half-expecting some sort of expensive cologne. "Intense. I was going to say intense."

"Okay, then."

"You've wanted to do that since you first met me?" Holly had to ask, and he laughed.

"I was precocious."

"I'll say."

She gave in to the urge to taste and opened her mouth to suck the warm skin of his shoulder.

A soft groan resonated through her as he reacted. His cock still pulsed, hard and needy.

"That was . . . only the beginning." He tangled his hand in her hair and tugged her head back. His mouth descended. "We are just getting started."

Holly was amazed as her body stirred back to life under the determined demand of his mouth.

His hands swept under her shirt and onto the skin of her back, exploring and discovering her skin inch by inch. They slid down to cup her ass and pull her tight into his erection. His fingers traced the crease of her butt, dipping between to stroke through her wet heat.

Holly whimpered softly as his fingers caressed her back to arousal. She moaned in protest as he stopped suddenly.

"These are going to have to go." He shucked his jeans and impatiently stepped out of them.

"And these." Holly grabbed his briefs and he yanked them off. *Holy shit.*

His cock jutted from between his thighs, heavy and tumescent, and she needed to feel him inside her.

He stepped between her legs, spreading them wide. He ran his hands from her knees, over her thighs, and into the soft thatch of hair. His expression intensified as his fingers slipped over her slickness and into her body, first one and then another.

"Ah, Holly, baby," he said. "You're so wet and ready for me."

Holly's body tightened around his fingers, greedily demanding more. He removed his hand and fit the head of his cock against her opening.

"Wait." Holly grabbed his wrist. "Protection."

"Shit." He reached for his jeans. His hands shook as he ripped a foil packet open.

She took it from him, stroking his erection, wrapping her fingers around it.

He groaned, frowning in concentration as she explored him.

"Please, Holly." He grimaced, and she slipped the sheath over his flesh. "Take me inside you."

He slid her onto his shaft.

Her body stretched to accommodate him, pulsing around him.

He eased into her slowly, his breath hissing between his teeth as he fought for control.

Holly writhed, her body needy and demanding, but he grabbed her hips and held her still until he was fully enveloped. The throbbing fullness inside her was incredible, a feeling of completion that shook her to the core.

"You're perfect, Holly, perfect." His eyes met hers and held her with his sheer intensity.

He moved, slow and shallow at first, allowing her body to get used to the invasion. He filled her completely, drawing out longer and longer strokes and pushing all the way back into her.

Holly's orgasm built deep and she grabbed onto him, her nails digging into the skin of his ass and his back as she urged him onward. Harder and faster he went, responding to the signals of her body, until with a shout Holly came.

He surged hard and strong, once, twice, and then he joined her, his body going taut as a bowstring above her as he climaxed. "Fuck."

Holly clung to his chest like a limpet, incapable of moving. His curse struck her as inordinately funny and she giggled.

"I think you broke me." He moved his weight off her and onto his elbows. The rumble of his laughter joined hers.

"It's been a while," she said.

"For you and me both."

Holly had trouble believing that, and she peeked up to see if he was lying.

He raised an eyebrow at her. "It's been a while for both of us."

It shouldn't have made any difference, but it did. It made her special somehow.

"I'll be back." Josh levered himself off her, strode through the door naked, and disposed of the condom in the bathroom. He walked back toward her.

She blushed, exposed and spread over the kitchen table like dinner. Holly sat up and reached for her clothes.

He snagged the T-shirt before she could put it over her head.

"Hey." Holly tried to grab her shirt.

"Uh-uh." He tossed the shirt across the room. "It took me long enough to get you out of this."

"Two days," Holly sneered.

"And the intervening years."

"Get serious." But his words caused a curious warm glow in the pit of her stomach.

He upended her and tossed her over his shoulder. "We're not done, you and I."

"What the hell are you doing?" Holly shrieked and stuffed her hand in her mouth. Portia was just down the hall. Guilt gave a small tug, but Holly stamped on it.

"I'm taking you to my bed, woman."

"Put me down," she said, torn between outrage and laughter. "This is such primitive, sexist behavior. This is a perfect example of men thinking they know what women want."

He trotted her down the hall and up the stairs to the bedrooms.

"For your information, women don't like these overbearing displays of masculine strength. They don't like being held ass over tip and jostled against someone's shoulder."

She was such a liar.

"I'm making notes here, Holly." He gave her butt a territorial pat. "Are you done with the lecture?"

"Why?" They were in a bedroom. It was novel, seeing a room upside down for the first time.

He flipped her over and she fell in an inelegant, panting heap across the huge bed. "Because," he came down on top of her, pinning her beneath his big body before she could roll away, "I want to get it on."

"Again?" Holly squeaked at him.

He lowered his mouth. "Hell yeah."

Chapter Eighteen

Josh lay still for a moment and absorbed the sensation of waking with Holly in his arms. He'd woken up with women before, but waking up with Holly was unique, as if he'd embarked on an entirely different adventure. He didn't probe the notion too deeply. A truth hovered outside of his willingness to look in that direction.

Instead, he turned his head to study his bunkmate.

She slept curled into a fetal ball facing him. Her legs pressed up against his side as if she simultaneously pushed him away and needed to touch him. She made him want to grin like an idiot. Vixen. It was a good word—small, feral, and absolutely savage.

He sat up. He instantly missed the physical contact. He was fucked. Here he was, thirty-one years old, one of Chicago's most sought-after bachelors, and he was chin deep in the shit. And why? Because she'd bustled back into his life and he wanted to keep her.

She murmured in her sleep. A line furrowed between her brows as if, even in sleep, Holly carried the weight of her burdens with her.

It was all rather predictable. The one woman who

wasn't chasing him. The one who got away. And despite thinking of himself as an individual and fiercely guarding his independence, he sat here, watched her battle dragons in her sleep, and planned how to keep her by his side. He'd got her into his bed last night with every intention of doing so again tonight, but for how long?

Ah, shit. The situation teetered on the edge of impossible. The helplessness fastened around his throat. He couldn't help Holly, and Portia was way outside of his understanding. He didn't see a happy ending here, and that really bothered him. Holly would need to choose, and he had a sneaking suspicion he already knew what her choice would be.

He avoided dwelling on the question and lumbered to the bathroom.

His reflection glared back at him. It was a good-looking face. People had been telling him that since preschool. He wasn't going to be disingenuous and pretend he had no idea. He'd certainly used his looks to his advantage since he stopped thinking girls had cooties and started taking a real interest in what girls did have.

Leaning down, he splashed water over his face. The cold hit him like a kick in the pants. Damn, he was awake now. His hands rasped along the dark line of his beard. He would shave later. He needed to go for a bike ride, try to clear his head. His triathlon loomed up on him. It had stopped mattering to him some time ago, but he was committed now. Beating Richard was as much a habit as his coffee in the morning.

Holly could tell by the way the light hit the blinds it was later than she usually slept. A strange sensation glimmered inside her. It took her a while to find a name for it. Good. She felt good. Not champing at the bit, raring to go, strong like a bull good, but a general feeling of well-being.

It made her want to roll over and burrow deeper into the bedding and stay there, clasping the feeling to her for a while longer. The linen smelled like Joshua and sex, and she took a deep breath. She stretched her limbs deliciously across the sheets and guessed their thread count was higher than her income statement.

Josh was such a big girl about his creature comforts.

She grinned and sat up. Where was he?

Deliberately, she tugged the comforter away and put her feet on the floor. She couldn't lie here all day. There was plenty to be done this morning.

And Portia.

A sour taste coated the back of her throat. She would have to come up with a plan for Portia.

She didn't rush to get ready, but she didn't mess around either. If something was wrong, Josh would have woken her.

Josh.

Last night had been incredible. She'd discovered a side of herself she'd never even suspected existed.

But it couldn't happen again.

Holly shook off the pinching sensation in her chest.

Portia was fixated on Josh, and it wouldn't take much to push her over the edge. They had taken a chance last night and gotten away with it. They might not be as lucky next time.

She slammed the door on the little voice asking *what about me?* Someone—she assumed it was Josh—had gathered her clothes up from the kitchen and left them draped over the bottom of the bed.

Holly pulled a face at the sight of her jeans. Even she was getting tired of hauling on the same pair of jeans day after day. Hanging around with a walking fashion plate chipped away at her ego.

Across the hallway was the bathroom, a mixture of modern convenience and old-world charm. The shower nestled above a claw-foot tub, and Holly stepped in. At least his mother didn't have his obsession with faucets, and this one she could operate.

After her shower, she followed the smell of bacon to the kitchen. A quick peek into Thomas's room confirmed Portia was still sleeping. If Portia was entering a depression, there would be a lot of sleeping. There would be days when her sister wouldn't be able to find the will to get out of bed.

Holly squared her shoulders. One step at a time was how they did this. First breakfast, and then she needed to make some calls.

Holly stopped dead.

There was an angel at the stove. The woman was exquisite. Blond, tall, and graceful, she moved in front of the stove and cooked what smelled like breakfast.

"Hey, beautiful." Josh's voice startled Holly.

The woman turned her head and smiled a big, wide, breathtaking beam of pure light.

Josh moved into Holly's sightline and sauntered toward the woman.

Holly stood, not certain what she was seeing.

Josh had been training. Again with the gleaming torso and no shirt.

"Look at you, all sweaty and smokin' hot." The woman had a rich, fluid voice with a shot of cognac to make it steam.

"Oh, yeah." Josh reached for her.

She giggled and tried to escape, but Josh grabbed her by the elbows and tugged her toward him, gentle but relentless.

Something tightened around Holly's throat and threatened to cut off her air.

The woman turned sideways as she tried to wriggle free.

Holly gaped. She was very pregnant. Not pregnant like swollen ankles and water retention, but perfectly, beautifully, and glowingly pregnant. The pair of shorts she wore stopped high up on her killer thighs, and the only place she carried was her neat, round, and adorable baby bump.

It was the baby bump that had all of Josh's attention as he spread his big, laborer's hands over her swollen stomach. "Hey, baby," he whispered to her enlarged belly. "Are you ready to meet the world yet?"

"Jeez." The woman rolled her eyes but allowed Josh to press his ear to her belly. His expression was one of rapt attention.

Some part of Holly clamored for an explanation but another wussed out and didn't want to hear it. All the old Josh stories rushed to the surface of her mind.

The woman wrinkled up her perfect nose and swatted at Josh's bare shoulder with a spatula. "You stink."

The red haze cleared. There was something familiar about the woman. Probably seen her on a billboard somewhere, or starring in a Hollywood blockbuster. She was that good-looking.

"Jesus, Joshua." A male voice interrupted them, but Josh didn't move. "Get off my wife. I swear to God, if I catch you with your grubby hands on her one more time, I'm going to break both your arms."

Holly almost whimpered with relief. It wasn't a good

reaction. She wasn't supposed to be getting attached to Joshua Hunter. Getting jealous and possessive of the man was a phenomenally stupid idea.

"She likes me better anyway." Josh tucked the blonde under his armpit. "She only married you to get closer to me."

"Gross." The blonde grimaced and pushed Josh away. "You're all sweaty."

Richard Hunter glared at Josh. "You're a dick."

"What?" Josh spread his arms wide.

"There she is." Richard turned and gave Holly his slow smile. It crept across his grave face like a surprise, all the more attractive for its unexpectedness. It changed his severely handsome features into those of a warm, approachable man. "I hope you managed to get some sleep."

"Yes, thank you." She got hit by an attack of shyness.

Josh gave her a sexy, intimate smile. "Babe."

Holly's face heated. Everyone in the kitchen could figure out what they'd done last night.

"Good morning." She dropped her eyes short of meeting his gaze and greeted the room at large.

Josh strode over to her, and Holly's heartbeat accelerated.

His mouth was warm on the skin of her cheek as he kissed her. "You were asleep when I left," he said, close to her ear. "I almost woke you up, but I took pity on you."

The woman was right; he did smell, but it was the sort of musky, male sweat smell.

"Come and meet my fabulous sister-in-law, Lucy." He grabbed her hand and tugged her deeper into the room. "Lucy is secretly pining away for me while she settles for second best and has babies with my brother."

"Not. Hi, Holly." Lucy glided over to her on her *Sports Illustrated* legs with her hand held out. "I've been hearing all about your adventures."

Gorgeous, pregnant goddess meet Frumpy, the eighth dwarf. "Er, hi."

Brilliant. Dazzle her with your wit, why don't you?

"You probably don't remember me." Lucy screwed up her face in an expression as enchanting as the last one. "I was in school with you."

"Lucy Flint?"

Another stratospheric beam of a smile as Lucy nodded. "We weren't in the same grade, but you were the dancer, right?"

"Right." Holly nodded, trying not to feel quite so absurdly pleased. Who could forget Lucy Flint? In sleepy Willow Park, Lucy Flint had been like a rock star, or one of those naughty royals who kept the tabloids filled. The school had hummed with the exploits of the gorgeous and infamous Lucy.

"How are you?"

"Great." Lucy and Richard had been an item in high school. "Are you still dancing?"

"A bit." Holly nodded. Steven didn't like her dancing; he thought it was demeaning.

"You were the most incredible dancer I've ever seen." Lucy waved her hands through the air. "You remember, Josh?"

Josh gave her his slow, sexy smile that warmed Holly from the inside out. "Sure I do."

"Joshua." Lucy brandished a spatula at his head. "You are such a dog."

"Why, thank you, Lucy." Josh ducked the spatula. "I'm glad you noticed."

"Go and have a shower," Richard said.

"And put a shirt on." Lucy turned back to Holly. "Are you hungry?"

Josh snorted with laughter, which Holly ignored. "I am, but only a bit."

"Thank God." Josh ambled out of the kitchen. "At least the rest of us might get fed. Between Lucy's gestating and your appetite, I was going to suggest Richard and I go for a burger."

"Hey." Lucy laughed as Josh retreated down the hallway. She indicated her large belly. "Making another person here."

Lucy focused her beautiful green eyes on Holly. "How is your sister this morning? You must let me know if there's anything I can do." Lucy's face said she meant it. It wasn't some mouthed platitude, to be forgotten before the words faded in the air. It made a place in the middle of Holly's chest warm.

"There's not much anyone can do," Holly said. "We're going to have to ride this out until I can get her back on her medication."

"She's not taking it?" Richard slid his arm around his wife's waist.

"No." Holly surprised herself by talking so openly about Portia's condition. There was something about Lucy and Richard, a complete lack of judgment, that made it easy. "There's no concrete proof either way for medication affecting the baby, but she doesn't want to take the chance."

"Understandable." Lucy touched her large belly.

Richard nodded. "But dangerous; I did some reading about it last night."

His interest touched Holly and she relaxed.

"There's every chance of a massive case of baby blues after she delivers." Richard's eyes met Holly's. She read understanding there, and compassion. "It's a very difficult situation."

Suddenly, Holly wanted to talk about Portia. The words came haltingly at first. Richard and Lucy didn't push or probe, and the trickle became a flow.

By the time Josh reappeared, showered and lovely in a pair of cargo shorts and a T-shirt, breakfast was ready and Holly was over her awkwardness.

Richard helped Lucy lower her bulk onto a seat and took up the one next to her. "Jeez, Luce." Her husband surveyed the feast. "I'm going to have to lose my baby weight by the time you give birth."

Lucy wasn't a yogurt and cup of strawberries girl— Canadian bacon, French toast, fluffy scrambled eggs, hash browns, and maple syrup. There were also strawberries.

Holly sat and took it all in.

Lucy grimaced at her. "I like my food."

"I think I love you," Holly said, and meant it.

"Well, that's good." Lucy bit her lip and flushed. "Because I've been presumptuous. Josh explained how you had lost everything in your car, and I brought you a couple of T-shirts and some shorts." She spread her arms to indicate her belly. "Because I'm certainly not using them."

"Um . . . thanks." Holly made a mental note not to attempt to squeeze her South American, short-girl curves into Lucy's clothing. There was a limit to how much humiliation a woman could take.

Chapter Nineteen

As the day got hotter, desperation drove Holly to try on the things in the package Lucy had given her. Locking herself in the bathroom, she prepared for all-out, total humiliation.

The T-shirt fit, and it was a great color for her. The woman in the mirror looked like her, only Holly as she'd never seen her before. The emerald green turned her skin sort of peachy. Feeling marginally better, she dug out a pair of linen shorts. They slid easily over her hips and fastened. Holly made a small huff of amazement and turned to examine her reflection.

The shorts were . . . quite nice. She pivoted to the side. Actually, they were very nice. She didn't look too suckish. She turned for the all-important rear inspection and made another small noise in the back of her throat. She pirouetted and examined the effect. The shorts hung low on her hips, but her stomach was nice and flat, and they made her look curvy and sexy. Her thighs appeared firm and taut beneath the drape of fabric near the top. There was a definite Jennifer Lopez thing going on here. She rather liked it.

Holly made a face of amazement in the mirror. Best

of all, she dug out a couple of bras in the bottom of the bag. Holly's breasts weren't large, but it was a relief to have them rounded up and pointed in the right direction. It seemed she shared a cup size with the fecund goddess as well. A jaunty pair of beaded flip-flops completed the outfit.

She sauntered into the kitchen. Looking good and feeling it.

Portia sat at the kitchen table, crouched around a mug of something, as if she were afraid someone was going to take it away.

"Good afternoon." Holly's ebullient mood disappeared like vapor.

Portia jumped and turned. Her hair tangled in a disaster around her head. Portia's eyes, puffy from sleeping most of the day away, tracked Holly into the kitchen. She scratched at her blotchy skin and went back to her mug.

"Did you sleep well?"

Portia shrugged one shoulder, her hair dropping over her face to hide it from view.

Holly gently took a handful and smoothed it to the side. "We have the same hair curse," she said. "Would you like me to tame the beast for you?"

Shrug.

So now what? Coffee. It would certainly make her feel better. `

"What have you got there?" Holly walked to the coffeemaker. Thank God, Josh's mother was a sensible woman and didn't go in for Italian stainless-steel beasts. She poured herself a cup and added cream.

"Is that coffee?"

Shrug.

"Should you be drinking coffee?"

Portia swirled the liquid in her mug before taking a sip.

All righty, then, intervention time. "Portia?" Holly took a seat opposite her sister and placed her mug carefully on the table. "You're in the middle of an episode."

Portia stared down at the table.

"We spoke about this. Emma and I would tell you when you were showing signs of being in an episode?"

"I can't think." Portia rubbed her head, screwing her eyes tightly shut. "My head is—I can't think."

"Okay, Portia." Holly waited for her sister's expression to relax before she continued. "But you know this is part of your condition. You get tired all the time and you don't want to do anything. This is how it is for you. We wrote it down on our action chart at home. Remember? We went to Dr. Foster and he gave us the chart to make notes of the warning signs and plans for what to do when we recognized them."

"I'm tired." Portia put her head down on the table.

Holly tightened her hands around her mug. Portia didn't do this on purpose. It wasn't personal either. It was important to keep that in mind or she would lose patience. "Portia, I know you're tired, but if you aren't going to take the medication, we're going to have to deal with this."

Portia stared unblinkingly ahead.

"We can break this down into small pieces and deal with them one at a time. Would that work for you?" Holly sipped her coffee and waited.

"It doesn't matter." Portia picked at the wood grain with one nail. "None of it matters."

"Of course it matters, sweetheart." Holly tucked a hair tendril behind Portia's ear.

Portia sat up, her expression suddenly keen and focused. "Do you think she knows I'm here?"

"Who knows?" Holly did a quick mental gear change. "Mummy?"

Everything inside Holly went on high alert. "Melissa's dead, Portia. Mummy—" Holly forced the word out of her mouth—"is dead."

"I know she's dead." Portia frowned, as if Holly had missed the entire point. "But do you think she knows I'm here?"

"I don't know." Carefully, Holly inched forward, not knowing where this conversation was heading. Melissa was dangerous territory. "Why?"

"Do you think anyone who's dead knows anything?"

Holly breathed a soft sigh of relief, Melissa averted.

"Again, Portia, I don't know." Talking about death with Portia freaked her out. Portia's halfhearted attempt to hurt herself very early on in the manifestation of her condition had served as a loud enough warning. Holly would be damned if she let her sister go the same way as their mother. "We need to talk about the baby, sweetheart. The baby you're going to have. We need to talk about what you want to do."

"I want the baby." Portia glared at Holly, as if expecting resistance.

"I gathered as much." Holly kept any reaction off her face. She'd had plenty of practice over the years. "And in that case, we need to talk about the father of this baby."

"Joshua is—"

"Josh is not the father." The trick was to be firm but gentle and stick to the truth.

"Why would you say such a thing?" Portia's face screwed up in consternation. "Ask them at the hospital. They'll tell you. Ask them, Holly."

"I don't need to ask them at the hospital, sweetheart, because Josh couldn't be the father of your baby."

"You don't know that."

"Yes, I do. Listen to me." Holly kept her tone carefully neutral. No judgment, no condemnation, and no unruly tail of emotion for Portia to latch on to, only the truth, spoken calmly. "You are fifteen weeks pregnant, Portia. Josh Hunter couldn't possibly be the baby's father, but somebody is, and that person is going to need to know."

"Why?" Portia's face twisted. "This is my baby. They might try to take my baby from me."

"Portia," Holly said before her sister could build momentum. "The father has to know." She locked eyes with her sister.

Portia looked away first. "How do you know I haven't told him?"

"Have you?"

"No."

Holly sipped her coffee. It gave her something to do with her hands. The bitter truth was, the father could be anyone. Hypersexuality was another one of those manic behaviors Portia could exhibit. It was a new one for her, but it meant her sister could be frighteningly promiscuous. And pregnancy was only one concern because Portia had, clearly, not bothered with protection.

Holly pushed the unwelcome thought aside. She would deal with this one thing at a time. She needed to establish who this *anyone* was, and if he was someone Portia and this baby could count on. Most especially the baby, because there might come a time when this child was going to need all the help it could get. Holly was willing to lay money on it.

"I want to keep the baby." Portia's face grew more animated. "I didn't plan it." Portia surprised her further. Her tone sounded reasonable. "It just happened."

It just happened? Three words that prefaced nearly every fuckup in history.

"Okay," Holly said calmly, instead of allowing the hot words to bubble up. Portia would refuse to accept any sort of accountability. In Portia's world, sex just happened. You couldn't fight her take on reality. "Have you thought what you're going to do now? I mean, in terms of your medication and the pregnancy?"

"Yes."

"That's good," Holly said. "Do you want to develop an action plan?"

"I already have."

Holly managed to keep the surprise off her face. The action plans were something they'd started on the recommendation of Portia's support group, but her sister generally hated them and her contribution was, at best, reluctant.

"That's good." The desire to see the plan throbbed like a festering wound, but Holly would have to wait for Portia to offer.

"I want you to tell me about Mummy."

"What?" Shock held her frozen. They never spoke about Melissa. "She died here in Willow Park, and before that she was sick for a long time."

"She wasn't always sick, though." Portia shook her head "There must have been times when she wasn't."

"There were." There had been long stretches, before the disease grew too marked, when Melissa had been almost like everyone else's mum. Only prettier and more bubbly, and Melissa had seemed younger and full of fun. Holly exhaled sharply and the tightness was gone.

"Tell me something." Portia leaned forward. "Something from when she was all right."

"She liked to bake." The anxiety of going back clawed through her belly. "Just like Emma does. She liked to bake and she was good at it. There were times when she would fill the kitchen with her baking."

The pain raked inside and Holly wanted to make it go away. Long-forgotten images tumbled through her head. "She would laugh when she baked and make the most beautiful cupcakes for us. She made butterflies on them and flowers and sometimes creatures like fairies and dragons."

The happy times hurt even more than the awful ones, because they always ended too abruptly.

Portia watched her with wide, shining eyes.

"And she liked to dance. She would put the music on and we would dance around the house, all day. All of us would dance everywhere we went."

"I don't remember her baking," Portia said. "I don't remember the dancing or the cupcakes. Only that she was sad a lot, and you and Grace would come and tell us Mummy needed some alone time and we were to try very hard to be quiet and good."

Guilt slammed into her. She'd hated that feeling as a child and, somehow, she'd managed to transfer it to her sister. "Sorry." It sounded inadequate, because it was. "It was all we could think of to say."

"You were kids yourselves." Portia shrugged. "I have no memories of her when she was well." She went back to staring at her coffee mug. "And now I'm like her."

"No, you're not." Holly's skin crawled. She took one of Portia's hands. It lay limp and motionless on her palm.

Portia had long, shapely fingers, their father's hands.

"Melissa was alone in her illness. She was totally alone and with nobody to help her or to try to understand what it was like for her. She had four children to manage with no family and no help. We kept moving from place to place, and it must have been torture for her. She was totally isolated, and the stress accelerated her condition all the time. You're not like her."

Holly shook the dead weight of Portia's hands. "You're not like Melissa because we're not going to let you be. You have an illness, Portia, but we've been managing. Haven't we?"

Portia took her hand back and wrapped it around her cup.

"I miss Emma," Portia said. "I want to go home to Emma. Emma understands."

She got up and slunk out of the room.

Holly rubbed the dull ache in the middle of her chest. It was all so damn hopeless. A doorway shut down the hall.

Portia would probably crawl back into bed and sleep for most of the day.

Holly would get up and check. Later.

She should know better, but the guilt was like an open nerve ending. In some festering place inside her, Holly knew she could've done something to prevent the condition manifesting in Portia. Doctors and therapists, counselors and experts had all said otherwise.

And Holly believed them.

Except for that dark little part that always believed if she could have done better; the same part that always insisted if she had been quieter as a child, an easier baby, a better daughter . . . perhaps?

Holly made a harsh noise and got to her feet. This was getting her nowhere.

"Holly?"

She jumped as Josh materialized beside her. How much had he heard?

"You okay?"

It was tempting to tell him how she was. To let it all hang out, and Holly hesitated.

There was real empathy on his beautiful, serious face. He did care, but she didn't have any idea what to do with that.

She understood how to be alone. She understood how you stood and managed on your own. This sharing was new and alarming. "I'm fine."

He went to put his arms around her, but she ducked to the side. If he touched her, she would shatter. "No."

One dark eyebrow shot up in response.

"We can't." She tried to gentle her tone.

He stilled, as if she were some sort of wild and unpredictable beast. "Can't what?"

He read her too well, and it annoyed Holly more than she could say. "You can't do things like that."

"Like hold you?"

"Yes." Holly stalked around the table to put the solid wooden barrier between them. "That and more."

"More?" His voice was a silky purr, but the lines of his face were carved and perfectly immobile.

She sensed the emotion he kept carefully concealed, and even his caution made her want to lash out. It certainly wasn't rational. "Portia thinks . . ." She had to remind both of them of that sickening reality or this would go too far, again. "You know what Portia thinks."

"But she's wrong."

"It doesn't matter." Was she the only person on the planet who got this shit? "The truth isn't important in Portia's world right now. It's what she thinks and feels that matter. She will react on those and . . . and we can't."

He rubbed the back of his neck.

She had to find the words, strong words that would end this thing. Forever. Last night she'd allowed herself to be swept away by lust or passion or whatever, but she couldn't afford to let her unruly hormones guide her.

Portia depended on her to do the right thing.

Holly always did the right thing. The pit of her stomach dropped like it was lead filled. And the right thing, right now, did not include the beautiful man looking at her intently.

She needed to end this thing between her and Josh. Holly didn't even know what to call it, and she resisted the idea of putting a name to it. Even in the privacy of her mind.

"You know . . . you understand . . . Portia? Me. You?" Holly swung around to break eye contact. She couldn't do this while he was looking at her. She was raw inside; she didn't want to put distance between them, but there was no choice. No fucking choices here but ugly ones. Holly massaged the dull ache settling above her breasts with her palm.

"I understand the situation is messy and difficult," he said.

Holly closed her eyes to try to block the effect of his voice. There was a lot he didn't say, but she heard it anyway. Holly desperately wanted to believe in the small flicker of hope he held out to her. She couldn't afford to, though. "Then you know why we can't . . . carry on."

"Look at me, Holly."

She shook her head.

"This isn't what I expected after last night." His quiet voice carried a steel undertone.

Holly winced under the impact, because throbbing under the anger was hurt. "Last night shouldn't have happened. This isn't about me." Her throat closed convulsively. It had been so easy to forget in the beauty of what they'd shared. "It's about Portia."

"And where does what you want fit into all this?" He said it softly enough, but it hit her like the sharp lash of a whip. "Portia is ill and I understand that, but there has to be a way for you to have a life outside of that."

Her legs were moving before she had fully formulated the thought. Her body escaped before her mind could catch up. She didn't want to hear it. He didn't know. He didn't understand. He couldn't know what went on in her mind. Her needs didn't matter. They hadn't mattered when Melissa was alive, and now they would get lost in the aftermath of their mother's legacy.

"I'm not giving up on you, Holly. We'll find a way."

She stalked away from him.

Josh had ended things with more women than he could recall. Some had cried, others had gotten mad, some even violent, and still others had quietly accepted what he said and slunk away with their dignity.

Laura, the sadness in her eyes impenetrable and soul deep. He'd failed Laura, too full of what worked for him to see her pain.

It sucked. It really, really sucked. And it was definitely worse being on the receiving end. His head reeled. The entire situation had spun out of control faster than he could blink.

Holly had been sitting at the kitchen table looking like a kicked mongrel. He'd caught enough of the conversation with Portia to know how much her last remark must have been like a kick in the balls. And, yes, his lady did have balls. She swaggered around like John Wayne wearing them, and her fierce independence, like some sort of badge of honor.

In his head, the scene had played something like: *he walks in, puts his arms around her. Holly sighs and leans her slight weight into his strong, manly chest and allows him to share her pain.* Josh laughed. The hollow sound echoed across the silent kitchen.

In the depths of the house, a door slammed shut.

Josh swallowed past the bile in his esophagus. Of course he could take his unloading with dignity and get on with his life. Except a woman like Holly deserved somebody by her side.

Holly Partridge thought she was done with him. One night of mind-blowing sex and *so long, sweetheart.* But there was this one factor she'd left out of her equation. Him. She needed his help and, dammit, she was going to get it. There had to be a way to manage Portia and for Holly to have a life of her own. And he had a growing certainty that he wanted to be part of whatever future Holly had planned.

Did she think he was going to calmly accept his dismissal like a good boy? Huh!

Of course the average stalker had much the same view.

His head hurt. His chest ached as well.

He could be coming down with something.

Chapter Twenty

Holly had been staring at the glow in the dark solar system on the ceiling for so long she'd made a pattern in the random collection of stars and planets. A younger version of Josh must have stuck it up there and his mother still hadn't gotten around to taking it down.

There was no reason for her to be awake, but it didn't seem to make any difference to her mind. Her brain kept on with its exhausting churning.

Portia had vacillated between utter despair and bleak despondency all day.

Holly had barely been able to leave her alone for a minute. It had taken some time to settle her down to sleep after a postdinner crying jag, and Holly had crawled into bed shortly afterward. She was as battered as if she'd done ten rounds with Mike Tyson.

Still, she couldn't sleep. She'd lain in the dark listening to the sounds of Josh moving around the house. Making a cup of coffee, the low rumble of his voice as he took a call on his cell, his footsteps past her door, and then the soft thud of a door shutting. Followed by the sound of running water as he took a shower. He'd been gone for most of the day and returned only after she and Portia had gone to bed.

But that had been hours ago, and the room next door had long since fallen silent. Yet she still lay here, looking at the Day-Glo universe. Had he put it there for himself or for the benefit of whoever he managed to get into this bed with him?

Holly stifled a giggle. It opened up a whole world of corny lines.

"I saw stars."

"The earth moved."

She groaned at herself and rolled over. A tired headache stirred, which was probably why it took her a while to realize the pounding came from outside her head.

She sat up and snapped on the light. It ricocheted off the back of her eyeballs, and she closed her eyes to accustom them to the glare.

The door next to hers opened, and the heavy tread of Josh's footsteps padded on the wooden floor.

The clock beside the bed told her it was well past the witching hour.

She silenced any incipient protests from her tired body as she rolled out of the bed. A light came on from the other side of her door, and Holly hauled a T-shirt over her panties. She might be developing a fondness for Hugo Boss tees. The fabric was soft and voluptuous on her skin.

Opening her door a crack, she pressed her ear to the gap.

Josh opened the front door. He spoke, the bass rumble of his voice, and then a lighter, higher note in reply.

A surge of outrage snapped her spine straight. A

woman visiting Josh at this hour? Was the son of a bitch taking booty calls?

Holly opened her door wider. She hung her entire head out the door to hear better. There was something familiar about the cadence of the female voice.

The front door squeaked as Josh opened it, and Holly crept to the top of the stairs.

Around the bend in the staircase, a pair of leather Jesus sandals appeared, partially concealed by the sweep of a long skirt. The toenails were unpainted, but a collection of toe rings glimmered.

Holly moved down the stairs at a rapid trot. Ah, shit, shit, shit.

Josh was closing the front door when she got to the bottom of the stairs.

"Emma?" Holly took a step forward. *What the hell?*

Josh staggered back as Emma barreled past him, through the vestibule, and deeper into the house.

"There you are." Emma greeted Holly with a scathing look, which swept Holly from her wild, sleep-tousled hair to her bare legs and back up. "And you're naked?"

"Emma?" Holly tugged the bottom of her shirt and cursed herself for doing it. Emma had always been a prude. "What are you doing here?"

Josh's expression remained carefully blank.

It was the first time she'd seen him since the scene in the kitchen, and Holly's hungry eyes drank in the sight of him. He looked sleepy and rumpled, and regret twisted in her. "Yours?"

Holly nodded.

Josh turned to study the new arrival.

Emma and Portia were fraternal twins. Emma was the shorter of the two. Closer to Holly in height, they also shared the same curvy, compact body. Emma had lucked out and got their father's straight, tamable blond hair. It hung as a long, silken curtain all the way to her waist. She invariably wore it braided, like now. Emma's hair never went insane, even when its owner charged into houses at three in the morning. The rest of Emma was more like an escapee from Woodstock.

"You might remember my sister, Emma." Holly tried to see her as Josh would. "Portia's twin."

"Ah." He turned to Emma with a charming smile. "Welcome."

It completely took the wind out of Emma's sails and she deflated. She fiddled with the beads around her neck as she stared at Josh.

Holly understood the feeling. It was a whole lot of eye candy for a tired girl to get her brain around.

He'd misplaced his shirt again and pulled on his shorts to answer the door. The hallway light glazed over him and bronzed his skin like some sort of pagan god's.

"You didn't call." Emma turned her head back to Holly. Her eyes followed reluctantly. "I was waiting for a call and it never came."

"It was late when we got back from the hospital—"

"Hospital?" Emma leaped on the word and her eyes grew huge. "What were you doing at the hospital? It's Portia, isn't it? I had this terrible foreboding. I drew the Brothers and Sisters card out of the Magical Unicorns and I was sure." She gave Josh a resigned look. "I knew."

"Of course you did," he said.

Holly shot a look at him over Emma's shoulder. She would bet her left arm he didn't have a clue what Emma was talking about. Yet here he stood, at something to three in the morning, looking like every girl's favorite birthday wish and being effortlessly charming.

"I got worried." Emma's gaze flitted back to him.

"Portia is fine." Josh gave Emma a warm smile. "She's upstairs sleeping."

Emma twisted a string of deep blue crystals around her finger as she eyed Josh suspiciously.

"You found her?" An expression of painful relief crossed Emma's features.

"We found her." Josh closed and locked the front door. "That's probably what the oracle cards were trying to tell you."

Now it was Holly's turn to stare at him. He knew what oracle cards were? "I texted you," Holly said. "I texted you on our way to the hospital."

"I don't like texts. You should've called and told me." Emma rounded on her with flashing eyes and a heaving chest. "You promised you would call."

"I know, Em." Holly cursed herself silently. "I'm sorry, but I was busy and it slipped my mind."

Emma didn't look in the least mollified, and Holly rushed to fill the loaded silence. "We found Portia yesterday. It took a long time to get her released from hospital and today she was unsettled. I didn't get a chance to do anything." She softened her tone a bit. "I was going to call you first thing in the morning."

"I haven't been sleeping." Emma's top lip wobbled. "She is my twin, you know, and we share this special connection."

Holly nearly snorted. The special connection was nothing more than a pact to keep things from their older sister. Portia wasn't the only one who believed her own bullshit.

"I knew I had to come." Emma tapped her breastbone with one beringed finger. "In here, I sensed Portia needed me."

"What time did you set out?" Too tired to get into it, Holly got matters back to the pragmatic.

"Just after you texted," Emma said. "I closed the shop and left."

"That was over fifteen hours ago." Holly gaped at her sister.

Emma stuck out her jaw. "I got lost."

"From London to here?" You could find the way blind-folded. "It's nearly a straight road all the way through."

"It's not well sign-posted," Josh said.

Emma threw him a glance loaded with gratitude.

Emma didn't need any more encouragement and Holly glared at him. She was almost sure there was a twitch around the corner of his mouth.

"I don't like to speed." Emma sniffed and smoothed a tendril of hair back over her scalp. "I'm an old soul." She looked at Josh. "We are naturally biased toward order."

"Yes, but you could have crawled faster," Holly said.

"It's not my fault I get anxious when I have to drive alone." Her mouth tightened as her expression grew alarmingly righteous. "I went to the address you gave me and you weren't there. I was worried. You know I don't like to be in strange places when I don't know where I am. You know that, Holly."

Emma's hazel eyes, also a gift from their father, filled with tears that spilled over and slid down her rounded cheeks. Emma, with her bohemian blouses, long skirts, crystals, and no makeup, could pass for sixteen.

Josh, a newcomer to the emotional faucet that was Emma, caved and immediately went to her and patted her shoulder. "I'm sure it was frightening for you."

"We left a message with the doorman," Holly said.

"Yes, but I couldn't find a parking space for the longest time, and I wasn't sure the building was the right one.

I had to go back to my car and check with the universe that I was on track."

"Did you consult the cards?" Josh dipped his head to Emma.

Holly must have woken up and stumbled into another dimension. That was the only explanation that made sense.

"No." Emma heaved a massive sigh. "Crystals. I checked the alignment."

"Ah." He gave a nod of understanding.

Holly gaped at him. Was he kidding her? He was listening to Emma, his handsome face grave and intent on what her sister was saying.

Emma gave him a mile-by-mile account of her journey—all four hundred–odd of them.

Josh listened, making the occasional encouraging noise.

Some of Holly's irritation melted away.

He treated Emma with the same courtesy he extended to everyone else. He didn't judge or reach superficial conclusions. He took everyone as they came. Was that because people always saw his perfect looks and made all sorts of assumptions? She didn't know, but she did know she liked this facet of Josh. It made him one of the good guys.

"I'm sorry; we should have known you would be desperate to know what was happening." Josh dug out some Kleenex.

"I drove all day and night." Emma wept softly. "I had to get here. I've brought the crystals with me in case I have to lay a grid for Portia's protection." She blinked up at Josh. "Perhaps I should lay the grid anyway?"

"Why don't we talk in the morning?" Josh handed Emma another Kleenex. "You're exhausted, and it's probably not a good idea to try to do something that intense."

Part of Holly wanted to smack him, but it wouldn't have done any good. He was just being Josh—gorgeous, kind, accepting Josh—and her heart did the leap thing. "Did you bring me some money?" she cut in to the love-fest before she did something stupid and jumped him.

"Oh, yes." Emma patted her burlap sack bag. "I have it with me."

"And some clothes?"

"You never asked for clothes." Emma glared at her. "You said to sort out the credit card, and I did that. And to bring money. You never said you needed clothes."

"No, I didn't." She'd got exactly what she'd asked for, and Emma wouldn't tax her brain any further than strictly necessary.

"Let's get you a bed," Josh said. "We can all get some sleep and talk in the morning."

Emma batted her sodden lashes at him and sighed, as if the weight of the world had been lifted off her shoulders.

Holly empathized. He had that way about him. It could make a smart girl go stupid every time.

"You can have Richard's old room." Josh gave Emma's shoulder a quick squeeze.

"You're kind." Emma swallowed and gave him a tremulous smile. "Grace and Holly always said you were a shit, but I don't think so."

"Thank you." Josh grinned. "Do you need me to get your bags out of the car?"

"Yes, please."

His eyes twinkled as he opened the door and let himself out.

Emma hissed at her as soon as Josh was out of earshot. "I thought you hated Josh Hunter."

"So did I." Holly led Emma up the stairs.

It didn't take them long to get Emma settled. Determination to get back to bed drove Holly to waste no time filling Emma in on the details. Finally, she slipped out of the room and closed the door behind her.

She was surprised to see Josh leaning against the wall outside Richard's former bedroom.

He oozed sexy with his tousled hair and shadow-darkened chin. He crossed his arms over his chest, bunching the muscles of his arms and shoulders. Brackets of muscles arched on either side of his lower belly and disappeared beneath the low rise of his shorts. "Does she have everything?"

"Yes." Holly dragged her eyes away from all that lovely man. Her mouth was like parchment paper and she swallowed. "I didn't know she was coming or else I would have asked."

He gave a careless shrug, as if it was no matter. His eyes strolled down her body to her toes. "Nice T-shirt."

"It's Hugo Boss." Holly's flush started on her cheeks and moved south. "They make a good T-shirt."

"So I've heard."

The silence hung in the hallway. He was close enough that Holly could reach out and run her finger over the horizontal lines of his six-pack. Or perhaps trace those hip brackets that girls didn't have. Did they have a name? There had to be a name. Something that mouthwatering must have a name.

"Oracle cards?" She forced her eyes upward.

"New Age girlfriend—don't ask." The corners of his mouth lifted.

"Ah. Thank you." Her voice came out deeper and

sounded like it was saying something different altogether. "For Emma and everything."

"No problem." His eyes burned hot into hers.

"I didn't see much of you today." The heat scaled her cheeks as she caught the unintentional innuendo.

"I was sulking."

"Oh."

"I'm over it now."

"I should go to bed." Holly waved at the empty hallway. The rest of her vetoed the idea.

"Yeah. About that." The small distance between them hummed with expectation. He uncrossed his arms and took a step closer. "I was wondering whether you might be lonely."

"Oh."

"Are you?"

"Am I what?"

"Getting lonely in bed all by yourself?"

He stood in front of her, and Holly let her head drop back against the wall behind her with a soft *thunk*. "Yes."

"I could help you with that."

She should say no and go back to bed alone. "Okay."

He took her hand and led her down the hall.

She reached for him before the soft *snick* of the door enclosed them in the privacy of the dark.

His hands speared through her hair and cradled her scalp, holding her head still for the thorough taking of her mouth.

"Josh, I—"

"No talking, baby. I don't want to talk anymore. We can talk more in the morning." His tongue tangled with hers in a mind-numbing duel.

The last vestiges of protest melted away as he crowded her toward the bed. She wanted what he offered, and morning would come soon enough.

He was true to his word. No talking. He made love to her with a ruthless, thorough determination that left Holly punch-drunk and clinging to him as he took her to greater and greater heights.

He drove her further with his hands and his mouth and his hot, hard body until she wasn't sure where he ended and she began. And then, later, she didn't care anymore, but gave herself over to his assiduous dominance.

By the time they lay spent, Holly got what it meant to be intimate with a man.

Josh lay at her side, his breathing deep and heavy as he slept. He kept a light touch on her, as if he couldn't quite bear to completely separate from her. He lay on his stomach, the pillow crushed beneath the side of his face and his hand heavy and slack across her belly.

Exhaustion snuck up behind her eyelids and mocked her intention to get up and go to her own room. She lay wrapped in a bubble of togetherness and couldn't move and break through the fragile membrane surrounding them. For a small while more, she wanted to lie here and pretend this was the way it could be. Just for a moment longer.

Chapter Twenty-One

Holly walked into the kitchen the next morning and straight into a full frontal glare from Emma. She'd dug out another pair of shorts and a tank top from Lucy's bag of magic. And although she didn't wear hot pink often, or never, it seemed to suit her. The shorts had a flat-fronted, forties cut, like a retro pinup would wear.

"You're sleeping with him?"

The rain on her parade sat at the kitchen table grimly eating something that should be fed to a horse. Emma ate strictly vegan and totally organic, which would have been fine if she could cook. As she couldn't, her diet generally consisted of rather dubious-looking bowls of brown-gray stuff. It was probably, in part, responsible for her pissy mood.

"Good morning." Holly walked over to the coffee-maker. Reality hadn't waited long to catch up with her.

Josh had already made coffee. It had to be Josh. Emma only drank herbal tea and Portia had yet to make a cup of coffee for anyone but herself. It was another of those small things that made it difficult to keep him at arm's length.

"If you're looking for him, he said to tell you he was going to train."

"Ah." Holly poured her coffee and fetched some milk from the fridge. "He's doing some sort of triathlon thing in a few days."

"He also told me to let you sleep. You were tired." Emma's eyes narrowed accusingly at Holly. "How would he know you were still sleeping?"

Holly bit back a sigh. Emma the nun wasn't going to quietly take the hint and drop it. Holly blew on her coffee and took a cautious sip. "I would say the answer is fairly obvious."

The man might not know how to cook, but he could certainly make a cup of coffee.

"What are you doing, Holly?" Emma shoved a spoon-ful of the unappetizing mess into her mouth.

"I'm drinking my coffee." Could she have one day without the drama? Only one. "I'm trying to get my sister back home safely, and other than that, I have no idea and am playing it as it comes along."

"Is it serious?" Emma swung her body around. "How long has it been going on?"

"No. Maybe. I don't know, Em. Now can we drop it?"

Emma examined her critically from over the top of her spoon of gruel. "And what are you wearing? Did you go shopping?"

"No." Holly was done with the interrogation. "These were lent to me. My clothes were stolen along with the car."

"Those don't look like natural fibers," Emma said. "In fact, I'm sure I saw those shorts in a magazine some-where."

"I doubt it." Holly sipped her coffee and hunted for

breakfast. She latched on to a paper bag full of fresh croissants.

Josh must have been up early.

"I'm sure I did." Emma hung on like a terrier with a bone. "That pink is one of the must-have colors this season. Everything is bright and vibrant this summer. Lots of florals and brights."

Say what? Emma, in her homespun pumpkin-colored dress that dropped from her shoulders straight to the ground, was talking about fashion trends? Talk about your parallel universe. "Is Portia up?"

"No." Emma pushed her bowl away. "And what about Portia? How can you even be thinking of getting involved with that man when he's involved with Portia already?"

"He isn't involved with Portia." Holly snapped her mug down on the countertop. Time to get this out in the open. "He says he has never been involved with Portia and I believe him."

She held up her hand when Emma looked like she was going to start up again. "Yesterday, Portia admitted as much. Any involvement between them is in her own mind."

Emma pursed her lips like a maiden aunt. "Still, you know Portia would be devastated to find out you're carrying on with him when she has feelings for him."

Guilt twisted the knife in her gut. "I know that. I didn't—" How could she explain her behavior?

Emma glared at her.

She should never have fallen into bed with Josh last night. She should have stuck to her decision to end whatever it was between them and get back to her real life. "I understand, Emma. Portia won't find out."

"How can you be so sure?"

"Because it won't happen again." And even as she said it, the reality pressed down on Holly.

Josh had been wonderful, a chance to be a different Holly for a while. A taste of something magical and transformative, but it was over now. Inside, way deep inside, the Holly forties pinup of this morning stamped her feet. Why did it have to be over?

Emma got to her feet and cleared her breakfast things away. "Good."

God, Emma was so calm and complacent. And smug. All was right in Emma's world again. The pinup broke free of the chokehold Holly had on her and the sense of injustice flared to life. "I am entitled to a life, Emma."

Emma's eyes bugged out. "You have a life, Holly. You have a good job at the university, a house you share with Portia and me, and a boyfriend. You seem to have forgotten about Steven."

"I haven't forgotten about Steven." The color leeched out of Holly's day. Her snappy outfit, which had seemed hip and sexy minutes before, felt silly on her now.

"This is not your life, Holly." Emma waved her hand in an encompassing gesture. "Here in Willow Park, in this house, wearing those clothes, and that . . . man. This is some temporary thing, and yet you want to risk Portia's sanity for it?" Emma turned away, as if the subject were closed. "I am going to check on my sister."

Emma sailed out of the kitchen.

A small knot of resentment hardened in Holly's belly. This life of hers Emma spoke about was suddenly as bland and unappetizing as Emma's breakfast.

But Emma was right. Her life wasn't here. She'd been kidding herself.

It could be. The Holly of last night stuck her head up carefully.

No, it couldn't, because men like Josh Hunter didn't go for girls like her.

Except he had and he was and he looked like he wanted to keep doing so.

The croissant on the counter lost its appeal and, for the first time in years, she didn't feel hungry. She was feeling sorry for herself and she hated that. It was the way Emma assumed she would carry on as if nothing had changed. They assumed she would because it's what she always did.

At what point had she made it her job to make up for the things the twins didn't get from their parents? And how come this was just occurring to her now? The knot of resentment grew into a bundle because she wanted something in direct conflict with the needs of the twins. She wanted Josh, but Portia was obsessed with him, and that put him out of the picture for Holly.

"Hey there."

Holly's heartbeat kicked up a notch as Josh appeared in the doorway. Not for her. A wan smile was the best she could dredge up.

"That's not the face you were wearing when I left you." Josh moved right behind her. His hands rested on her hips, his lips warm on her ear.

Make it go away like you did before.

Holly desperately wanted to lean back into his heat. She wanted it so fiercely she stood for a moment, every molecule of her being urging her to allow herself to take what he offered. Instead, she stepped away and to the side. He was hot and sweaty and gorgeous, and she couldn't stand to look at him right then.

"Holly?" As always, he read her like a book.

"About last night." Her voice was strained, wooden.

His jaw tightened. "You're going to tell me it was a mistake, right?"

"It was." She stubbornly stuck to her course.

"I don't agree." He shrugged. "We have something, Holly. It's new and I'm not sure where it's going, but there's a connection between us, and the more time we spend together, the stronger it gets."

His words pierced the part of her that wanted so badly it made her gasp. "But we can't."

"Because of Portia?"

She nodded. Saying it out loud made her want to cry, and she never cried.

"Or because of you?" Up went his eyebrow.

"What the hell is that supposed to mean?"

"Portia is sick, no doubt about that, and this situation has all kinds of trouble all over it, but if you're going to walk away from us, be sure it's not because you're frightened of what would happen if you actually grabbed on to a life of your own." He stopped in the doorway. "Because from where I'm standing, Holly, you deserve that and a whole lot more."

"Argh." Holly collapsed in a chair. She didn't want to argue with him. She wanted to fight with life. The life that said it was wrong for her to be with him. The same life that said it was her responsibility to take care of Portia.

Down the hallway, Josh greeted Emma.

Her sister gave a frosty response.

And there you had it. There was no point to this ridiculous uproar. She was going in a day or two. As soon as she had her passport, she was out of there. When they were back home, things would settle back down to the way they always were.

She wanted to cry.

Josh stalked into the bathroom and shut the door. He resisted the urge to slam it, repeatedly.

She pulled him close and then shoved him away.

He'd been stupid enough to believe last night meant something more, that Holly would give them a chance. She'd slammed the door on that idea.

He didn't like the feeling in the pit of his stomach; a jittery sensation that made him ask all sorts of uncomfortable questions.

He needed to know how she felt because right now he was strung out on a line. Vulnerable.

He turned on the water and stepped into the shower. Propping his arms against the wall, he let the water drum against his nape.

Her rejection hurt and he'd struck back.

What a fucking dick! Only a complete douche could resent her sisters because they stood between him and what he wanted.

Portia was ill and needed help. Emma was so fragile he was terrified of doing anything that would shatter her.

Holly. Brave, fierce, and loyal Holly, fighting to hold it all together like a one-man army. And here he was, having a mantrum.

He'd spent the last hour of his run working on the sort of fantasy that would top off his endorphin high. He wanted to slide his hands up under that oversized T-shirt and find that firm, ripe, gorgeous body. There was something about her baggy, oversized clothes. He was doing his best to get rid of them, make no mistake, but there was still something appealing about knowing he was the only one who got what a wonderland they concealed.

Damn, it was so much more than sex. Getting to know Holly was an adventure, peeling back the layers of who she was and finding the real woman beneath. She hid more than a kick-ass body beneath her big tees, and he wanted more.

Ah. Lest he forget: Steven the boyfriend, conspicuous by his absence.

But he wasn't here, standing beside Holly while she battled on alone.

Holly needed someone to stand by her, be with her. Not a man who only gave a crap about his own agenda.

Which brought him right around to himself and being a dick. He was doing the same thing he'd done all those years ago. The same thing his dad had reamed him out about: taking what he wanted and damn the rest.

For the first time in his life, he might have to consider the possibility he wouldn't get the girl. Josh snorted out loud at his own conceit. There were probably all sorts of people waiting for this day. What goes around comes around and all that.

He snapped the faucets off and stepped out of the shower. The mirror fogged and he wiped it clear. "Josh," he said to his bleary reflection, "this is Karma; Karma, meet Josh. You owe him a little something."

Holly put in her call to Grace.

"This is Grace."

"Hey, it's me." Her news wasn't going to go down well. "I wanted to let you know we found Portia."

"Yeah. I got your text." Grace sounded distracted. "That's good, Holly. That's very good."

"Gracie? Are you listening to me? I said we found Portia."

"And I said that's great."

Holly took a moment to absorb the rudeness. It was completely uncalled for.

Grace heaved a huge sigh. "I'm sorry, Holly, I'm a bit on edge. Tell me about Portia."

"Well, we were right, she's off the medication and has been for a while."

"What the hell?" Grace snorted. "Why can't she stay on the stuff? If you don't force it down her throat, I don't know if she would take it at all."

"Actually—" They might as well get this over and move on—"there's more, and it's not so good."

"Uh-huh." Grace's tone braced for impact.

"She's pregnant."

The silence hummed and snapped down the line.

"You are going to have to say that again," Grace said.

"Portia is pregnant and that's why she went off the medication."

"Motherfu—are you sure?"

"Yup. Doctor confirmed it."

Grace took a breath. "And the father?"

"Now is where the story gets interesting." Holly grimaced as she anticipated Grace's reaction.

"Oh, I can't wait to hear this."

"You know Josh Hunter? I said he was helping me?"

"Yes, but—" Grace choked. "You're kidding me? Josh Hunter and Portia?" Grace made a soft noise of sympathy. "Oh, Holly, I thought you and—"

"No." Goddamn. All she needed was Grace storming down the wrong road. "There is no Josh and Portia. There is only Portia saying there's a Josh and Portia."

"Don't play word games with me, Holly." The edge was back in Grace's tone.

Holly was walking on eggshells around Grace today. "Portia says Josh is the father of the baby."

"Is he?"

"Not unless he has supersperm that can get a woman four months pregnant instantly."

"It wouldn't surprise me if he did." Grace chuckled dryly. "Or at least thought he had. The Josh I remember ranked high on the self-esteem front."

"He's not like that anymore." She'd already jumped to that conclusion and tumbled off again. "He's different; kinder, more patient, and less full of himself." No, that was a lie. Josh was still full of himself, but there were so many other facets to him, and she was only beginning to sort them out. "He's . . . he's very Josh."

Such a lame finish.

"Oh?" Grace loaded the syllable to the point it should be wearing an abnormal warning.

Holly resisted the bait. She didn't want Grace delving into her feelings, or whatever, for Josh.

Bloody hell. She didn't even want to go there herself.

"I'm pretty sure Emma knew, but she hasn't said so. And Portia is Portia and won't tell me who the real dad is."

"That's screwed up," Grace said.

"I know." It made her head want to explode with how fucked up it was.

"What are you going to do?"

"What do you mean, me? What am *I* going to do?" Holly's throat tightened and resentment swirled like bile in her stomach. "Why is it up to me to do anything?"

"Get off it, Holly," Grace just about snarled down the line at her. "You don't get to play the victim."

"Really? And here I thought it was my turn." And didn't that just beat all? It was so grossly unfair. She wanted to yell and stamp her feet like a child, but that would get her nowhere with Grace. "I'm going to get Portia more stable, take her home, and help her take care of the baby. I don't have any choice."

"Yes, you do," Grace said. "You do have choices. I'm not saying the options are fantastic, but there *are* choices."

"That's easy for you to say." Why couldn't Grace get off it? Grace always lectured her because Grace always had the damn answers. Except Grace wasn't here, was she? Grace was off in Boston, living the beautiful life with her designer husband and her high-powered job.

"I don't want to fight with you, Holly," Grace said. "I know you shoulder virtually all the responsibility for the twins. I'm not insensitive to what that means, but I get frustrated for you. You have your own life to lead and you can't babysit them forever."

"I don't know what else to do." Holly deflated rapidly; her shoulders sagged under the weight and she leaned her elbows on the table. "If somebody doesn't take care of them, I don't know what will happen to them. I couldn't live with myself if Portia ended up like her."

It was an old argument that went round and round until they were both too bloodied to continue.

"I know." Grace sighed. Her voice softened abruptly. "You sound tired."

"I didn't sleep well last night."

"Stud muffin keeping you up all night?"

Whoa. Holly's face heated. "I don't know what you're talking about."

She winced as she ended up sounding like a Victorian maiden aunt.

"Sure you do." Grace chuckled. "You are so doing Josh Hunter."

"How would you know?" Holly was not sunken enough in deceit to go for an outright lie.

"I'm right, though." Grace wouldn't be Grace if she let it go at that. "I would bet my right arm I called this one."

Holly writhed inside. "I don't want to discuss it."

Grace roared with laughter.

Holly's face would burst into flames any moment. "Besides . . ." She raised her voice over Grace's chuckles. "Nothing can come of it."

"Why not?" Grace stopped laughing. "And if you say because of Portia, I'm going to reach through this phone and rip your heart out."

"Okay, then." Holly's heart bottomed out. "I won't say it, but—"

"Ah, Holly." Grace let out a long shaky breath. "Life is too short for this shit."

"Gracie?" Everything in Holly went on alert at her sister's tone. "Are you all right? Are you going to tell me what's going on with you?"

"No." Grace's voice flattened into a scary, dead calm. "I don't want to talk about it, and I am most definitely not all right, but I will be, Holly, I will be."

Holly got a nasty feeling in the pit of her stomach. She took a seat at the table. "What's going on, Grace?"

"Just some stuff." Grace was lying through her teeth. "Actually, a lot," she said. "But I'm sorting it out. We'll talk again, but not now, okay, Holly? Not now."

"Okay," Holly agreed reluctantly. Something was up with Grace and it wasn't good. But if she pushed, Grace would push back harder.

After hanging up, Holly sat there with the phone in her hand. And the hits just kept coming. Now Grace was in trouble.

Josh walked into the kitchen wearing a pair of khaki shorts and a loose cotton shirt.

Holly's entire body stiffened in response. How, in the name of all that was holy, could someone rock shorts and a shirt? He didn't even have any of that impressive muscle on display.

He indicated her phone. "More bad news?"

"I can handle it." The last thing she needed right now was another lecture from him.

He gave her a slow smile. "I know that, Holly, I was just asking."

He walked up to her and took the phone from her nerveless fingers.

"Hey."

He put it on the table and sank to his haunches in front of her. "I'm sorry, Holly."

"What?" She hadn't seen that one coming and it hit her like a truck. How was she supposed to stay angry with him?

"I said I'm sorry. I got pissy with you earlier and you don't need more crap on your plate right now. I want to help, not make life more difficult for you." He took a breath. "So, I'm getting out of your face, stepping back. You tell me what you need and I'll see what I can do to make that happen."

Her mouth must have dropped open because he reached over and shut it for her. "Have I actually rendered you speechless?"

"Uhngnhu."

"Somebody should get this down for the record books. This is the second time I've managed that amazing feat."

"No more . . . touching and stuff?"

He raised his hands to the sides of his head. "No pressure of any kind."

This is what she wanted. Right?

"Am I forgiven?"

"Uh . . . okay." *Way to go on the together thing, Holly.*

He grinned at her. "As a gesture of atonement, I've made an appointment for you at the Canadian consulate. I have a contact there who might be able to put a rush on your passport."

"A woman?"

"Yup." He rose smoothly, his face bland.

Holly wasn't born yesterday. "An ex-girlfriend?"

"An old friend." He turned the tables on her effortlessly with one of his big charm-school smiles.

Holly snorted as she got to her feet. "Stop messing with me."

"Okay and no, she really is an old friend. You look good." He gave her the top-to-toe sweep. "Is that one of the things Lucy lent you?"

Too smooth, too bland. He was up to something.

One of the things Lucy lent her? Right. She had her burgeoning suspicions, but his eyes gave the game away. She let it go.

An appointment at the consulate was good. It meant she could get her passport sooner and go home. And that was the best thing for everyone.

Chapter Twenty-Two

Holly's eyes popped open. *What?*

"Joshua, darling? Are you awake? I wanted to let you know I was here." A woman's voice, rich with the smoothed edges of a French accent.

To hell with this.

"It's not Joshua." Holly snapped on the light.

"Oh."

The woman stared at Holly.

Holly stared back.

There was a stunned silence. They both spoke, then stopped.

The woman was older than Holly expected; much older in fact. Her dark hair, liberally laced with silver, was cropped short and elfin around her face. It was an interesting rather than a pretty face, with a delicate but strong bone structure. "Who are you?"

"Holly. I'm Holly Partridge. Who are you?"

"Never mind who I am. What are you doing in Joshua's bed?"

That was a bit personal. "What are you doing in his house?"

The woman's chest swelled. "It's not his house. It's *my*

house, and I'll ask the questions. So, Holly, what are you doing in my son's bed?"

Oh, fuck. Recognition hit her like a ton of bricks. Josh's mother; what was her name? Donna. It would have been more helpful if she'd realized it a moment or so earlier.

"Oh. Hi." Holly pulled the covers up to her chin. She wanted to disappear beneath them altogether.

Donna eyed her speculatively.

Holly got the picture; a girl in Josh's room in the middle of the night. This couldn't be looking good from Donna's perspective. Holly desperately tried to think of a way to explain the situation, but nothing came immediately to mind. Nothing quick, anyway. "Josh said it would be all right if we stayed here."

Donna crossed her arms over her chest and gave Holly a decidedly unfriendly stare. "I'm sorry to tell you, Miss Holly Partridge, that I do not allow my son to bring his women to this house. You are going to have to get up and get dressed."

It didn't seem possible that petite Donna could have given birth to her three hulking sons. But she didn't need size when she had that look in her arsenal.

Holly gathered up her courage. "Actually, I'm not one of Josh's women. Not in that way, anyhow."

Those penetrating blue eyes didn't flicker or waver.

Holly squirmed like a bug on a pin. "Well, not now, anyway. I—"

"*Maman?*" Josh's voice came from the hallway beyond the door.

Thank you, Jesus. Let Mr. Smooth Talker come up with an explanation.

Donna stepped back and turned in the direction of his voice. "*Oui. Est-ce que c'est toi? Qui est cette femme?*"

Holly quelled the desire to giggle hysterically. It was like being a teenager all over again.

"What are you doing back?" Josh enveloped the smaller woman in a hug.

Donna returned the embrace for a moment before she freed herself and gave her son a slap on the arm. "Put a shirt on, Joshua." She straightened her linen blouse. "I came back a few days early. What are you doing in my house? And who is the woman in your bed?"

"I see you've met Holly." Josh jogged into the room, briefly framed by the light behind him in the doorway. "Holly, meet my mother, Donna." He gestured grandly. "And Ma, this is Holly, and it's not what it looks like."

They both murmured something suitable and continued to eye each other suspiciously.

Holly wanted to get out of bed, but she couldn't take the chance Donna would spot Josh's T-shirt in an instant.

A door opened down the hall and Holly tensed.

Josh glanced in that direction and back at her. He grimaced. "Portia."

Soft footsteps pattered in the hallway, and Donna's eyebrows hit her hairline.

Portia pushed past Donna and into the room. She rubbed her eyes sleepily. "Holly?"

And of course she wore nothing more than sleep shorts and a cami. Perfect.

All eyes snapped in Portia's direction.

Portia looked at Josh and Donna and, finally, Holly. "What's going on, Holly?"

"Yes, Holly." Donna finished her visual appraisal of Portia and raised her eyebrows. "It's an excellent question."

It was a bloody farce. Holly stuffed the edge of the

sheet into her mouth. She was going to start laughing like a bloody hyena. Another door opened farther down the hall.

"Portia?" Emma's voice reached them.

Ah, hell no. Not Emma. The funny side of the situation disappeared like smoke and Holly sat up straight.

Donna glared at her son.

He threw up his hands in surrender. "I can explain."

"Oh, I hope so," she said and grimly watched the newest addition.

"What are you doing up?" Emma appeared at Portia's shoulder. "And what are you doing in his bed?" Her eyes widened as she spotted Holly. "We talked about this. You said you weren't going to sleep with him anymore."

"You talked about this?" Josh fired a quick look in her direction.

"He wasn't in it with me." Holly hushed her sister with a hand motion. The farce had just morphed into a fucking nightmare.

Emma pursed her lips like a maiden aunt and folded her arms primly over her chest. "Oh, really?"

"What does that mean?" Portia blinked at Emma. "Holly?"

"I would like to know what all of this means." Donna crossed her arms.

Oh, God. Holly swallowed convulsively.

Josh tugged a T-shirt over his head. He ran a quick hand through his tousled hair. "Emma doesn't mean anything." He gave Portia's shoulder an awkward pat. "My mother surprised us, that's all."

"Holly?" Portia frowned at her in childlike confusion. "Why does Emma think you're sleeping with him? You can't be because Josh is with me."

Emma, Holly, and Josh all froze.

Donna narrowed her eyes.

"Did you just get back?" Josh's voice was too loud as he took his mother by the arm.

"Yes, about half an hour ago." Donna's gaze moved constantly between Holly, Portia, and Emma.

Josh tugged her arm lightly.

Donna snatched it away. "Stop pulling on me, Joshua. I am not going anywhere until I get an explanation."

"I will explain." Josh spread his hands wide. "But could we do this in the kitchen? The girls are standing here in their underwear."

"That is exactly what I want explained. Why is my house filled with nearly naked young women?" She poked him in the chest. "You may be thirty-one years old, Joshua, but this is still my house and my rules."

"Holly, who is this?" Emma stuck her chin up imperiously.

For the love of God, could Emma not shut up? Just once in her life, could she take her head out of her ass long enough to clue in to what was happening?

Donna smirked at Emma. "I own this house, *cherie.* I think I should be asking the questions, *n'est-ce pas?*"

"Oh." Emma's shoulders slumped and she dropped her head.

"I don't understand, Holly." Portia threw her hands out in a helpless gesture. "Why does Emma think you're sleeping with Josh?" She looked from Holly to Josh and back again. "You can't be sleeping with him. Josh is my boyfriend."

"No," yelled Holly and Josh together.

Donna's spine snapped straight.

"Not now, Portia." Holly tried for a stern, no-nonsense tone of voice. "Let's get dressed and give Josh a chance to tell his mother everything."

"I can explain all of it." Josh pushed a hand through his hair.

"I am sure you can." Donna kept her eyes on the girls. "And am I going to want to hear the explanation?"

Portia touched her belly. "He must tell her about the baby."

Ah, fuck!

Emma gasped.

Josh paled beneath his tan, and his jaw clenched.

Portia ran to Josh and placed her hands against his chest. She raised herself onto her toes. "Tell her about our baby, Josh."

"Whaaa . . ." Donna went as pale as her son and her mouth dropped open. *"Que veut-elle dire, Joshua? Tu ferais mieux de tout m'expliquer et rapidement. Est-tu le père d' un bébé? Avec cette jeune fille? Est-ce que tu a mis cette jeune fille enceinte?"*

The French was too fast for Holly to follow. The gist of it was that Donna wanted to know what the hell was going on.

Holly didn't blame her. Three strange women standing, nearly naked, in her house, and one of them claiming to be carrying her son's child.

"Don't worry, *maman.*" Josh pushed Portia gently out of the way and approached his mother. "It's not what you're thinking." He pulled a wry face. "I'm not sure exactly what you're thinking, but I can imagine, and it's not that. Only, can you come to the kitchen?" Josh took a deep breath. "Please?"

Donna followed without resistance as he led her away.

Not out of the woods yet, but getting there. Holly let out the breath she'd been holding.

"Why doesn't he tell her about the baby, Emma?" Portia turned huge wounded eyes to her twin. "Doesn't he want the baby?"

Emma bustled over and put her arm around Portia's thin shoulders. "I told you this would happen," she said fiercely to Holly. "Look what you've done now."

"Get dressed." One more word and she might give in to temptation and slap Emma silly.

Holly splashed water on her face, brushed her teeth, and pulled on the same clothes as yesterday. It was just past six thirty in the morning, but she didn't think anyone was going back to sleep. Except Portia, who could sleep most of the day away.

Josh and Donna were in the kitchen, talking quietly.

If only she'd stayed asleep a few minutes longer this morning.

Josh did most of the talking.

Donna listened and tapped her fingers on the table. Her expression was set and forbidding.

As much as it gave Holly the chills, she empathized with the woman. It didn't look good from Donna's angle. She braced for the worst.

"Hey." Josh gave her one of his beautiful smiles as she walked into the kitchen. "I was explaining things to my mother."

Holly's mouth dried. "Oh?"

"Yes." Donna's eyes stopped just short of hostile. "I do not allow my sons to treat my home as party central." She folded one hand over the other on the table. "I am not a prude, but I am also not running a motel. I was shocked to find you here."

"I can imagine." Her voice came out as a breathy whisper. Holly cleared her throat. Where the hell was her spine?

Josh gave her a small smile of encouragement. "I explained the situation, *maman*."

"I understand; however, it is temporary, and there

were circumstances that led to this point," Donna said in a hard voice.

"I suggested my mother move into the condo for a day or two. Just until we can get things sorted out."

Say what? Holly's stomach twisted. "There is no need." Kicking the woman out of her own house would put the final nail in her coffin. "You don't have to do that."

"I realize that." Donna pursed her lips. "I don't mind," she said in a cold tone. "I like Josh's condo; it is no hardship for me to stay there for a few days. I have not yet unpacked and it will suit me."

"I don't want to be responsible for ousting you from your own house." Holly threw a pleading look at Josh.

"You're not," Donna said. "I have no problem with this and I am very sorry to hear of your troubles. The matter of the baby, however—it needs to be sorted out."

"It will be, Ma." Josh frowned at his mother.

"Before people start talking about it, Joshua." Donna tapped her fingers on the table. "You have never had the best reputation with women. People will have no problem believing this is your baby and judging you accordingly."

"Since when have you cared about gossip?" Josh stuck out his chin and crossed his arms. "Couples who aren't married have babies together all the time."

"No, Josh," Holly said. Donna made a good point. "Your mother is right. You can't have people saying you got a young girl pregnant and walked away from her."

She nodded to Donna. "I'll make sure Portia doesn't spread her story around, and in the meantime, I'll make sure we get her to accept the truth. It's difficult, however. Portia can make up her own reality and live in it."

"I see." Donna shrugged her shoulder in a gesture marking her as French as clearly as a neon sign. "I do not like the situation, but I can understand your sister is very ill." She turned back to her son. "What I do not understand is why you are in this up to your neck. Do you know how this could end?"

Josh's face hardened and his cold, cold blue eyes blazed at his mother. "I'm in this because I chose to be."

"Then you are a fool." Donna slapped the table, and Holly jumped. "You could end up supporting a child that is not yours if you are not careful."

"That's not going to happen," Holly said, appalled Donna would think so, but not entirely surprised.

"So you say." Donna kept her eyes locked on her tall son.

Okay, then. She'd shut her mouth.

"Ma?" Josh's voice was laced with dire warning.

Donna shook her head. "I did not raise you to be such an idiot."

"Then you need to trust my judgment."

Holly's belly clenched tight as a drum. Should she say something? Or leave Josh to handle Donna? Her last attempt at an explanation hadn't ended well.

The standoff between mother and son lasted a few moments longer.

Donna dropped her eyes first. She got quickly to her feet. "Drive me downtown."

Josh nodded and grabbed his keys. His shoulders were tense as he stalked out of the room.

Donna followed him out. She paused in the doorway. "I wish you and your sisters well, Holly, but you will understand if I wish you well back in Ontario."

Chapter Twenty-Three

It was clearly a dismissal, and Holly left the kitchen as quickly as she could.

"Wow." Emma lurked against the wall outside the kitchen door. "What a bitch."

"She's protective of her son." God knows why she was defending the other woman. Holly nodded her head toward the top of the stairs. "How is she?"

"She's okay." Emma gestured to the closed door of Portia's room. "It would help if she took the medication, but she won't because of her pregnancy."

"Did you know?" Holly wasn't sure what difference it made, but it was suddenly important to hear Emma's response. "Did you know she was pregnant?"

"She never said a word." Emma's gaze slid away from hers.

Anger surged through Holly. Emma was lying through her fucking teeth. And not even brave enough to look her in the eye while she did it. So quick to point the finger was Emma, and as quick to loudly proclaim her innocence. "But you suspected?"

"The cards said—"

"You knew, didn't you?" She dared Emma to tell the

truth for once. To stop hiding behind her New Age jargon and be honest. "You knew she was pregnant before she left London. You knew all of it and you said nothing."

"I didn't . . ."

Holly wanted to puke. She'd had it with Emma's lies and her convenient rearranging of the truth. "And you must have known about the men."

"What men?" Emma flushed bright red.

The stupid girl knew all right. Holly didn't budge. She folded her arms over her chest and waited.

"She went out a lot, you know that," Emma said. "She went alone because I don't like to go out. She seemed like she was having a good time. It's not my job to chaperone her." Emma's gaze darted around frantically. Looking anywhere but at Holly.

Holly kept staring, compelling Emma to look at her. "And you never said anything to me about any of this?" Emma had her head jammed in the sand. It would take surgery to remove it.

"Why should I?" Emma shifted her feet. "You never asked where we were going or who we were going with."

"I trusted you." And didn't that make her as stupid as her sister? "I was trying to give you both some space."

"It's not my fault." Emma's eyes filled up like fish bowls and her lip quivered. "You can't make this my fault."

"I'm not saying it's your fault she's pregnant."

Emma wasn't a child. She was a grown woman of twenty-four, standing in front of her, crying tears aimed at drawing pity and feeling sorry for herself. This shit was getting old.

"It's nobody's fault Portia is bipolar, but we can't pretend everything is okay. You're the one closest to her. You're the one who would notice any deviation in her behavior. And you did notice, didn't you, Emma?" Holly took a step closer, and still Emma wouldn't look her in the eye. "You noticed and you said nothing. Why?"

"Maybe I'm tired of it all." Emma glared at Holly reproachfully.

Holly wasn't going on that guilt trip.

"Maybe I'm sick of looking after Portia all the time. Always worrying about Portia, always watching Portia." Emma heaved a large sniff and scrubbed at her eyes with the heels of her hands. "What about me?" She held her hands out to Holly like a supplicant. "I matter. I count. Not just Portia. I want to live my own life without having to worry about my sister all the time."

It was bloody ironic. Holly threw back her head and laughed. "'This is your life,'" she parroted back at her sister with relish. "Remember what you said to me?"

"You're being mean." Emma's tears continued to flow.

"No, I'm not. We may not like it, but Portia's disorder affects all of us. We have to shoulder our share of the burden."

"You're being so unfair," Emma wailed.

She was being unfair? "None of this is fair." Didn't Emma get it? Fair had bugger all to do with it. "To any of us. It just is."

"You can't expect me to babysit Portia for the rest of my life."

"Really?" Holly's anger vibrated through her until she almost hummed like a tuning fork. "Because it seems to me that's exactly what you expect me to do. You expect me to step in and take care of Portia *and* you. You two screw up and I get to fix it."

"That's not true." Emma's tears vaporized. "You take over everything and expect us to go along with it like good little girls. You treat us like children. Telling Portia and me what to do and whom to do it with. Lecturing away like you have the right to push us around."

Holly opened her mouth and shut it again. She had to leave before she said or did something she would regret. She yanked open the door and stepped outside.

It was barely eight in the morning but building toward a scorching hot summer day. It hit her like a wall as the door swung shut on her heels. The heat bled out of the sidewalk in sticky waves clinging to her hair and skin.

She walked through humidity thick as butter. She had no particular destination in mind, letting her vague memories carry her forward. She'd lived so many different places they blurred. Not that she confused one with the other. More like she stopped taking particular note of one as different from the others.

Willow Park stood out. It was here the disease finally won its battle with Melissa. There weren't many happy memories connected with this place. Mostly the Partridge girls had hidden in their house and concealed the extent of what happened behind closed doors.

Melissa's death had been devastating, but Francis hadn't allowed it to change the daily routine of their lives much. By that time, Holly was already in charge, and the other girls automatically turned to her.

And now Emma wanted her own life. Emma didn't want to be stuck with the responsibility of Portia.

Holly laughed.

Oh, she understood that feeling all right. She knew what it was like to be young and dragged down by responsibility all the time. People rushed forward with their lives around you, and you were stuck.

Emma didn't know the half of it. She and Portia would never understand. The twins had been sheltered because she and Grace had made sure. Emma and Portia were older now, but the habit of protecting and guarding was as intrinsic to Holly as breathing. And she had sheltered them so well the twins were lost in a permanent adolescence.

She'd been mother and father to them. She'd made decisions for them, guided them, and indulged them. And she had got exactly what she had created.

How could she not have seen this coming? Was Portia's pregnancy a rebellion? Had Holly, however unwittingly, set it up this way?

Grace had been saying as much for years.

She stalked to the end of the block, determined to ignore the heat. Past a veterinarian clinic and a florist she vaguely remembered. Across the street there was a woman's clothing store. The sort that sold highly priced wisps to women who looked like Lucy, so they could make the most of the gifts nature had showered on them. She was sure the store was new. It was the sort of place Josh would shop.

A thick layer of sweat lined Holly's skin as she turned the corner away from the main street. If memory served, there was a park down here somewhere. Lindens, maples, oaks, and ash cast deep shade over the road but did nothing to cut the heat. It was like trying to walk through syrup, but Holly refused to slow her pace. She wished she'd brought a bottle of water, but this charge along the neighborhood wasn't exactly planned.

She needed to think, to clear her head, and she couldn't do that with other people constantly underfoot. Her sisters were one thing, a nagging but familiar worry. The situation with Josh was another thing altogether. It was impossible and getting more so. She should turn around, pack up her sisters, and go stay in a motel until her passport came through. It was the logical thing to do, and yet she hesitated.

Sarah Hegger

She dressed it up to look like staying with Josh was more convenient and easier. Portia was better when she was kept stable, *blah, blah, blah.*

She didn't want to go. She liked him; she really, really liked him, and it wasn't getting any better as the days wore on. She wanted to trust the evidence he showed signs of a man looking for more than a sexual connection. He cared for her, he helped her, he made his own life difficult to help her. He'd even stood up to his mother on her behalf.

And still she hesitated, too scared to trust what she felt to be true and in too deep to do the logical thing and walk away. It was such a bloody mess.

Five blocks later the heat won, and Holly slowed down to a stroll. Her shirt stuck to her back and her hair hung heavy and sticky on her neck. She checked her pockets for something to use as a restraint. Nothing.

Holly grabbed a handful of hair and held it off her nape.

Emma did have a point. She was autocratic and dictatorial, and it had become a habit over the years. There was always so much to do and only her to do it. She had stopped asking for opinions and input some time ago.

It galled her to admit Grace might have called that one right as well. The twins had got totally used to having her run their lives for them. They sat back and let her do it, and she held the reins as tightly as she could.

Josh, on the other hand, didn't need her for anything. It was strange and unsettling. His life was fine without her at the helm. He didn't need her to bolster his flagging ego or keep him focused.

She had a calendar pinned to her fridge at home. Portia, Emma, and her own schedule neatly color-coded in careful columns. She also had Steven's life in a well-ordered column of its own, a bit like his mother.

Gross. She didn't need her two years of a psychology degree to unpick that one. No wonder their sex life was as tepid and inspiring as dishwater.

Josh treated her like a woman, a woman he desired and enjoyed. Yes, he had a tendency to want to rescue her, but he didn't lean on her. It was like she was playing a familiar board game by different rules.

She turned the corner. Thank the Lord, she hadn't forgotten.

The park sat at the confluence of six residential streets, an emerald-green oasis amid the houses. Ancient trees stretched their shading canopy over the small family groups clustered to enjoy the glorious summer day.

Small children clambered enthusiastically up and over the wooden castle and bridge of a central jungle gym. Where did they find the energy? A group of mothers sat in the shade, taking a welcome respite from their turbocharged offspring.

Holly headed straight for a large concrete culvert that formed a small shallow pool and water fountain, perfect for soaking tired legs and hot feet. The hardier souls braved the full sun and leaped in and out of the bubbling sprays lined up like soldiers along the length of the culvert.

She eased onto her butt and slipped off her flip-flops. The icy water brought instant relief to her hot feet.

"Holly?" called a soft voice with a touch of cognac hanging on the end.

Holly squinted up against the sun.

In the glare, Lucy's rambunctious blond hair clustered around her head like a halo. She lowered herself slowly to sit beside Holly and handed her a bottle of water. "You look as if you need this."

Lucy was an angel.

"What about you?" She didn't want to be responsible for the dehydration of a pregnant woman.

"I have another and mine's bigger." Lucy produced a larger version from her capacious handbag, with a grin so mischievous Holly was forced to grin back. "Richard is a firm believer in the daily constitutional." She indicated her walking shoes. "I come up here to look at the children." Lucy twisted the cap off her bottle and drank deeply. "I look at the children and their mothers and wonder why the hell I ever thought I would be any good at it."

"Really?" Holly turned to look at her. Lucy didn't seem the sort to have doubts about anything.

Lucy nodded and smiled. "I'm excited and terrified all at once. Thank God I have Richard to keep me on an even keel."

"He seems very special," Holly said.

"He's a keeper." Lucy winked. "I see my shorts fit."

Holly looked at the shorts and then at Lucy. She took a sip of her water. "Are we going to keep pretending the shorts are yours?"

She caught Lucy in the middle of a sip. Water exploded out of her mouth and nose.

It made Holly feel marginally better about the whole unmitigated gorgeous thing.

"No." Lucy spluttered into a laugh. "I suppose we aren't."

It was a sweet thing to do. "You have great taste."

"No," Lucy said, her green eyes wide. "No, I don't."

"Oh." She'd guessed Josh, the sneaky sod, was behind her transformation. It was kind of cute. Annoying, but caring. "I don't know whether to be grateful or kick his ass."

"That's men for you." Lucy toasted her with her water bottle. "So, what are you doing here?"

"Brooding." Holly kicked her legs up. Water droplets slid down her shins.

"Hatched anything good?"

"Not so good, actually." Holly pulled the corners of her mouth down. "I was pretty much beating myself up when you did me the favor of breaking up the fight."

Lucy watched a toddler of two or three try to catch the water jets in his chubby fist. "Anything you want to talk about?"

"I don't do the whole talking thing." Holly squirmed inside. She liked Lucy, but she didn't share.

Lucy smiled. "Okay."

And Holly got the feeling it *was* okay. The comfortable silence worked the kinks out of her neck muscles. "I met Donna this morning."

"Is she back?"

"Apparently. I don't know who was more surprised."

"I sense a story." Lucy bumped shoulders with her.

Holly's face heated.

Lucy crowed triumphantly.

"Do you get on with Donna?" It was easier to focus on Donna rather than the jumble of confused impressions and emotions fighting for space around Josh.

"Oh, yeah." Lucy smiled fondly. "I adore Donna, but I virtually grew up with her. I'm closer to Donna than I am to my own mother."

"Hmph."

"Now you're going to have to tell me the rest of the story." Lucy turned to look at her. "You can't open with a leading question and leave me hanging. It's plain cruel, and after I gave you my water." Lucy raised her eyebrows to add weight to her statement. "A pregnant woman gives you her water."

Damn, the other woman was good. "All right."

Lucy gave a smug smile and settled herself comfortably. "Even if you're not much of a talker. I'll get the story from Donna or Josh anyway." She patted Holly on the arm.

"I didn't make the best impression." She could still see Donna's face in her bedroom doorway. She gave Lucy the abridged version, and still her face got hot.

Lucy threw back her head and laughed.

After a few minutes, Holly managed a weak smile. It *was* kind of funny.

Lucy listened carefully when she glossed lightly over the kitchen this morning.

"There are three boys in the family," Lucy said after a pause. "Donna is a great mother to all three of them, but I think there's a special place for Josh in her heart. Richard was always his dad's son and Thomas is—" Lucy shrugged. "Thomas is his own man through and through. I don't think anyone has told Thomas what to do since he was two years old."

Lucy took a hefty swig of her water. "Josh was always Donna's little ally. And there's the fact that he's ridiculously beautiful." Lucy rolled her eyes. "Girls are always hanging on to Josh. I think Donna is more territorial with him than she is with the other two. Give her time. She'll come around. At the end of the day, she loves her boys and only wants what makes them happy."

"It doesn't matter." Holly's chest tightened. "I won't be here that long."

Lucy turned those glowing green eyes on her. "Really?"

It was as if Lucy could see right through to the soul of her. She certainly hoped not. It was a pretty dark and dismal place for the most part. Holly avoided it at all costs.

"Really." She dropped her eyes to her legs. "I have to get back to my life."

"What a pity." Lucy squeezed her arm. "Then we'll have to enjoy you while you're here."

Chapter Twenty-Four

Donna put down her book. She'd read the same line four times and still had no idea what was on the page. She lifted her glass to her mouth and watched the sunlight dance across the top of Lake Michigan. The large windows of the loft condo framed the serenity like a painting, and she paused a moment to appreciate the beauty. The condo was quiet around her, everything neat and in its place and about as welcoming as a hotel room.

She worried about Joshua and this curious detachment of his. He was everybody's favorite guy, especially the women. Even the ones he broke up with stayed in his life as friends. Josh always knew the right thing to say, the best form of comfort. He got the chocolate thing, he listened, and he was always ready with a timely rescue. He was everything to everyone and yet nothing to anyone special.

It didn't matter how many times she talked to Josh about Des, and how his father would have forgiven him within moments of the fight ending. Josh carried that scar on his conscience. Mostly, it was a good thing that kept him from hurting anyone else.

Since Laura and the subsequent argument with Des, Josh guarded his feelings so carefully he'd virtually embalmed his own heart.

Until Holly Partridge reappeared in his life.

Over the years, the women had come in all shapes and sizes. Josh didn't have a type because he genuinely enjoyed women. Of all of them, why did he have to choose this one?

Donna snorted and took another sip of her wine.

Okay, she was always going to be hard on whoever got her Josh.

Holly Partridge. She hadn't immediately recognized the woman who stared at her from Joshua's bed, but Donna remembered them now. The family had kept to themselves, but speculation had run rife through the neighborhood. Willow Park was a small neighborhood, and like most small neighborhoods, they knew each other's business. It was a point of pride.

Things had gone on in the Partridge house that had the mothers of the community clustered together and clucking over those four innocent chicks.

Holly Partridge, all hair and secrets in a tiny bundle of determination. Her eyes were what stuck with Donna the most. They had been the eyes of a woman twice her age in the face of a teenager. The eyes hadn't changed; the shadows still lurked in their depths.

Of course Josh had ridden to the rescue like the knight he was. Responding to some intangible call to rescue the damsel.

Women had spoiled Josh since the day he first batted those indigo eyes in his chubby baby face. They fell over themselves to make Josh's life a nicer place to be. He'd taken Holly's brush-off, all those years ago, as an affront to his considerable teenage ego.

Donna had heard the story of the Valentine's Day

dance from a variety of different sources. It was one of the harshest lectures she'd ever given her middle son.

The family disappeared after the mother died.

Until now. Now, they were camped out in her home, dripping complications all over her floors, and Josh was determined to make himself indispensable to them.

And she, Donna, was jealous. Pitifully jealous.

She'd never had to share her boy with another serious contender. She'd always been number-one woman in his life, and she was truthful enough with herself to own that she didn't want to share.

The play of light across the water soothed her.

Richard was happily settled with his Lucy, and now it looked like Josh had found his *one*. Whether she liked her or not, Donna had the strongest feeling Holly Partridge would be part of her life from here onward.

Josh wasn't happy with his mother. His anger in the kitchen and then the car had been unwelcome and unexpected. He had taken her to task for her treatment of Holly.

Another first.

Donna sipped her wine. She hadn't behaved well. Her reaction had been 90 percent shock at the situation and 10 percent mama bear. All right, maybe 50/50 was a little more accurate. She'd been tired and jetlagged, and the surprises had taken her by storm.

When pressed, Josh had been cagey about how matters stood between them. According to her son, it was Holly who wasn't keen on taking things any further.

And mama bear had come clawing out of the cage again. *My boy not good enough for you?* she'd wanted to yell. They never got much older than three in your mother's heart. The instinct to protect and swaddle was hardwired all the way to the bone.

Lucy had been easy. Donna adored Lucy, and she'd

assumed she would love whoever her other sons brought home. Holly, a small woman with a huge attitude who took crap from nobody, reminded Donna of someone.

Donna, baby, they don't come much tougher than you; you're my warrior. Des's voice resonated in her head.

Donna almost spat the Sancerre across the room. Holly reminded her of herself before life had softened the edges.

The doorbell peeled loudly in the silent condo, a welcome relief from the direction her thoughts were taking. She got to her feet and stretched.

The doorbell pealed again.

Whoever waited on the other side sounded like they were in a hurry.

Donna yanked the door open. "Yes?"

A young woman stared back at her uncertainly.

Of course there would be a woman at the door. This was her son's condo after all.

"Er . . . Hello?" The woman studied the address plate on the wall beside the door. She looked back at Donna. "Um, I thought—"

"Who were you looking for?" Donna placed the woman's age at late twenties. She scrolled through the women in Josh's life she'd met. It didn't take long. Despite his reputation and his past behavior, Josh played his private life close to his chest.

"I have the number right." The woman consulted an iPhone. "I'm terribly sorry, I think I might have the wrong address. I drove in from the airport, and the streets in this part of the city are confusing."

"It's the one ways," Donna said.

Her visitor was attractive without being pretty, the sort of face that would come to life in front of a camera. Flawless peach skin sculpted around high cheekbones and a pair of large hazel eyes. Her lustrous tortoiseshell hair moved from honey to brown and remained neatly confined to her nape.

"Who are you looking for?" A suspicion popped its head up in Donna's mind. The woman's exquisitely tailored suit draped her body perfectly, despite her claim to have been traveling, and Donna smelled a designer label worthy of Joshua.

"I was looking for Joshua Hunter." The woman confirmed Donna's growing certainty. "I have the right building, I checked with the doorman." The young woman frowned.

Donna had a feeling it was a habitual expression, like the weight on the girl's shoulders never let up. She had a sudden, completely inexplicable rush of maternal protectiveness. "Were you looking for Josh or Holly?"

The woman's face cleared and she smiled. It changed her from attractive to lovely in an instant. "I *am* at the right place, then?"

"You are." Donna nodded. "And you aren't. This is Joshua's condo, but they aren't here."

The visitor's face dropped.

"But you are lucky." Donna stepped back and opened the door. She motioned the woman to enter. "I am Joshua's mother, Donna, and they are at my house in Willow Park."

"They are?"

"They are." There had been four girls in the Partridge family. "Now I am guessing you are the other sister, right?"

"I'm Grace." She stepped through the doorway, wheeling a small, compact suitcase behind her.

"You had better get settled." Donna motioned toward the sofa. "Because we have a lot to talk about." She made for the kitchen. "I'll get you a glass of wine. You're going to need it."

* * *

His mother sitting on the front porch wasn't the last thing Josh would have expected this evening; however, it was unusual enough for him to get that prickling sensation at the back of his neck. He raised a hand in greeting as he approached.

She got to her feet and waited for him.

"Hey, Ma. How did you get here?"

"I got a lift. You look good." She gave him the maternal hawkeye.

"It's this insane training I'm doing." Holly would probably scoff at him, but he wasn't doing this to look good. Actually, he wasn't really sure why he was doing this anymore. Fuck. Richard was right. The only reason he'd signed up was to kick his brother's ass.

"You are still going through with this race?" Donna put her hands on her hips.

"I'm committed now." His mother had raised boys, but she still didn't get the male need to climb a mountain just because it was there. To be honest, it sounded dumb to him right now, too. "It's happening in a couple of days."

Donna made a rude noise. "You are entered and you paid your admission. That is not committed."

"I undertook this and now I have to finish it." Or Richard would never let him hear the end of it.

Donna gave him a hard stare. "I am your mother, Joshua, and you should never try to lie to me. You are doing this because Richard did it before you."

Busted! She was brutally accurate, and he should know better than to try to dance around the truth with her.

"And you are probably going to do it faster than he did and never let him forget it."

He grinned back and drank his water. "So, what brings you here? Here to fight with my girl again?"

"I did not fight with her." Donna blushed under his steady regard. She gave a Gallic shrug, as if her statement explained everything. "You are my son."

"I'm going to see her through this, Ma."

Donna kept her eyes locked on his. "I know that, Joshua. I would expect no less from you. But this is not the sort of thing you can fix with some charm and a big smile."

He dropped his head. "I know that."

"And I am not sure there is any space in her life right now for romantic complications," Donna said.

"You came to warn me I might get my heart broken?" Josh raised his eyebrows at his mother. Once a mother, always a mother. "There are some who might argue I'm due my fair share of heartbreak."

"They would be wrong," Donna said. "Laura was different."

Josh finished off the water. The guilt made it difficult to swallow. "Dad—"

"Your father spoke in anger. His words were harsh and I know he regretted them." Donna touched his arm.

Her touch seared like a brand. "He was ashamed of me."

"He was angry." She gave him a pat. "And you did not always treat girls as I would like when you were younger, but you are not that way anymore."

"No, I'm not that way now." He tapped the toe of his running shoe against the bottom step of the three stairs leading onto the front porch. He didn't want to hurt his mother, but they had to air this. "And what if Holly is my choice?"

Donna smacked his arm. "Do you think I am blind and stupid?"

Relief washed over him in a wave. He didn't need her permission, but it would be nice to have it anyway. "Anyway, like you say, she has enough to worry about with her sisters."

"Will you accept that?" She cocked her head like a bird.

Josh's gut tightened. Holly walking away from this thing between them was looking more and more possible. "I might not have a choice."

A worried frown puckered her brow.

"But I'm going to try to change her mind," he said with a forced bit of confidence that convinced neither of them.

"We will see." She gave him a small smile. "I am not here this evening to talk to you. I brought you a surprise."

"What is it?"

"Not a what." Donna drew the moment out with relish. "A who."

"Who?"

"Exactly."

He glared at her repressively. He wasn't in the mood to play Abbott and Costello. "Who is it?"

"I hope you are sure about this Holly because there just got to be more of her to love." She raised her eyebrow.

He shook his head at her.

She grinned back unrepentantly. "Your surprise is in the kitchen."

Josh took the stairs slowly. Any more surprises like Portia and he might toss in the towel. Oh, who was he kidding?

"Josh?"

The seriousness of her tone stopped him. *"Oui?"*

"Tu es sûr?"
"I am."

"Grace?" Holly couldn't believe she was here. Bloody hell, it was good to see Grace.

She looked phenomenal, but then Grace always did. She wore one of her power suits in a crisp mint with a pair of shoes even Holly coveted. It was like looking at a grown-up version of herself. "What are you doing here?"

"I took a plane and then I drove." A tentative smile played around the corners of Grace's mouth.

"You look great." God, she'd missed Grace. They used to be as close as two sisters could get. It was over two years since they'd been in the same room together. Grace and her husband liked to do Christmas somewhere warm. Holly was glad for any excuse not to have to make nice with Greg.

Holly wanted to reach out to Grace She hesitated, not sure the gesture would be welcome.

"So do you." Grace's tentative smile blossomed into a grin.

To hell with it. Holly closed the gap between them and pulled her sister into a hug.

Grace froze for a second before her arms came up.

Holly tightened her hold. The familiar feel and scent of Grace surrounded her, and some of the bleakness receded. "I'm glad you're here."

Her throat constricted on the words.

Grace nodded and tightened her arms briefly, then she stepped back. "This feels weird."

"I know." It was weird, but good weird. "Where's Greg?"

"Not here." Grace moved to stand over at the window.

"I never thought I would come back here. Ever." She kept her gaze on something outside the window. "Have you been to the house?"

"Yes." Holly joined her at the window. Outside, an elderly man tried to dissuade his dog's interest in an azalea bush. "You wouldn't recognize it, though. It's been completely renovated."

"Speaking of overhauls. You look great." Grace turned and studied her from head to toe. "No, I mean it. You look great."

"Yeah?" The compliment warmed her from the inside out. More often than not, Grace was outspokenly vocal on Holly's complete disregard for fashion. "I can't take the credit." Holly waved her hand breezily through the air. "I have a new consultant."

Grace snorted.

"I strongly suspect I am being managed," Holly said.

"You? Managed?"

"Uh-huh."

"With your full knowledge?" Grace's eyes narrowed. "Okay, who are you and what have you done with Holly?"

Holly laughed. "Don't get excited; it's only a temporary thing." She took a moment to study her sister's face. "I can't believe you're here."

"Me neither." Grace pulled out a kitchen chair and folded herself elegantly into it.

"Grace?" Emma stood poised in the kitchen doorway. "Is that you?"

"Hey, Em." Grace greeted her from the kitchen table.

Emma stayed in the doorway.

They weren't a tactile family. It had never occurred to Holly how little affection they displayed among one another. Josh was a corrupting influence, with his constant casual touches throughout the course of a day.

Emma floated over to where Grace sat.

They couldn't have been more different—Grace with her perfectly tailored suit and blouse, her killer heels tapping the floor, versus Emma in her tie-dyed cotton dress sweeping the ground over her bare feet. Their dissimilarity went all the way to the core.

"I knew you would come." Emma gave Grace a smug smile.

Grace narrowed her eyes. "Wow. That's incredible, considering I didn't have any idea I was actually coming here until I got in the car."

And Grace and Emma fit straight into their assigned roles. Tension oozed into the room.

"I wish you'd told me." Holly tried to lighten the atmosphere. That was her role in this. Emma and Grace went head to head and Holly soothed the waters. "I was blown away."

"I drew some cards for you." Emma patted Grace's hand. Her bracelets clattered against the wooden table. "I thought they were for me, but they didn't make any sense, so they must have been for you."

"Thanks, Em." Grace shifted uncomfortably.

"Don't you want to know what they said?" Emma never knew when to let something go.

"Maybe later." Grace gave her a weak smile. "So, tell me about Portia."

"Portia is fighting a war within herself." Emma blinked mistily. "The cards are cautioning her to take it easy and to be herself."

"She's bipolar," Grace said. "I don't think the cards cover that."

Emma stiffened.

"It's okay, Gracie." Holly stepped in quickly. "That's what Emma means."

"Then she should say so." Grace rose to her feet and stalked back to the window. "So, give me the facts."

"Portia is on a quest." Emma's eyes grew unfocused.

Grace made a growling noise.

"No, she's right. Sort of." Holly held up a hand to forestall Grace. "Like I said, I think this has something to do with Melissa."

Grace paled and leaned against the counter for support. "Melissa?"

"Why do you always call Mummy Melissa?" Emma looked from Holly to Grace.

"Habit." Grace motioned for Holly to continue.

"I think Portia's pregnancy is the reason for this sudden interest in Melissa." The old bickering made her tired. Holly took the seat opposite Emma. In as few words as possible, she told Grace more about the pregnancy and Portia's fixation on Josh.

"He's being rather understanding," she said. "But for everyone's sake, we need to get this sorted out."

Emma clasped her hands together on the table in front of her carefully, like a nun preparing herself for prayer. Her rings and bracelets rattled loudly against the wood as Emma lowered them to the table. "You mean for your sake."

"What am I missing?" Grace looked from one to the other.

Emma shook her head and continued to study her jewelry with a pious air of martyrdom.

"Emma doesn't approve of my—me and Josh Hunter." To put it mildly. Holly folded her arms over her chest.

Grace's eyes gleamed with lively curiosity. "Is there a you and Josh?"

"Yes. No. I don't know." *Brilliant answer, Holly.* "It's complicated."

"Tell me about it." Grace snorted.

Holly got the feeling she was talking about something entirely different.

"Have you been doing the wild thing with him?" Grace cut straight to the chase.

"Uh-huh." Holly's cheeks heated.

Grace threw up her hands triumphantly. "I knew it."

"I knew it." Emma's head shot up and her eyes narrowed on Holly. "I knew you were doing that with him instead of—"

"You go, girl," Grace said. "If he's as hot as he was in high school, you are my new hero."

Emma curled her lip. "It's disgusting."

"No, it's not." Grace glared at Emma. "It's high time Holly got some action."

"She has Steven." Emma's eyes widened.

"Steven." Grace managed to load the name with a huge dollop of contempt. "No woman in her right mind would choose Steven over Josh."

"Not the point, Grace." Emma smacked her palms on the table. Jewelry clanked and scraped. "What about Portia? I cannot believe both of you can be this selfish. This will drive her over the edge."

"She's already over the edge." Grace turned on Emma suddenly.

Emma gasped. "That's a horrible thing to say."

"Why? It's the truth." Grace stuck her chin out.

"I think what Grace is saying—"

"You're being awful and unkind." Emma shot to her feet, the bench screeching against the floor.

"Bullshit, Emma. She's ill, sick." Grace tapped her

temple with her forefinger. "In here, Emma, something doesn't work properly."

Emma gasped, her eyes going even wider.

Grace rolled right over her. "It doesn't make any difference what any one of us does or doesn't do. Because Portia is not going to get better. She's not ever going to be right again. *Do. You. Get. That?*" Grace's cheeks flushed and her eyes glittered.

Emma imploded on a sob and crumpled back onto the bench.

Grace dropped into her seat. "Shit."

"Gracie?" Holly approached her sister slowly. There was so much going on beneath the surface. Grace's reaction had shocked her as well. Her sister had a hair-trigger temper, but this was something else.

"Where did that come from?" Grace raked her shaking fingers over her cheeks and down, as if she could pull her skin off her bones. "Where the hell did that come from, Holly?"

"It's being here," Holly said into the silence. "It's being in this place and with Portia cycling. It brings it back."

Grace's eye entreated Holly to toss her this bone. "For you, too?"

"For me, too."

"Man." Grace exhaled loudly. "It's like Melissa all over again. Are we screwed up or what?"

Beside Holly, Emma stopped crying and looked from one to the other of them. "You never talk about her," she said suddenly. "About Mummy; you never talk about her."

Grace flinched at Emma's choice of words.

The word *mummy* jangled inside Holly, tightening her stomach and making her chest ache. "We can't."

Grace shook her head and shrugged.

"But—?"

"Leave it, Em." Emma had no sense of self-preservation. "Not now."

"Then when?" Tears spilled down Emma's cheeks. "Portia and I have the right to know."

Holly's heart sank as Emma lit the fuse that was Grace.

The menace resonated off Grace as she turned to Emma. "What did you say?"

"Grace." Holly didn't disagree with Grace. Emma and her whining about her rights and what mattered to her was enough to make a saint snap, but they had enough on their plates right now.

Grace shook her off.

"I said," Emma swallowed convulsively and stuck her chin out, "Portia and I have rights in this family, too."

"Rights." Grace threw up her hands. "Rights?"

"Yes," Emma said doggedly.

"Don't you dare talk to me and Holly about your rights." Grace rounded on Emma like a feral thing. "You had the right to be taken care of, to be fed, to wear clean clothes, to get to school, and we made sure of that. Holly and I, we gave up everything for your damn rights."

"Gracie . . ." Holly tried to reel her in.

"No." Grace shook her head. "She needs to hear this. She can't keep hiding behind you or the mystic shit she mouths off. We protected the two of them so well, Holly, but we forgot about ourselves. Who took care of us, Holly? Who? And who's stopping us from screwing up our lives now? They have you." She pointed at Emma. "Who do we have?"

Thunderous silence filled with the heavy choke of the tears Grace still didn't shed.

Grace's words sank in, finding the cracks in Holly's armor and widening them.

"I can't deal with this shit." Grace scraped her chair back loudly. "I've been traveling and I'm tired and sticky and I want to . . . I need . . ."

"I'll show you where you can get settled." Donna stood in the doorway with Josh.

Holly could barely look at them. She had no idea how much they'd heard and she felt stripped right down to the bone and exposed. The Partridge girls in all their dysfunctional glory.

Emma shot out of her chair and ran from the room. She pushed past Grace on her way up the stairs.

"This way." Donna led Grace out of the kitchen.

Holly was hollow, detached inside.

Emma would find Portia and comfort there.

Grace's words still rang in her ears. Who would comfort Grace? Who would comfort Holly?

"Emma and Grace, they don't get on." Holly raised her hand and dropped it again.

Josh was beside her. "Holly?"

"I'm fine."

He reached for her and she stepped away.

He dropped his hands and shoved them into his pockets.

He saw too much. She couldn't control it when he gave her his empathy. "Grace is angry."

He grunted his agreement, his gaze heavy on her.

She couldn't look up. If she did, it would be over; she would walk into his arms and the comfort they offered. It wouldn't change a damn thing, however. "She's been holding it together for so long she's frightened if she lets it go, it will overwhelm her."

Still he didn't move or speak.

"It's like this big sore festering inside her, and she's terrified of what will happen if she exposes it. It could poison everything around her."

"I don't think that will happen," he said.

"You don't?"

"No, I don't. Because she was strong enough to survive in the first place, and she'll be strong enough to handle what happens next."

"But you can't be sure." Holly turned to look at him, unable not to. "You can't be sure she'll be okay."

"Yes, I can, because she's strong." He stepped toward her. "She's stronger than she knows."

"No, she isn't." Holly gave a brittle little laugh. "She isn't strong at all. It's an act, and it's going to come crashing down around her ears any day now."

"Holly." He reached for her.

Holly shook her head and dodged him. "I can't." How to make him understand when her mind kept yelling its defiance? "I can't do any of it. You have to see that." Please, God, don't let him make her explain. "It's too difficult."

"Josh?" Donna appeared in the doorway. "Could you drop me home?"

Josh took a step back. "I'll come back later."

"No." Holly took the escape offered. "I need to go and see if my sister is all right."

"I put your sister in Josh's old bedroom." Donna headed for the door. "Feel free to use mine. There is room enough here for all of you."

Holly nodded, not able to meet the older woman's eyes.

Donna's footsteps drew closer. "He is right, you know. You have the strength for this."

"We were talking about Grace." They both knew she was lying, but the alternative was to break down and weep.

"Indeed." Donna cleared her throat. "*Bonne chance, ma petite.* You have more friends than you know."

Chapter Twenty-Five

Holly wanted to bust out of her skin.

Thankfully, dinner was over quickly. Grace sat nearly silent throughout and Emma sulked magnificently. Portia had put in an appearance and spent the entire meal pushing food around her plate. As soon as they finished, the twins excused themselves and disappeared upstairs.

Holly didn't even mind that they didn't offer to help with the dishes. She was glad to see the back of them.

Josh still hadn't returned from taking his mother home. Maybe he wasn't coming back.

She put the dishwasher on and tried to shake the flat nothing in her middle. She was a mess. Her family was in crisis, the girls at one another's throats, and she was worried she'd pushed Josh away hard enough to keep him away.

"Hey?" Grace came up beside her. Her sister had changed into a pair of shorts and a tank top. Even dressed casually, she looked like you could toss her down a runway.

"So, about earlier with Emma." Grace tucked her hands into her pockets. "I got pretty intense there."

"Uh-huh." Holly glanced at her out of the corner of her eye because there wasn't much she could say to that. It would be nice if Grace could back off, just this once, but Emma made Holly want to have a screaming shit fit, too.

"She gets me so mad." Grace shook her head. "She has this way of being unbearably self-righteous, I want to take her head off."

Emma's smug complacency wasn't easy to take, but Holly tended not to let Emma get under her skin. Perhaps through living with Emma, Holly had developed immunity to her.

"And now she's sulking." Grace's lip curled in disgust. "And she can keep that up forever."

"You know Emma." Holly wiped down the countertops. "She's got a different set of rules for the rest of the world."

Grace made a rude noise.

"Perhaps you could talk to her about it sometime." Even as she made the suggestion, she mentally kicked herself. Like hell Grace and Emma would sit down for a heart to heart.

"I said pretty much all I needed to say." Grace stuck her determined chin out.

And there you had it. Normally, she would have charged right in and made the bad thing go away. Now, she paused and waited; perhaps she didn't need to keep making everything all right. She shrugged and let the subject drop.

Grace poured them each a glass of wine. "Donna seems nice."

Nice? Not the word Holly would have chosen to

describe Josh's mother. She took the glass Grace offered. "She's not happy about the situation."

"Who can blame her?" Grace shot back. "None of us are jumping for joy."

True, that. Holly finished cleaning and sipped her wine.

Grace stared out of the window in a moody silence.

Holly searched for some clue to Grace's mood. "How long are you here for?"

"I'm not sure." Grace leaned her butt against the counter and folded her arms across her chest. "I didn't have any fixed plan to come. I packed a bag and worked out where I was heading when I was already on the road."

"That doesn't sound like you." Holly laughed. Grace used to plan the next day's outfit down to her hair bands.

"No." Grace sighed and shook her head. "It doesn't, does it?"

"Well, I'm still glad you're here." And she meant it, Emmagate aside. "Perhaps you can drive me into Chicago tomorrow, I have an appointment for a passport."

"Sure," Grace said and went back to her middle distance staring.

Holly couldn't contain the question any longer. "You going to tell me what's going on?"

"I'd rather not," Grace said, but softly and without bite.

"But there is something going on." Holly edged closer carefully. Grace was hair trigger at the best of times.

"Yes." Grace crossed one leg over the other "Can we leave it at that, Holly?" She looked up suddenly. "Do you think you can do that? Just know there's something and trust me to talk about it when I'm ready?"

"I could try," Holly answered as honestly as she could. "You know that's not my strong suit, but I'll do my best."

Grace's expression gave her nothing.

"Tell me if I should worry?"

"You always worry," Grace scoffed, but lightened it with a smile.

Holly rolled her eyes. Worrying about her sisters was as ingrained as all the rest of the crap. "Any more than usual?"

"No." Grace shook her head. "In fact, I think you should be glad—sort of. I think I'm better than I have been in a long, long, long time—sort of . . . I think."

"Oh?" Holly laughed on the inside, way down on the inside. "That clears things up nicely."

Grace gave a bark of laughter and sipped her wine. "Where's Josh?"

"He took his mother back to the condo and went to pick up some things." Holly refused to look at the empty driveway again.

"Is he staying here tonight?"

Holly shrugged. She wished she knew. "I think so."

"The question is . . ." Grace drew the words out. "Where are *you* staying tonight?"

"Ah, Grace." The million-dollar question, right there. "I wish I knew."

She needed some fresh air and stepped out into the cooling evening. Thank God there were no mosquitoes out tonight.

Grace followed her out. "Emma is full of shit, you know."

It was a typical town garden, neat and orderly with fast-blooming summer color. Large trees provided enough shade to make it comfortable for sitting outside.

"In the general sense or the specific?" Holly tossed over her shoulder.

"Both." Grace smiled. Then grew serious. "What I meant was you and Josh. You are entitled to a life. Your happiness doesn't always have to be sacrificed for Emma and Portia."

If only it were that easy. *Here Emma, here Portia, take your fucked-up lives and run with them. Take Grace with you while you're at it.* Holly lowered herself onto the grass and rolled over onto her back.

The sky spread from wall to wall in an aching arch of blue. The warmth of the evening sun crept like a caress over her skin. Holly closed her eyes and soaked in the calm around her.

It was impossible to relax. She could feel Grace beside her, always stewing and fulminating about something. Grace was exhausting to be with sometimes. Holly almost laughed out loud. Josh said much the same thing about her. "Do you think I should chill?"

"Duh." Grace stretched out beside her.

Holly let her eyes drift from one sister to another.

It was late and the twins had reappeared before going to bed to resurrect an old family ritual of milk and cookies. Even Grace and Emma tacitly agreed to a cease-fire.

Holly had been glad to see everyone gathered at first. It gave her a brief feeling of togetherness. The warm and fuzzy feeling had faded fast. Unsaid words hung heavy between them.

The crunch of cookies and the slurp of milk broke the silence.

Holly placed her glass on the table with more force than strictly necessary.

Portia jumped.

Emma grimaced and crunched at her cookie.

Grace raised an eyebrow.

She couldn't stand it. "Are we really going to do this?" Holly demanded of nobody in particular.

Emma flickered her eyes briefly in her direction but went back to her dignified stare.

Portia frowned in confusion. "Do what, Holly?"

Grace got it immediately, and a nasty grin spread across her face. "Of course we are, Holly." She plastered a big fake grin on her face and waggled her head. "We always do this. It's the Partridge girls, pretty as a picture and just as perfect."

Holly pushed back from the table. The frustration throbbed just beneath the surface of her skin. "Well, it sucks."

"You said it," Grace agreed heartily and pushed her plate away. Holly quelled the desire to yell. She was in serious danger of losing it. Portia, Emma, and now Grace, and it all felt like too much. And they sat there and crunched cookies.

The pretend thing had grown old. She wished she could rip off all the scabs and have them air all their shit for once. Instead, they followed in the picture Francis had created for them. Everything's okay here, as long as you don't look too closely. Added to which Josh hadn't come back, and it ate at her. And then it bugged her that it ate at her.

"I don't understand," Portia said.

"Sure you do." Grace tilted her head at Portia. "You're bipolar, not stupid."

Holly nearly swallowed her tongue. "Grace!" she and Emma yelled in sync.

Portia paled.

"You're right." Grace flushed and shifted in her seat. "Sorry, Portia, I know you can't help it."

"What do you suggest, then?" Emma's soft challenge to Grace hung in the air.

Holly waited for the explosion.

Grace simmered down again.

Surprising.

"I haven't got a clue." Grace pulled the corners of her mouth down in a rueful expression. "I never thought I'd see the day when I came back to this place."

"Why are you here?" Emma never knew when to quit.

Grace's eyes flashed a warning. It was too much to ask that she didn't react for a second time in as many minutes.

Holly opened her mouth to intervene, to soothe away the nasty, then stopped. Fuck it. Not two minutes ago she'd wanted them to air their crap. Why not let them have at it?

Emma and Grace stared each other down.

Surprisingly, Grace looked away first.

"I don't know. I honestly don't know." Grace made a face. "I don't want to be here, but I couldn't seem to stay away."

"It was the same with me," Portia surprised Holly by saying.

"None of us wanted to come back here," Holly said, without knowing why. "This place is full of ghosts for us."

Silence settled over the kitchen again.

"They put me on drugs for seeing ghosts," Portia said.

They turned to look at her.

Holly wasn't sure who started it, but all of a sudden they were laughing. Laughing as if they could never stop.

Grace collapsed her head into her hands on the table. Her shoulders shook so hard they rattled the table.

Holly laughed until tears streaked down her face.

Even Emma was laughing, hanging on to Portia and hugging her, but laughing.

It wasn't really funny, but the laughter felt good; it felt healing. Eventually they subsided. The atmosphere between them was less charged.

"Greg and I are getting a divorce." Grace's face stayed carefully blank.

Holly kept her head lowered. Relief flooded through her.

Grace would have her ass if she dared voice it.

It didn't surprise Holly that much. Grace and Greg were the perfect dual-income, no-kids couple, both lawyers, both pulling in big salaries, and both living the high life. And yet there always seemed to be something missing between them. As if Grace had constructed her marriage into the perfect picture.

A cold shiver snaked down Holly's spine. It sounded awfully familiar.

"Why?" Portia recovered first.

Grace shrugged. "I'm not sure."

"You have to have some idea?" Emma sniffed at her sister.

Grace managed a small laugh. "I know why we say we're getting a divorce. I don't know how and why we got to this point."

Holly understood perfectly. She nodded

"Why do you say you want a divorce?" Portia's brow furrowed.

"Because we both want different things from our lives. We've grown apart—yada, yada, yada." Grace got up abruptly and filled a glass of water from the faucet. She stood by the sink with the glass in her hand.

"Is there any chance of reconciliation?" Emma's lips puckered up. "Marriage is such an important commitment. Too many people today give up on their marriages. It's a thing you have to work on constantly."

Say what? Holly stared at Emma.

"You know, Emma . . ." Grace turned her hazel eyes on her sister like two death rays, "I would take this lecture more seriously if you had actually ever been in a relationship."

"I have relationships." Emma's voice quavered.

"Real relationships?" Grace leaned into her. "Where you actually have sex with someone?"

Emma went all shades of red from her neck to her hairline. "Having sex isn't the definition of a relationship."

"It relates to intimacy." Grace banged her knuckles on the table. "I don't think you've ever had anything close to an intimate relationship with someone else, man or woman."

Emma's eyes flooded and her lip quivered.

Here we go. Holly's gut clenched.

"Don't you dare. I swear to God, Emma." Grace leaped out of her chair and got right in Emma's face.

Portia jumped.

Holly bit back a groan. The peace was too good to last.

"If you start bawling," Grace slapped her hand on the kitchen table, "I am going to give you something to bawl about."

Emma stared at Grace, her mouth open.

Grace loomed above her, as tense as a bowstring. "If

Portia is supposed to be the depressed one, how come you're the one always crying?"

"I'm not always crying," A tear slipped down Emma's cheek and she dashed it away.

Holly needed to change the subject because the tension between them made her head hurt. God knew what it was doing to Portia. "What does Greg say?"

"He says I'm not the woman he married." Grace turned back to Holly. "And he's right. I'm not. The part I can't figure out is who that woman was and who she is now."

Chapter Twenty-Six

Holly wasn't waiting up for Josh.

She wasn't.

She was such a liar.

It was after one in the morning and she was out of reasons to explain her sitting in the kitchen and watching the door like the family dog. She'd gone to bed at the same time as Grace and spent the next half hour drifting fitfully in and out of sleep.

After her initial outburst, Grace had grown silent again. Holly was secretly relieved. They'd all had more than enough for one evening.

At some point she'd given up pretending to sleep and come downstairs. She shouldn't be here. She should stay upstairs and keep a distance from Josh. In the morning she was going to the consulate to get her passport, and then there would be no more reasons to stay in Willow Park.

She remained in the kitchen and made a cup of tea, which she didn't drink.

The throaty rumble of the XK-E made her look up. A door slammed.

He opened the door, his gorgeous face tired and

drawn. Dressed much like the first night she'd seen him in that bar on the Gold Coast, he wore beautifully tailored pants and a dress shirt.

He caught sight of her. "Holly?" He took a tentative step toward her and stopped, like a wolf scenting trouble. He dropped his car keys onto the counter. "Is everything all right?"

"No." She shook her head and leaned her elbows on the table. "I couldn't sleep."

He tilted his head. "Any particular reason?"

"Grace is getting a divorce."

"Wow."

"Wow indeed. And she won't tell me why. She and Emma are about ready to kill each other."

"That didn't take long."

"It never does." Why were they having this totally inane conversation? Oh, yeah, because she was too much of a coward to risk anything more. Holly huffed and fiddled with her mug. "Oh, by the way, Emma has been laying crystal grids across the house. Just in case you notice bits of rock lying around."

Way to go, Holly!

"Sounds painful."

"Only if you step on them." Holly forced a smile. "Or ask her how it works."

"And Portia?"

"Well." Holly laughed weakly. "We all know about Portia."

He nodded and shoved his hands deep into his pockets.

"How is your mother?" She should say good night and go to bed, but now he was here, things didn't seem as hopeless.

He shrugged. "Better than she was."

"Good." Holly clasped her hands around her mug.

The tea had gone cold. "That's good." *Stay with me. Do something manly, like grabbing me and kissing me until I can't think anymore.*

"Holly?" He stepped closer to the table. "Why are you sitting here at this time of the night?"

"I have no idea." She was such a liar.

"Okay." He walked to the door. "Then, I'll—"

"That's a lie." Holly couldn't let him go.

He stopped.

"I do know why I'm sitting here." She had a hard time getting this out. What if he laughed at her? Or worse, had changed his mind.

He tilted his head, a small smile playing across his lips. "Care to share?"

"I'm working up to that." Her pulse thumped. She pushed the cup farther away. With nothing to do with her hands, she tugged it back again.

"No time like the present," he said as she kept her eyes trained on her tea.

"I was waiting for you," she said before she chickened out. "I was waiting to see when you came home, if you came home, were you alone. That sort of thing."

"Ah, Holly." He moaned her name softly, as if it came from the deepest place inside him. "Do you care?" His hands bunched in his pockets as he rocked his weight from the balls of his feet to his toes. "Tell me, because right now I really, really need to know."

"It seems I must." Her voice strangled in her throat. "Because despite my attempts to send myself to bed, I am still sitting here."

"I'm trying, Holly." His head dropped forward. "I want to do the right thing, but you've got me twisting like a pretzel. You want me and then you don't. Sometimes you seem to need me, and the next you slam the door. I don't know what you want from me."

"Neither do I." She got slowly to her feet. The warning voice in her head went silent. This was what all of Holly needed. "I only know you have something I seem to need. I don't want to, but I do. There you have it."

A shudder ran through his body as if he felt her words physically. His eyes bored into hers, burning in their intensity. "Why?"

"I don't know that either." Her heart pounded and she pressed her forehead to his shirtfront. "I don't know." The heat from his body warmed her. "I only know that I do. I need you."

"And you have me." The words were dragged out of him. His arms came around her slowly, as if he was resisting all the way. He took her hand and pressed his lips to her palm. "Right here in your capable little hand. You have me."

"Show me." Her blood buzzed in her ears.

His eyes darkened and his hands tightened against her arm.

She wasn't too proud to beg. "Show me."

He kissed her like a starving man.

The taste of him went straight to her knees; beer and mints, but mostly Josh; the heady, husky flavor unique to this man. There were reasons, so many reasons, why she shouldn't do this, but they skulked away into the shadows of her mind. She wanted him too much.

Holly strained onto her tiptoes as she tugged his head down. She couldn't get close enough. Like a flame to kerosene, she caught alight, writhing and grinding against him. Impatient, needy sounds vibrated from her throat, crooning to him to hurry, urging him closer and faster. Her hands burrowed under his shirt to find hot, silky skin beneath. She spread her palms over his flesh, reveling in the feel of him against her palms.

Impatiently, she tugged at his pants until she could

delve inside. He was heavy and strained in her hand as she stroked his length.

"Holly." He ripped his mouth away from hers, panting. "I need . . . want . . ." He pressed his forehead against hers, flushed and sweating.

"Yes." Holly moaned as she claimed his mouth again. "Yes." She didn't want to wait, didn't need polite or considerate. Him, inside her, now, was all she wanted.

He lifted her thighs and parted them around his hips.

Her back hit the wall. Her body vibrated its approval. There was a distant thud and shatter as something fell. She didn't care.

He tugged her panties aside. His fingers slid over her.

Yes. She was ready for him, wet and hot against his hand, and he growled into her mouth. "Condom."

He barely took long enough to sheath himself before he was buried deep inside her.

Holly gasped as he thrust into her, taking him as deep inside her body as she could. She clung to him with arms and thighs as he moved, pulling almost completely out to plunge deeper and make her cry out, muffling the sounds against his neck.

Her orgasm hit her fast and hard. She bit down on his shoulder to keep herself from screaming. With one more thrust he joined her, his entire body clenched as he spilled himself inside her.

They stayed absolutely still. Their harsh breathing set up a counterrhythm to the distant tick of Donna's rooster clock on the kitchen wall.

"Shit, Holly," he said, still buried inside her. "Do you have any idea what you do to me?" He raised his head and kissed her gently on the forehead. He rested his brow against hers and sighed. "Let's take this upstairs."

"What?" Holly lay quiescent against him as her heart rate returned to normal. Some part of her mind registered a problem.

"I want you in my bed, Holly." He feathered soft kisses against her cheek and jaw. "I want to make love to you again and again. I want to wake up with you beside me."

"No." Reality washed over Holly in an icy wave. She wriggled against his hold as the last vestiges of intimacy evaporated.

He released her legs, one at a time. "Holly?" He tensed. His pants were pooled around his ankles and he bent and pulled them up.

"I can't." Shit, it ripped her apart to say it. She wanted to be in his bed so badly she ached with it. Wanted to have him hold her and take away all of this crap for a few hours. Holly dropped her head back against the wall. "I can't."

Chapter Twenty-Seven

Holly's eyes burned with unshed tears

"Say again?" An explosive stillness shimmered around Josh.

"I can't." Holly shivered as the haze of the afterglow burned away under the harsh misery of regret. "I can't go upstairs with you."

He stepped back and fastened his zipper. The sound seemed unnaturally loud in the kitchen as his eyes bored into hers.

"I'll sleep with Grace." She couldn't deal with this right now. She needed to retreat and get her head together. Holly slipped from between Josh and the wall.

"Why?" He caught her wrist.

Holly tugged at her wrist. *Oh, God*, he was going to make this difficult. "I have to."

He tightened his clasp, forcing her to stay where she was.

"I can't sleep with you. I can't be seen sleeping with you." He had to get it. Portia was right upstairs. You didn't have to be a genius to figure out what would happen if Portia found them in bed together. *Shit*. She shouldn't have given in to her need for him. "You know how things are."

He made a soft noise of disbelief in the back of his throat. "You're kidding, right?"

He was upset with her. There was nothing she could do about that. She'd made a big mistake. This was a terrible misjudgment on her part. Guilty color crept up her face. She couldn't compound the error now. "No."

She tried to free her wrist again.

He held tight.

What the hell? Holly stared at his hand on her wrist. "They can't see us together. Can you imagine what would happen if Portia saw us together?"

She couldn't believe she had to explain this to him.

He stepped closer and got right into her space. "We'll make sure she doesn't see us together."

"I can't take that chance." Holly had to tip her head back to maintain eye contact.

"I don't know much about this disease of Portia's, but how is keeping her twisted myth of me as her baby daddy alive helping her?"

Shit, she'd hurt him. She could see it clear as day in his eyes. He was mad, yes, but lurking underneath was a sort of vulnerability that twisted her inside. "There's a difference between keeping Portia grounded in reality and shoving it in her face. Emma already knows what happened and she couldn't wait to tell me all about it the next morning."

"You're thirty years old, Holly. Way past the age where you have to ask permission for a sleepover."

"I know that." His body warmth reached out to her. His chest was so broad and strong. She had to get away before she gave in to temptation and tucked herself against him. "You know it's not that. Portia would lose it if she knew you and I were . . . we were . . ."

"What?" His jaw clenched. "Fucking?"

Holly flinched. He made it sound so dirty.

"Don't you like that word?" She'd never seen him this mad. "I don't like it either because I didn't think that was what we were doing here. I thought it meant more than that."

"It was a mistake." His words twisted her inside. She wanted to crawl away and hide.

"What happened to 'I need you, Josh'?" His voice mocked her. "Did you get what you needed and now it's time to cut and run?" He crowded her back against the wall. "Is that what you needed, Holly, a quick bang against the kitchen wall? Why wait for me to get home? Anyone could have done that for you."

His mockery ripped straight through her. This was high-school Josh—abrasive, cutting, and cruel. Anger surged through her. He was being a bully. She shoved at his chest. "Don't be crude."

He didn't budge. "I'm good enough for fucking, but nothing more. You won't tell your family we're together."

"I can't." Holly thumped her hand against the immovable bulk of his chest. Her fist throbbed. "You know I can't."

"No." He didn't yell, but the anger vibrated through his voice. "I don't know. I know the situation is ugly as hell, but if you give me half a fucking chance I can work through it with you. But you won't, Holly. You keep pushing me away."

"That is . . . so unfair." His anger battered against her. Holly struggled to find the words; they snagged painfully in her chest. "That isn't true."

"Really?" His lip curled up. "You want me and then you don't want me. You let me in and then get scared and push me back."

"This isn't about me." But it kind of was, and her protest lacked conviction.

"Yes, it is." He cupped her face between his palms, firm but not rough. "You have to ask yourself if you're going to go the rest of your life giving up what you want for your family."

God, he was being so unfair. She pulled her face away from his warm hands. "I shouldn't have waited up tonight. I'm sorry if I gave you the wrong impression, but that doesn't give you the right to be nasty."

"No?" His eyebrow went up sardonically. "I want to be with you, Holly. This thing between us is special, and you're the one making it cheap and tawdry."

"I didn't . . ." Didn't what? Because she had.

He'd been honest with her from the start.

She was the one who couldn't stick to a game plan. It made her resent his anger even more.

"Decide, Holly; decide what you want. Do you want a life of your own? Or do you want to carry on paying some kind of screwed-up penance for your parents?"

It was like she'd been sucker punched. "That's not fair."

"Yeah?" His mouth curled down. "Well, I'm not feeling fair right now. I'm mad at you, Holly, and getting tired of having my chain jerked. You want me but you don't want to. You pull me close and you shove me away. How fair are you being?"

"I'm not doing it on purpose." She tried to explain, but she couldn't even make sense of it in her mind. "It just happens."

"Great, Holly, just great." He growled in frustration. "And such a cop-out. You know what I think?"

He was going to tell her anyway, and Holly was sure she didn't want to hear it.

"I think you want me as much as I want you and it

scares the crap out of you. Here you are, apparently grown up and doing the same thing now you did all those years ago."

"You don't know what you're talking about." Holly stamped on the little voice that whispered he had her nailed down.

"You're protecting yourself," he said, his face implacable. "Now you dress it up with different faces, but the truth remains. You're hiding in case you might have to actually risk. You don't know how to trust yourself, and because you can't do that, you can't trust anyone else."

His words cut deep and close to the bone. Cold anger rescued her. Holly shoved as hard as she could against him and he stepped back. "Thanks for the pop psychology lesson."

She took the gap at a run.

"Running, Holly?" His voice taunted her as her foot hit the first step. "How novel."

"You don't understand anything," Holly rounded back on him. God, she was such a mess, and he was being a total prick.

"I understand perfectly. Go on, Holly. Run away. Off you go, because you're going to anyway. You're going to take your sisters and go back to London. You can hide in Canada and carry on with your dead-end job and convince yourself you aren't using your sisters as a human shield."

"Screw you." Holly's anger lashed and boiled beneath her skin.

"You already did."

"It's easy for you to criticize." The self-righteous, smug asshole. Holly closed the distance between them in two long strides. "You spoiled, pampered shit. I've been taking care of other people while you've been doing exactly what you please." Her voice grew stronger as her sense of injustice bloomed inside her. "I didn't have any choice. I was all the girls had. Our mother was dead and our father couldn't give a toss what happened to us as long as it didn't require anything from him. I had two teenagers to take care of."

"I know it hasn't been easy for you, Holly." As her voice got louder, his got softer.

Hasn't been easy? Oh, man, that was a good one. "'Hasn't been easy'? You don't know the half of it, you with your gifted existence. I would have loved to go to university, get a degree, and do something bigger. The option wasn't open to me."

"It is now." His tone got less jarring, but his jaw was set like granite below his hard-as-gems eyes. "And you're bullshitting yourself if you say you didn't have choices. You're hiding, Holly; in plain sight, but you're hiding."

He hit her right where she was most raw.

He raked his fingers through his hair. "In the years since your sisters have grown up, you had plenty of chances to pick up your education. You're bright, Holly. Hell! You beat the pants off me at school. You could have gone back, studied at night, made a deal with them. No, Holly, you chose to keep your life the way it is, and you're choosing now to walk away from this." He gestured between them. "You're choosing to walk away from us."

"You don't understand." It came out as the hiss of a wounded animal. She backed away. Inside, she bled, but she would die before she'd let him know the power he had to hurt her.

"Yes, I do." Josh took a step forward and loomed over her. "I may not have your life story, Holly. And I'll admit you carry a burden heavier than most, but you've made a martyr of yourself. You won't let anyone help you. You take a sort of perverse pride in making this as hard for yourself as possible. Right now, you could send Grace to take Portia home and stay here with me and see where this thing leads. You could tell Emma where to get off."

He dropped his head forward as if he were suddenly weary. "All of us have stories, Holly. All of us have good reasons for being the way we are. It's what we do with them that defines our future."

Never in her life had anyone dared say such things to her. Not even Grace would go so far. "Who the hell are you to be handing out the truth?"

"I'm invested in this, in you."

"How novel." Her laughter jangled harsh and ugly. "For the first time since Laura, you've stepped out behind your self-imposed martyrdom and taken a risk."

He flinched as if she'd struck him, but Holly was way beyond caring. His words had cut deep and she wanted to carve a piece of him back. "Your father died being angry with you. Well, boo-fucking-hoo, Josh. My father left me to raise his children. My father let my mother die because he couldn't be bothered dirtying his hands trying to save her. I will die before I let that happen to my sister. Do you hear me?"

He went dead pale and his jaw muscle worked. "Holly—"

"You had your turn." She shoved him again. "You had your turn telling me what was wrong with me. You have your mother and your brothers and a whole host of other people who give a shit what happens to you. Portia doesn't. She has me. I'm it for her. I'm all she fucking has. Do you get that? Do you?"

For a long moment Holly stood frozen, and then she spun on her heel, taking the stairs two at a time. His words kept jangling on in her brain.

"Holly." The anguish in his voice almost made her turn around.

Screw him anyway.

Holly made it to the room she shared with Grace. Her hands shook and slipped against the handle as she closed the door behind her. Her ragged breathing split the dark quiet of the room. It felt as if there was a gash in the middle of her chest.

Footsteps went past and a door shut. The sound of running water followed.

She also wanted a shower. She wanted to scrub him off her skin. It was a pity no amount of water would wash away what he'd said.

Grace lay still, an unmoving lump in the bed.

Part of her wanted to wake Grace up and share. Except Grace would probably agree with Josh, and Holly couldn't stand that right now.

Screw all of them.

His words swirled around the darkness surrounding her. He was a judgmental, self-righteous prick who'd had everything handed to him on a silver platter. How dare he look at her life and pick it apart as if it were worth nothing?

Yes, her job was boring. She worked in the dean's office as a glorified file clerk, but it was a job. It had put food on their table and put the girls through school.

Somebody had to take care of the twins. They had their shop, which sold crystals and charms and New Age paraphernalia. It didn't do so well, and someone needed to keep them afloat. As the oldest, it was up to her to step in and make things work. Just like it had been up to her to run the house while her mother collapsed and her father worked.

It was all very well for him to talk about choices.

He had no idea what it had been like for her. Not a
bloody clue.

Josh let the water drum over his head. It didn't drown
out the echo of his harsh words. *Smooth, Josh. So fucking
smooth you amaze me.*

Her face haunted him. Holly would be horrified to
know how stricken she'd looked. Her eyes had almost
overwhelmed her face as she stared at him through his
tirade.

Talk about repeating bad behavior. *Jesus.* He should
take the log out of his eye, or however that went. Things
had always come easy for him, especially money and
relationships. He'd come from a great family, with two
loving parents who supported him. He hadn't had to
deal with the stuff Holly had taken on her plate.

Tonight he'd gone and indulged in what amounted
to nothing more than a tantrum because he'd had his
new favorite toy ripped away from him. Damn. He
snapped off the faucet and grabbed a towel. And he'd
lashed out. He hurt, and he wanted to share it around
until the pain eased.

He'd launched into his self-righteous lecture with the
conviction of a born hypocrite. He wiped the steam off
the mirror. All this time thinking he'd grown up, and it
took one five-foot-two bundle of baggage and complications to show him how skin deep his maturity was.

So now what? He toweled himself dry roughly. Now
he had to fix this thing. He was going to man up and
make it right. He was going to stop dancing around the
issue like a coward.

He was in love with Holly Partridge.

And not a little in love either. He was knock-down,
drag-out, head-over-heels in love with a woman who may

or may not feel the same. Deep down, he knew she had feelings for him. The trick would be getting her to admit it. She'd been hurt. She was frightened. She was hiding. It was true, but underneath was someone worth fighting for. Even if he'd taken several huge leaps backward.

Fuck, some ladies' man. He walked through to the bedroom, debating going to find Holly to fix this thing now.

She'd reamed him out good about Laura and his dad. Close enough to the truth for him to want to throw up.

What would his dad have said?

If you love her, son, you stand by her. You be a man and stand by her side.

"I fucked up, Dad." He spoke to the silent room, wishing some trace of his dad was still in this house and listening.

It's not about you, son, it's about her. A heart is a fragile thing; if she gives it to you, make sure you guard it well.

A woman stood in his room.

Portia.

Joshua froze.

She stood so still, he didn't see her at first.

"Fuck!" He reached for the towel, but he'd left it in the bathroom. He brought his hands up to cup his junk from her view.

Except Portia didn't even look down. Her eyes burned with a sort of unholy light as she glared through him. "How could you?" Her voice shook. "How dare you?"

"How dare I what, Portia?" Josh edged toward the door. There was an eerie stillness to her that had him wanting to run for Holly.

Portia moved swiftly, reading his intention and cutting off his exit.

Holly was down the hallway and Josh had the feeling

she needed to be dealing with this and not him. Portia, with that face, scared the crap out of him. And he'd had the sheer audacity to mouth off about Portia to Holly, as if he had a clue how to deal with her. He was way out of his depth. Sunk and going down further.

"I saw you." Portia's eyes narrowed into slits. "In the kitchen with Holly. I saw you."

His freaked-out brain struggled to take that in and process it.

The door shutting shook him from his paralysis.

Fuck. Fuck. Fuck. This was bad. This was going to get so ugly it made his flesh crawl.

He edged open the door.

Portia ran down the passage toward Thomas's old room. She slipped like vapor through the door and it shut behind her.

What now? Josh stood a moment, indecision tugging at him.

Man up, son.

He knew what his dad would have done.

Chapter Twenty-Eight

"Think, Emma; what did she say exactly?" Holly didn't bother keeping her voice down. She was fucking panicking.

Josh had found her ten minutes ago with the unwelcome news that Portia had seen them. The humiliation of being caught in the act by her younger sister was almost enough to have her pulling the covers over her head and staying there. The knowledge of what this unwelcome revelation meant got her out of bed.

"I don't know." Emma's eyes filled with tears. "I was asleep when she came in and I only woke up because she was making so much noise."

Grace was all for letting her go, but Holly couldn't. The guilt squeezed like a chokehold around her throat. She'd known all along what would happen if Portia found out about her and Josh.

A livid Grace paced the hallway outside the bedroom and swore.

Portia had made her escape in Grace's rented car.

"Where did she go?" Grace stuck her head around the door.

"I don't know," Emma wailed, the tears sliding down her cheeks. "I can't remember."

"Don't be fucking pathetic," Grace said.

Holly could slap them both silly. She swore beneath her breath as Emma imploded into a heap of misery on the edge of her bed.

Grace took a threatening step toward her.

"Don't." This had all the ingredients for an old-time Partridge girls fight.

Josh took Grace by the arm. "Let's take a walk."

"Fuck." Grace let him turn her back into the hallway.

"Emma?" Holly crouched down beside her sister. "You must have some idea where she's gone."

Holly blew out a breath as Emma stopped crying and turned huge eyes on her.

"I don't," Emma whispered.

"I'm sure you do," she said. "Remember the twin bond. You know where she is, Emma."

Emma shook her head again.

A scream of frustration built in Holly's throat. Not again. She wanted to open her mouth and yell it to anyone within hearing distance. They would have to hunt for Portia all over again. This time she had a car and there was no telling where she could get to before they caught up with her.

Emma sat up straighter. "Wait."

Holly froze and turned to stare at the other girl. Bloody twin bond indeed, but she would take anything right now.

"I do know where she is."

"That's my girl." Holly took her hand.

"At least I think I do." Emma bit her lip and sighed. "But I'm not sure."

"Just tell me where you think she is."

"I asked her what was wrong." Emma's eyes lost focus.

"And she told me she had seen you and Josh." Emma paused and glared at her. "I told you what would happen." She gave Holly a look loaded with reproach. "But you never listen."

"Emma." Holly got her back on track before she let rip with the blast of profanity bristling in her mouth. "What did Portia say then?"

"I asked her to sit and talk to me, but she said I didn't understand. She said that only one person understood and she needed to talk to her."

"Melissa." Certainty exploded in Holly's brain. "She's gone to see Melissa."

Josh appeared in the doorway. "She went to your mother's grave?"

"That's what I said." Emma crossed her arms over her chest.

"Why would she do that?" Josh kept his attention focused on her.

"Holly won't tell you." Emma tossed her head. "She and Grace never want to talk about Mummy. They always change the subject whenever we do."

Holly dropped her eyes. She didn't want to answer the questions gathering in his eyes. "Can you take me there?"

"Yes." He came to stand right in front of her. So close his big, strong shoulders beckoned. "Let's go find your sister."

"Portia came to Willow Park to find our mother," Emma said. "She needed to make peace. Before she had the baby, Portia said she needed to make peace."

Holly turned on her heel. She couldn't listen to any more of this. Not with Josh standing there looking like he was putting the pieces together into a neat picture. She didn't want to stand here dissecting the past. They had to find Portia.

Now.

Grace stood in the doorway, barring her exit and forcing Holly to stop.

"Melissa was like Portia," Grace said.

"Like Portia how?" Josh asked from behind her.

"Melissa was bipolar." Grace's voice went flat. "It got worse and worse as we grew older. Here in Willow Park, it finally got the better of her."

Holly's spine stiffened. It was out there. She should feel relieved, but a part of her still wanted to grab up all the snippets of information her sisters tossed around and shove them back in their box.

The mystery unraveled in Josh's mind. The final piece of the puzzle that was Holly Partridge clicked into place. The mother, Melissa, had been bipolar. All these years and Holly had carried this weight around on her delicate shoulders.

Her strength awed him and scared him at the same time. He knew she'd taken care of her sisters, but he hadn't really got how deep that responsibility ran.

There was so much to reevaluate in light of this new information. It went racing through his memory banks. He'd been sure he had all the information. Positive he had Holly figured out.

Deep down, he'd suspected all along. The times he'd trod near the subject of Melissa, Holly had checked him instantly. She was so guarded, especially about her mother. She carried a mammoth-sized warning: *Here be dragons.*

His words from earlier rose up to taunt him, and he wanted to puke in self-loathing. She had called it right. He really had no idea what her life had been like and no right to judge.

He took a deep breath. "Do you know where she's buried?"

"Oh, yes." Emma cheered up. "We know exactly where she is."

"I'll get the keys to my mother's car."

Relief punched Holly in the gut. Only one car in the parking lot, and it looked like Grace's rental. She guided them through the massive cemetery on autopilot.

Portia sat on the ground beside Melissa's grave, looking as if she were on a family picnic.

Emma ran on ahead.

Holly hadn't been here in years. Beside her walked Grace and Josh. She wanted to slip her hand into Josh's larger one and feel the instant reassurance of his presence. She cast a quick glance up at him.

His beautiful face was set in severe lines, cold and unapproachable. It was better this way. Now Josh knew the whole ugly truth and would want to be as far away from her buggered-up family as he could. She grabbed Grace's hand instead, and her sister's clasp tightened.

Her and Grace against the world. Again.

There wasn't much to mark the passing of Melissa Partridge, only a small granite square set in the ground among hundreds of others. No message from a husband and her children, just her name and the dates of her birth and death.

"She was thirty-eight." Portia looked up as they drew near. Her eyes gleamed clear and focused from her pale face.

Holly hesitated, with no idea of the correct response.

"She wasn't that old. In my mind, she was always older." Portia touched her fingertips to the engraving.

"You were very young when she died." Grace's grip on Holly's hand tightened.

"We were ten," Emma said. "I don't remember a lot about her, though. You would think I would remember more, wouldn't you?"

"She was like a ghost," Portia said. Her voice sounded eerie and otherworldly, and Holly's nape prickled. She had no idea what she'd been expecting, but this wasn't it.

Portia sat at their mother's grave and chatted, as if this was the most normal occurrence in the world. "I used to think of her as a ghost in the house. Holly was the one who took care of us. And Grace."

Holly's world wobbled on its axis.

"Holly took care of you?" Josh asked.

"Yes." Portia rubbed her hands over the gravestone. "She had the same disease as me, you know."

"Yes, I know," Josh said.

"There were bad days, like I get. Holly never said anything, but I could tell when the days were bad."

"Come on, Portia." Emma patted her sister's hand. "Why don't we get you home?"

Holly watched from outside like her life was a movie. She had this weird sort of disconnect inside her that couldn't understand why they were talking about this. The Partridge girls never did this, and certainly not in front of someone outside the family.

Yet there was something right about Josh being there.

Wrong, shouted her mind. He should not be here. *It's because you weren't strong enough to walk away that this is happening.*

"Do you remember the bad days?" Portia turned and asked her twin.

Emma nodded. "I remember the bad days because

those were the days when Mummy would stay in her room and Holly was in charge."

"Dad would stay at work." Portia nodded. "I would hear her at night, always weeping. It would go on and on for hours. There were times when I wanted to get up and yell at her to stop."

"I don't remember that." Emma frowned at her sister.

Holly's stomach churned. She was going to puke if they didn't stop. The memories screamed at her, demanding she listen to them, let them out.

"You don't?" Portia blinked. "We used to snuggle under our duvet and I could hear her through the walls. Holly would always go to her."

"I remember that part," Emma said. "I wish I remembered more about her."

"I don't think I want to." Portia looked up suddenly. "I think she was bad at the end, and I don't think I want to know."

As if Portia's words opened a floodgate, the memories came pouring out. Holly spent most of her adult life refusing to think about her mother. It hurt too much. As she stood there, pictures flashed rapid-fire through her mind. One after another the memories came, and she couldn't stop them. She stopped trying and let the past wash through her and over her. She'd been trying for so long to keep it neat and confined. In the raging chaos of her childhood, she'd created a ruthless, safe order.

"She killed herself, you know?" Portia said conversationally. "In the end it was too much and she killed herself."

Yes, Holly did know. She'd been there in that last race to the hospital, trailing the ambulance as it rushed their mother to emergency. She and Grace, hands tightly clasped, legs sticking to their plastic chairs, when the doctor had come out. She and Grace couldn't hear what he said to their father, but they had known. Melissa had succeeded in killing herself this time. Neither of them had cried.

"I understand how she felt," Portia said. "Sometimes I understand exactly why she did it."

"Shit." Grace took a deep breath.

The graveyard gave a sickening dip before it settled around Holly. The twins had known all along. She'd spent so much time hiding the truth. For nothing.

"What?" Portia looked from one face to another. "You didn't think we knew?"

Holly shook her head, not trusting her voice. "We thought it was better that you didn't."

"We've always known," Emma said. "Is that why you won't talk about her?"

Holly nodded. "And because it . . . hurts." Such a small word to encapsulate a huge, aching chasm of pain.

Portia laid both hands against the grave marker. "I'm just the same, just the same as our mother."

"But not today." The words spun out of Holly's dead brain and over her lips. "You aren't like her today and it's time to go home."

This wasn't how it would end for Portia. She would use every ounce of strength and determination she had to make sure it wasn't.

Chapter Twenty-Nine

Holly trailed her sisters into the house. A fog blanketed her mind and she needed time to make it go away. She would think more in the morning. Something important hovered on the other side of her conscious-ness, but she couldn't go there. Right now it was all she could do to keep putting one foot in front of the other.

"Holly?" Josh's voice stopped her and she turned.

He stood beside his car.

"Aren't you coming?" She motioned to the house.

He shook his head.

His face was grim, like a man facing a firing squad.

She shivered, suddenly terribly cold and exposed beneath the steady blue of his gaze. She walked back toward him slowly, not sure she wanted to hear what he had on his mind. Her heart thudded unevenly in her chest.

"I'm not coming in." Josh shook his head. "I think it would be better if I stayed at the condo tonight."

"Why?"

"I think it's better this way, Holly." He dropped his head.

He was giving up on her. Defeat was etched into every

line of his body. It hit her like a ton of bricks. She didn't want him to say good-bye. Maybe never. And it made no sense. But it was for the best. This thing couldn't go anywhere. Then why was everything inside her screaming in rebellion?

"Before I go . . ."

His lips moved and the words came out. Some functioning part of her brain got every word, but still the clamor grew inside her.

"I was out of line earlier and I was going to ask for your forgiveness, but Portia came in before I could. You were right; you are right." He shoved his hands into his pockets.

Holly wanted to protest. She wanted to look into those blue-as-forever eyes and lose herself there.

"I didn't know what it was like. I didn't know most of this stuff I just found out." He cleared his throat. "I fucked up, Holly, and you needed better from me. You were right. Other than the thing with my dad, I pretty much sailed through life, and in my arrogance I said a whole lot of crap that I had no right to say." He took a step closer to her.

Maybe he would hold her and make the terrible coldness inside disappear. Her body tingled in response to the implicit touch.

He stopped. "I'm still here for you, in whatever way you need. You only have to ask and I'll do it for you."

She swayed toward him, but he didn't move. Holly was bereft without the missing touch.

"I'm here for you. No strings, no payback, and no judgment." He held out his hands. "I know trust is hard for you, and I haven't exactly covered myself in glory there."

He made a circle in the air with his forefinger. "We've

circled around to the trust thing, and I get it now." His voice softened. "I want to be a part of your life, and if it's not too late, I want you to know that I'm going to try my best not to let you down again. But that's me and my shit, and it's not what you need right now. Not with everything else you have going on."

A soft noise of distress built in the back of her throat. She couldn't maintain eye contact.

"So I'll leave," he said.

Something chilly settled into the deepest part of her.

"You know where I am if you decide to give me that chance to make it up to you. To stand by you like you need me to. I wish I could make it different, but you don't get to keep what we have without a leap of faith, sweetheart." And then he said the thing she feared the most. "I love you, but we both have to take that jump. Just know if you make that leap, Holly, I'll be right there to catch you."

"I . . ." Conflicting emotions chased through her mind.

He loved her and that made her want to dance.

But right on its tail came a sense of defeat. It wrapped around her neck like tentacles. She needed a connection to him, and she reached out with one hand. It was impossible. She dropped her hand.

"I want it all, Holly, but I'll take what you have to give." His face had the sort of stark beauty of an archangel as he laid his soul bare for her. "And if that's nothing, I'll still help you as much as I can."

She shook her head. God, she wasn't worth this much love. She didn't deserve it or know what to do with it.

"Whatever you need." He turned and got into his car.

The penis on wheels turned the corner and disappeared.

Her heart went with it. Still, she was too much of a coward to yell for him to come back.

God, how could he say those things to her? Knowing what he did, he still thought she was worth it? It didn't make any sense.

Nobody got that sort of unconditional offer. Life didn't work like that.

Her sisters watched her as she walked through the kitchen, a silent vigil of three. She walked right past them and went to the room she shared with Grace. Her legs were shaky and she sank onto the bed. It had a bold geometric pattern on it in shades of blue and gray, and she played tricks with her eyes, trying to make it fall into repeat patterns.

Anything was better than thinking about Josh leaving.

It had once been Josh's room, but he'd long since taken anything of his out, and the room now belonged to nobody. Unlike Thomas's room, there were no posters or old photographs to map out the life of the occupant. Only the stars still stuck on the ceiling gave any indication of who had lived in this space.

Holly dropped over onto her back and stared up at the universe.

Josh was gone.

Holly could feel the lack of his presence in the very air she breathed.

He said he loved her. He didn't expect anything back in return. Things like that didn't happen, especially not to Holly Partridge.

A blessed numbness filled the space where her feelings should be. She was going to hurt when the numbness left her. It was like watching a car wreck come toward her in slow motion.

She should be glad he'd gone. He was trouble. He was a complication she didn't need in her life. She missed him already.

The door opened.

"Hey there." Grace stuck her head around the corner.

Holly held up her hands. "Just don't ask me if I'm okay."

"All right, I won't." Grace walked over to the bed and sat down beside her. "That was quite something."

She dragged her mind back to their newest mess. "Is Portia okay?"

"Portia is fine." Grace rolled her eyes. "It's you I'm more worried about."

"You don't need to be." Holly didn't even manage to convince herself.

Grace snorted with laughter. "No?"

"I don't want to talk about it." She prayed Grace would go away and leave her to curl into a ball of misery.

"Okay." Grace swung her legs up onto the bed. "I'll let it go for now. Do you mind if I talk?" She dropped onto the bed next to Holly. "I've been living a lie."

Holly stared at the ceiling. Grace in a sharing mood was rare. But right now Holly wasn't sure she wanted to hear it.

"I've been walking around half alive, convinced it was what I needed and wanted. I thought I could walk away from Mum and Dad and even you and pretend it was finished." Grace leaned her shoulder against Holly.

The contact eased some of the ache in Holly's chest.

"The only problem was, I carried you around with me. The more I tried not to feel, the more it fermented inside me. Lately, I've been behaving out of character. It totally freaked Greg out." Grace pulled a face. "It's like I had this stuff stored up inside me and someone shook the bottle. Greg asked what was going on with me and I told him. I told him all of it."

"All of it?"

"Every last sordid detail." Grace made a small sound of regret. "You know I never told him about us as children, growing up with Mum?"

"What did Greg say?"

Grace pulled a face. "Greg told me to get it together. He didn't want to be married to a hot mess."

"What a fuckwit."

"Precisely."

"So what did you do?"

"I did as he said and got myself together. I looked at our lifestyle and saw how barren and meaningless it was. I looked at Greg and saw a convenience, not a lover and a friend. I don't know." Grace shrugged. "I just woke up and knew I had to go back to the beginning. Greg didn't want me to come here. He said if I left, it was the end of us."

"Wow." Holly tried to think of something comforting to say and came up blank. That was plain fucked up.

"Wow indeed."

They lay in silence, both of them lost in their own thoughts.

"So, what happens now?" Holly asked.

"I haven't got the answers." Grace laughed suddenly. "Hell, I don't think I've even unearthed all the questions, but I've stopped running. I'm home again, Holly. I'm home to try to find some meaning in all of this. I thought if I ran fast enough, I could outrun the pain and you and Mum." She let Holly absorb for a moment.

"I thought I might start living my life, the real one this time, and see where it leads."

"And Greg?"

"I don't know anything other than that I'm not prepared to go back to a half life. I've made a break for it and I can't go back."

"I never really liked Greg." Holly didn't see the point in hiding that any longer.

"I know."

Holly tipped her head slightly until it rested against Grace's. This was how it used to be when they were kids. When the entire world was in uproar around them. In the hub were Holly and Grace, clinging to the stability of each other.

Shit, she was tired. Her heavy body melted into the bed. "Was it as bad as I remember, Gracie?"

"It was probably worse," Grace said. She took a deep breath. "The worst days for me were the ones when she couldn't get out of bed."

"Those were bad. I used to think if I was good enough or quiet enough it would make her better." Holly was right back there, the terrified little girl, all over again. "For me, though, the worst days were the high days."

"Yeah." Grace nodded. "It made you hope maybe this time she would be all right."

"He's gone." The words hid in the back of Holly's mind, in the place where she didn't like to wander too often.

Grace patted her hand. "He didn't go far."

"It doesn't matter." The numbness receded and she ached. "Even if I didn't chase him away, I can't be with Josh."

"Only if you tell yourself that," Grace said.

"Oh, come on, Grace." The bitterness crept into Holly's voice. "You tell me what's going to happen to Portia and Emma if I go sailing into the sunset with Josh?"

"I don't know, Holly." Grace sat up again. "I don't know what's going to happen to me, but I do know I can't go on as I was. Something in me has changed, and I can't change it back again."

The fight drained out of Holly and left her feeling like a dried husk. "Same here."

Chapter Thirty

"So, what are we watching?" Holly took a seat beside Portia on the sofa. There was no sign of Emma.

Grace shoved in next to her and Holly inched closer to Portia.

Portia jumped slightly and stared at them. She opened her mouth as if she wanted to say something, shut it, and turned back to the screen with a vague wave of her hand. "I . . . er . . . I don't know. I'm not watching it."

Holly kept her eyes on the screen. Her chest was full of a dull sort of ache. She couldn't get the last image of Josh out of her mind. She had never seen a man stand so openly vulnerable, with his heart in his eyes. He loved her. As incredible and unbelievable as it seemed, Josh Hunter loved Holly Partridge. It should be enough to make them a happy ending.

"Well, we'll not watch it with you." The strain showed in Grace's voice. Playing nice wasn't her thing.

The images flickered in front of Holly.

Portia sat coiled up on the other end of the sofa,

looking like she might spontaneously combust at any moment.

She should ask what was bothering Portia, but she couldn't. The will to open her mouth wasn't there. She was behaving like a sulky child, but for right now, she didn't want anything more to do with Portia and her feelings. Instead, she tried to apply her attention to the drama rolling out on the screen.

"Who's that?" Like she cared about some random beautiful person wearing too much makeup.

"That's Hope." Grace seemed to be making the effort to keep it chirpy. "And the one she's talking to is called Steffy. Hope is leaving town."

Lucky Hope. Holly tried to pick up the thread of the conversation on the screen. It was better than dealing with the dialogue in her head.

Hope's departure seemed important and had a lot to do with Liam. Then Liam came into it as well. Holly couldn't say how. He was a good-looking guy, this Liam, other than the strange goatee thing he had going on. He had nothing on Josh. A huge sigh built up in her chest and she released it.

Grace opened her mouth.

Holly didn't want to talk. Enough was enough, however, and she reached for the remote.

"I know it's not him," Portia said.

"Huh?"

Grace shrugged and looked past her at Portia.

Portia virtually climbed the arm of the sofa in an effort to put distance between them.

Holly turned down the volume and paid better attention. "What did you say?"

Portia's mouth wobbled and her eyes filled with tears. "I know it's not Josh." Her voice was so quiet Grace leaned forward. "You think I don't understand, but I do. I know it's not Josh."

Oh, fuck. Holly's head reeled. It was like a sucker punch straight to the gut. She opened her mouth and a strange strangled sound slid out.

Grace gaped at Portia for a long hard moment. From somewhere Grace dredged up an inside voice. Holly was impressed. She didn't have one of those in her at the moment.

"Yet you told everyone he was your baby's father?" Grace's body vibrated with tension.

The tears spilled over Portia's lids and slid down her face.

Holly watched her sister cry from a distance. There wasn't an ounce of pity in her.

"Josh and Holly love each other and Holly is going to let Josh go because she's worried about you," Grace said.

Thank God Grace still had the mental capacity to pursue this. Holly was floored.

"I know," Portia said in a choked whisper.

"And even when you could have said something, you didn't?" Grace's voice hardened. "You knew Holly and Josh had feelings for each other and you didn't do anything. I don't understand."

Grace was on the attack.

Normally, Holly would strap on her armor and protect Portia. Not tonight. There was nothing Grace said that wasn't the God's honest truth.

"I know." Portia's sweatpants bunched beneath her convulsive clasp. "I'm sorry. I didn't want Holly to have him."

Holly let the information sink in as she sat there.

Portia knew all along. She wasn't delusional. This had nothing to do with her being bipolar. Portia had known and left everyone to flounder around her. It defied understanding. Portia was sick. The excuse suddenly wasn't good enough.

The anger lit a slow burn in Holly's chest.

Portia had started this and then gone and made it worse with her ridiculous accusation. Not happy to let it stop there, she had finished the job with her latest bolt to Melissa's grave.

"Why?" Holly and Grace spoke at the same time.

The question hung there. Holly kept her attention transfixed on Portia and the answer. Every fiber of her being needed to know this.

"I wanted it to be true. I wanted to believe Josh was the father." Portia winced.

"Why?" The word shot out of her mouth in a harsh rasp.

"Because," Portia's breathing hitched like an asthmatic stutter, "he was nice to me. When I first came to Willow Park. I didn't know anybody, and I remembered him from when you were at school together. He was so nice to me."

Portia wiped her cheeks. "I saw him here in Willow Park, like I told Emma. But he didn't recognize me. He said he did, but I could tell he didn't. It was only when I said I was Holly's sister that he remembered. He bought me something to eat and asked about Holly. I wanted to see him again. He said he didn't think it was a good idea."

"You're going to have to give me a bit more." Holly's jaw tightened as she clamped down on the hot angry words threatening to spill out. Her stomach lurched.

"I was scared. And he was like some kind of fairy-tale prince. He was the father I wanted my baby to have. He was the sort of man I always dreamed of having and I wanted it to be real."

"What happened?" Grace took over the questioning.

"I found him at the bar the next night and the next night. He was nice to me."

Josh hadn't shared this part, probably because he had tried to spare her feelings. Holly's chest ache sharpened and twisted. He had been so patient. Portia put him in a crappy position again and again.

"He told me I should go home." Portia sniffed and reached for a Kleenex. "He wasn't unkind, but he wanted me to go home, and I got sad. I got so, so sad."

"And you lied?" Holly barely hung on to the rage. It simmered and spat beneath her skin. Portia had fed them one lie after another and let them grow and grow until the pile toppled over and crushed her and Josh.

"Yes." Portia blew her nose. "And now Holly and Josh are mad at each other and it's my fault."

"You're right." Her voice sounded totally alien. Josh loved her. This amazing, beautiful man loved her and now he was gone. The pain lanced through her. Gone.

Grace gripped Portia's hand. "Part of it is your fault—a big part, and you're going to have to fix that part—but Holly did her share."

Another sucker punch. Grace's betrayal added a fresh sharp pain to the constant ache. Holly opened her mouth and shut it again.

Grace's gaze didn't waver. "You had choices, Holly."

"What should I do?" Portia asked from behind her.

Holly dragged her eyes from Grace.

Portia's eyes were huge and childlike.

Holly wanted to lean over and slap the look off her face. The anger rose up, swift and fierce. She'd been getting the look for years. *What should I do, Holly? Help me, Holly, Make the bad thing go away, Holly.* It was crazy and bizarre and sickeningly familiar. It was like listening to Melissa. It didn't make any sense unless you were sitting right in the eye of the storm and feeling what they were feeling.

"Somewhere your baby has a real father," Grace said.

"Yes." Portia nodded and blew her nose.

"He needs to know, Portia," Grace said. "And he has a right to know. This is his child you're carrying. We're going to need the help financially." Grace pressed her. "And maybe he even wants to be involved."

Portia's bottom lip quivered and she sank her teeth into it. "Maybe."

"No, Portia," Grace said. "There is no maybe about it. The guy needs to know and he deserves to know." Grace frowned. "Portia, do you know who the father is?"

"Yeees."

Grace swore softly.

Holly gave a sharp bark of laughter. It beat the alternative of having a screaming shit fit.

Portia cried, and Grace handed over another Kleenex, and another, before she spoke again. "You tell me what you can remember and I'll see what I can do about finding him."

Holly could barely hear the conversation past the buzzing in her ears.

"I'm scared," Portia whispered. "Gracie, I'm scared."

"Really?" Holly wanted to start laughing again.

Portia was scared?

Holly exploded off the couch. "That's not good enough."

Portia and Grace stared at her.

Holly didn't give a crap. "You're scared and I'm supposed to tell you not to be scared, everything is all right?" Once she opened her mouth, the words wouldn't stop. "Well, it's not all right. You're sick, Portia, and it's not your fault, but you have to quit using your condition as an excuse to do whatever the fuck you want."

"I can't help it." Portia turned huge, pleading eyes on her.

"Yes, you can." Holly was so fucking tired of this. "You can take your medication and you can take responsibility for your condition, instead of waiting for me or Grace or even Emma, for that matter, to do it for you."

"Why is Holly yelling?" Emma's voice reached her, but Holly raged on.

"You had unprotected sex." Holly took a step back before she shook Portia. "You had unprotected sex with some man who you either don't know or won't say. Never mind getting pregnant. What about STDs? The average sixteen-year-old knows better, and you did know better, Portia. You did."

Holly clenched her fists together so hard her fingers ached. "Christ. Even Emma the nun knows better than that."

"Hey." Emma's protest was weak.

Holly swung toward her. "And you?" Some part of her brain tried to tell her to get it together, but the anger roared on and swept caution with it. "You thought it would be a good idea to let her go on some asinine fucking pilgrimage to find Melissa. You have your head stuck so far up your ass it's a wonder you can breathe."

"Holly?" Grace got to her feet. "You need to calm down."

"I need to calm down?" Holly's head reeled. "Is that your opinion? From all the way across the country? You think I should calm down? Tell me." Grace and her self-righteous opinions made Holly sick. "What other words of wisdom do you have to offer from behind those walls you've put up?"

Grace's eyes went hard as steel. "Now you're being a bitch."

"Yes, I'm being a bitch." Holly reveled in the newfound

feeling. "And I like it. You," she turned back to Emma, "need to get a life, and not one I make for you. And you," back to Grace again, "you need to decide, are you in this family or not, because I'm done with this pussyfooting around the outside. And as for you." Holly had to pause as she ran out of air. "You are going to be a mother. Not me, not Emma, and not Grace, but you. You are going to have to step up and take responsibility. I have already raised another woman's children and I'm not doing it again."

All three sisters stared at her with a mixture of shock and resentment.

Grace's nostrils flared like she was ready to wade right in.

Good. Holly welcomed the fight. Disappointingly, Grace got it under control again.

"Man up," Holly snarled at them. "All of you can fucking man up, because I'm done."

Grace wasn't sure whether she wanted to slap Holly silly or applaud her. As tantrums went, it had been rather spectacular.

Absolute silence reigned as Holly stalked away. She stomped up the stairs, and a door slammed and reverberated through the house.

Beside her, Portia jumped.

"Wow." Emma sighed and settled between her and Portia. "That sucked."

It struck a chord through Grace that rang right to the core of her being. And she laughed.

Emma and Portia stared at her with wide eyes, and it made Grace laugh even harder.

"Stop it." Emma glared at her.

"I can't." Man, this was it. She had finally lost her mind. Grace Burrows née Partridge had lost the plot.

"What are we going to do?" Portia wailed.

Grace, barely, managed to get it together again. "We're going to man up."

Wasn't she the one who had been telling Holly that for years?

Portia's eyes were huge in her pale, tearstained face.

Shit. Portia was pathetically childlike, and a fierce wave of protectiveness swept through her. Grace wrapped her arm around Portia's shoulder.

"What if I can't do it?" Portia hiccuped. It was as if a dam had opened, and she cried in earnest now, great big racking sobs that shook her entire frame.

Grace held on tight, handing over the Kleenex and waiting for the storm to pass. Holly had been doing this for years. Respect.

"What if I can't do any of it? Have this baby, be a mother, stay stable enough not to fuck this baby up?"

"Hey." Grace shook Portia's shoulder gently. "There's no need going down that road because you're pretty much past that point." She took a pause and gave Portia a look laden with meaning. "And as soon as this baby is born, you're going back on your medication. You're going to do it for this baby. You're going to take your medication because you know what growing up with Melissa was like and you can do better."

"Okay." Portia shredded her Kleenex and scattered them over the floor.

"Look at these." Grace gently clasped Portia's arms and waggled them in front of her. "Look what I have here. Do you know what I have?"

"My arms?" Tears spiked Portia's lashes together and made her cheeks blotchy. She stared at Grace as if one of them had lost her mind and she wasn't sure which one it was.

"Yes, your arms." Grace nodded and gave them another waggle. She was totally winging it. "Your two strong arms." She wrapped Portia's arms over each other in her lap. "And that is how you're going to do this. With your two strong arms."

Portia blinked her sodden lashes at her, frowned, and turned to study her arms. Then she shook her head, and her hair crowded over her face, clinging to her damp cheeks. "What if they aren't strong enough?"

Grace wiped the hair off her face tenderly. "What if they are?"

Portia drew a shuddering breath.

"And if there are times when they're not, then know there are times when everyone's arms are weak. And look what I have here." Grace waved her own arms in front of Portia's face. "I have another set of arms to help."

"Oh, come on, Grace." Portia managed a small laugh. "I'm not a child anymore."

"No, you're not, and you're in a very adult predicament." This shit was so serious it hurt Grace's head to even think about it. "But these arms will still help you when yours fail, just like when you were a kid. And," she pressed her forehead against her sister's, "I know for a fact Emma has a pair just like them. And when Holly gets over her mad, she isn't going to toss you to the wolves."

"You're such a dope." Portia sniffed.

You have no idea. Grace held back a sigh. "I was thinking—" she kept it calm and controlled—"we might give Holly's arms a rest for a while."

Portia sniffed. "So she can be with Josh?"

"There you go." Grace kept it positive. This was for all of them. "You catch on fast."

"Is Josh completely gone?" Portia asked eventually.

"I don't think so." Grace unwrapped her arms from around her sister. "We might need to give Holly a good shove in his direction, though."

"I don't get it," Emma said.

"Which particular part don't you get?" Grace tried to keep it pleasant, but it came out sounding pissy. She was going to have to do better if she was going to take this challenge on.

"Why Josh left."

"Why do you care?" Grace rolled her eyes. Emma had done everything but push the man out the door. She would be running for her life if she were Josh. "You had a shit fit about Holly and Josh."

"That isn't what we're talking about." Emma gave a regal wave. "And it does nothing to explain why Holly let him go."

"Holly needs to figure that one out." And she would, with a little help from a kick-ass sister.

Emma snorted. "Gee, thanks, Yoda."

Grace shut her mouth and counted to ten. One day at a time. That was how they were going to do this.

Chapter Thirty-One

Holly must have dropped off to sleep because she woke to find it growing dark outside. She'd spent a good part of the day locked in this room, and ping-ponging between righteous indignation and guilt. Nobody had disturbed her, and she liked it that way.

Outside, the long, slow meander into night of a Willow Park twilight lit the sky. Warm air ruffled the drapes in bursts of enthusiasm.

Holly rolled to her feet. She couldn't hide in here forever.

Downstairs, her sisters were preparing supper. They looked up briefly when she came in.

Portia handed her a knife and Holly took over chopping.

They worked in complete silence, but it wasn't uncomfortable, just cautious.

"So," Grace said from the oven, "we were talking."

The smell of roast chicken filled the kitchen, but Holly wasn't hungry.

"Oh?" she feigned polite interest. It was the best she could do; she was wrung out. She'd dreamed of Josh.

Only in her dreams, he was still with her, smiling at her and teasing her out of a mood.

"Yes." Grace turned from the oven. "About the manning-up thing."

Holly's throat jammed up and she kept her eyes on her chopping board. She'd been such a bitch, but she didn't totally regret it. It had been kind of liberating.

Grace pushed a glass of wine in front of her. "I thought I might move to Ontario."

"Really?" Holly's hands shook as she reached for the glass. All of her sisters in one place made her want to run in the other direction.

Grace put the chicken on the counter and took off her oven mitts. "Greg and I are splitting up. There's no reason for me to stay in Boston."

"What about your job?"

"I can get another one." Grace picked up her wine and took a sip. "It's not like I loved it in the first place."

"Yes, you did." Only a small part of Holly was engaged in the conversation. There was nothing but a big black hole where her feelings should be.

"No, I didn't." Grace pulled a face. "It was part of a lifestyle I thought I wanted. Anyway, I have enough saved up, even after Greg and I are . . . over. I can wait to find something else."

"Oh." Holly had sliced an entire cucumber, and they didn't need that much for a salad. She reached for a tomato. "What will you do in Ontario?"

"The first thing is to get Crystal Clear turning a profit." Grace snorted.

"We do fine," Emma said.

"You do not." Grace jammed her hands on her hips. "You piss around and play at being a shopkeeper. Well, you can be sure that's going to change."

"Nobody asked you to interfere." Emma tossed the lettuce she was washing into the sink.

"They didn't need to," Grace said. "We discussed this, remember?"

"Yes, but I didn't think it would mean—"

Grace glared at her.

"Fine, but don't think you're going to start jackbooting all over me." Emma tore the lettuce into shreds.

"Grace won't bully you." Holly didn't know why she bothered. Why didn't she let them have at each other? In future, she would. She stared at the tomato and belatedly started to quarter it.

"Portia can stay with me until the baby is born," Grace said. "And then she's going back on her meds."

"And she'll stay on them," Emma said. "Once the baby comes, we know she's going to have the baby blues, but even once we get through that, she needs to stay on her meds. For the baby."

"Emma and Grace said they'd help me. I'm having an episode right now, but I'll come through this," Portia said. "One day at a time."

"That's great, Portia." What the hell was wrong with her? Portia was voluntarily offering to go back on her medication and stay that way. She was showing signs of being able to take care of her own baby. Holly should be dancing for joy, not sullenly chopping vegetables.

"Portia and the baby can live with me," Emma said from the other side of the table. "Grace and I will never be able to share a house, but Portia and I will be fine."

Grace and Emma in a house together meant blood on the walls.

"And I'll be living nearby," Grace said.

"Carrots." It popped into Holly's head and out her mouth.

All three sisters gaped at her.

"We need carrots." She bent her head to her chopping. Her eyes grew foggy and she couldn't see the board clearly. She'd lose a finger at this rate and she blinked to clear her vision. Something plopped onto the chopping board beside her knife. Where was the water coming from? Another drop hit the chopping board. What the hell was that? She touched the wet spot with the tip of her finger.

The board and knife blurred before her eyes. She tried to blink, but it made it worse. Other droplets joined the first two.

Someone is crying.

Portia took the knife out of her hand and laid it on the chopping board.

"There, there, Holly." She put an arm around Holly's shoulders.

It was her. She was crying, which was impossible because Holly Partridge never cried. That's what she'd told Josh; she never cried. The tears increased their flow down her cheeks. She tried to remember the last time she'd cried and came up blank.

Then the anguish hit her in a roaring, gusting storm of hurt that flooded through her. It swept her up in its path and tossed her along in its current.

Grace joined Portia and Emma stood on her other side.

Holly surrendered. The tears came from a place she'd long since forgotten about. She'd stored them for years, crying on the inside and forcing them back. The dam broke and there was no stopping the flood.

She cried for the lost years and the little girl who grew up too fast. She cried for the days of misery and fear and uncertainty. She cried for the youth gone and the opportunities wasted. Holly cried for the missed chances and the wasted guilt. She cried for the beautiful man who'd said he loved her. Holly cried and then she cried some more.

Clustered around her, Holly's sisters clung to her and kept her afloat as Holly cried her river. They were her life preserver.

When it was done, she was still breathing, wrung out and depleted but standing, and her sisters were standing with her. The one person she wanted wasn't there, however, and it was now her move.

"I think . . ." She gave a huge sniff. Her nose was blocked and her eyes puffy. "I think it doesn't matter what you do."

"Nice." Grace snorted.

It drew a sodden laugh from Holly.

"What I mean is, I think I've been hiding as much as the rest of you, and it's time to stop." She blew her nose on a Kleenex Emma handed her.

"Really? You don't say?" Grace rubbed her back.

"And?" Portia's eyes were hard to meet in their quiet intensity.

"And I think I have a man to go to get."

Emma sniffed. "We're back to that man again, aren't we?"

"You're not back to any man," Grace said over Holly's head. "You need to meet one first."

Through her tears, Holly began to laugh.

Chapter Thirty-Two

Holly used a key she'd found at the house and let herself into the still apartment. Through the windows the glitter of the city lights reflected off Lake Michigan. She crept through the dark like a thief. She'd die if Donna woke up and caught her sneaking around.

She guessed Donna would be in the same room Holly had used when she stayed there. Holly pressed her face through the crack in the door. The faint scent of Donna's perfume lingered in the air.

Nope, not going in there.

She opened Josh's door slowly. She still had no words, only the compelling need to be near him.

He slept spread-eagled across the bed like someone had flung him there. Moonlight gilded his skin and he was breathtakingly beautiful. This man loved her, and Holly still couldn't quite believe it to be true, but she was done quibbling.

She stripped out of her clothes and slid cautiously onto one side of the bed. For once she was glad she was compact, as she found a small space for her body under his outflung arm and above one of his legs. Slowly, she eased a pillow under her head and then, as slowly, got the sheet up to her waist. The smell of Josh surrounded her like a blessing, and Holly lay perfectly still for a moment and absorbed it.

He groaned softly in his sleep and moved.

Holly held her breath.

He rolled onto his side. Suddenly, he flung one arm over her waist and hauled her tight against him, her bottom cradled by his hips. His breathing was deep and even, as if he were still sleeping.

Holly stayed as still as she could.

His breath tickled the back of her neck and his body bracketed her from neck to toes. The warmth of him crept through her muscles inch by inch until she relaxed and melted against him. From this position, the world seemed much less harsh and daunting.

"What took you so long?" His rough murmur startled her.

"Just stubborn, I guess."

"Hmph!" His breathing returned to the deep rhythms of sleep.

Holly's eyes drifted shut as she relaxed and gave herself over to the safety and comfort of his embrace.

I love you. Holly tried the words in her own head and they fit. She whispered them softly into the night. "I love you."

"That's convenient," he huffed against her neck, "because I love you, too. Now go to sleep; got a race in the morning. Got to be faster than Richard."

Holly entered the kitchen cautiously.

Donna nodded a pleasant enough greeting, but Holly's every instinct warned her to tread warily around the older woman. She slid up to the counter and out of the way.

"Coffee?" Donna's eyes were lighter than Josh's, less indigo and more arctic.

Of course the deep freeze could have absolutely nothing to do with her physiognomy and much more with recent events. "Yes, please."

She moved forward to fetch a cup from the cupboard behind the coffeemaker.

Donna moved at the same time, and they narrowly avoided a collision in front of the dispassionate glare of the stainless-steel Saeco.

Holly backed off first. "Sorry."

Donna nodded and grabbed a cup. She expertly twisted dials and knobs until the aromatic bite of fresh-brewed beans hit the air. The machine gurgled and burped happily into her cup.

"Cream? Milk?"

"Cream, please."

"Sugar?"

"No, thank you."

Donna doctored the cup with the efficiency of long practice and slid it across the granite toward her.

"Thank you." Holly pulled it closer.

The silence shrieked around them, and Holly took a careful swallow of her coffee. She almost burned her throat trying not to fill the silence with something like a slurp or a loud swallow.

"How is it?"

"Great." Did she have to sound so bloody enthusiastic? A little over the top for a morning cup of coffee, but it would have been perfect if they'd been discussing, say, a cease-fire in the Middle East. Holly had a whole new appreciation for the tired old journalistic workhorse: *the situation is poised on a knife's edge.* There they were, two women, both of them loving the same man— *poised on a knife's edge.* It sounded rather depressingly apt.

Donna stood in front of the fridge and surveyed the contents. "Are you hungry?"

"No." Enough was enough, and Holly took a bracing sip of coffee. Cowering here under the displeasure of the woman who might or might not be playing a significant role in the rest of her life wasn't going to fly—unless of course Josh could be made to see the expediency of shallow graves.

"No, thank you." She eased back on the throttle. All indications were Josh adored his mother.

In for a penny, in for a pound. Poised on a knife's edge.

"You don't like me very much." Holly lobbed her first grenade and braced for the explosions.

"I don't know you well enough to say," Donna counterattacked with a swift and lethal passive-aggressive strike. She turned to look at Holly, her face stony. "But you're right," she said suddenly. "Given the way my son is suffering at the moment, I don't like you very much."

Who was the idiot who said honesty was the best policy? Holly took a deep breath and blew it out slowly. "Fair enough."

"I'm a mother." Donna turned back to the fridge. "Someone hurts my child and I get feral. I know you understand."

And she did. Holly nodded. Not all mothers gave birth to their charges. Some fostered someone else's offspring.

"The thing is . . ." Holly wasn't entirely sure why she was bothering to explain this, but she wanted the other woman to understand. "I'm not very good with this sort of thing."

Donna raised an eyebrow in question.

"The relationship thing." Oh, hell, she sounded like

an idiot. "I get frightened, and it doesn't always bring out the best in me."

"Relationships are scary." Donna pulled out a carton of eggs. "We put ourselves on the line for them and we are all frightened of being hurt."

"True." Josh had said much the same thing. "But some of us aren't as brave as others."

"Some of us have a good reason for being cautious." A flicker of something that was nearly a smile touched one corner of Donna's mouth. "But that's not an excuse, merely an explanation."

"Right you are." Talk about a tough room. "I'll try to do better."

"Try hard." Donna glared at her.

"Will do." Josh's mother could scare the pants off anyone.

Donna took the eggs out and laid them on the counter. She dug through drawers until she found a pan. "I was going to meet Josh at the finish line later today." She cracked the eggs into a bowl.

His triathlon. Holly hadn't given it a thought when she'd crawled into his bed last night. *Selfish. Selfish.* Clearly, Donna was right. She had some serious ground to cover before she got any good at this relationship thing. "I should have waited until it was over."

Amazingly, Donna didn't react, which proved she was either warming up to her or Donna had decided she couldn't get much lower and had zero expectations. Not a cheery thought.

"Would you like to come with me?"

"Yes, I would." It was so unexpected, Holly's mouth dropped open and she blinked at Donna stupidly for a long moment. "I would like that very much."

"And Joshua would love it." Donna heaved a huge sigh that seemed to come from the depths of her being.

So. They weren't exactly soul sisters, and Donna wasn't delighted about the situation, but it was something. And, there were way too many eggs in the bowl for one person. Things were looking up already.

Josh could honestly say the best part of completing an Ironman was when you stopped moving. The swim went well, the cycle was exhausting, and the marathon was nothing short of mind over very, very sore matter.

He sat in the competitor's tent and looked at the other exhausted bodies around him.

Richard came in with Lucy tripping along beside him, looking like an advertisement for fertility.

Even in a tent full of exhausted, aching men, heads jerked and turned. Some could only move their eyeballs, but they moved.

Cocaine, Richard had once called his wife, cocaine for straight men.

"How you doing?" Richard clapped a firm hand on his shoulder.

Josh grinned weakly. "I don't think they work anymore." He twitched a finger in the direction of his legs. Nothing else could or would move.

Richard smiled and squeezed his shoulder. "Did you get your time?"

"Nope." Josh shook his head. He didn't even have it in him to give a shit. "All I registered was 'finished.'"

"Well, then, allow me to be the first to tell you that you did it in ten hours and sixteen minutes."

Josh threw himself back in his chair and sucked at an energy drink. "Great."

"You beat my time by forty minutes." Richard gave him a broad, happy grin.

"Whoopee." Josh worked on the straw as if his life depended on it. Sweet electrolytes burst over his tongue and down his sandpapered throat. "Did you bring any drugs?"

There had to be advantages to having a doctor for a brother.

"Sorry, bud." Richard shook his head. "But I'm not on duty here. Besides which, it's frowned upon when we doctors whip out needles and start jabbing people indiscriminately."

"Even family?"

"Even family."

"I'm not too proud to beg."

Richard laughed and crouched down beside his chair. "Well done, Josh. Fantastic effort." And he meant it.

Josh smiled back, warmed by his brother's praise.

Richard grinned. "You looked powerful right to the end."

"Powerful?" He'd settle for anything better than pathetic.

"All sexy, sweaty stud," Lucy said.

His fellow competitors stirred into life.

Lucy gave him her beautiful smile. "There's a surprise waiting for you outside."

Josh didn't want any surprises, wonderful or otherwise. He wanted to go home and crawl into bed and have Holly crawl in beside him until the hurting stopped. Just like she had last night. He'd been sleeping, all the time feeling like a part of him was missing, and then there she was. Slipping in next to him with her own unique brand of *everything's going to be all right; just let me finish extracting this tooth.*

The tiredness went way deeper than his muscles. "Let's go home."

"You don't want to stay for the event afterward?"

"Hell no." Josh rocked his weight forward and stopped. "You're going to have to help me up." He glared balefully at his brother, daring Richard to make some smart-ass comment.

Richard hauled him to his feet.

Josh had never fully appreciated the mechanics involved in taking a step, the collection of muscles that would need to contract into action. Now that every one of those muscles ached, he understood very clearly what was involved in moving one step forward.

Richard chuckled softly and took his elbow in a light clasp. "You might want to man up here a little," he said, softly enough for only Josh to hear. "Your lady is outside."

"Holly's here?" Josh had the ridiculous urge to cry.

"Yup." Richard nodded calmly. "She came with Ma earlier this morning. They've been here most of the day."

Josh closed his eyes to bring back the sweet feel of Holly in his arms. Her even sweeter words of love and, as suddenly, adrenaline pumped through his muscles and he walked. Well, more of a hobble, but at least he was mobile.

And there she was, and it was better than a shot of anti-inflammatory straight into the thigh.

She stood beside his mother, shorter even than Donna, dressed like a bag lady with her wild, wild hair making a break for freedom any place it could. Her T-shirt was at least three sizes too big and probably a Walmart reject, her cargo shorts were straight from the Sears boys' department—and she was perfect.

Holly Partridge, the most beautiful girl in the world, saw him coming and sent him a smile so sweet and full of apprehension that he melted. One look and he was putty in her managing little hands.

"Hey, pretty boy." She beamed up at him. "You were amazing."

He beamed back at her. She was right, he was. Abso-fucking-lutely amazing, a magnificent pagan god, a colossus among men, and, most of all, the man who got to take Holly Partridge home.

He tugged her closer to his side. "Are you impressed?"

She didn't seem to mind he was sweaty and filthy. She snuggled up beside him and tipped her pretty face up to him. Her mane tangled over his hands and tickled the skin of his forearms and he threaded his fingers through it—just because he could.

"You did great." She tapped his chest possessively. "It was rather gladiatorial and primal."

He grinned like an idiot. "That's good, right?"

"Sure." She grinned back. "If you're looking for the mate who will pass on the strongest DNA."

"So." Josh's eyes gleamed down at her. "Am I your chosen sperm donor?"

"Gross." Lucy poked him in the back. "As lines go, Josh . . . ergh." She made a few retching noises.

"Yes." Donna reached over from his free side and kissed him on the cheek. "You might want to remember your mother is present." She patted his cheek gently. *Formidable, mon fils.*

"Where's the rest of your tribe?" Josh asked as they hobbled toward the car.

"Grace has them under her thumb." Holly opened the door for him.

He clambered in with the grace and dexterity of a rhinoceros.

Donna drove and Holly helped him into the back and rode shotgun.

"And what will happen to them now?" Donna asked.

Here it came. Josh tensed.

Holly merely shrugged and threw him a soft smile over her shoulder. "That depends on what happens when Josh and I sit down to talk."

Chapter Thirty-Three

Josh felt no pain. A hot bath, a couple of magic tablets left for him by his brother, and peace and love reigned. And a sweet Holly was pure honey.

She seated him comfortably on his bed and poured him a very fine glass of red wine.

The rest of the house was silent. The other sisters were off doing something.

Josh didn't ask any questions, too scared he'd jinx the thing. Tonight he had Holly all to himself, and life couldn't get much better.

A surprise she'd promised him in her raspy voice with a glint in her eye had made him hard just thinking about it.

Candles lit the room, their bodies glowing warm amber and honey as they perfumed the air. The light flickered in golden silhouettes against the wall.

A voice ululated gently against a soft, throbbing beat. An *arghul* lifted its reedy voice across the bass throb and sent tendrils of haunting sound drifting through the incensed air.

His exhausted brain had to be making this shit up.

Holly floated in with the melody stroked across the strings of a *kanoun*. But Holly as he'd never seen her, wrapped in gauze, her hair hung in loose waves to the curve of her waist.

He almost asked her what she was doing, but she began to dance.

Josh swallowed his tongue.

Her body inhabited the sensual rhythms of the belly dance, undulating and wrapping the silken skeins of seduction around him.

His gaze stuck. A part of him wanted to laugh, it was so unbelievable, but the larger part stared in silent amazement.

Light and shadow caressed the curves and crevices of her body, shifted and settled and shifted again as she moved.

The music pulsed within the room like a heartbeat, and Holly moved through and with it. The candles gilded her skin to molten gold as she moved. Tiny bells tinkled from her ankles and wrists and coins shimmered as they moved against the skin of her belly. Their sound hit the air in a sweet susurration, weaving a spell around him.

The scent of jasmine lay heavy and teased him with possibilities.

Holly wove and twisted wraithlike through the flickering light. The soft clash of the coins dancing across her belly and the slow, dreamy float of gauze through the air held him captive.

His lids dropped, and he forced them open, but they went right back down. The perfumed air coddled him in a warm embrace as the music settled into the slow beat of his heart.

Josh's eyelids flickered. He'd swum over two miles,

followed by a hundred-and-twelve-mile bike ride and, finally, run a full twenty-six-mile marathon. He jerked his eyes open and fixed his gaze on the fascinating woman who moved like a sensual mist through the laden atmosphere.

Maybe if he rested his eyes for a moment . . .

Holly paused to look at Josh. Her mouth dropped open with a huff of surprise.

He was fast asleep. Not dozing, but man-down, out-for-the-count asleep. His head had dropped to the side and his mouth hung open, noisily hissing air down his throat.

For a moment Holly considered stuffing her gauze scarf down his open maw, but her better nature won out. She'd had big plans for tonight. She'd been belly dancing for eight years now, but this was the first time she'd ever done it for someone. It was the first time she'd ever told a man she loved him. Leave it to Josh to disrupt her best-laid plans. Lucy had helped her set the whole thing up, even found the outfit for her. The other woman was going to have to wait on the details. Actually, Lucy was going to die laughing.

A snore sawed through the air, and Holly laughed.

She approached the bed slowly, her bells clinking softly as she walked.

His breathing came deep and even. Even with his mouth hanging open, Josh Hunter was every girl's dearest wish.

And this beautiful man was hers.

A secret thrill chased down her spine.

He loved her. God knows why and quite possibly he

really needed to get out more, but he loved her. She would never get tired of knowing that.

Quietly, she moved about the room, snuffing candles as she went.

Josh blinked his eyes open to discover morning. He shut his eyes and opened them again, just to make sure. The last thing he remembered was Holly and the belly dancing; he'd shut his eyes for a moment and—

Oh, fuck.

Two things hit him simultaneously, both of them with the approximate force of a Mack truck. Jesus, he'd screwed up with Holly. The second thing sent him reeling back onto the mattress again, as he paid the price for an Ironman time of ten hours and sixteen minutes.

Every single muscle in his body ached. At. The. Same. Time. It even hurt to blink. He lay there and whimpered at the effort it took to pull air into his lungs. The door opened, and he manfully bit back a monster groan and struggled into a sitting position.

"Good morning." Holly smiled at him.

It was the sweetest, loveliest smile she'd ever given him. A warning niggled in the back of his brain and then went silent.

She carried a tray with a glass of orange juice and the bottle of magic Richard had left behind. And—thank you, Lord—a cup of espresso.

"Good morning." His voice came out in a god-awful croak.

"Richard thought you might be feeling a bit rough this morning."

"I'm sorry, Holly." Best to get the groveling over quickly.

She gave him another sunny smile. "What would you like first, juice or ibuprofen or both together?"

"Now I'm sure I love you." His eyes fixed on the little blue pills and stayed stuck.

"You have to get out of bed to get them." She grimaced sympathetically. "Richard said to get you up and moving."

Josh nearly let the pills go, but in the end he managed to heave himself, hissing, groaning, and moaning like an old truck going uphill all the way. She didn't seem to mind his nakedness, so he didn't do anything about it.

In fact, she looked at him like he was walking chocolate. Apparently there were a few muscles not too sore this morning.

Her eyes widened appreciatively and she gave him a smile laden with promise.

He swallowed two of the pills and drank the juice in one long gulp.

Holly took the glass from him and handed him his espresso. She put the glass down and sashayed back to him. "There was something I didn't get to last night."

She came up behind him and pressed her breasts against his back. Her hands slid around his waist and spread over the ridges of his abdomen.

Josh's pain melted away as she planted hot little kisses across his shoulders. Her teeth against his shoulder bit hard enough to get his attention but not cause any real discomfort.

"You are a very beautiful man." Her fingers trailed across his abdomen and left little trails of heat in their wake. She moved around to the front of him and pressed her nose against the skin of his neck and breathed.

Screw Richard's pills, this was what he needed.

"You smell wonderful." Her mouth replaced her nose and she sucked gently. "Just like my man." She bit him and then licked the mark to take away any sting. Her hands drifted over his chest, grazed his nipples, and moved lower to stroke the arrow of hair from his navel.

Her soft hands grasped his cock. Heat shot through him. It got better as she stroked her hands up and down his length. Her other hand cupped his balls in a firm grasp.

Slowly, without taking her eyes off his, she sunk to her knees in front of him.

Josh stilled.

She dragged her mouth in a slow, sliding caress down the skin of his chest and then his abdomen as she went. Her mouth was wet and hot, and the soft rasp of her teeth was sweet, sweet torture on his sensitive skin.

She stopped level with his cock. It jumped in her hands and strained toward what he wanted.

Josh forgot to breathe.

She dipped her head. Her hot pink tongue shot out and licked the tip.

He groaned as she blew against the moisture, his hands so tight around the espresso cup it might shatter.

She palmed him firmly and guided her mouth over him.

Josh hissed and tensed as the searing heat of her mouth opened over his erection. Jesus, he was in heaven as she sucked him deeper into the hot, wet cavity of her mouth.

She took him deep and then withdrew, her tongue making lazy circles over the sensitive tip.

As she took him even deeper, his eyes rolled back in their sockets. Her mouth was a thing of glory, wet and scorching as she worked the length of him in and out. Her other hand cupped his balls as her tongue stroked him.

"Holly, baby." He hung on by a thread. "I'm going to come if you keep that up."

He tried to grip her head to stop her, but she moved faster, and his fingers tangled in her hair and kept her where she was.

His orgasm built from the very end of his toes.

Her mouth disappeared.

She rocked back on her heels, her beautiful face alight with trouble. Josh reached for her, but she dodged quickly out of his hands.

"There's a good boy." She stood and gave him a swat on his bare ass. "Payback's a bitch, isn't it? Don't fall asleep on me again."

She sashayed through the door and shut it behind her. She'd left him here with his balls ready to burst and she wasn't coming back.

Ah, hell no.

Josh flung the bedroom door open and charged down the stairs. Into the kitchen he stormed.

The sisters, clustered around the table, stopped and stared. They took one look at him and scattered, clucking and squawking like hens in battery cages.

Josh tried to cover himself with his hands, his face so hot it was ready to spontaneously combust.

And then he got a look at Holly.

Her dark eyes glinted, evil with mischief and ripe with the challenge.

He reached her in two easy strides.

"You're naked," shrieked one of the sisters, probably St. Emma.

"It's my house." He didn't give a shit as he locked in on his target. "Look away if you don't like it."

Emma was already doing so and Portia stood like a

deer in the headlights, while Grace crossed her arms and grinned at him.

He dipped his shoulder and hauled Holly up and over.

She gasped and laughed through a protest. "It was payback." She wriggled like a trout on the hook. "For falling asleep on me."

"It's about time you learned who's in charge here." He jostled her on his shoulder and strode up the stairs. He was breathing fast by the time he reached the bedroom. He slammed the door shut with his foot and dropped his flushed, laughing bundle onto the bed. He came down on top of her before she could move.

"Stop." She giggled and tried to fend him off with her hands.

Josh grabbed both tiny fists in one of his and held them over her head. "No way." He loved the way she squirmed and wriggled beneath him. "We're just getting started."

"I can't believe you charged into the kitchen naked." She collapsed into a jellied mass of spluttering, snorting laughter. "You should have seen the look on Emma's face." That brought about fresh peals of laughter.

"Hey," he said in protest as her body shook with laughter beneath him. "Pay attention here; you're about to be ravished."

"Ravished? Who says 'ravished'?"

"Fucked senseless?"

She went still under the profanity. Heat replaced the amusement in her eyes.

"So?" *Gotcha!* "Holly likes it when I talk dirty."

She wriggled beneath him, pushing against him impatiently with her hips. "You might have to practice a bit to make sure."

He got down to the matter at hand. "I have the rest of my life, Holly."

Epilogue

Josh heaved a sigh of relief as the taillights of Grace's SUV disappeared around the corner. Grace and the twins were on their way back to London, Ontario. Holly, his Holly, was still here, tucked under his arm and waving her sisters good-bye.

Grace would stay with Portia until the baby was born.

Emma had received the news with trepidation. Tough shit, Emma, because Grace had turned her formidable energy in the twins' direction.

Josh suspected their lives were never going to be the same.

Holly had loose plans to stay here in Willow Park with him for a while longer and then go home. Then they would take it as it came. London was less than a day away, unless Emma was driving, and there were lots of reasons to stay in Willow Park. Josh was working on one more.

"You should marry me, you know?" He pulled her body in front of him and cradled her from behind.

Holly snorted rudely. "Why would I do that?"

"At the very least, you would get a good wardrobe out of it."

"You aren't going to go Pygmalion on me, are you?"

She nestled under his chin like a small bird going to roost. "Because I'll fight you."

"I expected no less." He leaned his cheek on her head. She was exactly where she belonged and where he needed her the most. "But you know you looked good in those shorts."

"What crap."

It was still early in the morning and the neighborhood lay peaceful around them.

In a moment they would go inside and she'd get him to make her a cup of coffee, but for now they stood still and listened to the stirring of things in the trees and grass.

His!

His arm tightened around her middle. "Those jeans will meet with an unfortunate laundry accident."

"Stop trying to change me," she growled.

Josh hummed a few bars of Billy Joel before he got an elbow in the gut. "You know," he said to the top of her head, "they're going to kick you out of the US if you don't marry me eventually." He wasn't too proud to use every weapon in his arsenal.

"I know that." She laughed softly and wriggled in his hold.

Josh loosened his arms enough for her to turn to face him.

"Are you sure your mother isn't going to come to live here?"

"Trust me." The only person who wanted that less than Holly was his mother. "My mother has been trying to get her hands on my condo since I bought it. The trouble will be getting her out of it." Not a total lie, and they had time to work on the rest.

"Are you going to get a job or something?" She narrowed her eyes up at him.

"Or something." He grinned back unrepentantly. "Sooner or later something new will grab my attention and then I'll do that. You worried I won't be able to support you while you go back to school?"

"No." She shook her head. "I'm worried you're going to be under my feet."

"*Cherie,*" he whispered next to her ear. "It's not your feet I want to be under."

"Don't even try with the French. I know for a fact you only know enough to get a woman into bed."

"Doesn't do it for you, hmm?" He pulled away from her slightly and grinned. "Then how about I promise to fuck you hard and fast—"

"Get your pretty boy ass into the house right now, mister. Don't make me embarrass you in front of your neighbors."

Keep reading for an excerpt from

NOBODY'S PRINCESS,

the next Willow Park Romance
from
Sarah Hegger,
on sale in March 2016!

And don't miss

NOBODY'S ANGEL,

available now.

Tiffany needed a man, about six two with blond hair and a tan. Right now, or life as she knew it was over. *Teeny* exaggeration but she was desperate and one man, how hard could that be? It wasn't as if she needed anything unusual. One white male, twentysomething, handsome, light-eyed, and ripped and cut like every girl's dirty dream.

In Chicago, a city of a shade over 2.7 million people, forty-eight percent of them male, and thirty-one percent of them white. Of course, to accurately calculate the chances she'd need to break that down into how many of the male residents were white and between the ages of twenty-five and thirty-five. If she could get five seconds to write this all down in her book, she could do it.

"Did you get hold of the casting agent?" Piers fussed with his camera, his face already the telltale pink prefacing a meltdown. Dear God, not that. Piers could throw a time-chewing tantrum to rival a toddler. Time was not her friend today. Where the hell was her white male?

"No." Tiffany snapped her book shut and hit redial. She kept Piers in sight in her peripheral vision. *Please, let the woman be there.* Piers was going nuclear any second now. If Piers lost it, the shoot would run over. Her new life started in a little under three hours and she couldn't be late for that.

"Hi, you've reached the voice mail o—"

"Shit." Tiffany ended the call. She refused to let this stop her. If necessary, she'd march outside and drag the next blond man in here, but she was going on her date. Tonight. "I'll keep trying." She smiled apologetically at Piers. As if that would stop a meltdown. *Not.* "Okay, let's get the rest of you ready."

It was so unfair, she had all the other models—Asian, Black, Hispanic, Indian—and Franco, who was Italian, but had the bone structure and sleek, long hair to pass for Native American. Tiffany wasn't sure his real name was Franco. Maybe he wasn't even Italian.

"Tiffany?" Piers tapped his foot impatiently.

She spun toward the cluster of hotness lounging about, looking effortlessly gorgeous. Except that much perfect took serious work. The fresh bagels she'd fetched this morning lay untouched—two hundred and fifty calories per bagel, another fifty for the cream cheese. She moved the bagel plate to the other side of a dish of strawberries. One dish aligned to the right of the cream cheese, another to the left. She snatched up a strawberry and popped it in her mouth. Four calories. You had to love numbers.

The models shifted to their feet in a tidal wave of undulating muscle. Pumped up, made up and ready to shoot. Six two, six four, six one—no, the order didn't work for her. Tallest to shortest or the other way around would be better. Maybe even tallest in the middle and descending in height order on either side. If Piers ever asked her opinion, she would tell him so. This was not her job, however. Her job was gofer, as in go for this and go for that. Shut your mouth, do as you're told, and show up looking fabulous. She took a deep breath. Two hours and fifty-five minutes to the launch of New Tiffany.

"Give me beautiful, darlings." Piers glanced up from his camera. "Get me that casting agent," he yelled at her. "And for Christ's sake get them oiled down." Piers winked at the models. Flirting with the "meat" his soul prerogative. "I need muscle. Big, shiny, I want to lick it, muscle."

Didn't they all? Tiffany patted the side pocket of her Dolce & Gabbana tote, reassured by the feel of her notebook in the side pocket. Daddy always made sure she had the best of the best.

"A Princess always looks the part."

She hit redial with one hand and grabbed the bottle of body oil with the other. God, she'd stroked more abs than any girl could fantasize about. Pretty much her only job perk. Six models each with a six-pack, did that make it thirty-six abs or eighteen? It would depend on whether you considered one ridge of muscle as consisting of two separate . . .

"Lower," Franco purred in her ear.

"Oh, puh-lease." Tyrone grabbed the bottle from her and oiled himself. "There's nothing down there, sister." He rolled his eyes at Tiffany dramatically. "And, believe me, I've looked. Now, if you really want to—"

She slapped a handful of oil onto the nearest corrugated stomach. Her gaze drifted to the hot-pink corner of her book peeking over the edge of the tote, the abs calculation forming in her head. She needed to write it down before she forgot. A tiny moment of sanity hovered, right there between those special pages. Later.

"Time?" Piers shouted.

Tiffany checked her phone. *Shit.* "Two forty," she called back and braced for impact.

"Christ on a stick, Tiffany." Piers started his meltdown.

Tiffany counted slowly backward. *Five, four, three, two, one and*—"Fucking twenty to fucking two. Shit. Fuck. Bum. Bugger. Willy. Dick."

The models suppressed a snicker or two. They couldn't help it. With his British accent, it never sounded that bad when Piers swore. It sounded sort of cute. The cuteness wore off fast, and after seven years of working for Piers it wasn't even mildly amusing.

"Get that silly cunt from casting on the motherfucking phone and ask her where my fucking white boy is. Tell her to get his pale arse down here or he will never work in this motherfucking cesspit of a fucking, fuck nose shitting town again."

"Impressive," one of the models murmured beneath his breath. This must be his first Piers shoot.

"He's just getting started." Tiffany grabbed the oil and smeared. The waves of rage emanating from Piers almost made her hands shake. She tried the casting agent again. Shit, she had only booked the studio for another two hours and fifty minutes. Her schedule was sliding straight into the toilet.

"Adjust the package on . . ." Piers clicked his fingers as he came up blank on the name. "Um . . . number two."

"Tyrone," number two helpfully supplied.

Heat crawled over Tiffany's face. Her gaze dropped automatically to the bulge of Tyrone's crotch. Tyrone spread his arms out and grinned. "Go ahead."

Sinfully beautiful, and Tyrone knew it. She couldn't resist grinning right back. Such a pity he was gay. And she was in a steady relationship with the most wonderful man. In. The. World. Everybody said so. Ryan was perfect. Maybe not exciting, but she'd had exciting and look how that had ended up? Disaster. No, Ryan was the one for her. No more wild, crazy rides. Her phone buzzed in her hand. "Is that the casting agent?" Piers demanded.

"No." Tiffany glared as Lola's name lit up her screen.
The woman's timing couldn't suck more. As much as she
needed to speak to Lola—and she really, really needed
to speak to her—she didn't want to answer the call now.
Five days she'd waited for Lola to call back. Of course,
Lola pretty much ignored every call she didn't feel like
taking. Conversely, when Lola wanted to speak to you,
she wanted it now and would blow up your phone until
she got hold of you.

She hit IGNORE and slipped the phone into her pocket.
Why today of all days? It must be some kind of cosmic
joke. Could you calculate coincidence? You must be able
to. Nearly everything broke down to numbers in the
end. Her gaze strayed toward the tote again. Her book
seemed to shimmer and pulse for attention. Perhaps she
could just quickly . . .

"Hi, I'm looking for Tiffany?" A deep voice spoke from
behind her.

Tiffany whirled on her four-inch heels and looked up.
And up some more. *Oh, thank you, sweet Jesus.* Her white
boy was here and he was totally gorgeous. His blond hair
was cropped close to his scalp. It brought all your attention straight to that face. And what a face. You could
break rocks on that jawline. The straight blade of his
nose rescued him from pretty, but the mouth beneath it
curved full and etched, made for nibbling on.

Tiffany did a quick, happy two-step. He even had
beautiful blue eyes. He might be a shade on the tall side,
but they could fake that a bit. Not as young as she'd first
thought, but makeup would fix that. Two vertical lines
between his eyebrows gave off a sort of "don't mess with
me" vibe. She beamed at him. "You're perfect."

He raised an eyebrow, and returned her smile cautiously.

Oh, yes, yes, yes. He had one of those smiles, all innocent on the outside until you looked into those bad boy

eyes. Scrap the Botox, those laugh lines were totally dreamy. So unfair, men got yummier-looking as they aged. She did a quick body scan. *Nice. Very nice.* If he looked as good out of that tight T-shirt as he did in it. Seriously, where had this boy been hiding himself?

Tiffany patted the sort of forearm that could be best friends with a jackhammer, and mentally forgave the casting agent. "Okay." She stretched her fingers to capacity to grip his arm. Wow! And this from a girl who worked with wow every day. "We are going to have to hurry. Strip and let's get you all pumped up."

"Where the hell have you been?" Piers snarled. "Your call time was one thirty."

Blondie opened his mouth to reply. Tiffany spun him toward makeup. It did no good to argue with Piers when he was on a tear. A waste of time they didn't have. Things were turning around. The white boy was here, and he was smoking hot. The shoot would finish on time, and then she could deal with Lola. And still have time to prepare herself for *the night.*

Blondie stood there giving the other models a thorough eye scan. Gay. What a shame.

She shook her head at herself. What did it matter? She was practically an engaged woman.

Blondie hovered at her side.

Tiffany rolled her eyes. Clichés sucked, but some of these boys had no brain between all that brawn. Hooking her hands beneath the hem of his T-shirt, she tugged. "You have to take this off for makeup."

"Are you taking my clothes off?" Blondie folded his huge paws around hers and stopped her. He had a great voice, like hot chocolate laced with rum. The sort of voice that would do great bedtime stories.

She hauled back on her thought path. "You have to strip."

He looked right at her. Not past her or around her, but right at her as if he wanted to see straight into the center of her. A snap of something she didn't want to put a name to crackled through the space between them. A shiver snaked down her spine, but she didn't seem able to break his eye lock.

"Strip?" Up went one eyebrow.

Sweat prickled her palms. Her hands were still fisted around his shirt, exposing about two inches of stomach. He had a garden path trail of hair disappearing below the low-slung waist of his jeans. That would have to go. Pity. Tiffany dragged her stare off his navel and focused on the writing on the front of his T-shirt. It read: NEVER TRUST AN ATOM—THEY MAKE UP EVERYTHING.

Cool shirt. She and Blondie were probably the only two people in the world who thought it was funny. The shirt needed to come off and now, before Piers went into orbit. "Yes, strip."

She pulled at the shirt and his hands tightened over hers. Tiffany glared up at him. An attack of modesty? Unbelievable. Did he think he would be modeling undershirts and long johns? "You have to take it all off."

"Normally I get dinner first." Those bad boy eyes danced at her, inviting her to share the joke. For a second, she badly wanted to.

"Tiffany, sweetie." Tyrone appeared beside her. "That's not your model."

"What?" Tiffany stared at Blondie. Of course he was her model because otherwise she was stripping . . . a whimper caught in her throat.

He looked back at her.

Tyrone took her by the shoulders and spun her around. "That's your model."

He pointed to a beautiful Rocky (as in the Picture Show, not Sly) lookalike talking earnestly to Piers. Piers lapped it up. Waving one hand through the air and patting the pretty, blond boy on the arm.

"I . . ." Tiffany peered over her shoulder. Please let the last two minutes be a figment of her imagination. Her figment grinned at her and tucked his hands into his back pockets.

"Tiffany," Piers bellowed. "Get Mark into makeup. And get him a cup of coffee. The poor boy has had a horrible day."

"I'm so sorry I'm late." Mark approached her, his big blue eyes awash with apology. "I'm new in town and I got lost."

"Sister," Tyrone cut across him. "Save it for the preacher and get your ass all prettied up. We are not getting any younger over here."

"Yes, of course." Mark scurried over to makeup, leaving Tiffany standing with Blondie.

"Well." She hoped she wasn't blushing as much as she thought she was. A red face would seriously clash with her hot-pink top. "I thought you were one of the models."

"Thank you, I think." His voice held enough of a laugh for Tiffany to see the funny side. The corners of her mouth tilted up.

"Tiffany," Piers demanded from across the room. "Do we like the color of these?" Piers waved his hand over a pair of briefs and frowned.

No, no, no, no, no. And just when things were looking up. Thank God she'd had the foresight to pack different colors. "You don't like them?"

"It's just . . ." Piers plucked at his bottom lip, thrust one hip out, and stared down at the models' skimpy underwear. "He has this lovely skin and I don't think these do anything for it."

Tiffany clenched her belly in protest. Piers looked ready to take one of his stands. This would throw her whole schedule off. There wasn't enough of those briefs for anyone to give a shit about the color. And the model wearing them had an honest-to-God eight-pack, all carved out of his deep chocolate skin. She went with the tried-and-true response, guaranteed to win the argument. "That's the color the client wanted."

Tiffany held her breath as Piers glared at the yellow briefs. *Take the shot, Piers. Please, please, please, take the shot.*

"I don't know why I must always work with people who have such fetid taste." Piers stalked over to his camera. Tiffany let her breath out.

"I wouldn't wear yellow underpants if you paid me." Blondie's heavy baritone stroked her eardrums. His voice sent goose bumps frog-marching up and down her spine.

"Well, we're paying him." She turned to frown at him. "If you're not a model, then what are you doing here?"

"Looking for you."

Goddamn it. Her phone slipped out of her hand. Blondie caught it in one paw.

"Do I know you?" Tiffany snatched her phone back and tried to do the same with her dignity.

"Nope." He shook his head slowly. "We've never met. But I know *of* you. I'm a friend of your husband. Lola told me where to find you."

"What?"

"I'm a friend of Luke's. Your husband?"

That's what she thought he said. Her heart skipped a beat. "Ah, fuck!"

GREAT BOOKS, GREAT SAVINGS!

When You Visit Our Website:
www.kensingtonbooks.com
You Can Save Money Off The Retail Price
Of Any Book You Purchase!

- All Your Favorite Kensington Authors
- New Releases & Timeless Classics
- Overnight Shipping Available
- eBooks Available For Many Titles
- All Major Credit Cards Accepted

Visit Us Today To Start Saving!
www.kensingtonbooks.com

All Orders Are Subject To Availability.
Shipping and Handling Charges Apply.
Offers and Prices Subject To Change Without Notice.

Books by Bestselling Author
Fern Michaels

__The Jury	0-8217-7878-1	$6.99US/$9.99CAN
__Sweet Revenge	0-8217-7879-X	$6.99US/$9.99CAN
__Lethal Justice	0-8217-7880-3	$6.99US/$9.99CAN
__Free Fall	0-8217-7881-1	$6.99US/$9.99CAN
__Fool Me Once	0-8217-8071-9	$7.99US/$10.99CAN
__Vegas Rich	0-8217-8112-X	$7.99US/$10.99CAN
__Hide and Seek	1-4201-0184-6	$6.99US/$9.99CAN
__Hokus Pokus	1-4201-0185-4	$6.99US/$9.99CAN
__Fast Track	1-4201-0186-2	$6.99US/$9.99CAN
__Collateral Damage	1-4201-0187-0	$6.99US/$9.99CAN
__Final Justice	1-4201-0188-9	$6.99US/$9.99CAN
__Up Close and Personal	0-8217-7956-7	$7.99US/$9.99CAN
__Under the Radar	1-4201-0683-X	$6.99US/$9.99CAN
__Razor Sharp	1-4201-0684-8	$7.99US/$10.99CAN
__Yesterday	1-4201-1494-8	$5.99US/$6.99CAN
__Vanishing Act	1-4201-0685-6	$7.99US/$10.99CAN
__Sara's Song	1-4201-1493-X	$5.99US/$6.99CAN
__Deadly Deals	1-4201-0686-4	$7.99US/$10.99CAN
__Game Over	1-4201-0687-2	$7.99US/$10.99CAN
__Sins of Omission	1-4201-1153-1	$7.99US/$10.99CAN
__Sins of the Flesh	1-4201-1154-X	$7.99US/$10.99CAN
__Cross Roads	1-4201-1192-2	$7.99US/$10.99CAN

Available Wherever Books Are Sold!
Check out our website at **www.kensingtonbooks.com**

More by Bestselling Author
Hannah Howell

More from Bestselling Author
JANET DAILEY

Calder Storm	0-8217-7543-X	$7.99US/$10.99CAN
Close to You	1-4201-1714-9	$5.99US/$6.99CAN
Crazy in Love	1-4201-0303-2	$4.99US/$5.99CAN
Dance With Me	1-4201-2213-4	$5.99US/$6.99CAN
Everything	1-4201-2214-2	$5.99US/$6.99CAN
Forever	1-4201-2215-0	$5.99US/$6.99CAN
Green Calder Grass	0-8217-7222-8	$7.99US/$10.99CAN
Heiress	1-4201-0002-5	$6.99US/$7.99CAN
Lone Calder Star	0-8217-7542-1	$7.99US/$10.99CAN
Lover Man	1-4201-0666-X	$4.99US/$5.99CAN
Masquerade	1-4201-0005-X	$6.99US/$8.99CAN
Mistletoe and Molly	1-4201-0041-6	$6.99US/$9.99CAN
Rivals	1-4201-0003-3	$6.99US/$7.99CAN
Santa in a Stetson	1-4201-0664-3	$6.99US/$9.99CAN
Santa in Montana	1-4201-1474-3	$7.99US/$9.99CAN
Searching for Santa	1-4201-0306-7	$6.99US/$9.99CAN
Something More	0-8217-7544-8	$7.99US/$9.99CAN
Stealing Kisses	1-4201-0304-0	$4.99US/$5.99CAN
Tangled Vines	1-4201-0004-1	$6.99US/$8.99CAN
Texas Kiss	1-4201-0665-1	$4.99US/$5.99CAN
That Loving Feeling	1-4201-1713-0	$5.99US/$6.99CAN
To Santa With Love	1-4201-2073-5	$6.99US/$7.99CAN
When You Kiss Me	1-4201-0667-8	$4.99US/$5.99CAN
Yes, I Do	1-4201-0305-9	$4.99US/$5.99CAN

Available Wherever Books Are Sold!

Check out our website at **www.kensingtonbooks.com**.